Granger retreated, slowly, glancing down at the ground as he went. Nervously, he checked around him in case he set anything off. Too late he heard the cracking sound below, then the next thing he knew he was being yanked upwards, the net closing in around him and pulling him into the air. His gun fell out of his hands, the mike from his head. He felt his stomach roll as he was hoisted up, only stopping when it reached a certain height.

There he was left, dangling. He took deep breaths, calming himself down. *You're still alive, still alive. Just caught in a net, that's all. You can get out of this.*

Even as he thought it, someone passed by beneath him wearing a hood. He paused to look up at Granger, and the youth thought that was it – his time was finally up. Then the hooded man went on his way, disappearing into the undergrowth as if he'd never really existed at all.

An Abaddon Books™ Publication
www.abaddonbooks.com
abaddon@rebellion.co.uk

First published in 2008 by Abaddon Books™, Rebellion Intellectual
Property Limited, Riverside House, Osney Mead, Oxford, OX2 0ES, UK.

Distributed in the US by National Book Network, 4501 Forbes
Boulevard, Suite 200, Lanham, MD, 20706, USA.

10 9 8 7 6 5 4 3 2 1

Editor: Jonathan Oliver
Cover: Mark Harrison
Design: Simon Parr & Luke Preece
Marketing and PR: Keith Richardson
Creative Director and CEO: Jason Kingsley
Chief Technical Officer: Chris Kingsley
The Afterblight Chronicles™ created
by Simon Spurrier and Andy Boot

ISBN: 978-1-905437-76-4

Printed in Denmark by Nørhaven Paperback A/S

THE AFTERBLIGHT CHRONICLES

ARROWHEAD

PAUL KANE

Abaddon
Books

WWW.ABADDONBOOKS.COM

For Mum and Dad who helped me find my path through the forest, and for my darling Marie who coaxed me out of it

In the first decade of the new millennium a devastating plague swept the planet, killing all but those with the blood group 'O negative.' Communities crumbled, society fragmented and in its place rose the rule of tyrants and crazed cults lead by dangerous religious revolutionaries.

This is the world of The Afterblight Chronicles...

The spirit of Robin Hood
Lives forever in Sherwood Forest
And in the hearts of those who seek him...

CHAPTER ONE

The arrowhead embedded itself in the wall just millimetres from his left temple.

Thomas Hinckerman had screwed up his eyes as the crossbow was raised, flinching only slightly when he heard the impact; in one way relieved to still be alive, in another wishing this ordeal would be over soon, one way or the other. The apple on top of his head wobbled slightly. There was a wetness running down his face. He assumed it was sweat. But when he opened his eyes and looked down – carefully, so as not to dislodge the fruit he was balancing – he saw the spots of red on the floor. The bolt had nicked his skin...

And seconds later there was pain.

Not that he could feel it much – this latest wound paled into insignificance compared with his others: the bullet hole in his shoulder, for example, the fingernails dangling off, pulled with pliers, the missing teeth, or how about the cigar burns on his stomach? Still, he'd fared better than his friends, Gary and Dan. Their bodies were still cooling on the floor near the entrance to the station.

It had been his idea initially, taken from those stories of refugees trying to enter Britain simply by walking, long before the virus came and took its toll. Before The Cull. Back then those people had wanted in, but now it seemed like a much better idea to get out of the country before things grew even worse.

Thomas suggested it to Gary, a former scrap metal dealer, and Dan, who used to be a butcher, because they felt the same. He'd met them at the local impromptu meetings just before The Cull, when everyone was still trying to figure out what could be done about their loved ones, their neighbours, those who were dying all around them. They weren't the kind of folk Thomas would have mixed with before all this, not the sort of men you'd see hanging out at the library where he had worked. But fate had thrown them together, and they'd stuck like glue: through all the madness that had followed.

Now they were dead. Just like he would be soon. Thomas was under no illusions about that, not after he'd seen them murdered in cold blood. His last memories of the men he'd trekked thirty-one miles with, sharing adversities he never would have thought possible, were Dan's brains exploding all over his own shirt, feet still twitching as he hit the ground, and Gary dancing like a puppet as he was riddled with bullets from a machine gun.

The three of them had emerged from the tunnel and into the station at Calais that morning, their torches almost out of batteries, supplies exhausted a day ago, glad to be free, glad to be back above ground. They'd passed dormant trains, their yellow noses rusting, glass at the front smashed. They'd seen no one, not until they reached the station. There Gary spotted a lone figure sitting on one of the benches inside the foyer.

They must have been watching from the start, though; because as the trio walked over to make contact, Dan was already dropping, a bullet coming out of nowhere to blow half his head away. And then the other men emerged – a half dozen or more, heavily-armed; one with silver hair carrying what looked like a sniper's rifle. That's when they'd pulled Gary's strings...

They'd been waiting, too, he found out. Waiting for someone like him to come. Thomas had been left alive – just clipped with a bullet – to tell them what he knew.

He was dragged to his feet by two men, one with a paunch, the other smoking a cigar. Their leader wasn't a huge man, but carried himself well. He had the air of someone much larger. He was dressed in grey and black combats, and was wearing sunglasses. When he took these off and stared into Thomas's face, he saw that the man's eyes were just as black as his glasses. There were jewelled rings on most of his fingers. He spoke with a French accent and his first question was: "Are you in pain, Englishman?" When Thomas nodded, the man smiled with teeth as yellow as the noses of those trains. Then he stuck two of his ringed fingers into the hole in Thomas's shoulder. His whole body jerked, but he was held tightly by the men on either side.

When Thomas had recovered enough to speak, he whispered: "What... what do you want from me?"

"Information," said the man.

"A-about what? I don't know anything."

He smiled again. "We will see."

Thomas was introduced to a broader man with olive skin and short, cropped hair. Thomas was told that his name was Tanek. "When Tanek was in the army," the man in combats told him, "his speciality was making people talk." The Frenchman nodded firmly, and that's when the pliers had come out. Tanek had gone to work on his fingernails first, grasping the little one on his right hand firmly, then yanking it off, the nail splitting and cracking as it went.

Thomas let out the loudest scream of his life. Even getting shot hadn't hurt like that. Through the tears, he saw the outline of the Frenchman's face again. "I need to know about the place you've come from," he told Thomas.

"W-What...?" Another nail was pulled. "*Yaaaaaahhhh...*"

The Frenchman slapped his face. "What is the situation in England? Do you understand me?"

Thomas shook his head.

"How organised are the people over there. Are there communities? Are the defence forces still operational?"

Thomas laughed at that one, which earned him another lost nail. "Everything's gone to shit," he shouted back at the man. "It's chaos. Fucking chaos! Why do you think we came through the tunnel? It's like being back in the dark ages."

The Frenchman chuckled this time. "I see."

They continued to question him for at least a couple more hours, asking him everything he knew about Dover, where they'd entered, about the surrounding areas of Kent, what he'd heard about London and other regions of England – which was very little since The Cull. Thomas had no idea why they were putting the questions to him, but he answered as honestly as he could, especially when Tanek pulled out his molars, then snatched the cigar from one of the men holding him and used that too. He'd cooperated as well as he was able and his reward was to be handcuffed to a notice board, ruined fingers dangling limply, while some of the men took it in turns to play 'William Tell' with a crossbow Tanek handed around, and an apple – a fresh golden apple that would have made Thomas's mouth water had it not already been filled with blood. And had his mouth not been taped over because they were sick of hearing his cries.

As he opened his eyes now, he saw that motorcycles were being wheeled into the station, six or seven in total. He also heard one of the men call out their leader's name: De Falaise.

The man came to join Tanek, just as another bolt was clumsily fired from the crossbow. It wound up in Thomas's right thigh. His muffled grunt caused much amusement amongst the group.

De Falaise raised a hand to stop the game for a moment, walking towards Thomas. "I thank you for your help, it was fortuitous that our paths should cross," he said. "From what you have told us, it would appear there is much in the way of opportunity for people like us in your land. Unlike the situation we leave behind... Your people are weak; we are not."

It was then that Thomas knew what he had in mind. De Falaise and his men were going to use the bikes to make the same trip he'd done, but in reverse, shooting up the tunnel and into England just like one of the bolts from Tanek's crossbow. And they would probably do just as much damage.

"In return, my gift to you, Englishman," said De Falaise. Thomas looked into those black eyes, and thought for just a moment the Frenchman might let him live, let him go. Then he saw that smile on De Falaise's face, and struggled against his bonds, the apple falling from his head. De Falaise stepped aside and there was Tanek, with his weapon now fully loaded – aimed at his head. Unlike the others, he would not miss.

In seconds it was over, and De Falaise was already giving the order to move out, to take the bikes down to the tunnel so they could be on their way. Tanek paused before leaving, to pick up the apple and take a bite.

"Come," said De Falaise, laughing again as he led the way. "There is much to do, much to see. And a country just as ripe for the taking."

CHAPTER TWO

The hunter had been crouching in the undergrowth for almost two hours when the creature finally wandered into the clearing. His prize. After tracking it for the best part of a day, he knew that this was one of its favourite haunts. This would be the place where he'd look into its eyes, where he'd feel that familiar adrenalin rush from bagging such a fine catch.

So he'd settled himself down to wait.

He was a patient man. And, besides, it wasn't as if he had anything else to do, was it? No going down the pub for a pint and game of darts, no cosy nights in front of the TV. Those days were long gone now, a distant memory... most of the time. The problem with waiting was that the mind needed ways to amuse itself. Against his will, he found himself drifting back, remembering. Thinking about the man he used to be and the life he'd once led. It felt like a dream.

"Read to me some more, Dad... please..."

Mentally, he tried to shake the memories from his head in the same way his old Golden Retriever used to shake himself dry. How little Stevie would laugh when Max did that – he could see the boy's face now on that holiday in Wales. They'd left the campsite and taken a walk down by a long river. Then they'd let the dog off the lead to run around and he'd immediately jumped in the water to chase a fish he'd seen. After swimming with his head held high, Max had finally realised there was no way on Earth he was going to catch the thing. He'd sprayed them all when they ran across to him. Stevie had laughed and laughed, as Joanne held up her hands to...

"Robert... Robert, come back to bed. It's Sunday

morning."

They were random, these recollections. That one was from back when they'd first got married, back when they used to lose themselves in each other every weekend. Back before Stevie came along and would climb in with them on a Sunday morning, bringing the papers with him. His son would read the comics while Robert took the sports section and Joanne would comment on what was happening in the world; which usually involved some soap or pop star spending thousands on rehab when everyone knew they'd be back on booze and drugs within a month.

"Listen to this: the government are stating categorically that there's nothing to worry about, Rob... That the people infected are 'isolated incidents', and there's only a slim chance of it becoming airborne."

He squeezed his eyes shut, but the images didn't disappear. Robert went way back now, to his graduation from training college in fact. Remembering how proud his parents had been of him that day; at least he'd given them something before the crash two years later. And he had to admit to feeling a swell of pride himself as his name was called.

"Would you please step forward, Constable Robert Stokes." He could see the crowds of people, the flashes of cameras as they snapped pictures. The applause was deafening. He thought he could change the world back then, make a difference.

Fast forward to the riots when the system was breaking down. The stones and half bricks that were hurled, terrified people hitting them with lead piping, with sticks. So many faces, so much panic.

Robert and his family had moved out of the big city a long time ago, when Stevie was only four. Joanne had argued that she didn't want her husband on the streets facing gun crime and goodness knows what else. She didn't want Stevie growing up without a father (a sick joke when he thought about it now).

"You ready?"

"Push the swing Dad, come on!"

"Okay, you asked for it."

"Higher, higher! Can we go on the roundabout next?"

"Sure thing."

"You're the best, Dad. The best."

Of course, he'd argued that there were pockets of violence everywhere, but he could see it from her point of view as well. In the end he'd listened and they'd upped sticks from the place where he was born and bred. But he hoped to return one day.

They hadn't really gone that far. Robert put in a transfer to a market town north of Nottingham called Mansfield, taking out a mortgage on a house between there and Ollerton. They'd been so happy there. He enjoyed community police work well enough and they lived in one of the most beautiful areas of England, only a short distance from rolling green fields, from woodland and forests – plenty of places to take Max out for walks. Yet close enough to 'civilisation' that Joanne could go shopping if she wanted, and pursue her ambitions to run her own accountancy business now that Stevie had gone to school. She always had been a whizz at maths, even when they were young...

"Hi, my name's Robert – I'm in the class above you."

"Joanne. You're friends with Tracey's brother, aren't you?"

"Yeah, that's right. A bunch of us are going out on Saturday, to the pictures. I was wondering...Well, do you want to come?"

It was ironic that the violence and the death found them all those years later. But it was the same countrywide in those dark days just before The Cull.

If the time prior to that had been a dream, then surely what came next was a nightmare; one from which he was constantly praying he'd wake. As friends on the force stopped turning up for work, as kids from Stevie's school were kept off sick, as more bullshit about the virus appeared in the papers and on the TV news... Nobody had taken it that seriously at first, not after all that business with SARS and Bird Flu. All that changed when they were smacked in the face with it.

Grimacing, Robert relived that night when Joanne had suddenly begun coughing in bed. Turning on the bedside lamp, he'd rolled over to find her holding a tissue up to her mouth. When she brought it away again, there was a bright patch of red there. And her eyes, *God in Heaven, her eyes...*

"You've got the most beautiful eyes, do you know that?"

"Charmer."

"It's true."

She was looking at him, petrified. They both knew what it meant – had seen enough about it to recognise the symptoms. Then they'd heard the coughing coming from Stevie's room as well.

The scene was playing out in his mind in slow motion: slamming open the door and snapping on the light; seeing crimson splattered all over the ten-year-old's duvet; Stevie crying because he didn't know what was happening to him; Max barking at the foot of his bed.

He'd bundled Joanne and Stevie into the car, knowing it was no use phoning for an ambulance. He and some of his colleagues had waited four or five hours for one to show up just a few days before. Tearing down the country roads, and thankful for all those lessons about how to drive at speed when in pursuit, Robert was soon brought to a halt when he reached the nearest hospital.

The car park was overflowing. People had left their vehicles on grass verges, double and triple parked; wherever they could. He'd had to abandon his vehicle half a mile away from the building itself, then he'd carried Stevie on his shoulder, holding up Joanne with his other arm as they made their way to the Accident and Emergency department. The place was heaving, packed to the rafters with patients, some on trolleys, sitting or laying down – or both – some making do with a couple of chairs for a bed, but most were strewn around the reception area and the corridors like beggars hoping for a handout. It was like something out of those history books from school, monochrome etchings which showed people suffering from the Black Death. Doctors and nurses wearing scrubs and masks flitted about in front of him, so Robert grabbed the nearest one and demanded that the man examine his wife and child.

"Look around you, mate – all these people need attention, and they were all here before you."

"I'm a police officer and–"

"You think that matters anymore?" shouted the man in scrubs. "You think it matters whether you're with the police, the emergency services or... or..." The man coughed. "People are dying... people..." He coughed again, except this time it was loud and wracking, chorusing with the others. The doctor pulled the mask away from his mouth, revealing the blood inside it. Then he looked up. "Oh Jesus," was all he said.

It was at that moment the penny dropped. It really didn't matter anymore: nothing did. Because they were all fucked. The medicos didn't have a clue how to stop this, not even the government – of this country or any other – knew what to do.

Reluctantly, Robert returned home with Stevie and

Joanne, made them as comfortable as he could, trying to force cough mixture and paracetamol down them as if they had a common cold or a dose of the flu. Robert waited it out with them, just like he was waiting here today. Knowing that any minute now, because he'd been exposed to the virus as well, he'd start coughing up blood. They'd all go together if they were going to go at all. He watched his wife and son pass their final few hours back in bed, in each other's arms, heaving up their liquefied lungs, fighting for breath. Max lay beside them on the mattress, whining as if he could sense what was about to happen. Robert had spent his whole life trying to protect people, and now he couldn't even protect his own family from the microscopic bastards that were ravaging their bodies. As they slipped away from him – Joanne first, taking a final, wheezing breath, followed by nothing; then Stevie while he stroked the boy's blond hair, not knowing how to answer his questions about why he felt so ill or why Mum wasn't coughing anymore – Robert cried until he thought his tear ducts would burst.

"Help me, Dad... it hurts... make it stop!"

Max licked at Stevie's face, trying to bring him round. The boy didn't move.

Robert slumped over their still bodies, clutching their clothes, screaming at the universe, at God, at anything and everything, before finally exhaustion took him. Conversely now he didn't want to wake, to face what had just happened. But when he did at last, realising that this was all real, wrapping them in the blankets they'd died beneath, he held on to the one and only shred of hope left.

"Stop wriggling about, Stevie, you're taking all the covers. And let your Dad read his sports section."

"Kay."

Robert waited once more, it must have been days...

maybe even a couple of weeks, but he didn't feel the passage of the hours. This time it was his own death Robert anticipated. He willed the cough to come, the blood, for the virus to take him. He was ready for it. Oh, was he ready.

Robert existed on what was left in the house – tinned food mainly that Joanne had squirreled away; she was a terror for keeping the cupboards overstocked. Though he hardly felt like eating or drinking, his survival instinct was too strong to simply let himself starve to death. He fed Max, but left the door open so the animal could supplement his diet elsewhere if he chose. Or perhaps for another reason altogether.

"You're going to have to find a new owner soon, boy," he'd tell the old dog daily, "because I'm not going to be here for much longer."

Then even that was snatched away from him by the men in gas masks, the hooded yellow-clad figures in their wagons, sent to scoop up the dead that littered the streets in a vain attempt to halt the spread of this infection. Even this far outside the towns and cities, the pavements were covered. The men broke down the doors of houses, checking inside, coming for the victims of the virus, spraying crosses on walls of buildings to be gutted with flamethrowers. Robert heard them approaching down the street, the megaphones blaring, but it hardly registered. Not until they were actually inside his house, waving their guns around, did he acknowledge their presence.

Max leapt at one of them, clawing at his plastic suit. The man struck the dog on the side of the head with the butt of his automatic rifle. Max fell to the floor with a whine and lay there twitching. Robert jumped out of his chair, but when a rifle was swung in his direction, he froze. He watched anxiously as a couple more men ascended the staircase. Was this what had become of the authorities in his absence, Robert wondered, bully boys throwing their weight around?

"Two of 'em up here," came the muffled call from upstairs. "Been there a while as well by the looks of things."

"Leave them where they are," Robert warned the man pointing the gun at him. "I'll be joining them soon enough."

The fellow gave a cold laugh. "You not seen the news lately, or what passes for it these days? If you haven't got it by now, chances are you never will. You must be O-Neg."

"O-Neg?" Robert gaped at him.

"Completely immune, you lucky bastard. Though it's a wonder you haven't caught somethin' else off them stiffs."

He couldn't take it in. He wasn't going to die after all – leastways not from the virus. But Robert felt far from lucky: he'd lost everything he ever cared about and now he just wanted this all to end.

The men came back downstairs and told him he'd have to go with them. They were looking for people like Robert, apparently. Someone in 'power' thought they might actually be able to develop an antidote from them.

"And what... what's going to happen to Joanne and Stevie... My house?" Robert asked.

"Same as all the others with infected dead inside. *Poof*," said one of them, opening his fist like a flower in bloom. "The rest of us can't run the risk of catching it when we've gone to all this trouble."

Tears welled in Robert's eyes as a man to his left grabbed his arm, attempting to drag him outside. "I'm not going anywhere," he told them.

"Oh yeah?" the first man brought up his rifle, aiming at Robert's head. He took a step towards the barrel, pressing the cold metal against his forehead.

"Do it, get it over with."

They all looked at each other. "He's too valuable," said the second man, shaking his head.

"Don't you understand, I don't want to live anymore!"

"Tough shit," said the third man, and they began to drag him out through the door. Robert elbowed one, lashed out at another, but all this earned him was a punch in the stomach.

Outside, two of them held Robert while the third sprayed a red 'X' on the front of his house and signalled to a truck behind. Robert looked on through the tears as more men climbed out with flamethrowers, tanks strapped to their backs. While he struggled, these 'firemen' disappeared inside, only to emerge moments later, leaving a trail of flames in their wake. And then, as if the rest of it hadn't been enough, something crawled from the spreading conflagration, looking for all the world like a demon emerging from Hell. Fur alight and whimpering with pain, Max made it a few steps down the path, before collapsing into a burning heap. They hadn't even bothered to check he was dead before setting the house on fire; or maybe they just didn't give a crap.

It was too much to bear. Robert reached up and pulled one of the men's gas masks off, then swung it at his other captor.

"Oh-shit-oh-shit-oh-shit-" gibbered the man whose mask was hanging off, fumbling to replace it, while Robert wrestled out of the other one's grip. Then he ran.

"Get him!"

The third man shot into the air, careful not to hit their prisoner, but at the same time powerless to stop him.

Robert made it round the corner, glancing back over his shoulder only once. His house and everything in it was a blazing inferno, much like many of the others nearby.

"Goodbye sweetheart," he whispered to his wife. "Goodbye son. I love you both very much."

The men would come after him, he knew that, but they wouldn't kill him. Instead they'd take him away somewhere to be prodded and poked, to provide a cure for the men in the masks and their superiors. People he'd once served (*no, not like that... never like that!*). So Robert ran, harder and faster than he ever had in his life. He didn't have a clue where he was going, just that he had to hide – he needed to get away from people: the living and the dead. Robert calculated that if only those with O-Neg blood were immune, as the man back at his house had said, then most of the population had already been wiped out. Joanne would probably have been able to give him a more precise estimation... if she'd been alive.

On his journey he came across a small abandoned army surplus store, which had been partially looted, the window smashed and whatever was in the display long since stolen. That wasn't what interested him. Robert climbed through, hoping that there might be at least some of the things he'd need: a change of clothing for starters. He found a pair of tough khaki combat trousers, a green t-shirt and a hooded top that fitted him, plus a long, waxy outdoor coat. All that remained was to find a decent knife, a compass and some twine. Once he'd scrounged them up, he left whatever money he had on him by the till.

In the end it was a logical choice. Head for the woodlands at Rufford where he'd spent so much time with Max, where he'd taken Joanne and Stevie occasionally at weekends and bank holidays. Robert would let the oak, silver birch and ferns hide him from what was left of society, live out his life until death took him from natural causes; hopefully soon. Maybe he'd just slip and break his neck one day...

Until then, he would get by. Robert would draw on the survival training he'd gone through as part of his job. He'd thought it was daft at the time, all those role-playing exercises, the team building out in the middle of nowhere. But he'd picked up quite a few things on those courses without even realising it. Unlike some of the lads, he'd actually been paying attention when the tutor had explained about things like making shelters and hunting if you were stranded. In fact, the first thing he'd done when he got to the woods was construct a simple lean-to between a couple of trees. He'd whittled down branches to make the poles, tying these together with the twine, then he'd covered the framework over with all the foliage he could find in the surrounding area. A new home, designed for one.

For water, to drink and to wash, he visited the huge lake at Rufford or trapped rain – filtering it through material torn from his disused clothing, then boiling it over a fire. This Robert made when it grew cold at night with a bow and drill, spinning the sharpened piece of wood on a fire board until it caught light. Using kindling, he'd build it up and warm himself.

For food, he picked edible mushrooms to begin with, then set simple snares and drag nooses to catch small animals, placed over trails or runs, attached to poles. These were large enough to comfortably pass over the creatures' heads, but then grew tighter as they struggled to get out. In his former life he might have felt some guilt about doing this, but it was a different world now. He was a different person. Plus which, he'd eaten meat all his life, hadn't he? Just never thought about where it came from. Now that was his responsibility, because Robert couldn't allow himself to become weak, not when the men might still come after him. He would also catch ducks and geese by the water, using a bolas – two stones connected by the twine and thrown, after some degree of practice, around the bird's necks to weigh them down. And he'd hunt small game with a sharpened spear, not throwing it as you might see in the movies, because that was a good way to lose the weapon, but jabbing at his prey. Then he'd cook whatever he could find over a spit beside the lean-to.

But the bow he used to light the fire gave him other ideas as well. Robert selected a hardwood – dead, dry wood as opposed to greenwood – branch about two metres or so long that was relatively free from knots and limbs. With his knife, he scraped down the largest end so that it had the same pull as the smaller one. The wood had a natural curve to it and he was careful to scrape from the side facing him, knowing that otherwise it might snap the first time he used it. Robert spent ages attaching the twine and getting the pull of the bow just right. Moving on to the arrows, he used the straightest dry sticks he could find, scraping and straightening the shafts. For the arrowheads, he used sharpened stone – then attached feathers from his previous hunts to the shaft, notching the ends. In many respects all this was the easy part, because Robert only had limited experience with a bow and arrow, amounting to the handful of times he'd taken Stevie for archery lessons on holidays.

So he'd practised; for many hours. Drawing back the bow, letting the arrows fly into a target carved on a tree. To begin with Robert had been miles away from the trunk, let alone the target, but gradually his aim improved.

Just like darts... only with bigger arrows, he'd tell himself.

He recalled the day that he hit the bull's eye – he'd been determined to do it before the dark skies emptied their load. The sense of satisfaction was tremendous, and for a split second he'd almost forgotten where he was and how he came to be there, turning and expecting Joanne and Stevie to be behind him, clapping.

"Way to go, Dad, way to go."

"Quite the outdoorsman, now, aren't we?" Joanne's beautiful eyes were filled with love, not terror. Her smiling mouth not stained with blood anymore.

But all was quiet except for the usual sound of birdsong.

As the first spots of rain came down, Robert had hung his head, pulling the hood up. Then he'd returned to camp for the night, walking past the cloth catchments which were collecting the water.

Once again, the days blurred into each other – and Robert could only go by the fact that the grass on the once neatly-trimmed golf course and the parks was now knee-length, that the beard he'd begun growing was thick and bushy, that he'd had to begin stockpiling meat in the ice houses at Rufford, man-made stone buildings set into mounds of earth that would keep it chilled, and insulated by the soil. He'd busted off the barred doors to these and used them as his own personal larder.

The meat mainly came from sheep in the fields, in particular the shaggy Hebrideans that had been introduced to the scrubland before The Cull: easy, slow-moving targets. But he'd noticed that deer were running free now too in the woods, and this was a chance to really put his new-found skills with the bow to good use. The first time he'd attempted a kill, he'd completely messed it up, stumbling through the undergrowth like the most uncoordinated of bulls blundering into Ming vases, alerting the startled deer to his presence. Since that day, he'd learnt to be very stealthy, and adept at blending into his surroundings. He'd bagged more deer and sheep than he could remember, ensuring enough to eat through the past two winters at least; and enough skins and wool to keep him warm during the colder months.

But today he was hunting something altogether different. Something that was worth all the waiting, the crouching, the memories that had come flooding back. Because there, in the clearing, was the magnificent sight of a stag: its strong grey and white torso moving fluidly as it paused to sniff at the air.

Robert held his breath. It was the ultimate test of his hunting skills; one false move and he'd tip off his quarry. Through the long grass and ferns, he looked at the animal, and he was so sure it was looking back at him. All hunted creatures were aware of being watched – if only on a subconscious level – he'd observed. It was the same thing he'd seen when he was just about to give chase to a pickpocket or bootlegger. They'd make a break for it just a fraction of a second before spotting Robert. The trick was to be quicker than them.

If he was going to make his move, it had to be right now. Robert rose, breaking cover: the leaves, twigs, and branches he'd used to camouflage himself falling from his body. Though he'd been hunkered down low, unmoving all this time, his legs were far from stiff and his muscles held him steady. Simultaneously, he raised his bow, which could easily have been mistaken for another branch, another piece of camouflage, were it not for the taut twine attached to its length. Robert and the stag exchanged a glance, the merest of heartbeats and yet lasting forever.

Hunter and prey.

It was only during this time that he felt something akin to being alive again, felt a surge of energy that reminded him he wasn't just a shadow, simply a ghost of his former self.

But in this animal, he also recognised a kindred spirit; a once proud creature reduced to a victim by circumstance.

Robert lowered the bow, nodding to himself and to the stag. The animal stood there stunned for a second or two, not understanding how it could still be alive – the hunter had him in his sights. But it didn't question this for long, running off back into the woods; vanishing from sight.

Robert watched it go, knowing that another kill had never really been the purpose of this exercise. He didn't need any more meat, and didn't hunt just for sport – Robert didn't have a trophy room in the lean-to. They'd shared something in that one brief moment, the stag and him. Both knew what it was like to be on the run, what it was like to escape.

Above all else, both Robert and the stag knew that he could have taken that life, but chose not to.

All of which meant that the hunter, the hooded man, was still the victor.

And so it was his turn to disappear back into the trees.

CHAPTER THREE

How had this happened? How had they gone from being the hunters to the prey?

One minute, they'd been the top dogs around here, now they were facing a serious ultimatum. Granger still couldn't quite believe it, back to being pushed around again, just like when he was growing up. Back to following orders.

In the past it had been his mother's boyfriends issuing them, a succession of no-hopers who seemed to view him as their personal slave half the time. His mother said nothing to them, mainly because she did the same: *fetch me this, fetch me that, make us something to eat, get us something to drink.* And if he didn't comply immediately, he was looking at being beaten around the living room of their tiny council flat in Finchley. Granger might have blamed it on growing up without a father, except that particular 'role model' would probably have made things worse from what little he'd heard. That's if he could have stayed out of jail long enough.

None of the boyfriends had lasted, not once they'd got what they wanted out of Granger's mum: somewhere to stay rent free for a while and someone who wouldn't complain in the bedroom when they forced her to do the most depraved things. He could hear them at night, no matter how much he pulled the pillows up around his ears – the moans and the screams, and, sometimes, the crying afterwards. That was when he wanted to go to her, when he felt what you were supposed to feel for a mother. The last boyfriend, Jez, had been the worst of the lot. He'd even been dealing from their flat. And, once, when they were alone in the place together, Granger had

said something back to Jez so he'd pulled a handgun
on him, one of those customised replica imports from
abroad.

"You're a smart kid, aren't you? Got a smart mouth...
How smart are you now, eh? Eh?" he'd said, turning it
on him. Granger closed his eyes, fully expecting the man
to shoot. Luckily, his mother had come home at that
moment, and Jez had tucked the gun quickly back away
in his jeans.

It wasn't even as if school was an escape from what
was going on. His teachers barked at him because he
hadn't done his homework – especially his old French
teacher, Mr Dodds. When did he ever have time? Where
was he supposed to work? As for the other kids, he never
fitted in with them either. They all had their little gangs
and they made it abundantly clear he wasn't welcome
in any of them, pounding it into him when he didn't get
the message. As for girls, well, who would look at him
twice?

When he'd left home at sixteen, bailing as soon as he
could to move into a shared digs only one step up from a
squat – his mother's cries of "You ungrateful little sod!"
still ringing in his ears – it had been the people down
the dole office who'd lorded it over him. They sent him
to interviews for jobs he so obviously wasn't qualified
to do. Until, eventually, he'd been taken pity on. Hired
as a labourer: paid peanuts for the privilege of being a
dogsbody to the other workers on the building site.

"Hey, streaky bacon," a site manager called Mick
always used to call across, in reference to Granger's
gangly teenaged frame, "we're parched over here – fetch
us another round of tea, will you. Come on, move your
skinny arse!" Then, when he brought the tray across,
they'd make fun of him again, getting him to pick up
tools from the floor, then kicking him over. It was just a

bit of fun, they said. That's all.

Granger used to wish they would drop dead; wished every last one of them would just drop dead, in fact.

He'd never expected his wish to come true.

People hacked and coughed in the streets, spraying blood over pavements, falling where they stood in some cases.

And while everyone else got sick from the disease they were calling the AB Virus, Granger finally got a break. Instead of coughing up blood, his actually saved him. Against his better judgement, he'd called round to see his mother while she was still alive... just. Even when she was dying, she'd ordered him to fetch her stuff; bring pills so she could get better.

"There isn't anything that can do that," he'd told her.

"You... *ack*... you fetch me something right now you... *ack*... you fucking–"

"You ain't going to get better, Mum!" he said, finally losing his temper. "There isn't a medicine on this planet that can cure you. How d'you feel about that?"

She coughed and spat blood in his face, though whether it was intentional or not Granger didn't know.

"I'll be seeing you," he told her as he began walking out, knowing full well that he never would again. Then he'd gone to the bathroom and washed his face, drying it on the towel. It was as he was doing so that he noticed a shape behind the shower curtain. Granger jumped, but the thing didn't move. Slowly, he reached out and pulled back the plastic curtain. Jez was lying there in the bath, a needle sticking out of his arm and sticky redness dribbling from his mouth. He'd OD'd rather than face the final stages of the virus. Granger had seen plenty of dead bodies lately, but not up close like this. He shook his head, remembering what a bastard this man had been. Bending down, he cocked his head and whispered, "Who's the smart one now?" Then he lifted the body, checking the back of the man's jeans for the pistol he always kept about his person. Taking it, Granger had turned his back on Jez, his mother, and the place where he'd grown up.

To Granger's mind, he was at last reaping the rewards of years of misery. During The Culling Year, when those in charge had attempted to stop the spread of the plague, there had been rich pickings for the likes of him. Rumours flew around of soldiers trying to take control, even of something big taking place on Salisbury Plain, but it hadn't affected Granger's plans. He'd moved relatively freely from place to place, taking whatever he liked from the shops, stuffing his pockets with money (it never occurred to him at the time that this would be useless later on) and generally having the time of his life... while everyone else was losing theirs.

And he encountered more like him, young men who saw opportunity in the wake of this new turn of events. Granger befriended a few – like Ennis, who he found working his way through the entire stock of beef burgers in a deserted McDonald's: it was where he'd used to work before it all hit the fan. Others he gently 'persuaded' to join him. Just having the pistol helped in that respect, though later they found all the weapons they needed when the men in yellow suits who were supposed to be cleaning up the streets came down with the virus too. Their numbers grew, all with a common goal – to help themselves to everything they'd been denied before. Granger finally had a gang to call his own and, though he knew there must be more in other parts of London, beyond that even, they ruled the roost in their little corner of the world. They called themselves 'The Jackals' and operated out of Barnet's council offices in Whetstone. Granger liked the irony of that; sticking it to the owners of his former home.

Girls, the ones that were left alive – and the ones who needed protection from other dangers on the streets these days – suddenly found Granger irresistible. Some of them were pretty good looking, as well, the kind he wouldn't have stood even the remotest chance with before.

At last they were the ones on top. None of them, especially Granger, would ever have to take another order or do as they were told ever again.

Or so they'd thought.

Then came the night of the attack. The first Granger knew about what was happening was when he got a garbled message over his walkie-talkie. It was Ennis, on watch outside, screaming that a bunch of men had come out of nowhere and taken down a handful of Jackals in one fell swoop. Granger, who was in the middle of making paper aeroplanes out of old council records, rushed to the window to see that Ennis was right.

Men on bikes were shooting at the building, making passes and picking off the Jackals on guard duty downstairs. They were much better trained than his gang. Older too, nothing like the punks they'd fended off in the past.

"Ennis..." he shouted into the mouthpiece. "Ennis, get back inside and bring the rest of the guys with you! We'll hold them off from up here." But, even as he said it, he heard windows smashing from several different directions at once. The men were entering the building right now, giving them no time to prepare. Looking back, Granger would realise just how amateurish The Jackals had been – how much more they could have fortified the building in readiness for just such an attack. Though even then, he doubted whether they'd have stood a chance against merciless professionals like these.

Granger called to the rest of his 'men' further inside the open-plan office, telling them to group at the stairwell, just by the lift doors. There were hardly any replies.

By the time he got down there it was all over. Those Jackals who hadn't been shot were on their knees in the entranceway to the office itself, hands behind their heads. Yet more were being marched down the stairs, along with some of the girls who'd been keeping them company. Granger raised his pistol, the one he'd taken from Jez so long ago and which he always kept about him – mainly as a reminder that he would never be pushed around again.

Several automatic rifles swivelled in his direction, clacking, ready to fire. Granger's gun hand began to shake.

"Gentlemen... Gentlemen... Écoutez!" came a voice from the doorway. There was a distinct accent that Granger recognised from those French lessons with Mr Dodds. "Hold your fire. This is obviously the very person we have come here to speak with." The man the voice belonged to came forward. He had dark eyes, which bored into Granger, making him feel cold inside. He smoothed down his black and grey combats as if he were wearing a Savile Row suit.

"Get out," shouted Granger, his voice wavering. "Get out now or..." But he had nothing to back the threat up with.

The guy facing him, their leader – he could tell by the way he was carrying himself – smiled chillingly. "Oh, I believe we will stay for a while. Won't we?" he said to his men, and the closest half dozen – obviously his elite – nodded their heads. "After all, we have a lot to discuss."

Discuss? Granger couldn't see much room for manoeuvre in that department; it was a pretty clear-cut situation. This man had them by the balls. "What... what do you want?"

"What does any of us want?" answered the man.

"Respect, loyalty... Fear."

They both knew he had the latter, and probably commanded the others through it. "I'm... I'm listening," Granger told him.

"Of course you are. All right, my proposition is simple," explained the man, taking off a pair of black leather gloves and revealing the rings on his fingers. "It's one I have put to several little 'operations' like yours, on the way to London and through it. Some listened. Some didn't."

Granger raised an eyebrow. "Proposition?"

"Yes. Un choix. You understand? A choice." He walked past one of the girls being held captive, who was only wearing a shirt, and ran a finger down her cheek. She flinched and he gave a small laugh, revealing hideously yellow teeth. Looking back over at Granger, he said, "You and your people can either join us or..."

"Or what?" Granger demanded, albeit half-heartedly, regretting this even as the words were tumbling from his mouth.

"Tanek?" called the leader to one of his men. The crowds parted and a huge, bulky soldier with olive skin and short hair stepped forward. Granger couldn't help thinking that he should drop the 'e' in his name and just go with 'Tank'. He held Ennis by the scruff of the neck, was practically carrying him like that, the boy's feet barely touching the floor.

"Granger... I'm sorry, I–" Tanek threw him down on the ground.

"Now," began the man wearing the smart combats, "show our friend here what the alternative to joining us would be."

Tanek unhooked the crossbow that was dangling on a strap from his shoulder, and aimed the weapon at Ennis's head.

"No!" shouted Granger, raising his pistol.

There was a nod from their leader, and Tanek turned in Granger's direction. Quicker than anything he'd ever seen in his life, the larger man had fired, the bolt catching Granger's gun hand, sending the pistol flying out of his grasp and then pinning his hand to the wall. He shrieked in pain as the bolt drove itself through his palm. Tanek then turned the crossbow – so unusual in its design, not needing to be reloaded it seemed – back on Ennis. He looked up pleadingly at Granger, then the bolt was fired directly into his head.

Granger howled, the pain in his hand forgotten for a moment. His friend, his 'second in command' was dead. The girl in the shirt was shaking and crying, the other members of The Jackals – how stupid that name sounded now – gawked at Ennis's body in disbelief.

"You bastard!" Granger spat.

The man in combats pointed to his chest with one finger, like it had nothing to do with him. "You asked. We gave a demonstration. As simple as that." His accent grew thicker with each word. "Now, what you have to ask yourself is, can we get past this and work together?"

Work together? He had to be joking. After what he'd just done to Ennis... But Granger knew what the option was. When this man had said there was a choice, he'd been lying. Really there was no choice at all.

"So, your answer, if you please." The man clasped his hands behind his back, tapping one booted foot. "I am waiting."

Granger, still in agony from the bolt in his palm, hung his head, nodding.

"Excellent, then allow me to introduce myself. My name is De Falaise. My aim is to bring order to this country, oui? Like your comrades here, England is on its knees. I intend to offer it the same choice I gave you: a killing blow or the chance to serve."

Granger stared at him; this guy was insane.

"Myself and my men are heading north," De Falaise continued, visibly enjoying his speech. "As my ancestors recognised, the seat of true power is not the capital at all. That, mon ami, is just for the tourists. It is from another place entirely that we will expand. We will reach out to every corner of this island, crushing any form of resistance. You are now a part of my army, making history, as it was once made long ago. In years to come people will look back on this moment as the start of something truly wondrous."

He actually believes what he's saying, thought Granger. *He wants to become like the King of England or something...* But then, stranger things had happened. And wasn't it only what Granger himself had done on a smaller scale? Hadn't this been his kingdom until De Falaise came along? Now, instead, he was one of the subjects in another man's realm – or maybe even the fool?

De Falaise returned Granger's stare. "So, do we understand each other?"

Granger nodded reluctantly again.

"Then answer me."

"Yes," Granger whispered. "We understand each other."

"Louder."

Granger gritted his teeth then raised his voice. "I said we understand each other."

De Falaise grinned. "Good." He reached up and yanked the bolt out of the wall, and Granger's palm. The younger man screamed again as blood flowed freely from the wound. "You may want to bandage that before we set off."

Granger, breath coming in hisses, gasped: "S-Set... Set

off?"

"That is correct. We leave for the army base at Hendon within the next half hour," De Falaise informed Granger, then told the rest of them: "Make yourselves ready."

As his men escorted The Jackals out, Tanek joined De Falaise standing in front of Granger. De Falaise handed the bloody bolt back to its owner, who wiped it with a cloth. "Do you know, I can see this being the start of a beautiful business arrangement, non?"

Granger sneered at him and De Falaise laughed.

He laughed long and hard, almost until it was time to leave the council offices at Whetstone.

CHAPTER FOUR

At first he thought they had come for him, finally.

Robert was aware of voices before he saw the group of men. They were skirting the edge of that particular section of woodland, about seven or eight of them in total. He'd been checking some of his snares when the sound of their talking carried to him. Robert had frozen. He hadn't heard another human voice in as long as he could remember – not since the men in the yellow suits...

"You must be O-Neg... Completely immune, you lucky bastard..."

"He's too valuable..."

"Get him!"

Surely they couldn't have tracked him down after all this time? There would be a certain irony to it if they had. If the hunter was again being hunted.

Leaving the looping trap, and stuffing the last wild rabbit into his skin-pouch, he'd moved swiftly and silently along the edge of the wood, before climbing up a tree to gain a better view. The first time he'd tried this it had been like being a kid again, doing something forbidden, and he heard his late mother's words in his head: *"Come down from there at once, Robert, before you really hurt yourself!"*

There was a part of him that wanted to get hurt this time, wanted to get hurt severely, in fact. Fall down and crack his skull open; wouldn't that be nice? But there was just as big a part of him that really didn't want to break his back and not be able to move, laying there dying slowly. Not a good end.

Better than Joanne's. Better than Stevie's.

It was like the bow and arrow: the more times he'd

done it, the better he'd become. Now, Robert was so used to it, he could scale even the largest of oaks. Up through the branches he went; strong hands, roughened by the elements, hauled him higher and higher. The tips of his boots found notches and ridges, much like a mountain climber scaling a rock face.

When he was high enough, he looked down at the scene. It was then that he actually saw the men. No yellow plastic suits, no gas masks or flamethrowers. Just blokes dressed in ordinary clothes, if a little the worse for wear: trousers, shirts, some in jumpers. They were carrying bags, had backpacks slung over shoulders. They knew each other well, were chatting and... yes, even laughing once or twice. Robert's eyes scanned the men but he could see no sign of rifles, automatic or otherwise. Which begged the question, who were they and where were they going?

He decided to find out. Call it a policeman's curiosity, which he didn't even know he still had, or an attempt to find out as much as he could about a potential enemy. Whichever way you looked at it, he was on the move.

Robert leaped from one tree to the next, trailing the men at height until they headed out across a field. If he wanted to know where they were going now, Robert had to break cover and follow on foot. But this didn't mean exposing his position. The men would still have no idea he was behind them.

As he crested a small hill, Robert saw where they were making for. In a big field just off the road, folk were gathering in fairly large numbers – large for post-virus times at any rate. Dozens of them: men, women and children. Some brought sacks, some trunks, some holdalls. From his hiding position behind a hedgerow, Robert noticed there were a couple of cars, a couple of vans, but these were few and far between. He guessed petrol was a rare commodity these days, with nobody to keep refilling pumps, without anyone to bring it over from abroad.

Some had reverted to using horses for transportation. Robert watched as a woman dismounted her steed, swinging a bag down as she went. Set up here and there were makeshift tables, trays with legs, or blankets laid on the ground. People were getting things out of their bags to place on these, arranging them carefully.

My God! It's a bloody car boot sale. Robert thought to himself. To his surprise, he found the corners of his mouth curling up. *An honest to goodness car boot sale!*

Only there weren't enough 'car boots' to justify the name. It was more like a market, just not as well laid out as those in Mansfield. The purpose was the same, however. Except Robert saw that here the traders were swapping items rather than paying money for them. In this 'society' what use were coins and bits of paper with the Queen's head on them? This part of England, at least, appeared to have regressed back to the barter system. Having seen nothing of his fellow man in an age, Robert was suddenly engrossed in the unfolding dramas; the flurry of activity as people from miles around gathered to do business. He'd completely forgotten what it was like to be in the proximity of other human beings, to have that contact with them. Was there a part of him now that missed it? No, it was better that he shut himself away, pretended the rest of the world didn't exist. Live out the remainder of his life ignorant of how the human race was getting along. It had no need for him and vice-versa.

But the same twist of fate that had saved him, killing the two most important people to him in the process, had other ideas.

Robert had been so distracted by the ad hoc market, he didn't notice the man behind him until it was too late.

"What ye doin' skulking about there?" said a voice with a thick, Derbyshire accent. "Aye, you there – you with the hood on. Get up and turn yessen around. And don't get any funny ideas about that bow yer carryin'."

Robert rose slowly, trying to stop himself from shaking. Was it fear or just excitement at being addressed after so long, at having someone other than a wild animal acknowledge his existence? He heard the distinctive click-clack of a gun being primed for action. And, sure enough, when he turned around, he was greeted with the sight of a man – early 40s, though he might have been younger, it was hard to tell after what he must have gone through in the past couple of years – and he was holding up a double-barrelled shotgun. It was a farmer's weapon, probably wielded by an ex-farmer. There'd certainly been enough of them round these parts. The ruddy complexion had faded somewhat, but Robert could tell that he must still spend a lot of his time outside. The pigeon-chested man wore a checked shirt beneath a tank top with holes in it, his trousers were loose as if he'd lost weight, and his boots had definitely seen better days.

"I'll say it again. What ye doin' spying back here?"

Robert said nothing, not even when the man lifted the shotgun higher, not quite aiming at him, but not pointing it away, either. Robert held up his hands to show he meant him no harm.

"What's a matter, can't ye speak or summat? Bit slow, eh?"

Robert shook his head to indicate that there was nothing wrong with his faculties. It had just been so long since he'd spoken, he wasn't even sure if he could anymore. Carefully, he began to reach across into his open coat.

"Keep yer hands where I can see 'em," instructed the man, moving forward.

"I..." began Robert. The sensation of talking felt odd;

alien even. The look of shock on his face must have registered, because the man frowned.

"Just what's yer game? We don't want no trouble at the market."

"No game. No trouble," Robert assured him. With each word, his voice grew stronger. "I've just come along to trade."

"That so?"

"It is. If you'll let me...?" Robert reached into his coat again, very slowly, the shotgun trained on him the whole time. "Easy... easy... See, in my pouch."

The man drew nearer to get a better look. "Rabbits?"

"Rabbits," repeated Robert.

Then the 'farmer' began to laugh: long, hard chuckles that caused his frame to shake. "Oh, that's a good un," he said eventually. "Rabbits... Judas Priest! What yer thinking of swappin' for them scrawny devils?"

Robert shrugged, pulling down his hood. "Whatever I can."

Lowering his shotgun, the other man wiped the tears from his eyes. "Aye, I'd be interested to see it an' all. Well, come on. Let's take yer down there, then, before all the best bargains are gone."

For a second, Robert hesitated, the very thought of meeting, of mixing with that number of people was terrifying. What if the men after him should happen by? "Is... is it safe?" asked Robert.

The man frowned. "Safe? What yer talkin' about?"

He didn't have a choice, he had to ask. "The... the men in yellow suits. The ones who set fire to the bodies."

He looked at Robert like he was insane. "Where yer bin, on Mars or somethin'?"

"Something," admitted Robert.

"They haven't bin round for ages, that lot. Not since the early days."

"What happened to them?"

"Dead," said the man, his face stern. "Like everyone else."

"So there was no cure?"

"Cure?" He laughed again, but there was a bitterness to it this time. "There were never any cure. Look, are ye comin' to the market or not? I haven't got all day."

Robert gave a small nod, and they began to walk across the field. The closer they came, the more he wanted to run – even though he knew the fear was irrational.

What if he's wrong – what if they're still out there somewhere, looking for you?

You heard what he said, they're all dead. Only the O-Negs are left. It's the grand total of the human race.

But...

"So, yer a poacher?" the man said, interrupting Robert's argument with himself. He nodded at the bow to emphasise what he meant.

"Can you poach something that doesn't belong to anyone anymore?"

"I meant before, like?"

"Not exactly," Robert said. *And you wouldn't believe me if I told you.*

They were nearly at the market and Robert could feel all eyes turning upon him. He wasn't a regular here, and everyone knew it. It was the same feeling as when he used to enter an unfamiliar neighbourhood to make an arrest.

"Well, 'ere we are then," said the man. "My name's Bill, by the way. Bill Locke." He stuck out his hand and Robert examined it for a moment before looking back up at his face. Such a simple act of humanity, of friendship, and it threw him completely. Then he reached out and shook it. The man's grip was rough and firm, once again emphasising that he'd worked with his hands all his life;

Robert couldn't compete with that – too many years of domestic bliss before embracing the wild.

He noticed the man was waiting for something, then realised he hadn't told him his own name. "I'm..." *I was... I used to be a man called Stokes. But what am I now? Who am I now?* "They call me Robert."

"How do then, Rob."

Bill finished pumping his hand, then let him go. Robert noticed that the people in the market seemed to accept him more now that they'd seen the handshake. Whatever Bill did here, whether it was organise the events, provide security, or simply trade, he was well respected.

Robert looked around at what was on offer. On one stall there was hand-made pottery, plates and cups; on another knitwear. A young woman of about twenty was selling these, but Robert imagined some old lady with O-Neg blood, sat somewhere knitting with whatever wool they could get her. And there were piles of other clothing, manufactured before The Cull: no dresses and skirts for women now, though, only more practical fare like trousers and jackets. One man had axes, knives, hammers – tools of various sizes and shapes – set out in front of him, obviously scavenged from hardware shops. A few batteries caught Robert's eye, mainly because he hadn't seen anything even remotely technological in so long. He found medical supplies on another blanket, antiseptics, pills – some identifiable, some not – plasters and bandages. There were suitcases, haversacks and holdalls, which at first he thought were just what the items had been carried here in, but then he saw people bartering for these, too.

There were tins of food, just like the ones Joanne had stockpiled and on which he'd lived after his family had died, but there was more fresh food to be found than anything else. Fruit and vegetables, which looked more appetising than anything he'd ever seen in a supermarket. Someone had taken their time growing these: ripe tomatoes, apples, runner beans, potatoes, most of them sold by a willowy woman with auburn hair. Very few pieces of fruit from more exotic climes, Robert noted, such as bananas or oranges. Hardly surprising now that there were fewer people to bring them in from overseas (*and just what was happening over there anyway – were they in the same state as this country?*). Everything here smacked of a survival instinct he could relate to, of human beings making do in the face of adversity. The ones that were left behind were obviously slowly forming communities of their own. He could tell that by the handfuls that had been sent to represent them at the market.

The meat – pork, beef and chicken – looked mouth-wateringly good, and now Robert understood why Bill had laughed when he showed him the rabbits. They weren't even skinned or properly prepared. Maybe next time he could bring some tastier treats from the ice houses.

Next time? What the hell was he thinking about... Robert couldn't come back here again. Couldn't allow himself to get drawn into the world again, to make friends, to talk with other people. Even if it were true and the men in those gas masks were no longer a problem, he still had his waiting to do, was still sworn to live out the rest of his life – however long or short that was – alone.

"Your first time here, huh?" said someone to the left of him. Lost in his thoughts, Robert gave a start. Then he looked over and his mouth dropped open.

Stevie?

He blinked once, twice, then saw the reality of who was in front of him.

The boy was twelve or thirteen, with a scruffy mop of hair that had once been blond – possibly could be again given a proper wash – and deep green eyes. He was wearing a baggy tracksuit, with a belt round the middle that had numerous pockets attached. He looked like he was playing superhero, but Robert knew full well that every single pocket would be filled with something important. The lad had a rucksack slung over his shoulder, which appeared to be full.

Robert opened his mouth, then closed it again, having completely forgotten what the kid had said.

"I haven't seen you here before," he continued, not put off by Robert's silence. The boy looked him up and down. "Would've remembered you, that's for sure. You have much to trade?"

Robert shook his head.

"That's a pity. It's a good market today, lots on offer. Isn't always that way, you know. Have to make the most of it while you can. I'm Mark, by the way."

Again, Robert just gaped at him. Was there a resemblance, or was it just in his head? True, Mark had a similar hair-tone, but his eyes were a different colour and he was much thinner, the cheekbones less padded with puppy fat.

"Who you here with, Mark?"

"What do you mean?"

"Your parents–" began Robert, then kicked himself when Mark looked down. Of course they were dead. Everyone was dead. "I'm sorry... Look, haven't you got anyone who takes care of you?"

Mark scowled at that one. "I take care of myself," he replied indignantly. "I'm not a kid."

Robert shook his head. "That wasn't what I meant."

"I find stuff myself, bring it here myself, trade it myself. Just like the others."

"There are more like you?" said Robert, barely able to conceal the shock from his voice.

"'Course. We're not professional collectors, mind, just snatch what we need to get by from the towns and cities." He appeared very proud of his profession. "We can get into places other people can't. And we're small enough to hide if there's trouble. I've got plenty of hiding places, me. So we go in, we come back out again. Easy."

"My God," Robert whispered to himself. He'd once seen a documentary about orphans who lived on the streets – or more specifically in the sewers of Bucharest, Romania. As the people had filmed them for the news report, bottles floated past in the dirty water and cockroaches climbed over the pipes where they slept. They were called 'The Forgotten Children'. When Robert looked at Mark he saw the same thing. In the wake of the virus, The Cull, these were England's forgotten children, left to fend for themselves, because if they didn't they would die. What kind of future did they have to look forward to?

"It's no big deal," said Mark, smiling. He reached into his bag and pulled out a chocolate bar with a purple wrapper, then proffered it to Robert. "You want one? I got dozens."

Robert held up a hand to say no, then reconsidered. How long had it been since he'd tasted chocolate? Far longer than he'd been in the woods. It used to be his weakness at Christmas and Easter. Part of him was tempted now, but another part was linking this small pleasure to those times in his life when he'd been happy; seeing Stevie opening his presents, his eggs, Joanne playfully threatening that she'd take the box of Dark Delicious away from Robert as they sat watching the holiday movies. What right did he have to that now? "No," he said to Mark, "thanks, but no."

Mark shrugged and opened the bar, biting off a chunk with the same glee that Stevie always did.

Stevie.

Robert was suddenly aware that he could no longer stay here. That if he did he might just break down and start bawling his eyes out in front of all these people, in front of Mark. The pain was still too real for him, still too close.

"I've got to go," he said, voice shaky.

"Wait..." Mark started, but Robert was already walking away from the boy, from the market.

"I'm sorry," Robert called back over his shoulder, pulling up his hood as he went. He strode past Bill, who was haggling with another man over the 'price' of an onion.

"Off s'soon?" said Bill. "Any joy with them rabbits?" When Robert didn't answer him, he laughed and said: "Thought not. Better luck next time, eh? We're 'ere most Wednesdays, all day..."

But the voice was fading as Robert broke into a run. He sprinted across the field, not daring to look back. He just needed to return to the safety of the woods, the cover the trees and foliage gave him.

Just like Mark, he had his own hiding places.

CHAPTER FIVE

As De Falaise sat back in the seat, he'd pull down his sunglasses occasionally and glance in the wing mirror of the Bedford armoured truck. From this angle it was difficult to see the extent of the line, but he knew it stretched right back along the motorway, zigzagging its way around the stationary cars with skeletons at the wheels. From the air it would have looked like a convoy: one of the wagon trains from the Old West, or even an army during the crusades (as a student of history, these kinds of comparisons amused him). But instead of being on horseback or in wagons, his men were encased in Challenger 2 battle tanks, Warrior Mechanised Combat Vehicles, Hummer muscle jeeps, Land Rover Wolves, open top WIMIKs, and other Bedfords: some capable of carrying up to twenty troops. Keeping them all in line were motorbikes patrolling the length of the convoy, ridden by his trusted elite brought across the Channel with him.

Like Tanek, driving this truck. The olive-skinned man stared ahead at the road, changing gears every so often, but never taking his eyes off the route ahead. De Falaise admired his single-mindedness. It reminded him of his own. He recalled the first time he'd come across the soldier, in a small provincial town in Turkey. De Falaise had been engaged in a highly illegal gun-running operation when the virus struck, and was quite grateful that people began dropping like flies because he'd been well on his way to getting caught... or killed. He subsequently decided to make his way towards Istanbul, with a plan to somehow travel through Europe and get back home to France. The plan wasn't very clear in his mind, mainly because it was every man for himself in the region at that precise time. What money he had acquired from the deal meant nothing, and De Falaise was beginning to regret handing over the firearms he'd snuck across the borders of several countries. Bullets now seemed to be the only way to get anything, and the only way to stay alive.

He certainly hadn't expected to run into his soon-to-be second-in-command outside a small watering hole there. The bar had been quite full, some of the men inside immune to the disease that was sweeping its way across the world, some of them in the later stages of it and desperate to drink themselves to death. De Falaise had realised long ago that there was no point in attempting to outrun the virus, nor was there any point in trying to avoid the people who were coughing up blood everywhere. If it was his time, then so be it; he'd meet the Devil and shake his hand. Who knows, maybe he'd even get a line of congratulation or two for services rendered. As it turned out, De Falaise was one of those spared, so perhaps his 'good' work hadn't gone unnoticed after all. *The Devil looks after his own*, isn't that what they always said? If so, then he'd also looked after this hulking great brute of a man who'd been taking on all comers in that very bar.

Drawing nearer, the Frenchman watched, increasingly impressed, as the fighter picked up men and swung them over his head, using moves he'd never come across before to floor others (De Falaise had later found out this fighting style was called krav manga, a martial art taught by the Israeli army, which Tanek had adapted to suit his own purposes). Breaking one man's nose, driving his fist so hard into it that there was nothing left of the bridge, Tanek had incapacitated another by arcing his forearm and crushing the man's windpipe with a crack that made De Falaise wince. It was then that De Falaise spotted an attacker creeping up on Tanek, knife drawn and ready to spring. He shouted out to the big man to warn him, but Tanek was already pivoting – with a grace that belied his size – and was unslinging what looked like a rifle. It wasn't until the two bolts had been fired, striking the man squarely in the chest, that De Falaise recognised it as a crossbow; but no ordinary one (modified by Tanek himself based on ancient Chinese Chu-ko-nu repeater designs, able to fire from a magazine without the need for single bolt reloading). The rest of the men fled from the scene after that, leaving Tanek and De Falaise alone.

Tanek had raised the crossbow, inserting another magazine, and for a moment De Falaise thought he might shoot him too. But no. Tanek walked over, kicking fallen chairs and bodies aside, and stood before him. Then, in that hybrid Southern European-Middle Eastern accent of his barely anyone got to hear, Tanek thanked him for the warning.

Taking a couple of bottles of whiskey and two glasses from behind the now deserted bar, De Falaise and Tanek drank and talked, though the larger man would only disclose the least amount of information about himself that he could get away with, all in that monotone voice of his. Information like the fact that he'd once worked as a torturer and knew every single pressure point on the body, especially those that caused the maximum of pain. De Falaise, in turn, told Tanek why he was there, what he was doing, and what he was about to do next.

"I've been in this business for some time, mon ami, but have always had a craving to see the guns I sell put to better use. To build up an army of my own." He recalled joyous times as a child, playing with toy soldiers – when he wasn't constructing gallows out of Meccano, much to his parents' dismay – sending his troops into 'battle', relishing the authority it gave him even at that young age. "It strikes me that we can look upon this little...

incident as either a setback or an opportunity," De Falaise had said, knocking back a shot of the whisky. "And I, for one, have always been an opportunist. There is much to gain from being organised where others are not, from being able to take advantage of a certain situation and use it fully. History teaches us that, if nothing else." And to emphasise his point, he quoted the Carpetbaggers at the end of the American Civil War, who had come from the North, exploiting the South's weakened state to gain money and power. He laughed when he saw Tanek's eyes glazing over. "I apologise. The subject has always fascinated me. History goes in cycles, that is what my old teacher once said. Now he was a dying breed of patriot."

The more he talked, about moving up into Europe, about gathering a band of men as he went, about taking their fair share of the glory on offer, the more De Falaise convinced himself that night. Before, he hadn't really had much of a clue what to do, but now, as he explained the basics of his spur of the moment plan, the more it sounded like the one and only course of action.

There was scope here to take control fully. But where to start? Germany? Italy? Or – De Falaise's dream – his homeland of France? But, as they were to discover, it would not prove so easy to achieve. Others, just like De Falaise, had already had the same idea. They were professionals and they'd organised themselves more quickly than he'd had a chance to. It was true that he'd recruited his core group during this sweep of Europe – like Henrik the German with a passion for fine cigars, silver-haired Dutchman Reinhart, an expert marksman, the Lithuanian Rudakas, the broad Italian Savero, and Javier, originally of Mexican descent but now operating out of Spain, who in spite of his belly was a mean fighter. All were former mercenaries, their allegiance given to power and riches, rather than any flag. But together they hardly constituted the army De Falaise had envisaged. And though they'd been lucky in acquiring some weapons and transportation, the group finding bikes easier to manoeuvre in the heat of guerrilla warfare, they'd also been thrashed any number of times and been forced to retreat, losing many good foot soldiers in the process.

All of which meant that by the time De Falaise and his officers entered France, they were in no mood for the resistance they met there either. On the one hand, it made him proud that his people hadn't just rolled over and given in. But on the other, it meant that De Falaise would be denied the role of Governor here as well.

"Merde," he'd muttered to himself as they were driven out of Paris by the most powerful gang in charge there. "It was such a good plan, too."

But there was still hope. Whispers reached them that across the sea, the once 'Great' Britain was but a shadow of its former self. And something about that definitely appealed to De Falaise, as it probably would have done to his old history teacher. Just like in 1066, when William the Conqueror's Norman army had landed at Pevensey beach and then defeated Harold at Hastings, De Falaise would claim the place as his own. William had quashed all the rebellions after he was crowned King, so why shouldn't he do the same? It was also the chance to put right a few wrongs. The outrages of the Hundred Years' War, for example, when repeated attempts to take over France had failed – and then, of course, there was Napoleon's defeat at Waterloo. That still stung. The one-time Emperor's downfall after that had been swift and marked a turning point in the war between Britain and France that straddled the eighteenth and nineteenth Centuries. A war which, at its heart, went back much further.

De Falaise had to know for sure, however, what condition the island was in. Which was why they'd made the effort of staking out the Channel Tunnel. Sooner or later, he realised, someone was bound to come through it from the other side and then... well, they'd get first hand information about the situation.

"Everything's gone to shit. It's chaos... Fucking chaos. Why do you think we came through the tunnel? It's like being back in the dark ages."

How appropriate, thought De Falaise.

So they'd made the trek to Britain, penetrating the island at Folkestone and working their way up to the Nation's capital. What they'd found en route backed up everything the tortured Englishman had told them. Small groups of thugs roaming the streets, with no imagination, no sense of the 'bigger picture'. Here and there certain areas were 'ruled' by tin-pot dictators, but their troops were few in number and there was no sense of working together for a common goal; at least not on the scale De Falaise was aiming for. In London itself, they found the same thing – nebulous gangs with no one person in charge of all of them. When he came along, all of that soon changed. He'd offered them a simple choice: life, under his leadership and protection, or death – which could either be swift or not, depending on what mood his men were in. Tanek did like to keep his hand in, to practise his skills. Back in the early days, De Falaise had once seen him keep someone alive for a week in constant agony. There was a talent to that, an art.

But this hadn't been their only reason to visit London. De Falaise needed information. He remembered the day they entered Parliament, the ease with which they'd dispatched the mob that had taken it over; its defences already immobilised at some point in the past. Those morons hadn't had the first clue about defending their position. He could have held the building and stayed there, or perhaps staked his claim on Buckingham Palace.

But De Falaise was much smarter than that. All he was after was paperwork: not the documents these street thugs had managed to rip to shreds in their boredom, but the really secret stuff hidden in safes that De Falaise cracked with plastic explosives. He found nothing about the AB Virus, but then he wasn't expecting to here. The politicians had probably known just as little as everyone else and the real secret of what had happened – whether it was man-made, natural or whatever – was probably tucked away in some covert location long forgotten about now, in whatever country its origin lay. Anyway, that didn't interest him.

De Falaise was more concerned with finding a list of all military installations – Army, Air Force and Navy, plus any American bases – which he eventually did. Especially secret barracks, Special Ops and the like. The defence systems had all been computerised, but when the electricity failed these reverted to multiple key lock systems, which his men got through with explosives. Quite a number of places had already been cleaned out, they found, and when they came across a couple of ex-squaddies still laughably trying to defend one of the installations, they discovered why. Operation Motherland: a botched attempt to round up all military weapons when the dust of The Culling Year had barely settled. Unorganised and misguided, the authorities thankfully hadn't had enough manpower to reach every UK base, particularly further up north. At various sites they found such weaponry as SA-80A2 assault rifles, Enfield L86s, MP5s, M4Comp, Colt Commandos and M203 machine guns, along with Milan Anti-Tank missile systems, LAW 90 anti-armour weaponry, bazookas, grenade launchers and plenty of grenades. At US installations around Northamptonshire, plus USAF Molesworth, and the RAF/USAF Alconbury Air Base, they came away with M16s, Remington combat shotguns, Minimi machine guns, Colt, Berretta and Sig Sauer handguns.

And so, on his way to the Midlands, the real seat of power for any invasion, De Falaise not only swelled his ranks, he also built up his arsenal. Clothed in a strange mixture of uniforms and kept going by food supplies and untapped fuel reserves they'd needed to power the vehicles they were driving today (including additional Honda and Suzuki motorbikes loaded onto the trucks) the men he'd picked up along the way didn't seem to regret their decision. Once they were armed to the teeth – though not without a little training 'on site' at the ranges – and had full bellies, they were content enough. Some of the pressure had lifted, they didn't have to think for themselves anymore. They were finally his to command.

Which brought him back to the present and their last drive up the motorway. He was taking his ever-burgeoning army to set up a headquarters, from which he could spread outwards. But where would they go? That was the question he had thought long and hard about. Buildings like the council offices in Whetstone, like Parliament, were not that easy to defend anymore, as they'd proved. What they really needed was something designed to repel attacks. Tailor made to that one specific purpose.

So De Falaise once again looked to the past.

According to guides of the United Kingdom he'd picked up on his jaunt through the capital, there were several castles to choose from in the central area of England that might suit: Castle Howard, for example, North of York; Conisbrough Castle, near the town which featured in Sir Walter Scott's novel, *Ivanhoe* – and just to the west of Doncaster; or Bolsover Castle, dating from the seventeenth century. But in the end it was a very easy decision.

The sign on the motorway showed that they were

nearing their junction, and Tanek radioed to the rest of the convoy that they would soon be branching off for their target. Their truck led the way into the city itself, down roads that were more densely packed with abandoned cars: so much so that one of the Challengers had to overtake and plough them out of the way, parting the metallic sea like a khaki Moses. It made sense for this behemoth to be in front anyway, now that they were heading into potentially hostile territory again.

The vehicles made their way into the middle of the city, but saw very little in the way of action until they'd almost reached the bus depot, passing red brick buildings, some with square windows, others arched, many with looted shops below. The square grey building, which looked like it housed a multi-storey car park as well, was obviously being used as some sort of HQ. And the people inside, who leaned over and started firing at the vehicles, were also quite well armed.

Bullets pinged off the tanks, the trucks and the APCs, as the motorcycle escorts zipped just ahead of the shots.

De Falaise radioed to Henrik, who was driving the tank up front. He could imagine the man, still chomping on one of those cigars he loved so much, loading a live shell and then working the tank gun so that it pointed at the depot. The thunderous roar that accompanied the blast was deafening. It took out a chunk of the building's side, and with it most of the people who'd been firing at the vehicles. When the smoked cleared, a blue sign with a white 'P' on it was dangling from the corner of the wounded building.

More gunfire, this time from the ground level. Men and women emerging from the white classical-looking buildings to the left. De Falaise's men returned fire using the range of rifles they'd amassed which, even in their rookie hands, were more than a match for cannibalised handguns and shotguns. Some hostiles were even using air rifles!

The skirmish lasted all of ten minutes. It was obvious that, as elsewhere, no one was anywhere near ready to fight such a superior foe.

That proved to be the case again as they carried on up towards the market square, its fountain long-since dried up. Packs of armed people used the city's buses and trams – some of which had been tipped onto their sides – for cover. More shells from the tanks caused them to calm down and a series of rockets were launched at the square's council house, cracking the grey-green clock tower dome and the pillars that stood out front, while the stone lions that guarded the entranceway looked on. Its inhabitants raced from the building, fleeing like mice from a skirting board. They held their hands in the air, not saying a word as De Falaise's men took them prisoner. Each would be offered the same 'opportunity' to serve in his employ.

Onward they went, trampling what little resistance they encountered like a size fourteen boot stamping on an ants' nest. To De Falaise's surprise and delight, he found the main object of their campaign virtually untouched. Not one person appeared to have had the same notion as him, to use this as their base – when it seemed such an obvious candidate. They entered through the black metal side gates round the corner from the main arched gateway, letting their vehicles inside.

Once his men had established that there was nobody in residence, De Falaise and Tanek stepped out of their Bedford to survey the area. The gardens were in turmoil, now that there was nobody to maintain them: in fact they were creeping over onto the path, snaking their way towards his future residence. To his right, De Falaise spotted a war memorial, the names of the dead who'd fallen in action. And he could just see some steps behind all the foliage, beneath which were two archways set into the rocks.

But there would be time to explore both the grounds and the inside later. For now, De Falaise just wanted to drink this all in.

The grand majesty of the square, cream-coloured building – not the original one, by any means - was steeped in history, and had reinvented itself several times over. It was also still here to tell the tale; standing in front of him for a reason.

"So," he finally said to Tanek. "What do you think?"

Tanek grunted, but De Falaise couldn't really tell whether it was in approval.

Then, turning to the rest of his men he said with a sense of pride: "Gentlemen, is she not magnifique? Our new home. I give to you the famous... Nottingham Castle."

CHAPTER SIX

It was their new home, and they were very proud of it. Life was good.

Clive Maitland stepped back, took off his glasses, and wiped the sweat from his brow. Although he'd complained before, he'd never worked as hard as he had in the time since the virus. Back then he'd only had paperwork and a handful of unruly children to contend with. Now he was getting this community back on its feet; a new community that was made up of what was left of many others. He was proud of the fact that he'd drawn them all together, that were it not for his efforts they might have just faded away, not quite sure what had happened to the world, but positive that they wanted nothing whatsoever to do with the new one they'd found themselves in.

They'd lost more than he could ever imagine. Loved ones dying right in front of them, and there was nothing they could do about it. Clive had been single, had never really had a relationship that had gone past the 'let's be friends' stage, and had no surviving family save for an aunt who now lived in Canada. Or at least she had lived in Canada, until the virus caught up with them over there. His Aunty Glenda had been type AB Rhesus Negative, he was pretty sure of that because his Mum used to comment on how rare a group it was.

Much rarer than O-Negative.

In a funny sort of way, though, he'd had the most to lose of all. None of the kids that he'd taught had survived, leastways he didn't think so; he'd certainly never come across any of them in the post-Cull period. Sometimes he saw their faces in his dreams; his nightmares. *Christ*, what a time that had been...

He'd seen registration in the mornings dwindle down to virtually nothing. Then again, there were hardly any teachers reporting for duty either. In the weeks that followed it soon became apparent that the human race was facing its toughest test since the floods of Biblical times. Only instead of drowning in water, people were drowning in their own internal juices. It didn't take a genius to work out what would happen next.

So, when the authorities had tried to round up survivors, burning the dead in the streets or in their houses, Clive had driven away from the towns and cities, his estate car laden with cans of petrol, food, and bottles of water. He'd driven as far north as he could, finding, quite by chance, a tiny little village – if you could even call it that – out in the middle of nowhere. The kind of place they put on picture postcards advertising Britain to tourists. The authorities hadn't touched it, and Clive doubted whether they'd ever get round to it in time. But, like everywhere else, the dead were in the streets, and they were in their homes.

The stench was incredible, but he'd covered his mouth with a scarf and dragged the bodies from the two main streets – all this place boasted – into one of the fields. Then he'd gone into the houses, carrying out men and women, parents, grandparents (one old man had died alone in his cottage, just sitting in his rocking chair, blood staining his light blue shirt), and children. They'd been the worst of all, because again it brought back scenes of the playground, the classroom. But Clive had to be strong. They weren't coming back and there was a definite risk of other diseases if he just left them as they were. Diseases that the survivors could catch if they weren't careful. Wouldn't that beat all, dying from a secondary virus? The dead would have their revenge after all.

Whether there hadn't been anyone with O-Neg blood

in this village or they'd simply left, he had no idea. All Clive knew was that there wasn't another living soul here, which suited him fine for the time being.

After burning the bodies, careful to do it in the most secluded spot he could find in case the smoke should draw unwanted attention, he set about biding his time.

When he'd been a teacher, the most important subjects had always been Maths and English – even the government said so. People who taught stuff like he did were virtually second-class citizens; that's how he'd always felt, anyway. But what good was Shakespeare right now, and why would you ever need to work out a quadratic equation when faced with the end of the world? Clive's subject – Sociology – had suddenly been promoted to one of the most important, along with Woodwork and Metalwork (sorry, Technology, as they called it these days), people who worked with their hands. Not to mention the domestic sciences, and those who also knew how to grow food.

Clive was more than familiar with how the structures of society operated; realised that it would be better to sit out all the violence and mayhem which would follow the collapse of reason and logic. Without law and order, without the police and judicial systems, everything would go to rack and ruin. One day, a dominant force or authority might well take control, hopefully for the better good – but meanwhile it was time to build up smaller communities so that the values of civilisation were not lost for ever. It was time to go back to basics.

First things first, Clive had to gather that community. This he did eventually by travelling round other rural areas, searching for survivors. It was in a medium-sized village just outside Derby that he came upon Gwen, a young woman who had also decided to live rather than just give up. He first saw her sitting at a bus stop as if waiting for a number 22 to come along. Thin, but naturally so, she was dressed in jeans and a jumper, her auburn hair tied back in a ponytail, and she was smoking a cigarette.

"Hi," he'd called from his car. "Are you okay?"

She took a drag on the cigarette, looking over at him. When she stood up, Clive saw the bloodstained carving knife at her hip.

"Look, I don't mean you any harm. I'm searching for other survivors."

There must have been something about the tone of his voice, perhaps the kindness in it – or maybe it was his inoffensive appearance? – that told her she didn't need to defend herself this time. She'd gone over to the car and, after a moment's hesitation, climbed inside. When he'd coughed at the cigarette smoke, she'd thrown it out of the window. "Sorry, I had quit before..."

Clive nodded.

She told him her story, of what it was like in Derby now – exactly how he'd pictured it. Gangs of hooligans were in charge, acting like animals. With no fear of reprisals and after seeing people they cared about die in such a horrific way, the darker side of human nature had emerged. Like him, Gwen had been single, and she'd tried to hide away in her house, down a street not far away from the Metro Theatre. There she pretended everything was okay. It was when a trio of men broke in and tried to attack her that she'd had to defend herself with the knife. She'd got out the back window, and run – away from the house, away from the city. That's how she'd lived since that day, alone, on the run.

As Clive drove, he explained what he was trying to do and asked a) if she wanted to join him, and b) if she would help in the search. Gwen had thought about this for all of ten seconds before replying yes. All she really wanted now was a chance at normal life, or as close to normality as anyone got these days. Clive could relate to that.

Together they'd scoured the outlying regions of Derby, Mansfield, Sheffield. There had been some frightening moments, like the time Clive had stalled the car just as a nutter brandishing a cricket bat had appeared to start battering the vehicle.

"Six... Six...?" he'd shouted as he hammered the paintwork. "Umpire, he's out, surely?" One look at the man's wide eyes and slavering mouth told them that he'd lost his mind completely. Fumbling with the ignition, Clive had restarted the estate and backed it up away from him.

However, slowly but surely, they grew in number, bringing the sane and willing people they found back to the safe haven Clive had created for them. As he said to each and every one of them, it didn't matter what the place had been called before: now the village was named 'Hope'. They'd even made a sign, which they planted on the main street.

It was a name Reverend Tate definitely approved of. They'd found this very special man one day, on his knees, praying inside a vandalised church. The thugs that had been desecrating the building were strewn around him. Tate had crossed himself and risen, leaning on his thick walking stick, asking what he could do for the newcomers. When they just stared at the felled men, Tate's explanation had been, "The Lord moves in mysterious ways." (Later they learned that the Reverend actually taught self-defence out in the community to the vulnerable. "God helps those who help themselves," he'd explained, patting his stick. "But not that way.")

The small, squat man, who walked with a slight limp and looked like he'd probably been bald since his teens, had hesitated when they'd asked him to come with them, arguing that he couldn't leave his flock. When Clive pointed out there were precious few of those left, and that the new flock he was gathering would need religious guidance, Tate finally agreed.

Clive was pleased he had, because he enjoyed his late night chats with the holy man, who suggested that there was a rhyme and pattern to all of this, that it was part of God's plans for them.

"Everything happens for a reason," Tate often said to him, "even if we can't see what that is right now."

"You really believe that?"

"Don't you?" the Reverend threw back at him. "He spared you, spared all of us for some purpose. And I think you might well have found yours, Clive. Your brains, your leadership qualities have saved these people. Saved us all."

It was true that without him the community of Hope would still be out there, lost. He'd organised them, found out what people's strengths were and put them to practical use. For example, June Taylor was a former midwife, so she had medical knowledge. Graham Leicester used to work in a garden centre, but as well as cultivating flowers he'd also had his own allotment. Clive worked in conjunction with him, at first taking over one of the large greenhouses they found in someone's back garden, but then on more ambitious schemes such as planting crops out in the fields. This is where Andy Hobbs, who used to be a gym instructor, and Nathan Brown, who had worked as a farmhand one summer, came into their own: ploughing the fields so that Hope would have a good harvest this year. It was only recently, in the last six months or so, that Clive had got wind of the markets where food and other items could be traded, so every now and again they would visit these with produce or whatever else they had to offer. Already, the 'economy' – however rudimentary – was getting back on its feet it would seem, society finding a way of rebuilding what had been destroyed. This also proved an opportunity to touch base with other burgeoning communities.

Though they were small in number, maybe thirty people at most (others were much, much smaller), they all got on and were working towards something together. Without Clive's influence and guidance there would have been none of that.

And without his pro-action he would never have met Gwen, who, over the course of time they'd known each other, had become extremely important to him. In the days before the virus, Clive doubted that a woman as good looking and kind – and, let's face it, pretty much perfect – as Gwen would have even looked his way, although she always told him he was wrong. Now, in this bubble, this experiment – a micro community really – he was rapidly becoming her whole world. They'd already 'adopted' a couple of the little ones they'd found on their searches, some no more than five or six, alone and scrabbling about for food or water. But one day, Clive realised, there would come a time when he and Gwen might start a family of their own. They'd even talked about asking Tate to marry them. They weren't the only ones, either. Folk, of all ages, were pairing up, whether it was for companionship, or love, or a human instinct to carry on the species.

Which was why he was out here today, working on turning the tiny village hall into an even tinier school. He was fixing up the place with the help of young Darryl Wade. The lad was barely into his twenties, but had been trained well by his handyman father before he'd died – in the hopes Darryl would take over the family business one day. It was this kind of passing down of skills Clive sought to encourage. The world no longer needed IT experts, estate agents or insurance brokers.

Outside in the sunshine, Clive was sanding down the first set of desk tops. He'd been working hard all morning and was looking forward to the communal dinner they would have outside the local pub, with freshly baked bread (that was one of Gwen's talents) and fresh meat picked up just recently from one of the markets: lamb today, if he wasn't very much mistaken. And as he placed the glasses back on his head, bringing a figure walking towards him into focus, Clive smiled a greeting at Gwen. All things considered, life was good in Hope, and much better than the alternative.

"Hello you," said Gwen, carrying a tray of blackcurrant juice across from the house they'd picked out together. She looked over at the desks, then at the work he and Darryl had done on the door to the hall. Gwen nodded, suitably impressed. "Been working hard, I see."

She placed the tray down and Clive gave her a kiss. She was wearing a flowery summer dress, even though they were barely into the spring, her auburn hair loose, flowing over her shoulders, and Clive thought that he'd never seen anything so beautiful in his life. He slipped a hand around her waist and she placed an arm over his shoulder. They both looked at the hall, knowing that in years to come it would probably become the true embodiment of Hope.

"Who's looking after Sally and Luke?" Sally was their little girl's real name, Luke was the one they'd given their boy when they found the poor mite.

"June's got them; they're happy enough playing out in the garden. Where's Darryl?"

"Inside; he's taking a look at the rafters. Apparently there was quite a bit of rot up in the roof. That's something else which'll need sorting out."

"There's time," Gwen told him.

"There is," he agreed, kissing her again. "For all kinds of things. Gwen, I–" There was a noise in the distance that made him pause. "Do you hear that?"

Gwen cocked an ear. "Sounds like an engine."

Clive listened again. "Sounds like *lots* of engines."

"Might just be someone passing by up on the main road," she offered, but her expression told him she was worried. They never had visitors to Hope – not even from the other communities they'd made contact with – and that was the way they preferred it.

The noise was drawing closer.

"Does... does that sound like a motorbike to you?" asked Gwen.

Clive took her hand and ran down the street, rounding the corner. The people of Hope had come out of their houses to see what was happening. Andy and Nathan had heard the racket and ventured down from the upper field. Graham Leicester was approaching from up the street, running towards Clive. "Men..." he spluttered, out of breath.

But then Clive saw for himself. They rode up the small street behind Graham, just as Clive had done all that time ago when he first came upon this place. There were three on bikes, the rest in jeeps. All wore uniforms, but as they got closer Clive could see they were a mishmash of Army, Navy and Air Force, British and US; obviously stolen. As were the weapons they were brandishing, heavy duty rifles and pistols. Some looked uncomfortable handling them, others looked very much at home. One of the soldiers on the bikes stretched out a leg and kicked Graham over into the dirt when he passed.

It was now that Clive realised his fundamental error. In seeking to gather together people who could make this community flourish, leaving behind the violent and the psychopathic, he'd left this place wide open to attack from the same. Hope had no defences whatsoever, and they'd been too reliant on its isolated location to shield them from the outside world. Now that outside world had found them, and they were about to pay the price.

Several men climbed from the jeeps, their boots stomping the street. And their apparent leader, his paunch so big he only just fit inside, got out too. Andy ran at one of the soldiers, swinging a hoe, knocking the man to the ground. For his trouble he was hit in the back of the head with the butt of a rifle. He went down hard and stayed there.

The man with the belly waved his hand, giving the signal to open fire. There was some hesitation, but then muzzles flashed, spitting bullets at the cottages which housed the people of Hope. These men didn't appear to care whether there were folk inside or not. Windows shattered, walls were pock-marked. The sign they'd made came crashing down to the ground. From somewhere Clive heard screaming, but couldn't tell if it came from a man, woman or a child. Gwen held on to him, and he pressed her head into his shoulder, covering her ears.

How could I have been so stupid?

The fat man gave another signal and Clive watched as small objects were tossed at the cottages, and at the pub. Seconds later, the first of the grenades exploded. There followed two or three more, drawing out the rest of the inhabitants of this place. They fell to the ground, covering their heads. Behind Clive and Gwen, Darryl appeared, his mouth gaping open. Then Clive saw June with the kids; she had Luke in her arms, crying, while Sally was holding her hand.

This isn't what I promised them.

Their leader held up a hand for them to cease, simultaneously pulling a pistol from a holster with the other. "That's enough," he shouted. Clive detected a slight Hispanic accent when the man spoke. He walked down the small street, eyes darting left and right, as if daring anyone else to trying something.

"So, people of..." The man looked down at the fallen sign they had made. He chuckled. "People of Hope. My name is Javier. Major Javier. Who here speaks for you?"

Clive made to move forwards, but Gwen tugged at his shirt. She shook her head, but he patted her hand to tell her it was okay. "That would be me," Clive called out.

Javier looked him up and down, perhaps wondering how such a man could have banded together the group; how he could have commanded such respect and loyalty without the threat of fear. "And you are?"

"Clive Maitland," he said, trying to toughen up his voice but failing miserably. "And I demand that you–"

"Demand? You *demand?*" He lifted his pistol and pointed it at Clive, who bit his lip. "Well, let me tell you what I demand, little man. I represent the new power in the region and he has sent me out to meet his... subjects. In fact, he's sent out many more of his men to do the same. His name is De Falaise of Nottingham Castle, so remember that. In the years to come everyone will know it. Cooperate and things will go smoothly for you. Oppose him, and they will not."

"What does this De Falaise want with us?" Clive asked.

"Your fealty, your tribute," came the answer. "You have stocks here of food?"

"They are for trading, for feeding my people."

Javier wagged a finger. "Except they're not your people anymore, are they? Were you not listening, Señor Maitland?" He waved a hand around to indicate the community of Hope. "They belong to De Falaise: just as this village is now under his 'protection'."

So this was what would fill the void. He'd been expecting something one day, but not this. Not a return to the old days that history warned them all about. "He's like a monarch, then," observed Clive. "Or would he prefer Sheriff?"

Javier thought about this for a second. "Sheriff? Yes, I think he would like the sound of that title very much. We will take most of what you have to feed our troops." He rubbed his inflated stomach. "Like me, they are all growing boys."

Clive stepped forward. "But how are we expected to eat? There are children here."

Javier paused before answering. "That is not my concern. But if you keep this up, we might well be tempted to take a few... other things back with us as well." He leered over Clive's shoulder at Gwen. "She's yours, yes?"

"She doesn't belong to anybody!" snapped Clive.

"What did I just say? You all belong to De Falaise. And I think he would be more than happy if I brought her back for him." Javier pushed Clive aside and made for Gwen. Darryl looked like he was going to do something, but the raised pistol dissuaded him. Clive knew that Gwen no longer carried the knife she'd once used to protect herself. If only he'd left her at the bus stop, she might have been safe. Or she might be dead already, he told himself. At least this way they had a fighting chance.

"Wait... wait," said Clive, following Javier. "Look, take the food – you're welcome to it. We'll manage somehow." There were a few gasps from the villagers, but he knew they'd understand. This was one of their own at risk, and any of the women could be next.

Javier turned. "I don't need your permission. And the more I think about it, the more De Falaise will be pleased if I bring back such an elegant lady." He stepped forward, reaching out to touch Gwen's cheek. Her face soured, then she bit the hand he was proffering.

"Ahwww!" screamed Javier, sticking it under his arm. "You'll regret that!" He struck her across the face with the pistol, sending her reeling back.

"Gwen!" shouted Clive and dove at the fat man. He didn't want to join the rest of the survivors in their grieving, couldn't bear to lose the only person he'd ever truly loved – not now, not like this. But sensing the imminent attack, Javier spun and fired a single bullet. It hit Clive in the ribs, tearing into him and out the other side. He dropped to his knees, glasses falling from his head. Clive clutched his side, bringing one hand up and seeing the blood there – his blood, spilling out of him like juice from a punctured carton. The people of Hope gaped, horrified. Gwen lay on the floor, blood and tears pouring down her face.

"I have to ask myself, is it brains?" said Javier as he approached Clive. "Is that why they follow you? Is that why she looks at you that way?"

Clive didn't know how to answer.

"I think it is." Javier leaned over him and snatched the glasses from his head. "You want to see them, Señor Maitland? Want to see those brains?"

"No!" shouted a voice. Someone, a blur to Clive, was moving towards them. It was too big and bulky to be Gwen, that was for sure. He squinted and saw the outline of Reverend Tate there. "In God's name, no!" He brought down his walking stick hard across Javier's shoulder blades. The Major let out another cry, then spun on his second attacker. Clive saw Javier raise his gun, but Tate grabbed his arm. The two men wrestled for control of the weapon. Other soldiers were coming across to help, but not quick enough. Javier was struggling to bring the pistol up, Tate attempting to stop him – but it was obvious who was winning.

"Please! This serves no purpose. Can't you see that?" Tate shouted.

The figures were just fuzzy outlines to Clive now. Then there was a sharp bang, followed by a scream from Gwen. Tate fell back, leaving Javier standing above him.

He's killed him, thought Clive, *that bastard's killed the Reverend.* But then he was aware of a cold sensation spreading over him. His sight was no longer fuzzy, it was dim. Fading. There was a pain in his temple, only the briefest of twinges. But there was no time to register anything else.

Clive didn't feel himself toppling over – though in the final few milliseconds of his life, Tate's words echoed all around him. "Everything happens for a reason."

He was at a loss to understand this one, he had to admit. He'd never see Sally or Luke, never see Gwen again: never hold her in his arms, feel her lips brushing against his.

Clive wouldn't feel the loss now, but she would. He knew she'd mourn him, and he was truly sorry.

But none of that mattered anymore. It was all going black, completely black.

And never before had he realised the true significance of what he'd thought earlier.

Life was indeed good.

"You evil... evil thing," the Reverend Tate hissed from the floor, several rifles trained on him. "He was a good man and now..."

Javier walked over and looked down at what he'd done. Clive Maitland's brains were spilling out onto the sign he'd helped to make, the name he'd given to this place. "There are no good men anymore. And there is no hope."

A tight smile played on his lips at the double meaning of his words. Turning back, he said: "It is fortunate for you that you are a man of the cloth; it is bad luck to shoot a holy man."

"May you burn in Hell for what you've done."

Javier snorted. "Look around you," he said, pointing to the fires with his still smoking pistol. "We're already there, together. Now, if you will excuse me." He nodded to the men to pick the catatonic woman up off the ground, her eyes still fixed on the dead man. "Put her in one of the jeeps."

Two of the soldiers grabbed Gwen by the arms, dragging her up and along the street.

"Christ who art in Heaven," said Tate, "how can you allow this?" It wasn't the first time he'd asked since the virus had struck, but the first time his faith had been shaken in such a way.

Though Tate thought he detected the Mexican flinching when he'd mentioned the Saviour's name, Javier ignored his words and made to follow his men.

Tate clenched his fists and repeated his question, looking away from Clive's body as he did so, towards June and the children Gwen and Clive had been looking after – both now in tears. Then he thought about what Javier had said. That there were no good men left, that there was no hope...

And prayed to God that the man was wrong.

CHAPTER SEVEN

The lake stretched out ahead, a mirrored surface. He was walking around the edge of it, strolling along without a care in the world. Gorgeously green foliage surrounded him, and across the other side of the lake trees whispered in the faint breeze. Robert took in the view, breathed in the sweet air.

He looked down at his hand and found something in it. He was clutching a brightly-coloured ball. Robert frowned as he examined it more closely. There was a barking to the side of him. Now Robert saw Max, waiting for him to throw the object. Robert pretended to toss the toy for him, laughing when the dog began to scamper after nothing – then he threw it for real.

"Fetch!"

The ball swerved off to the side and landed in the lake, but it didn't matter: Max happily jumped in after it and started to swim. Clamping the ball between his teeth, the dog paddled back to the bank and clambered out. Max shook himself, spraying lake water everywhere. Laughter filled the air. But it wasn't Robert's.

A young blond boy held up his hands to shield himself from the deluge. He was laughing so hard he was almost doubled over. Robert froze.

"Stevie?"

The spray continued, as did the laughter. All Robert wanted to do was join in. He was moving forwards, virtually running towards the boy, who was pulling the ball out of Max's mouth, preparing to toss it into the lake once more. The boy brought back an arm, then let go of the object. It spun in the air, catching the sunlight for a moment, and Max was after the thing before it had time to hit the surface. The blond boy laughed hard again when Max finally splashed into the lake.

Robert was drawing near, only metres away. "Stevie... Stevie, is that really you?"

"Read to me some more, Dad... please..."

But he could see subtle differences now. As the child turned, the cheekbones were slightly less curved, the brow more stooped, shielding green eyes. This boy was a bit older than his Stevie, as well.

Robert's mouth formed the name, but he couldn't say it out loud. Mark...

No, it couldn't be. Because if he acknowledged that this was the boy he'd met at the market, then so many things were wrong with this picture. And yes, as soon as he'd thought it, Robert saw Mark pointing out across the lake. Except it wasn't filled with water anymore.

Max was bobbing up and down, ball now in his mouth – but he was swimming in a lake of fire. The flames lapped at the dog, but he didn't seem to be taking any notice.

"Max!" screamed Robert, rushing to the bank. The heat from the rising blaze drove him back. The dog, however, was still swimming towards them through it all – its fur all but burnt away, patches of blistered skin clearly visible.

Robert expected to see the men with the flamethrowers at the edge of the lake – surely they must be the ones doing this? But no. Instead, he saw the vague outline of figures, could hardly make them out, except for the fact that they were holding weapons of some kind.

One of them began walking across the surface of the lake, the flames hardly touching him. The man was wearing sunglasses, grinning madly as he approached. He pulled out a pistol, his fingers covered in rings, and aimed it at Max... Except it wasn't the dog anymore, it was something else. Something with antlers...

That didn't seem to matter because the man fired three times without any hesitation, blowing it away.

Now gunfire turned the scene into a war zone. Flashes from across the lake. Robert ducked, turning to see if Mark was okay. The boy was crouching, hands covering his head, tears streaming down his face.

Robert gritted his teeth. "No. No, I can't. I've got to go..." he said.

"Wait... please... please help..."

Robert turned and began walking away, his back to the scene, to Mark. "I've got to go. I've got to go..." he kept on repeating, then finally: "I'm sorry."

"Help us!" The boy's cry followed him, but Robert had to ignore it. Yet could he? Could he just walk away? Robert began to turn.

There was one last loud bang and–

Robert jerked awake, breath coming in short, sharp gasps. He sat up under the shelter of his home, a much improved and portable version of his original lean-to, adjusting back to reality. Robert inhaled more slowly, reaching for the water he kept by the side of his bed of grass and leaves. He drank greedily.

It had been the same dream – or a variation of it – ever since he'd visited the market, seen Mark. Robert never used to be able to remember his dreams, but out here they were so much more vivid, more intense. The boy had looked just enough like Stevie to affect him, like seeing a ghost made flesh. And now this. If he'd thought he might be going insane before, then this was putting the finishing touches to it.

He would have been lying if he'd said he hadn't thought

about going back again. It wasn't that far, and it was almost a fortnight since the last market – he'd marked off the days on a fallen branch, the only time he'd ever bothered to keep a track of the time. He'd stayed away the first week but it was almost Wednesday again, almost time. He could trade some of the meat he had, some of the better meat – there were things he'd seen there that he could use.

Again, he wrestled with his conscience. How could he allow himself such luxuries when his family... If his stay in the woods and the forest was his penance, his time to wait before joining them, why should he make life easier for himself?

He shouldn't. He couldn't.

Yet there was Mark. All Robert could think about was the boy asking for, pleading for his help. It was only a dream, but it felt so real.

Robert put down the water and lay back again. He wouldn't sleep now, he knew that – but dawn wasn't that far away.

He just hoped he could hang on till then.

The market was busy that week, but there was something missing.

Bill Locke knew most of the regulars by sight and there was a stall that was conspicuous by its absence: one that offered fruit and veg, mainly. Sometimes it would be manned by the woman with auburn hair, sometimes the fellow with glasses, sometimes a vicar. Bill didn't know their names because they preferred to keep themselves to themselves, which was fair enough. He wasn't in charge here, after all. Nobody was. This was a free and open market – he just liked to see that things went smoothly, that's all. Keep the peace. It was a little foible of his. Bill guessed that people saw him as the boss because he'd been one of the first to set these markets up, but it seemed pretty logical to him, just an extension of what he'd been doing for years.

It was rare that he'd have to break up any trouble, though. Only minor disagreements about what things were worth. Usually it could be resolved, especially when Bill stepped in, the very sight of his shotgun enough to make people agree on a reasonable settlement.

Apart from the missing stall, everything was relatively normal – the same faces, the same names. Like Mark, the kid who scavenged in the cities and towns for items to trade. He was good at it, too. There was a part of Bill that felt sorry for the lad, left all alone in the world. But Mark was getting by, the only way they knew how. He was the next generation, the ones that would grow up in this world, whatever shape it would eventually take. He was learning early, that was all.

Mark caught him staring, smiled, and offered him a sweet from a bag he was chomping his way through.

"Those things'll rot yer teeth," said Bill, but took one all the same. "Better off eating some o' that beef or pork over there."

Mark pulled a face. "Next you'll be telling me to eat my greens."

Bill laughed softly. "Cheeky bugger."

The boy stiffened, and at first Bill thought it had been what he said. Then he could see that Mark was attuned to something he couldn't yet perceive.

"What is it?" asked Bill, but then he heard the engines himself. The people with the fruit and veg stall, maybe, showing up late? was his first thought. But they tended to arrive in an estate car. This was the sound of more than one engine.

Before anyone knew it, the motorbikes were in the field – at least a dozen of them, churning up the grass. The open-top jeeps followed next, handling the soft terrain with ease, men hanging from the seats, carrying weapons Bill hadn't seen outside of pre-virus news reports about the troubles abroad.

"This is an illegal gathering," came an electronic voice, some kind of megaphone system attached to one of the jeeps. "By order of your new lord and master, High Sheriff De Falaise, all goods here will now be confiscated. Resist, and there will be serious consequences."

"Bloody Sheriff? What's he talkin' about?" Bill looked down and sensed that Mark would have taken off at that point, if there had been anywhere to hide. But this wasn't the city, this was open countryside. And there were precious few places to find cover out here. Bill hoisted up his shotgun, not really knowing what good that would do when – not if – this turned ugly.

Without any provocation at all, the men on bikes raced round and round the stalls, shooting into the air. Others were climbing from the jeeps, knocking people to the ground and pointing rifles at them so they wouldn't move. Some of them snatched food. Bill saw one young man grab a hunk of cheese and bite down into it, waving an automatic pistol at the owner, daring him to do something. A pair of people did run, in fact, off across the field to get away. Apparently that counted as resistance, because one of the soldiers threw a grenade at them. It exploded just a few feet away from the couple, blowing them several metres into the air. When they landed they weren't moving.

"Yer bunch o–" began Bill, moving towards the men. Mark got behind him, perhaps reasoning that if he couldn't hide in a building he'd hide there. Bill raised the gun to his shoulder, then let off a round that hit one of the bikers squarely in the chest. The rider slumped over the handlebars, and the machine he was on smacked straight into the side of a Sierra belonging to one of the marketeers. The body was flung over the bonnet to land in a slump on the other side.

Bill let off another blast. This time it only glanced across the front of one of the jeeps. Several rifles turned in his direction, but something made them hold their fire. Bill cracked open the gun and loaded up two more cartridges. "That's it, yer bastards, ye do well to be frightened."

He was aware of Mark tugging on his jumper, trying to get him to turn around. When he did, Bill understood why the men had held off. The noise of the engines had masked the approach of something else: a great beast of a thing, rumbling over the hill. Bill gawped at the tank, blinking as if that might make it go away. He'd never seen one up close like this. But it was real, it was solid, and the cannon on the front was swinging in his direction.

"Judas Priest!" said Bill. Mark tugged at him to run, to get out of its path. But Bill stood there, raising his shotgun again. "All right then, bloody well come on!"

As Mark fled, Bill shot at the tank twice, both barrels having as much effect as a wasp sting trying to penetrate a suit of armour. The tank carried on advancing; it must have looked like some kind of surreal modern twist on George and the Dragon, or even David and Goliath. Only Bill was out of stones for his slingshot.

The tank rumbled up and didn't stop until the cannon was inches away from Bill's head. He looked down that black hole, expecting at any minute to be on the receiving end of a live shell.

Mark ran; he hated leaving Bill but didn't know what he could do if the man wouldn't budge. He'd be dead in seconds if that tank opened fire.

The boy was aware of a bike riding up alongside him. A quick glance to the side told him a boot was kicking out, trying to knock him over. Mark ducked and rolled away, but the bike swerved round, readying itself for another pass. Mark reversed direction, aware that the bike was gaining rapidly on him.

He looked up and saw that another one of the riders had decided to join in the game. That one was coming after him from the front. He was being hemmed in.

On the first pass, he managed to dodge sideways, hoping the two bikes would just slam into each other. It wasn't going to be that simple. Avoiding one another, they rode now in a pair, leaving a gap between to squash Mark. He ran as fast as he could but knew that he wouldn't be able to get away from them this time, that he'd be crushed beneath one set of tyres or another.

Then something odd happened.

Mark heard a whizzing sound, felt the brush of something flying past him. He heard a loud bang as the front wheel of the bike to his left exploded. He risked a look over his shoulder, just in time to see the spokes and mudguard of the bike bite into the field, sending the rider over the handlebars.

But Mark couldn't stop running. The second bike had weaved out of the way, and was still chasing him, unwilling to give up on this cat and mouse fun just because his partner's tyre had burst. In fact, the rider had a grenade in his hand and was getting ready to toss it at Mark.

Another couple of whizzes and this time Mark saw the arrows hit the bike and its rider. They went down heavily, leaving Mark to throw himself out of the way, just as the grenade the man had been holding went off.

Mark felt a searing heat, then there was a ringing in

his ears.

Shapes passed overhead, arrows flying through the air. Two more soldiers crumpled beside him. Mark finally got to his feet and attempted to track the source of the arrows, but he could see nothing.

Panicking, they began firing every which way, because that's where the threat appeared to be coming from. Now that Mark's hearing was coming back, he caught barked orders, and more than a few scared yelps.

Someone had got these people spooked even with their guns and their armoured vehicles.

The same someone who had just saved Mark's life with a few of bits sticks.

Bill heard the explosion at the same time as the tank crew, it appeared. To begin with he thought it was the soldiers killing more people from the market, but when he looked properly he saw it was one of their own bikes that was in flames.

The cannon swivelled away from Bill, chasing the person who had done this. It couldn't find anyone – and neither could Bill. To his right, a couple of soldiers holding rifles dropped to their knees. No bangs, no gunshots – nothing. But now Bill could see they were clutching at arrows protruding from their chests.

Farther down the field, a jeep had stopped dead – its two front tyres useless now that they had been punctured. The men inside were climbing out, rifles poised, but already three had gone down.

Bill grinned.

He took this opportunity to get out of the tank's way, rushing back towards the market. One soldier was heading in his direction, but before he could bring his rifle up, Bill had already whacked him in the face with the butt of his own gun.

The top portion of the tank was still swivelling, and Bill observed the hatch opening up on top. A thickset man smoking a cigar emerged. He was trying to get a bead on whoever was firing those arrows. Then he pointed, shouting in a German accent: "There, you idiots, he's over there!"

It was the man Bill had met a fortnight ago, but hadn't forgotten. The 'poacher' with the rabbits.

The man called Robert who'd worn a hood.

Henrik couldn't believe how incompetent these foot soldiers were. Granted, there were only a handful of properly trained men to spread around the units (hence the fact he was doing the job of three – tank commander, loader and gunner – while his driver, chosen for his previous experience with tracked diggers, sat behind a 10 mm partition up front). The rest of their 'army' was made up of dregs they'd struck the fear of God into on their journey. But surely even they should be able to handle one man using such a primitive form of weaponry?

Yet he was running rings round them; running, ducking and hiding behind bushes. *Bushes for Heaven's sake!* Henrik couldn't get a shot off fast enough with the cannon, so he dropped back inside and ordered his driver to lead the rest of his squad down towards the figure, or at least where they'd last seen the man firing.

Looking through the viewfinder, Henrik saw the remaining vehicles not only following, but getting ahead of them, taking the hunt to this cretin with the arrows.

And there, yes, Henrik could see the speck running. He wouldn't get far, not on this terrain, not with bikes, a jeep, and a tank in pursuit. He'd picked the wrong people to play tag with. He was outnumbered and outgunned.

They followed him over the next small hill, and it was then that Henrik saw what the man had in mind. He was trying to get back to cover. He was going back to ground.

If he made it there, they might never find him. And he'd never let a kill get away.

Henrik bit down on his cigar, then ordered the Challenger driver to speed up.

Rory Wilkes didn't even know what he was doing here.

He'd gone along with all this since the armed men had arrived in his home town of Coventry – let's face it, they hadn't really given any of them an option. But now people were getting hurt; and there was a good chance he might be as well. While he had to admit the feel of the combats, the weight of the M16 in his hands, did feel good (what little boy hadn't wanted to play Action Man at some point, even after he'd grown up?) this was all getting a bit too serious for his liking.

Rory had been impressed by the ease with which they'd taken Nottingham, De Falaise's words as they moved into the castle like something from an old movie. But if one man could now send them into confusion like this...

As the jeep bounced up and down, in pursuit, Rory and the other men in the back looked ahead at the bloke they were after. He was running fast, hard, towards the trees. *We should let him reach them, then we won't have to deal with him at all*, thought Rory. But the man was spinning around, not even stopping – running backwards even while he was notching another arrow.

The projectiles bounced off the front of the jeep, and Rory ducked in case any found their way inside. One of the bikes flanking them went down. Rory looked around to see the unfortunate man get crushed under the tracks of the Challenger tank that their 'commander' was operating. *God Almighty, enough was enough, wasn't it?*

Obviously not, because they were still in pursuit of the running figure Then the hooded man was gone. The woodland absorbed him, sucking him inside itself like he was an extension of it. Surely they could give up now?

Rory felt their jeep slowing, the bikes and the tank behind doing the same. All the vehicles stood at the perimeter of the woodland, as if expecting the man to emerge again and give himself up. No such luck.

In the end the silence was broken by their unit leader who appeared from out of the top of the Challenger. "Inside," ordered the man, "after him on foot!"

If the men with him hadn't known the consequences of disobeying, they would have turned the jeep around and just driven off. But going in there was preferable to having a tank turn on you... just about. And there was no way any of them wanted to mess with Henrik. Not one of them could take him; Rory doubted whether all of them put together could, in fact.

Reluctantly, they climbed out of the jeep, climbed off their bikes and, holding their weapons in front of them, walked up to the edge of the woods. Rory hung back as far as he could.

"I said inside!" screamed Henrik from behind them. "Right now!"

The men all looked at each other, not really knowing what to do for the best. Then one of them made the first move into the undergrowth. The next man followed, then the next. Soon there was only Rory left. Swallowing, he stepped forward into the line of trees.

It wasn't as densely packed as some woods that he'd seen – though admittedly, his experience was fairly limited in this respect. It was thick enough, however, to hide the person they were tracking. As the men in front of him walked further in, they automatically fanned out – partly to give themselves some room if anything happened, partly because they didn't want to be standing too close to anyone who might be a target. Rory could feel the beads of sweat trickling down his face.

There was a rustling off to their right and one of his group opened fire, splintering the trees. When the sound died down, there was nothing to see.

"Where'd he go?" Rory heard one guy say.

There was no answer to that, none of them had a clue. Then the person who'd asked the question went silently down, falling over as if fainting. It wasn't until Rory looked more closely that he saw the arrow sticking out of the man's side.

More dropped like this, only a couple getting a chance to let off a round or two. Rory spun, looking for a direction the arrows might be coming from. He saw nothing. It might as well have been the trees firing them.

Then the guy to his left let out a piercing scream, dropping his rifle and clutching his leg. There was a huge knife sticking out of his thigh; the man hissed a swear word before dropping to the ground. The group that had gone in were already half their number and the rest began to open fire randomly – in the hopes that they'd get off a lucky hit, maybe wing their enemy.

Not much chance of that. Even as they were firing, the arrows flew – and one by one the noises died down until the last person who'd been firing was silenced.

That just left Rory. He was no hero, he hadn't signed up for this – hadn't signed up for anything, actually – so it was time to get out of there, whether the mad German was waiting for him or not.

Turning to run back out, he came face-to-face with the man they'd been hunting. Or rather, the bearded man who'd been hunting them. Only he couldn't see much of that face because it was obscured by his hood. There was a strap around his shoulder which held a handmade quiver, and this still had a few arrows left in it – but he'd made every single one of his shots count. There was also one in the bow Rory was looking at, pointing at his head.

He dropped the rifle on the floor, holding up his shaking hands in surrender. "Please... please don't hurt me, I had no choice. He was going to kill me. Kill us all!" Rory was almost in tears.

The man raised his head, looked directly at him. His eyes were narrowed, but whether he was readying to fire or just didn't believe a word of Rory's excuse was unclear. Then he lowered his bow.

"Who?" asked the hooded man.

"What?"

"Who was going to kill you?"

"T-the Frenchman. H-his name is De Falaise."

"Get out of here," he said to Rory. "Take the ones who can still walk with you." Then he went over and pulled the knife out of its home in the felled soldier's leg.

Rory gave a quick nod, searching for any survivors. There weren't many: two, three at most. Rory helped the guy whose thigh was pouring with blood, half dragging him along as he seethed in pain.

Rory risked one last glance over his shoulder at the man, who was now bending over some of the fallen soldiers. A single guy, but he'd managed to take out most of their group in no time. He had never seen anything like it... and never wanted to again.

Head down, he half-carried the injured man out of the woods.

Henrik tapped his seat, keeping his eyes on the panorama ahead of him.

He had never been very good at waiting. Everything had to come to him yesterday. It was one of the reasons he'd thrown in with De Falaise. It was a quick route to the top: to power, to influence over this new world. The man had made such an impassioned speech about his plans that Henrik would have been a fool not to listen. Yes, he could have tried to build up an army of his own, he supposed, but that would have taken longer. De Falaise already had Tanek, Savero, and a handful of other loyal followers – this would be the easier route to success. Then later maybe...

Things had been going well. They'd been spreading out from Nottingham, tracking down small communities that had set themselves up and obliterating any thoughts of resistance. The local people would serve them or they would die. Which was why these markets had to be stopped; free trade meant independence, and De Falaise could not allow that. The villagers would work for him and him alone, and he would take whatever they had to offer without recompense.

That was why they'd been dispatched to this area. It was why they'd come down on these people so hard: fear equalled respect.

But it had only taken this one 'spoke' in the wheel to cast doubt on their mission. One survivalist who thought he was pretty handy with a bow and arrow. Henrik grunted. *Amateur.*

He sat up when he saw movement in the woods. Two

figures emerged, one dragging the other. His team had done it; they'd killed the primitive and were bringing back the body. No, wait, the body was still moving – not only that but he was dressed in their unique uniform, a combination of colours and styles that De Falaise had chosen himself. He was certainly not hooded. A couple more of his 'men' staggered out behind them. The useless dickheads had failed, and now they were returning with their tails between their legs.

Henrik almost chomped through the cigar he was smoking. He climbed up through the hatch, cursing them in German.

"Incompetents! Where is he?"

"I'm here," came a voice from the woods, strong and loud. In spite of himself, Henrik flinched. But if the man had wanted him dead, then wouldn't he be already – an arrow between the eyes?

"Then show yourself, coward. Come out of your hiding place and we will discuss this."

There was a pause before the reply came. "You come out of yours."

Henrik thought about this. Seriously considered hopping down from the Challenger, going to meet this man at the edge of the woods and pounding him into the ground. No weapons other than their fists. They would see who won then.

But why give up the advantage? Pride was something for romantics, not mercenaries. "I give you thirty seconds to come out, or I will come in after you... personally."

"Go back to your Frenchman and tell him this is over," came the reply. It was not the voice of someone easily intimidated.

This man was more infuriating than all of his ex-wives put together! Henrik didn't even give him the thirty seconds. He just slipped back inside and fired off a high explosive shell into the woods, hoping to obliterate the insolent fool, but also clearing some space for them to enter. "Forward!" he shouted to the driver, who reluctantly obeyed.

The hulking thing trundled into the woods.

I will teach this man a lesson!

Henrik would knock down or blow up every single tree in this place to get to him if he had to. He swung the 120 mm gun around and was just about to load up another shell when...

Suddenly there he was, the fellow with the hood, standing ahead of him, bow over his shoulder. He was holding something in his hand, something small and round, like a ball. Henrik watched as the man drew back his arm and tossed it at the tank. It hit the front and bounced off, rolling underneath the Challenger. He felt the explosion, though it didn't rupture the shell of the tank. *Damn him, he must have taken grenades from my troops!* "Forward!" Henrik yelled to the driver, but the tank was going nowhere. The explosion had clearly disabled the treads.

When he peered through the smoke all he could see were trees.

The bastard had left him little choice but to come out now, to kill him the old fashioned way. But Henrik didn't intend on using his fists. Picking up his machine gun, he opened the hatch and stuck his head out, mindful again of the fact that the man could very easily fire off an arrow. He scanned the area. If the hooded man so much as moved anywhere within sight, he would be dead.

Henrik was aware of something above him in the treetops, something big. A figure. He ducked back down into the hatch, gun poised and ready to fire upwards. An object dropped into the tank, hard and round. He was still about to fire when his mind registered what had just happened. Henrik's eyes grew wide and he let go of the rifle, scrabbling around for the grenade that had just been tossed inside.

"Fetch!" he heard the man shout as he dropped. The hatch slammed shut. Henrik could hear the driver's voice shouting something, but he wasn't listening – he was still looking for the grenade, not caring that he didn't have the pin, nor that he couldn't toss it out of the top anymore...

There it was!

Henrik was actually reaching for the thing when he realised it was too late; he'd taken too long, there was no way he would survive. Just before the explosion came, a phosphorus blast that would set off all the ammo and cook the entire inside of the tank, the cigar fell from Henrik's open mouth, one of the few times he'd ever been without one in his adult life.

And, it was safe to say now, the last.

Bill and Mark finally made it down the field.

Even from a distance they could see the smoke from inside the woods, curling up into the air. On the outskirts the bikes were left abandoned, one jeep limping off at a snail's pace with maybe three or so people inside it. Of the tank there was no sign, but they could both see where it had pushed its way into the green.

"Judas Priest!" whispered Bill as they drew even closer. "Better wait out here, lad." Mark was having none of this, and Bill had to admit he'd earned the right to see how this thing had played out. They both had.

So, following the trail of the Challenger's tracks, they made their way into the wood. It wasn't long before they came upon the remains of the metal beast. Bill made the mistake of opening the hatch at the top and looking inside.

"Trust me, ye don't want to see in there," he warned Mark before the boy got any ideas.

"It's over," said a voice from behind them, "there's nothing to see here."

Bill and Mark spun around, and spotted Robert.

"Sound like a copper," commented Bill.

"Go home. It's over."

Mark was still looking from the tank to Robert, but the man was trying desperately to avoid his gaze.

"They'll be back," Bill told him. "If this De Falaise thinks he's lord of the manor. And there'll be a lot more folk needin' help, an'all."

"Go home," Robert repeated and began to walk away, into the trees. Something Mark said made him stop.

"What home?"

The man in the hood, with his back to them, hesitated only briefly. Then he blended in with the green.

CHAPTER EIGHT

De Falaise stood on the balcony, hands on the rail, and surveyed the city below him. There was a glass information plinth – cracked, but still quite readable – which told him exactly what he was looking at, or the major landmarks at least: The view from Castle Rock, south to west, from what had once been the Inland Revenue building, disused now, to Wollaton Hall. Built for Sir Francis Willoughby in 1588 (the year of the Spanish Armada's defeat), that was almost as saturated with history as the site on which he stood.

De Falaise's initial explorations of the castle and its grounds had taught him much about this place, all of which had earned his respect and confirmed that it was the best location he could have possibly chosen to mount his takeover.

Surprisingly, the castle had been left relatively untouched by those still alive in the City. As expected, there had been some vandalism – such as spray paint on the side of the castle and various colourful phrases inscribed on the wooden doors that opened into the main souvenir shop, as well as defacement of the busts that guarded the door. Lord Byron would definitely not have been happy that they'd turned him into a buffoon with a moustache and a red nose. And the vandals had done some damage inside, too, beginning with the shop – its contents strewn about the place: books about the castle shredded, plastic figures torn from their packaging.

Once it was ascertained that nobody was in residence, De Falaise had insisted on taking his initial tour alone. The ground floor contained the remains of a museum. Glass cabinets that housed examples of metalwork, ceramics and woodwork, had been smashed, their contents tossed aside. Security grilles over the windows in the shape of branches and leaves remained intact, but ironically useless since the doors had been breached. In one room De Falaise discovered a children's mural depicting an ark, which asked 'Can you Help Noah Find The Animals?' There were bloodstains smeared over the simplistic paintings of a horse, lion, elephant and toucan.

Similarly, the exhibition called simply 'Threads' had been ravaged, the clothes from various centuries broken out of their cabinets and tried on, then discarded as if part of some high street shop sale. Dummies were on their sides, some headless, some stamped on till they were flattened.

But it was on this level that De Falaise also found one of his favourite rooms, containing items from the history of the Sherwood Foresters Regiment. The glass cabinets here had been broken into, as well – presumably so that people could reach what they thought were working weapons inside. Upon finding they were either too old, or merely replicas, they'd left them behind. De Falaise was surprised that they'd also left the rather lethal-looking sword bayonets and knives, but then he had no way of knowing how well armed the people who'd broken in here had been. If they'd already had guns, they probably wouldn't have felt the need for such close combat weaponry.

He'd noted that the case containing the book of remembrance had also been smashed, the book itself thrown on the ground. De Falaise had stooped to pick up the tome, placing it back where it should be, when his eye caught a pair of dummies wearing full dress uniform: red jackets, white shirts, bow ties and cummerbunds. They were standing in front of a couple of silver cups, worthless now. But, if nothing else, this reflected the more civilised side of war. *To the victor, the spoils*, thought De Falaise absently, making a mental note to come back and check what size the uniforms were.

Parts of the wrecked café could be salvaged and used as a mess hall for the men – though as their numbers grew this might have to be reconsidered. In the South Hall he found the long, regal-looking stairs, the white banisters dirty and the grey steps chipped. There were torn posters for an exhibition on the upper floor, which must have still been running when the virus struck Nottingham. De Falaise gazed up at the images showing historical characters who may or may not have existed, but had become legend. The exhibition was all about the latest TV incarnation of these characters, information about each one contained on huge cardboard standees.

It took him through into the long gallery, once a place where the great masters hung: home to Pre-Raphaelites and Andy Warhols alike. The paintings that had run the length of this airy room, its creamy walls smudged with dirt, had now either been slashed or stolen. It upset De Falaise a little, not because he was any great lover of art, but because he loved the 'idea' of it. He'd always imagined himself surrounded by the finer things in life. And art was a connection to the past, to history.

Descending into the bowels of the castle, he found one of the most interesting areas – and one remarkably still intact. If there was anything he needed to know about the history of the Castle or the city, it was down here. When the castle had power, a movie theatre had played a twenty-minute film. 'Relive the excitement of battles, intrigues and power struggles' it announced on the sign, and De Falaise wished that it was still working. Of all the things on this level, De Falaise found three the most fascinating. Firstly, there was a model of the castle as it was in its prime, a natural fortress – at its highest two-hundred feet – protected by three sheer rock faces. Many of the same principles of defence still applied, and it would help him considerably when he came to position guards.

Secondly, he found skulls and bones behind glass: 'Evidence from Cemeteries'. He crouched to look at the long-dead, those who had made their mark in history – pledging to do the same. Down another flight of steps, he found the more recently deceased – or pictures of them, anyway, next to a gigantic representation of one of the lion statues from the Council House they'd fired upon. 'Meet You At The Lions' this display was called, revolving around a focal point in the city where people would get together. Metal rods held plastic squares with photographs of people and messages. Men, women, children: families that were long gone now. De Falaise stared into the faces of the dead citizens, snapshots of a frozen moment in time.

"Rather you than me, mes amis," he whispered to them.

A side exit took him back into the open air. He wouldn't stay there long, because he was desperate to check out the famous caves. Man-made, carved out of the rock, he'd had to smash some of the locks that kept out intruders – nobody had bothered before; why should they want to come down here? – and he'd made use of the industrial-strength torches they'd brought with them. Down in the western defensive wall he found a chamber that had been meant for a medieval garrison, and 'David's Dungeon' where King David II of Scotland had once been held captive. It hadn't been used for this purpose for quite some time, but De Falaise fully intended to put that right. In fact, walking up some steps and outside again, he found a pair of stocks that would also be ideal for his needs.

Down yet more steps, just off from the café, was another man-made structure. De Falaise navigated the sandstone stairs which took him into 'Mortimer's Hole', a lengthy tunnel named after Roger Mortimer: an Earl of March once taken captive by Edward III (who'd used the passage to enter the castle). The first thing De Falaise would do would be to secure the entrance at the bottom of the tunnel, at Brewhouse Yard, so that nobody could do the same to him. The castle was only vulnerable at points like these – leaving the iron side-gate and the arched Castle Gateway the main causes for concern. As soon as he was satisfied he knew the castle inside out, De Falaise had ordered those defensive positions fortified.

He left the balcony rail now and strolled round the property, along the East Terrace. A glance up to the rooftop revealed the barrel of a sniper rifle, ably handled by Reinhart. Men were positioned at various points along the balcony and armed guards patrolled on a constant basis in shifts. As he made his way along to the steps De Falaise looked out over the piece of overgrown grass that had once been the site of the Middle Bailey. Now that, and the small car park behind, were home to just a few of the vehicles they'd brought with them – those not out and about, that was.

De Falaise smiled. He thought about the troops already in circulation, making 'contact' with the small communities that had banded together, letting the people know that there was a new force to be reckoned with. They would not just be left alone to get on with things, but would have to bow down to him if they wanted to live. As in Nottingham, as in all of the places over here they'd ploughed through, they'd encountered little resistance. Most saw the wisdom of giving him his tribute, especially with a couple of deaths to illustrate the alternative.

Like the community Javier had reported back on, 'Hope'

its residents had optimistically called it. Their leader had tried to put up a fight, though from what Javier had said the man hadn't been any kind of threat – which was probably why his people were mourning him right now. Javier had also brought a little unexpected gift back from Hope, the thin, auburn-haired woman who waited inside for him. She'd apparently had a spark in her back at the village, though now she was just like a rag doll which he would use as he pleased; her eyes dull, resigned to the fact she was a possession. It was how he preferred his women to be: malleable. De Falaise took great pleasure in dressing her up in some of the gowns he'd found inside the castle, imagining himself back in the past. He'd tire of her eventually, but for the time being it amused him to have her around. Hands behind his back, he made his way to the nearest doors.

His plans were coming together nicely. And there was nothing or nobody to stand in his way.

The boy had skirted around and was now standing in his way. This kid had been silent, he'd give him that – and quick.

Robert had been running away, been desperate to get away in fact – when Mark had appeared in front of him. He hadn't wanted to get involved, wouldn't have done if he hadn't heard the explosions and gunfire coming from the direction of the market. The fact that he'd been hanging about on the edge of the woods, determined not to attend the market, but somehow gravitating towards the place, had nothing to do with it.

Instinct, that's all it had been: a throwback to his years on the force. His curiosity and the fact that people might be at risk was what made him break cover again. Or was it the idea that Mark might be in danger? He dismissed that, because it was dangerous thinking. Whatever the reason, once he'd seen what was going on at the market, he'd had little alternative but to act.

Robert had to admit he'd been shocked. He'd never seen tanks and guns like that outside of visits to museums. And definitely never in action. What did he have to fight these people with? Only the bow and arrows he used for hunting, his knife. They'd cut him to ribbons before he got anywhere near them. (A part of him actually found this appealing.) But then he got to thinking: it was all a matter of hunting, wasn't it? Maybe he didn't need to get anywhere near them to pick a few off. And if he kept on moving, perhaps they'd miss him initially.

He'd been lucky.

The more adrenalin that pumped through him, the more he used skills he didn't even realise he had: hearing keyed into every bullet fired, every bike or jeep engine; muscles lean and strong, thanks to nothing but exercise and eating from the land; eyes sharp enough to pick a target, enough practise with the bow to hit it faultlessly. It wasn't until now, when he looked back on what he'd just done, that it felt real.

Lucky, that's all. Pure luck.

That and the fact the majority of the 'soldiers' appeared to be novices. Barely a step up from some of the thugs he'd dealt with on a daily basis during his early years on the beat. They knew how to handle their weapons, but that didn't make them fighters. Pin them down and all they really were was scared.

And you killed some – badly injured others...

It wasn't his fault, he reasoned. It was this... what was his name? De Falaise, the Frenchman. And that bastard in the tank, another European. What was this, some kind of invasion?

Not your problem, Robert told himself. *Stay out of it and go back to waiting. Waiting for your death.*

But Mark was preventing him from doing that, barring his path. He pulled off his hood and sighed. "Look, move out of the way, will you?"

Mark shook his head. "I'm not going anywhere."

"Fine," said Robert, stepping to the left in an effort to get around the boy, "then I will."

Like a shadow, Mark sidestepped with him. He could be just as quick as Robert, probably quicker due to his size. Robert backed up and tried to go right. Mark was in his way there too, having slipped around him in the other direction.

"Oh, come on!" Robert shouted, quickly getting fed up with this game. "Let me through or–"

"Or you'll what?" Mark challenged. "Do to me what you did back there to them? I don't think so. You saved us."

"Maybe that was a mistake." He regretted the words as soon as they'd tumbled from his mouth, but couldn't take them back. Mark stuck out his bottom lip – more child than canny adolescent now. "That came out wrong, I didn't mean..."

"S'okay," Mark said, rubbing his nose on his sleeve. "I understand."

"No, you don't," Robert told him. "I meant maybe I should have just left well enough alone. If Bill's right and they do come back then I could have made things ten times worse for you all."

"They were shooting up the place. They were running me down with motorbikes! They had a tank for fuck's sake–"

"Watch your mouth," snapped Robert instinctively, chastising himself almost as he did so. He had no right to tell this kid off.

Mark looked at him, confused, then added softly: "How much worse could it be than that?"

Robert considered this for a moment. "More men; more guns; more tanks. People like that always come back stronger than ever."

"Then you agree with Bill?"

That was clever – Robert had walked right into that one. If he agreed that De Falaise's troops would return in larger numbers, then didn't he have an obligation to help out? Hadn't he just admitted his own guilt in the next stage of whatever this was? Robert said nothing for fear of digging himself a deeper hole.

"It weren't no surprise, anyway," Mark said eventually to break the awkward silence.

"What are you talking about?"

"The men coming. You hear things touring round, y'know? I knew something was going on, just not what – or that it would reach out here."

"So this is already happening in other areas?"

Mark nodded. "Lots. Food, clothing, all sorts taken. Even people sometimes."

"Why didn't you tell..." Robert had forgotten himself for a moment and Mark punished him for it.

"Tell someone? What, you mean like the police?" He knew Mark was studying his face for some kind of reaction; what Bill had hinted at just ten minutes ago had obviously stuck with him.

"No. I meant... Isn't there someone..."

"I told you before," Mark said, hurt in his voice. "There isn't anyone. I haven't got a regular place to stay. Nobody to take care of me..."

"I thought you said you didn't need anyone to do that," said Robert, turning the boy's own words back on him.

"I don't," snapped Mark, puffing up his chest, then: "But..."

"What?"

"It's hard sometimes. Being on my own." Mark looked down. For all his bluster, this kid missed having a home, having parents. Missed TV, games, holidays.

"Read to me some more, Dad... please..."

Robert shook his head. "I don't know what you want me to say."

Mark nodded at the woodland. "You live out here, don't you? All by yourself."

"Yes."

"Don't you miss... y'know, people? To like, hang out with and stuff?"

Robert thought back to the men in yellow with the gas masks, then in his mind a picture of the men with machine guns flashed up. Nothing had really changed in all that time, had it? If this was the case then the answer had to be no. But how could he write off the rest of the dwindling population when there were still people like Bill out there, the men and women from the market. And Mark. "I... I try not to think about it," was the only answer he could muster.

There was another awkward pause before Mark came right out and said what was on his mind. "Can I come with you?"

So many emotions flooded through Robert at that moment he couldn't really make sense of them. But chief amongst them was fear. He'd felt oddly calm as he'd dodged the bullets and gone up against the German in the tank. Now this simple question petrified him. How could he let Mark come with him, how could he risk spending any time with him at all, when he could be snatched away at any moment like Stevie had been? Robert had come here to wait, not to be an adoptive father.

"Out of the question," he said at last.

"I know people in lots of places, I could keep tabs on

what's going on and get back to you with–"

"Didn't you just hear what I said?" Robert's tone was harder now. "I can't... Look, I just can't. Okay?"

Mark frowned. "I'll pull my weight, honest. I'm a hard worker."

"No," Robert told him.

Mark pulled items out of his bag now, as if he was trading at the market. "Please. Here, you can have it all... And I have other stuff, stashed away, really cool stuff that–"

"I said no!" Robert surprised himself with the harshness of his reply.

The boy's face fell sharply, and for a moment Robert felt sure he was going to cry. As he'd suspected, that streetwise attitude was simply a front, and now Mark had let Robert see too much of the real him. Slowly, the lad began to gather the things back into his bag.

"Listen, I'm sorry," began Robert, reaching out a hand as if to place it on Mark's shoulder, then quickly withdrawing it. "It's just that... I can't let you come with me."

Mark stared at him. "Why?"

It was a simple enough question, but the answer was so complicated. "I can't tell you that, either. Go back to Bill, Mark. You'll be safe with him." Robert pulled up his hood and stepped around the boy. This time Mark didn't try to stop him.

What are you doing? said a voice in Robert's head, the small part of him still connected to the past: to his family, to his job. *He needs help... they all do.* But he'd 'helped' enough for one day, caused more trouble than he'd prevented, probably. *So what, you're just going to run away now and let them get on with it?*

Robert tried to force the thoughts out of his head, but they persisted. *Can you do that? Can you really? Have you strayed so far from who you used to be?*

He was tempted to look back over his shoulder at Mark, but gritted his teeth and told himself that the kid would be better off without him; a dysfunctional excuse for a human being. Robert couldn't give him what he so obviously wanted, someone to look up to, someone to admire.

After a few minutes Robert broke into a run and pretty soon he was swallowed by the wilds he now called home.

De Falaise never liked to be interrupted when he was entertaining. Especially when the news was of this variety.

The knock on the door of the 'converted' office was light, but curt. It had been followed by a cough, then: "My... my Lord?"

De Falaise answered the door dressed in his robe. He recognised one of the young men they'd recruited on their travels – he didn't remember his name (it began with 'G'... Granville, Grantham possibly?) but he'd been a member of that ridiculous gang that called themselves The Jackals, and De Falaise did remember ordering one of his friend's deaths. Yes, there was the scar on the back of his raised hand, where Tanek's bolt had found its mark. Now the only thing that had stopped De Falaise from grabbing this silly boy by the throat and carving onto his chest 'Do not disturb' was the use of his new title, a mark of respect he was owed.

"Ahem..." said the young man, attempting to keep his eyes dead ahead, and not on De Falaise's lack of clothing, nor what was beyond him in the room. "My Lord, I bring news of an incident involving one of our units."

"What kind of incident?"

"We're... we're not quite sure. Tanek sent me to fetch you, he said it would be better if you 'talked' to one the survivors yourself. He's down in the stables."

De Falaise caught the youth gazing past him, at the woman on the bed. "Tell Tanek I will be with him momentarily, oui?" The youth made to leave. "Oh, and next time you see too much, I will take out your eyes. Do you understand?"

Granville or Grantham, or whatever his name was, nodded. There was no hint of disobedience anymore, just terror – pure and simple.

"So, run along, run along." De Falaise clapped his hands to get the moron moving, then closed the door and prepared to get ready.

Ten minutes later, after dressing and posting a guard to watch the woman from Hope, he'd joined Tanek and a handful of others in the former stables. He was not at all surprised to see that the big man had already put the stocks there to good use, but he did raise an eyebrow when he saw that the youth occupying them was wearing a uniform. As De Falaise joined them, Tanek explained that this 'soldier' and a couple of others – currently being held down in the caves – had been caught trying to flee the area by one of their routine patrols.

De Falaise bent slightly and asked the man his name.

"R-Rory," he gasped, obviously having trouble breathing in the stocks.

"Was he not in Henrik's unit?" De Falaise asked Tanek. The larger man nodded.

"What happened? Why were you trying to escape?

At first Rory didn't answer, but then De Falaise gestured to Tanek, who grabbed hold of the captive, yanking his head up by his sweaty hair. "Answer!"

"*Gak...* I was scared... Scared of... of what you'd do to

me."

"I see," De Falaise said, "as opposed to what we are doing now, you mean? No one has the option of walking away from my army, my young friend, I thought I had made that abundantly clear?"

Tanek pulled Rory's head back further and he let out a frightened choke.

De Falaise leaned in, his face inches from Rory's. "Tell me what happened. Tell me what was so... frightening that you could not return."

Rory's eyes flitted from Tanek to De Falaise. "Our... our unit...wiped out."

De Falaise raised another eyebrow. "A whole squadron of men, with jeeps, motorbikes and a tank?"

Rory tried to nod, but Tanek's grip held him fast.

"And your commanding officer?" De Falaise enquired.

It was barely a shake of the head, thanks to Tanek, but it was enough.

"Impossible! Henrik was one of my best!" De Falaise searched Rory's features for any hint that he might be lying. "How could this be? A gang, a group of resistance?" Had the people of the region banded together to fight back so quickly? If so, it was serious news indeed and they would require wiping out. Then another thought occurred to him. "Or did you organise this yourself, perhaps? Kill the rest of the men and then make a run for it?"

Again, Rory attempted to shake his head, his breath coming in quick gasps.

"Then what? I need to know!"

"A... A man."

"What? Just one man? You're lying."

Rory forced out the words. "No. A man... one man did it all. He came from the trees."

"The trees? What on Earth are you talking about?"

"A man wearing a hood. He was like a ghost."

De Falaise frowned. "Where did this skirmish take place?"

It was Tanek who informed him this time that the incident had occurred not far from Rufford. De Falaise stood up and felt the corners of his mouth rise slightly. In spite of himself, and in spite of the fact he'd just lost one of his most capable and trusted fighters in Henrik, De Falaise was smiling. Then that smile turned itself into a chuckle, the chuckle a laugh. Suddenly De Falaise was guffawing like he'd just heard the funniest joke ever. Rory gaped at him, then stared upwards at Tanek, who appeared equally mystified.

"Can none of you besides myself see it?" De Falaise asked as he looked from the captive to Tanek. "Someone else is playing the game." They looked at him blankly. "Do you not understand? A man wearing a hood... A hooded man? Just like the statue outside this very castle!"

He waited for it to dawn on them. This all made sense now, especially when you factored in what Javier had told him about Hope; about the name De Falaise had acquired there. If he was to play the role of the Sheriff of Nottingham, then someone was auditioning for the part of his arch nemesis. Someone who was a little too enamoured with the old legends of this place.

"Gentlemen, history is repeating itself, is it not? But there will be a different outcome this time. History is written by the victors, and it has painted my 'predecessor' in a remarkably bad light. That will not be allowed to happen again. This hooded man must be destroyed at once, before news of what has happened reaches the rest of the towns and villages. Before we really do have rumblings of rebellion."

De Falaise ordered Tanek to extract as much information from Rory as he could about what had happened. "Use any means necessary; and when you are finished with him, work on the rest. Then we will send out as many men as we can spare."

"Where to?" Tanek enquired.

De Falaise grinned once more. "Where else would we send them to hunt for the hooded man, but to Rufford. Rufford at the heart of Sherwood Forest!"

CHAPTER NINE

It wasn't an easy thing to do, but Robert was putting what had happened behind him. Not the big thing, not the thing that sent him out here in the first place, but the thing that had happened a couple of days ago at the market. He'd returned to his life as 'normal', busied himself with the everyday, with catching food and living out his time. At night he still dreamt of the men, of his son, of Mark, but on waking he was able to slot them into some hidden compartment of his brain. He'd quietened the voices that told him he was leaving Bill and the others to fend for themselves against overwhelming forces; armed men that he'd brought down on them. It was none of his business – *Oh, so suddenly it's nothing to do with you? Weren't saying that when you were rushing to their defence, were you?* – it didn't matter anymore what happened, he of all people should know that.

He could just keep on running, keep on hiding. It was for the best.

But Robert should also have known, especially after the amount of times he'd done it himself standing by the huge lake at Rufford, that when you cast a stone into the water it creates ripples. He could no more run from his destiny than he could commit suicide after losing Joanne and Stevie.

A few days later he spotted an intruder near to his camp.

Or at least he thought it was an intruder – he'd been on edge since his encounter with De Falaise's men, for which no one could really blame him. Robert had been bringing back some of the day's spoils when he spotted movement in the undergrowth not far from his tent. Robert had done his best to camouflage his home, and doubted whether any passers by would see it from a distance. But what if they were looking for it?

Relax, he told himself, *might only be an animal.* Though it hardly ever happened, deer had been known simply to walk into his camp before now. They never stayed long, though, and counted themselves lucky that the times they'd done so had been when he'd had more than enough meat to last him.

But it wasn't an animal. As Robert crouched down he saw the shadow cast across the trees. Leaving the catches where they were, he began to move around, encircling the camp, keeping low and loading a freshly-made arrow into his bow at the same time. The approaching figure was stealthy, but over time Robert had become the master. When he was close enough, he rose up out of the woodland, aiming his arrow at the intruder's head. His finger twitched, almost releasing the missile.

What he saw made him stand down, ease up, and let the tension of the bow lapse. There, holding his hands in the air, was Mark. "Don't shoot!" he urged, a little too late. If Robert had decided to do so, there'd have been nothing he could have done about it.

Robert let out a long sigh. "What are you doing here? I could have killed you."

"I..." Mark began, the implications only now sinking in. "You could've as well, couldn't you?"

Robert's gaze never faltered. "I still could," he informed him. "Why have you come here when I specifically told you not to?"

He wasn't expecting Mark's answer. "To warn you."

"What?"

Mark nodded. "They're coming for you, Robert. De Falaise's men."

"How do you know?"

"How do I get to know anything?" Mark said with a smile. "I keep my ear to the ground. And right now I can hear marching feet."

"Let them come."

The boy moved closer. "You don't understand, they're coming in mob handed. De Falaise got wind of what you did and he's going to take you down before you cause any more trouble for him."

"Is he now?"

"Yes," said Mark. "And they're on their way from Nottingham. You have to get out of here."

Robert gave a hollow laugh. "I'm not going anywhere."

"Don't you understand? They're going to kill you!"

"I understand, and what I said the other day still stands. Get out of here – go where it's safe, Mark."

Mark scowled. "After all that? After risking my neck to come and tell you, you still–"

"Sshh," Robert told him, holding his finger to his lips.

Mark froze; he'd been too busy talking to notice. "What?"

"Gunfire," said Robert. "They're already here."

Maybe it was the fact that he'd been the one to deliver the news that had landed Granger in this mess. Here they all were, entering a forest, looking for someone who had taken on a whole unit of De Falaise's men and won. Granger thought of them as De Falaise's men rather than his own now, though there were a few other former members of the Jackals here today with him. They'd been through too much on the road up north to ever be the same again. If the virus and The Cull had changed them the first time around, banding them together against what they saw as the former system, then meeting De Falaise had changed them back again into drones of another 'machine'.

Every night when he slept – when he could even get to sleep in the crowded makeshift barracks on the upper floor of the castle – he saw the bolt entering Ennis's head. Saw what that git Tanek had done to him on De Falaise's orders. He'd wake, sweating, the scar on his hand throbbing.

And he'd seen many more die at their hands when they'd refused to sign up for this mad army, run by an even madder dictator. Christ alone knew what he was doing to that poor woman in his bedroom.

You can hardly talk, what about the girls that The Jackals took in? That was different, he argued with himself. *They needed protection, they knew what they were doing and got something in return.* The woman brought back from that village by 'Major' Javier – the man leading them into the forest today – had been virtually catatonic. He'd seen her eyes when they ushered her into the castle. They were dead, like a zombie or something. Whatever had been done to her, even before De Falaise entered the picture, must have been enough to bend her mind.

So here he was, serving that lunatic, calling him 'Lord' just so he wouldn't do the same to him that he'd done to those men they'd caught deserting. One poor sod was still hanging in the stocks after he'd been tortured for information, his screams heard throughout the grounds as Tanek had done things to him Granger didn't even want to think about. The others had been interrogated down in the caves.

It was how they knew what they were up against

today: a single bloke who'd shot out the wheels of bikes and jeeps just using arrows. Who'd killed that psychotic cigar-smoking kraut, Henrik, blowing up his toy tank in the process.

Yep, they were looking for bloody Rambo out here.

Given the option, Granger wouldn't have been present at all – he would have been cheering this guy on from the sidelines. This man had the guts to take on De Falaise and obviously had him rattled. So much so that he'd sent along a bunch of heavily armed troops to bring back the man's body. De Falaise was definitely taking no chances.

Something rustled in the undergrowth to their left and, almost in unison, the men turned and fired. The forest came alive with light, the muzzles of machine guns flaring. Even before Granger had a chance to aim, the order had been given for ceasefire. Javier stepped in front of the men, examining the shredded bushes and trees.

"It's nothing, false alarm. Just a hare or something," he said to his men by way of headsets.

Granger groaned. So they were shooting at Thumper now? What next, Bambi's mother?

"I don't like this," muttered a soldier to Granger's right. He knew what the guy meant; even with their firepower, it felt like they were sitting ducks, felt like they were the ones being targeted. And they'd just told whoever was out there exactly where to find them. Smart.

They moved forwards, following Javier, knowing that they didn't have a choice in the matter. The overweight Mexican was De Falaise's eyes and ears; he might as well be him. If they revolted, more men who had no choice would come after them. Granger knew that, they all did.

"Why don't you try picking on someone your own size?" came a voice out of nowhere. It echoed all around them, impossible to trace. "If you can find anyone."

"There!" shouted Javier, "It's him!" He pointed, and the men opened up on the trees once more. Except for Granger. He had his finger on the trigger of his weapon but something told him he'd be wasting his ammo.

When the gunfire died down, he was proved right. All was quiet and still for a moment or two, then came the voice again. "Nice try."

"Bastardo!" spat Javier, red faced.

There was movement again in the foliage – but this time Javier himself was on it. He brought up his M16/Colt Commando, firing an incendiary from the grenade launcher fitted underneath. He laughed crazily as the forest burst into flames, burning everything ahead of him. "How does that suit you, my friend?"

There was no answer this time.

Suddenly there was movement again, this time from a completely different direction. Javier pointed, ordering a handful of his men into the trees, Granger included.

Shit! he thought. *More orders, more trouble.*

Granger held well back as the troops moved in. They crept along as they scanned the area. A guy on his right was the first to go down. Granger heard a snapping sound and turned, quickly enough to see that the man had stepped into a snare, the noose around his ankle yanking him sideways as the branch it was attached to dragged him away into the foliage.

"Place is booby-trapped. He's led us into a fucking trap!" shouted another man, right before his leg disappeared into a small hole that had been covered over with bracken. He cried out in pain, eyes watering. Another ran across to help him, tripping some twine on the floor, which in turn dislodged the stick holding a weighty branch in place. This swung down and hit the man squarely in the chest, sending him reeling backwards, rifle flying out of his grasp.

Granger didn't see how the next soldier set off the trap, but he spotted all too late the spear that was fired from what looked like a huge bow. It hurtled across the green into the man's shoulder, with such an impact that it carried him back a few steps before he eventually fell.

More cries came as the rest of his 'comrades' experienced the same. Spears, snares and tripwires caught them out. Set in a concentrated area to catch animals, they were now decimating their number. Another fell when a homemade bolas wrapped itself around his neck.

Granger retreated, slowly, glancing down at the ground as he did so. Nervously, he checked around him in case he set anything off. Too late he heard the cracking sound below, then the next thing he knew he was being yanked upwards, the net closing in around him and pulling him into the air. His gun fell out of his hands, the mike from his head. He felt his stomach roll as he was hoisted up, only stopping when it reached a certain height.

There he was left, dangling. He took deep breaths, calming himself down. *You're still alive, still alive. Just caught in a net, that's all. You can get out of this.*

Even as he thought it, someone passed by beneath him wearing a hood. He paused to look up at Granger, and the youth thought that was it – his time was finally up. Then the hooded man went on his way, disappearing into the undergrowth as if he'd never really existed at all.

Javier had heard all the screams through his headset and scowled.

It was one thing he hadn't anticipated, although he probably should have. Having led men into battle in the jungles of South America, he should have thought more about the possibility of traps. But who would have expected the quiet English countryside to be like those war zones? These were different times, though, weren't they? This was post-Cull Britain and anything was possible. The man they were dealing with was a hunter, of course he'd know how to lay traps! Now a good chunk of his squad had been incapacitated, probably killed.

Bastardo!

Javier shook his head. He couldn't let some fucking Englishman with a sense of the theatrical get the better of him. He still had over a dozen well-armed men and–

There was a noise. It sounded like something whistling, travelling fast. "Take cover!" screamed Javier, but his warning came too late. A single arrow was already flying. But it didn't strike any of the men as he'd expected. Instead it hit the ground, some distance from where they were standing.

What is he doing? thought Javier. *Either he's a very bad aim or...*

"Get up! Get up and get out!" Javier barked his orders, but they were too late.

The explosion was loud, a live grenade attached to the arrow suddenly detonating. The nearest men were thrown into the air, pulled as if performing a circus act on wires. Smoke was everywhere.

Through the smog, he saw a figure. It darted between the trees, entering the arena of battle, taking on those who were still standing, making the most of their confusion. Javier could have warned them but instead wanted to observe his enemy in combat, get the measure of him. The hooded figure was trained well in the defensive arts, that much was obvious by the way he handled himself. Deflecting punches with his forearms, kicking, throwing men onto the ground and winding them. One pulled a Browning pistol out of his holster and the hooded man spun around, grabbing the soldier's arm and bringing it down over one raised knee until the gun was relinquished. He fought as if he didn't care what happened to him, and yet at the same time Javier recognised some sort of survival instinct there. It was a curious and very dangerous combination.

By the time the smoke had cleared, Javier had brought his grenade launcher to bear again, letting off another incendiary in the hooded man's general direction. And, just as he hadn't anticipated what had happened with the traps, he didn't see what came next, either.

The hooded man cowered from the spreading fire.

Could it be that... Yes! He was actually afraid of the flames. Javier grinned. The hooded man held up his hand to protect his face, stumbling backwards, his mouth open in fear.

This wasn't any ordinary aversion, Javier could see that. Rather, it was as if the fire held some kind of special significance for him – some private terror that only he knew about.

It didn't matter. He'd burn the bastard to a crisp and take his remains back to De Falaise. Javier could imagine what the Frenchman might say: "You have done well, Major. Pick a county and you will rule it as my deputy." It was why all of them were with the man, wasn't it? Power? A chance to rule? Or maybe he should take the hooded man back to De Falaise alive so that he and Tanek could have some of their special brand of fun?

Javier had only let his mind wander for a moment or two, but it was enough for everything to change. Suddenly, out of nowhere, there were other people there. One of the rising soldiers was struck across the face by what Javier thought at first to be a piece of wood, a branch of some kind: another trap the hooded man had set? No... now he could see it was a walking stick, brandished by a squat, bald man, who was even now attacking again. He looked very familiar.

And who was that on the other side? Smaller than the rest, throwing stones at a couple of the other soldiers. A rock caught one man a glancing blow across the temple and he collapsed to his knees.

So he has friends, then? Javier mulled. As he suspected there was no way he'd been able to do all this on his own. *No matter, I'll fry the lot of them.* He brought up his weapon one final time, then felt something hard pressing into his cheek.

Javier's eyes swivelled left and down. They traced the end of the shotgun to another man. "How do," said the ruddy-faced man in the checked shirt and tank top. "I'd be droppin' that about now if I were ye. We don't want no accidents, do we? Nice and slow."

The Mexican began to lower his weapon, which the man with the shotgun took off him.

"When De Falaise learns of this, you will all be in big trouble," grumbled Javier. Even to his ears, it sounded lame.

"That so?"

Javier nodded, but the ruddy-face man just laughed. The battle – the hunt – was over and they'd lost. Javier knew it, his enemies knew it. But the next thing he knew was blackness, as the man turned the gun around and hit him hard with the butt.

Once they'd dealt with the fires and tied up all prisoners left alive, the trio turned their attentions to Robert.

He had barely said a word; just sat propped up against a tree, eyes staring out from beneath his hood. They knew it had been the incendiary from Major Javier's weapon that had done this to him, but none of them knew why. None of them dared to ask. Instead, they discussed what should be done about De Falaise's men.

"I know what I'd like to do to that one," said the Reverend Tate, leaning on his stick. He pointed across at Javier, still spark out and helpless as a baby. A complete reversal of the last time they'd met. "He took a friend of mine away, killed another."

Bill nodded. "Aye. But could ye really do that? A man of God and all?"

"An eye for an eye, the Bible says." But Tate conceded the point. "All right, maybe just a bit of a pummelling, then."

"I'm worried about Robert," interrupted Mark. They both looked at the boy who'd brought them here today, who'd sent word that De Falaise's men were on their way to the forest and that Robert might need their assistance. In spite of the fact the man had turned his back on them earlier on that week, Bill knew that he owed him a debt. And when news reached Tate, even though he hadn't met the man, he came. Maybe it was partly for revenge – a concept he wasn't supposed to believe in – or was it something else? To meet the man who'd taken on De Falaise's troops at the market, the person that people in neighbouring villages and towns were already talking about. The Hooded Man. Someone they might be able rally behind? A figurehead?

A hero?

He didn't look like one at the moment.

"Perhaps I should talk with him?" offered Tate. "I'm used to it after all. Giving counsel. I can be quite persuasive when I need to be."

Mark and Bill both shrugged, then watched as the holy man walked over to the tree where Robert sat gazing at nothingness. They could just about hear the conversation between the two men, which was woefully one-sided to begin with. Tate introduced himself, explained what had happened in Hope, the things Javier and some of his men had done there, when all the community had really wanted was to start over again.

That had done the trick, woken Robert from his stupor. "Start over? There is no starting over. No forgetting the past."

Tate frowned. "No one's suggesting we should forget what's gone before, my son. It's just that–"

"Don't you understand, there's no going back!"

"And where would you go, if you could?" asked Tate, resting on his stick. "To somewhere before the virus, hmm? To save someone you loved? Is that why you're out here all alone?"

Robert's lips were a straight line.

Tate waved over his shoulder. "And those people back there, Mark and Bill, do you not think they would give everything they have to turn back the clock? Don't you think they lost people they loved as well?"

"It's not the same," Robert said. Then, more quietly: "Not the same."

"How can you say that? For each and every one of us, it's personal. I lost parishioners, people I cared about a great deal," Tate continued. "And for a time, the briefest of times, I almost lost my faith as well."

"Faith," huffed the man in the hood.

"That's right. Don't think I haven't questioned what all this was for, what it was about. But still I have to believe there's a purpose to it. That something good might come out of this yet."

Robert looked up, the shadows disappearing from his eyes. "What purpose, what good?"

Tate shook his head. "I honestly don't know. But I do know one thing, if we stand by and let men like De Falaise have their way, then this world hasn't got a chance."

"What exactly do you expect me to do about it?"

Tate leaned in further. "I saw what you did back there, or at least some of it. And I heard about what you did at the market, the people you helped. In spite of what you might say, I know you care. Now, you have a choice. You can turn your back on them." He looked over at Bill and Mark once more. "Even though they came here today to warn you, to help you. You can turn your back on everything again, in fact, detach yourself from the hurt, from caring about anyone ever again. Or..." Tate paused. "Or you can save them. You can lead them. You can stop De Falaise. Now, ask yourself what the people you lost would have wanted you to do."

Robert didn't answer Tate, he just sat there deep in thought. Then he got up. Trying hard not to catch Mark and Bill's eyes, the hooded man strode over to where the prisoners were tied up. He examined their faces one by one, the men he'd attacked, those who'd fallen foul of his traps.

One of them, a soldier Robert had last seen dangling from a net, stared at him. He couldn't have been more than twenty.

"Please don't kill us." The young man spoke with a Southern accent.

Robert pulled down his hood. "You want me to let you go, is that it? So you can return to De Falaise?"

The youth thought about this, then shook his head. "Not after what he did to the others. The men you let go last time..."

Robert remembered what another young man had told him in similar circumstances, almost in tears. "Please... please don't hurt me, I had no choice. He was going to kill me; kill us all." Then Robert looked across at the other troops, saw that they were terrified of the same thing.

"You did these things, joined De Falaise's army, because you had no choice, right?"

He nodded.

"Okay, now I'm going to give you one," Robert told him.

The youth looked puzzled.

"What's your name?"

There was a moment's hesitation before he replied: "Granger."

"All right, then, Granger. I'm going to offer you, offer all of you, a choice." He looked back over his shoulder at Tate. "You can join me... join us. Help take down De Falaise, provide information so that we can put an end to his operation. Or you can take your chances out there."

Tate limped over to join him. "Hold on, what are you doing? This isn't what I meant. They were sent here to kill you, Robert."

"They're scared."

"They can't be trusted," argued the Reverend. "They've committed terrible acts."

"Many of them because they were forced to. Because De Falaise rules through terror, not trust." Robert undid the bonds that held Granger. "If we're going to do this, that's not how it'll work here." Robert held out his hand. "So, what do you say?"

Granger looked at the outstretched hand, as if not quite sure what to do, as if nobody had ever shown such faith in him before.

Then, finally, he reached out with his own scarred hand and shook Robert's.

CHAPTER TEN

It had been rich pickings that day.

In the front seat of the truck, Savero nursed his rifle and smiled. De Falaise would be more than happy with the hoard his unit were bringing back to the castle. As specified, they'd started up near a place called Worksop a few days ago and wound their way down the map, back towards Nottingham. De Falaise – as per usual – had guessed correctly that the most productive communities had actually sprung up away from the major towns and cities, in countryside like this. It made sense for people to gather together out in rural areas, away from the attention of the gangs and violence that characterised the larger, urban localities. These were the communities using a network of markets and trading to get by. England had indeed been thrown back to the Middle Ages in some respects, to a time before rail networks and airports. People had to be self-sufficient, which suited De Falaise and his army well... because they weren't. Why bother, when they could just go around creaming off food, clothing and any other useful items they might want from less well organised – and less well armed – factions?

Just outside a place called Sutton-in-Ashfield, in fact, they'd come across a clump of people who'd gone back to their roots. They thought the world had forgotten about them, off the beaten track, but what they didn't know was Savero and his troops were actively searching for such places. They'd steamrollered in, the three jeeps, four bikes and two trucks, enough to put paid to any resistance from the inhabitants. In the face of uniformed men with automatic weaponry, they'd handed over their goods without complaint. Savero had organised the collections, ordering the men to take whatever they could find that might be of use, loading it up into the back of the Bedfords for transportation to the next location, and then finally on to their base.

They used the back roads mainly, as it was easier to spot the houses that might be hidden by trees or in the dips of hills. A couple of times they'd come across isolated farm houses, with only a handful of people gathered there. It always amused Savero to see how the 'men' of the villages and households crumpled when confronted with people armed to the gills. Now and again you'd get one who fought back, but usually only with crude weapons like knives. England's pre-Cull gun ban ensured that only criminals and those from large cities had any halfway decent weaponry. Certainly nothing compared with De Falaise's arsenal.

Savero hated using the old cliché, but it really was like taking candy from babies. It was just as De Falaise had promised when he recruited the Italian. The practised speech he'd given when they met in Parma might have come across as so much hot air had anyone else been speaking the words. But the Frenchman's impassioned plea, the way he carried himself, and the way he had already inspired loyalty in the men he'd recruited to his cause, made Savero take his words very seriously indeed.

"You have balls, Savero. Come with me, work for me," De Falaise had said, "and I promise you won't regret it."

Savero hadn't in the slightest, not even when they'd been in the heat of battle. Because his life had turned around at that moment. He was no longer on his own, scrabbling for survival, fighting off the nuts stupid enough to approach him, avoiding the gangs that had sewn up pockets of Europe. He felt a part of something special, however small, and now look where that decision had taken him, look how it had all grown. Savero was an officer in De Falaise's army, had men under him once more. Just like the old days in the Esercito Italiano – the Italian Army – before the lure of money persuaded him to go AWOL. Granted, they weren't the elite he'd fought with then, but there was strength in numbers. And they were petrified of him, of De Falaise. With good reason. Savero watched his driver for a moment, a man in his late twenties, dressed in the uniform of a soldier but with the uncertain look of a new recruit. Even more uncertain the longer Savero stared at him, uncomfortable under his scrutiny.

No, there was something else. Something his driver had spotted down this country lane they were following towards Nottingham, fields, trees and hedgerows on either side of them. Savero faced front again and saw what the problem was. Up ahead, just as the lane hit a kink, was a car... Wait, it was a jeep. Not only that, it was one of their jeeps, a Wolf similar to those accompanying his unit today. It was blocking off the narrow road, bonnet up, a couple of uniformed men examining the inside as if there was something wrong with the engine.

Savero ordered the truck to slow down – they were going nowhere till this was sorted out. He wound down the passenger window and stuck his head out.

"Hey, you – what's the big hold up?" he called out to the soldiers by the broken down vehicle. One of the men standing by the bonnet came forward, shielding his eyes from the mid-afternoon sun. He shrugged, pointing back to the jeep. Savero sighed deeply. He could see there was something the matter with it, he wanted to know what. Opening the door, he clambered out. He was going to leave his rifle on the front seat, but at the last second took it with him. It was habit. A good soldier always kept his weapon with him at all times.

Savero walked towards the young trooper, even more fresh-faced than his driver. "What's wrong with it?"

The man shrugged again, this time adding, "No idea. Don't know much about engines. It just started making this funny noise and..."

Savero wasn't really listening to him anymore. He was listening to his instincts instead. Something wasn't right here. Something didn't add up. "What are you doing out here anyway? This was our designated route back."

"Routine patrol, sir," said the soldier, but there had been a brief hesitation before answering.

"Who's in charge? It can't be you."

Another one of the soldiers, the guy with his head in the engine looked up at the pair of them. Suddenly Savero saw it, the panic in his eyes.

"Er..." began the first lad. "In charge... er..."

"I asked you a question!"

"That would be... him." The soldier nodded behind Savero, and even as he turned, raising his eyes at the same time, he saw the shadow dropping down from the overhanging trees to land on the roof of the truck.

He swore, preparing to fire at the hooded man. The soldier jostled him, spoiling his aim. The man in the hood ducked sideways as the bullets completely missed their target. Savero spotted more men emerging from behind the hedgerow, armed just as they were... because they were them: soldiers from De Falaise's ranks. What was happening here, some kind of revolt?

Before his own men could react, these rebels had pulled them from their jeeps, prodded them off their bikes with the ends of their rifles.

Savero spun back around, training his gun on the youth who had knocked his arm. But before he could fire, the man on top of the truck leaped down on him.

Savero was pushed forwards, the rifle knocked from his clutches. It was quickly picked up by the traitor who had led them into this trap.

"Figlio di puttana!" cried Savero, wriggling out from under his attacker. He was up in seconds, but then so was the bearded man in the hood. "Who are you?"

The man didn't answer him, which only infuriated Savero further. He went to punch the man in the stomach, but his opponent shifted his weight slightly so the blow landed east of where it should have.

The man brought down his own fist and the Italian moved towards the blow, angling himself so that his forehead took the full force of the punch. But he didn't stop there. Savero continued to bring up his head so that he caught the man's chin from beneath, knocking the hooded man sharply backwards. His enemy stumbled a few feet, shaking his head.

Savero grinned. "You won't win." By now he saw that people had gathered round, his own men and those who had come out of the hedges. He also spotted a couple of people out of uniform, one who looked like a farmer holding a shotgun, another – unarmed – limping with a stick. They were all fixated on the fight.

This is more than just a brawl, realised Savero. Whoever wins this will have their respect... *But you can take him. He's just some guy who thinks he can play in the big leagues.*

He launched himself at the hooded man again, attempting a roundhouse punch to the ear. The bearded man bent, not allowing the blow to settle, then responded with an uppercut, which snapped Savero's head back. It was his turn to shake himself, his vision slightly blurred. Savero saw that the hooded man was rolling up his sleeves, ready to go again.

He didn't give him the chance.

Savero ran at him, grabbing him by the middle, shoving him backwards into the truck. The air exploded out of his opponent's body. Savero stepped back again, watching with satisfaction as the hooded man crumpled. Then he took a run up, to kick the winded man. Instead, he found his foot being grabbed, then twisted and pushed back so that he lost his balance completely. Savero fell onto his shoulder blades; hard.

"Merda!"

Rolling onto his side, Savero noted that the hooded man was climbing to his feet. Getting a knee under himself, he rose as well, but not quickly enough. The man was on him, not letting up for a second. Savero was being pummelled with blows from the left and right. He held up his arms to defend himself, swinging blindly. In the end he tried to push the man away, but after a few seconds the punishment continued. Savero reached down to his belt, loosing the knife he kept there. He brought it up in an arc, slashing the hooded man across the chest, though not deep enough to penetrate his clothes.

Now, squatting down, he slashed at his enemy again. But then he saw the hooded man produce his own knife: a hunter's blade with serrated edge. Savero acknowledged this with a tip of the head. They circled each other, two sets of eyes fixed. Savero watched for any sudden movements, and he knew the hooded man was doing the same. At last, it was the Italian who moved first, running at his enemy and bringing down his blade. The hooded man blocked him by raising his forearm, linking the pair together so that neither could strike. They pulled each other around, as if in some kind of crazy dance, until finally the hooded man brought up his knee and levered Savero back. The Italian was not fast enough to avoid the slash that cut open the top of his right arm, and he let out a wounded shout.

Through clenched teeth, Savero cursed the man again. Why won't you just lie down? Why won't you die? In all his time he had never encountered an opponent so reluctant to give an inch, so hard to read. It was as though he wasn't bothered about dying; and if he wasn't frightened of death why should he be scared of Savero?

When the Italian came at him this time, he made a false play, pretending to go in one direction, then dodging back behind the hooded man, snaking an arm around his neck so that it was in the crook of Savero's elbow. The knife point dug into Hood's chest. One false move and he'd drive it downwards into his heart.

"Ah, that's it... " he grunted in the man's ear. "You're mine n–"

Savero was aware of a numbness. Something warm and wet was leaking into the crotch of his trousers, and for a bizarre second he thought he might have somehow wet himself. But a wave of pain was spreading outwards; enough for him to let go of his captive. Savero looked down and saw the knife sticking out of him, right in the 'V' of his legs. It was almost as if the sight, the knowledge of what had happened made things so much worse, caused the pain to increase a million fold.

Savero dropped his own knife and his hands went to the other one. He thought about it, but daren't touch the thing, let alone pull it out. He saw the faces in the crowd, the 'thank God that's not me' expressions, and he stared at the hooded man, uncomprehending. It was one thing to kill him, to die in battle – it was quite another to do this to someone.

Savero staggered a couple of feet, but the pain when he moved was tremendous. He knew the blood was draining out of him rapidly – the femoral artery sliced. Wincing, he dropped to his knees, then fell over sideways. Tears were streaming from his eyes.

The shape of the man standing over him was indistinct, the pain that had been so sharp a minute or two ago was now dull and throbbing. *So this is what it's like*, Savero thought to himself. In a funny sort of way he welcomed death, for what kind of a shameful life would he be able to lead after what had happened.

Something De Falaise had said that first time they met came back to Savero. "You have balls..."

He would have laughed, or at least chuckled at the dark irony, had he been able.

Robert took no great delight in what he'd done.

It had been kill or be killed, and once again his survival instinct hadn't allowed him to give up. Breathing hard, he gazed down at the dead man, curled up on the road in a foetal position, then at the people who'd been watching the fight. Their mouths hung open. They'd never seen anything like it, not even during The Cull. He knew he had to say something – anything – to break the silence.

"Check the back of the trucks, see what we've got... and where we need to return it."

They all continued to gawp at him. He'd said only recently that he didn't want to be like De Falaise, couldn't rule through fear, and yet here they were all so scared of him they could barely move. Thank goodness Mark hadn't been here to see this; Robert was grateful he'd got him to see sense about staying out of harm's way, if only this time. The kid had probably seen worse, out there on the streets, but still...

His opinion of you matters, doesn't it? Go on, admit it.

"Didn't you hear me? Check the truck, I said. We have work to do." This time they snapped out of their reverie, welcoming the chance to leave the scene. Robert nodded at Granger, who'd been the bait in this particular hunter's trap. "You did well," he told him.

The young man blinked and nodded back. "Thanks."

"You're in charge of talking to the men from this unit – finding out whether we can trust them or not, weeding out the bad bets."

Robert had to admit, he still hadn't been a hundred per cent sure about his men until they'd come out from behind their hiding places, until Granger had pushed the commander's arm when the man was firing at him. Now he knew he'd been right to do what he did, freeing them, giving them the option of walking away or teaming up with him. He'd seen wayward kids like Granger before on the beat, who needed to be shown trust before they could trust. Given the right circumstances – and motivation – they could be turned around.

But that hadn't been what changed Robert's mind. Nor that little pep talk Tate had given him, right after he broke down in the face of those flames.

(All he'd been able to see was his house burning, his wife and son being cremated inside, his injured dog crawling out of the door on fire... *Jesus, it was enough to make anyone seize up, wasn't it?*)

Though Robert had to declare that something Tate mentioned sparked the turnaround. He asked him what Robert's family would have thought, what they would have wanted him to do...

"Read to me some more, Dad... please..."

It was then that it all fell into place for him. It was all connected, he saw that now. Even down to how he'd chosen to dress, where he'd picked to hide away from the world.

"Read it to me again, read the part about where he robs from the rich to give to the poor."

Somebody, somewhere, was playing a game with him –
providence was having its own little joke. Robert Stokes's
life was now the equivalent of a storybook. Only an idiot
couldn't spot the parallels, and only an idiot couldn't
figure out what he had to do next.

"Read the bit where he defeats the evil Sheriff..."

What would his family have wanted him to do? Joanne
would have wanted to keep him safe, of that he was
certain, but she was also so very proud of what he did.

*"You help people. It's what you do, it's who you are,
even without the uniform."*

As for Stevie, he'd been trying to tell Robert all along.

"Read to me, Dad, go on."

That's when he'd got up and walked across to the
captured men. That's when the decision had been made,
not even really by him, but by two people he'd loved
so dearly and lost so suddenly. If he was to wait it out,
bide his time until he could be with them again, then
he might as well do some good while he was at it. But
if Robert was going to bring down this new 'Sheriff of
Nottingham' he'd need men. And he was banking on
the fact that Granger and his lot could be persuaded to
switch sides.

Some had been unsure, of course, and some Granger
had marked out as being dangerous; the ones who
hadn't needed any threats to throw in with De Falaise.
Robert would still let them go, in spite of Bill and Tate's
protestations. He was, after all, a man of his word.

The others had told him all they could of De Falaise.
What the set-up was like at the castle, what his plans
were – which Robert had pretty much guessed anyway –
and roughly how many troops he had. The answer to that
one was too many, not all of which could be relied on to
do what Granger had done, especially in the core group
that De Falaise had brought with him or had bribed with

promises of power and fortune.

Which brought them to Javier.

"Let me talk to him," Tate had practically begged Robert. "I can get you all the information you need."

He'd hesitated, taking note of Bill's shaking head, before finally relenting and giving the Reverend his time with the man. Tate promised not to hurt him... much, though it was very hard to tell whether the holy man was serious or not. They'd left Tate all alone with the bound Javier, splashing water in his face to wake him up.

Three hours later, Tate had fetched Robert. As good as his word, there hadn't a mark on the prisoner that hadn't been there before. "He's ready to talk now," Tate said. Which the fat man begrudgingly did, detailing De Falaise's operations that he knew of, routes back to the castle, routes the patrols took in the area, villages they were planning on targeting in the near future.

"How did you do that?" Robert asked him later on.

Tate merely smiled. "I can be very persuasive, as you know. I also have God on my side. There were just the three of us there in that forest today."

"Faith again."

"Faith," Tate confirmed. "It can move mountains. Ultimately Javier is more frightened of divine retribution than anything De Falaise might do to him."

Robert shook his head. "Do you ever think that's what all this might be about?"

"Sorry?"

"The virus. Divine retribution, for 'man's sins'? After all, God didn't do much to stop it, did He?"

"Perhaps. All I know is that He is at work here, in you and in me. We have to trust that He knows what he's doing."

Pursing his lips, Robert held his tongue and walked away, unwilling to get into another debate with the holy man. He had too much to do. For starters, he had a trap to set. They'd tackle one of De Falaise's supply lines, striking where it would hurt the most (especially, as it turned out, in the case of the Italian in charge).

"There's something else you should know," Tate called after him. "My friend, Gwen, who was taken from Hope. She's still alive and in the castle, a plaything of De Falaise."

Robert paused, head turning to the side. "Then you pray for her, Reverend. And while you're at it, pray that we succeed in our endeavours." He'd continued walking. Robert hadn't wished to sound callous, he just didn't see what he could do about the woman right now. One step at a time was how they'd have to take it, and that meant not rushing to attack the castle if it was as heavily fortified as Granger and his men had described.

Once this first step, first attack, had been figured out, he'd ordered that Javier and the ones who wanted out – or Robert didn't want in – to be driven back to the outskirts of Nottingham in their own vehicles, then sent on their way. It amounted to about four or five men in all.

"I reckon you're makin' a mistake there," Bill had informed him when he learnt of the releases. "Why should we let 'em go?"

"What do you suggest," said Robert, "hold them prisoner here, feed them and keep a watch on them in case one escapes and kills us all? Or maybe just murder them in cold blood?"

"They're bound to be spotted by patrols and they know too much about where we are."

"They know we're in the woods, in the forest. De Falaise knew that already. Don't you see that this sends him a clear message?"

"Aye, come and get us."

"Let him come," answered Robert firmly. "We'll be

ready."

One of his men interrupted Robert's thoughts, bringing him back to the present. He'd found a list of villages that this unit had passed through on its expedition. Robert had heard of a lot of them and Bill knew the rest. In any event they had a map they could follow, replacing what had been stolen from people in those communities. It would be a long job, but splitting up would make it easier. And at least the people out there wouldn't starve. Then they'd do the same again with any other supply lines to the castle.

"Right then," Robert said. "Let's get all this stuff back to where it belongs."

In his head he heard that voice again: *"Read it to me again, read the part about where he robs from the rich to give to the poor..."*

It hadn't come as a total shock, of course.

News about the bound men walking through the streets of Nottingham, had been radioed in from look-outs near the train station more than fifteen minutes ago. Orders had come back to leave them be, and so they'd walked past the red brick of the Gresham Hotel, over the bridge, past derelict shops, making their way up towards the centre of the city.

So no, it hadn't come as a complete surprise to De Falaise, who was now standing on the roof of the castle, but it was still a somewhat unexpected turn of events. To his left, the Dutchman, Reinhart, was on one knee, leaning over the side. De Falaise had swapped his sunglasses for powerful binoculars and was watching the tiny group of men shuffling along the road towards the Britannia Hotel, wrists tied in front of them: trussed up like Christmas turkeys. All that was left of the assault team he'd sent to dispose of the hooded man.

Right at the very front was his Major, Javier, looking like the sorriest turkey of the bunch. Around his neck was a crudely painted sign. The message read: 'You Missed'. How could the simpleton have let this happen? De Falaise stamped his foot., his ringed fingers tightening around the binoculars. Reinhart watched through the scope of his sniper's rifle.

"He failed me," griped De Falaise. "And I don't like to lose."

"What would you have me do?" asked Reinhart.

De Falaise thought about this for a moment. "Wing Javier somewhere... uncomfortable, but not fatal. Kill the rest." Before the man could fire, De Falaise laid a hand on his shoulder. "No, wait, shoot the others first. I want Javier to see them die."

The Dutchman closed his left eye, centring a soldier's head in the crosshairs. He pulled the trigger as De Falaise observed. The soldier carried on walking for a second, then stumbled and fell, the contents of his skull leaking out onto the road.

The other men only really began to register what was happening when two more of their team went down. They ran then, not so much turkeys now as soon to be headless chickens. Javier looked around him, screaming as more men were picked off.

"What is he doing?" asked De Falaise, watching as Javier dropped to his knees "Is he praying? I don't believe it, he actually is! How pathetic."

"What should I do?" Reinhart enquired.

"You have your orders.

The Dutchman picked a spot on his target, the side of Javier's head. It would take all of his skill and precision; very delicate shooting indeed. Reinhart blew away the

Mexican's right ear. Though neither of the men on the roof could hear his cries from this far away, they almost felt they could. Javier clutched at the red mess the bullet had made, hands shaking.

"No, it is far too late to repent, my friend," De Falaise said in hushed tones, then he radioed the troops he had on the ground, ordering them to bring the injured Javier to him at the castle..

CHAPTER ELEVEN

It came again, the dream of water and fire.

Of De Falaise and his men.

But something was different this time, something that gave Robert hope. When the soldiers appeared brandishing their weapons, when De Falaise began his walk across the lake, Robert realised he was not observing it alone. Not only was Mark by his side, Robert was joined by others, too. Bill was there, as were Tate and Granger, plus another man that wasn't so well defined. Behind them all stood a further line of defence, the new recruits who had chosen Robert over their former master. De Falaise's face fell when he saw this united front. He was no longer dealing with just one rebel, but a group.

It came to the point in the dream where the Frenchman was about to shoot Max – but Robert was ready for him this time. Hands tried to stop him, but he ran across the lake of flames – towards De Falaise – the burning liquid somehow solid beneath his feet. Max was morphing into the stag once more, but the stag was also transforming. It was like watching one of those old Universal movies where the wolfman changed in dissolves under the influence of the full moon. The stag was taking on human features. De Falaise appeared totally oblivious to this – still intent on shooting the creature.

"Stop!" shouted Robert, notching an arrow. For some reason he felt sure that if the stag-man died, everything would be lost.

De Falaise laughed. Then pulled the trigger.

Robert could see the bullet leaving the chamber, as though it moved in slow motion, but he was powerless to stop it. The stag had changed into a man, though it still wore its antlers. The creature turned just before the bullet struck.

Robert drew in a sharp breath when he recognised the face. The features were his own.

He recoiled in terror, the bow falling from his grasp as he witnessed his death at De Falaise's hands. But more than that, Robert was now the one facing the bullet, was now in its path, helpless to get out of its way.

Time speeded up and the darkness was deafening.

Robert was being shaken.

"Wake up—"

Robert was not only awake, he was also holding his knife blade to this person's throat. He tried to focus on whoever had interrupted his sleep. It was one of his new 'guests', a member of Granger's old gang. After seeing what Robert had done to their unit, anyone would have thought he'd take more care. Robert asked him what he wanted, lowering his weapon.

"S-S-Someone." stuttered the lad, eyes still on the knife. "Mark says he saw someone enter the forest, told me to get you quickly."

Robert let him go, pulling the weapon away. "Tell him I'm coming." He watched the envoy scramble back and out of the tent, glad that he hadn't accidentally hurt him. But he still wasn't used to having people around, even after a week or more and a move deeper into the mature woodland areas of the forest. It would take a while to adjust.

The suggestion had been put forward that they make use of Rufford Abbey or the visitors' centre at Sherwood itself – at least then there would be a roof over their heads. Robert had reminded them that they would be one of the first places De Falaise's troops would search, and would be infinitely harder to escape from.

"You want a siege on your hands, that's the right way to go about it," he told them. "Here you have cover, roughly 450 acres of forest, and you have the element of surprise. It was how I got the jump on you lot, remember?"

In truth that centre held too many memories for him. It was one of the occasional bank holiday haunts he and Stevie would visit: going in the shops and buying souvenirs; taking photos; walking the trail to see the Major Oak, its branches being held up by poles now because of age. His son would marvel at the history connected with it, would imagine the outlaws hiding their stolen goods there before tackling the Sheriff's men.

Robert never thought that he'd be doing it for real.

He grabbed his bow and arrows. Walking through the camp he saw Granger and some of the others asleep in the army-issue sleeping bags from the trucks, the blackened remains of the fire from the night before now a charred heap. He'd show them how to build their own shelters at some point, along with a few other things, but for now he had other matters to deal with. Like the figure Mark had spotted. The kid was turning into quite the little lookout.

Seeing Mark, Robert went over to him.

"What is it?"

"A bloke, really big. He came into the forest not long ago."

"Did he see you?"

"Naw, I kept well away. Looked like he meant business by the way he was sneaking through the trees."

"Was he armed?"

"Couldn't really tell." admitted Mark. "What're you thinking?"

"I'm thinking the Frenchman has sent an assassin. He couldn't get me by brute force, so he's trying the complete opposite. All right, take me to the last place you saw him."

"You're going up against him alone?"

"Better that way, only myself to worry about."

"I don't think you understand how big this guy is. I mean, he's fu... well, he's huge."

Robert didn't show that the size bothered him, but he was thinking back to what Granger had said about De Falaise's men – about one man in particular he'd called Tanek. "Just take me there," he said to Mark. The boy nodded, then led him into the undergrowth.

They'd been travelling ten or fifteen minutes, heads down, moving swiftly but silently, when Robert heard the noise. The snap of wood underfoot. A foot far too heavy to be that of a woodland creature. Robert tapped Mark on the shoulder then signalled for him to stay and keep low.

Robert nimbly climbed the nearest tree, bow slung over his shoulder. From the upper branches, he surveyed the scene, and didn't have to look too far to see the trespasser. Mark had been right, the man was gigantic! If anything, the description he'd given had been an understatement. He wasn't dressed in a uniform like the rest of De Falaise's men, but instead wore clothes pretty similar to Robert's, designed to camouflage him. A cap was pulled down low on his head, obscuring his features.

He couldn't see any weapons but Robert knew they could well be concealed about his person. Robert shifted his weight on the branch and notched an arrow. Best to take this bloke out in one, clean shot, he thought. But before he had time to pull back the string, the man turned and threw something in Robert's direction. A stone came hurtling towards him.

Robert flung himself out of its way, but in the process lost his footing and tumbled from the tree. He forced himself to relax as he fell and managed to land without breaking anything. When Robert looked up, he discovered he'd rolled right into the big man's path. He reached for his bow but he appeared to have lost it in the fall.

The behemoth leant down and hoisted Robert above his head.

Knife. Go for your knife, he thought to himself, but as he reached for his belt he was thrown through the air.

Robert landed awkwardly this time, the air driven from his body by the impact. He shook his head, dazed, but he was given no chance to recover. Something was falling on him. At first his confused mind thought it was one of the trees toppling over; then he realised his attacker was dropping with all his weight behind him. Robert twisted out of the way at the last moment, as the big man flopped heavily onto the ground.

Robert staggered to his feet and adopted a defensive stance. The man suddenly reached out and grabbed his arm, swinging him around. He crashed up against the nearest tree. The edges of his vision began to blur but he managed to shake away the haze in time to see the big man charging with his shoulder raised. He was going to ram Robert. If he wasn't careful he'd end up being the filling in a very painful sandwich.

Robert twisted away just as the man rammed the trunk. The goliath cried out in agony and Robert could have sworn he heard the wood creaking as though the tree might collapse.

All I've done is make him angry, Robert thought as he again went for his knife. But even as he was sliding it out, his opponent was slapping it from his hand, leaving Robert with no way to defend himself... unless....

As the man came at him again, Robert ducked sideways and picked up a fallen branch. It was almost as tall as he was, and strong with it. He hefted it like a staff, jabbing at the bigger man who kept trying to wave it away.

Robert slammed the staff forward with both hands, but the man grabbed it and pulled. Bringing a knee up, he shoved it into Robert's stomach and flipped him over, losing his cap but gaining the staff. The man grinned.

It was his turn to jab at Robert, who snaked left and right to avoid the blows. Robert dropped and scrabbled around in the foliage. His fingers brushed another branch, not quite as big as the first, but beggars definitely couldn't be choosers. Robert snatched it up and met the man's blows, the stick almost splintering with the force. Wood smacked against wood and, suddenly, Robert spotted his chance. He lowered his weapon and struck the man's knee, causing it to buckle. Then he hooked the bigger staff with his own, flipping it out of his enemy's hands and catching it. Robert dropped the smaller branch and raised the huge staff. He was about to bring it crashing down on the man's head when–

"Wait! Hold on, I know him."

Mark came rushing out of the undergrowth towards them, hands flailing to stop Robert delivering the final blow.

"I told you to stay hidden back there," Robert said.

"But now I can see his face," Mark continued. "I'd know him anywhere. And those moves."

Robert cocked his head, looking from the boy to the giant. "You know him?"

Mark nodded enthusiastically. The man on the ground, nursing his sore knee, looked just as mystified as Robert.

"Of course. Don't you?"

Robert studied the man's features – the curly hair, the goatee beard – but couldn't recall having ever seen them before.

"That's Jack 'The Hammer' Finlayson," said Mark. "You're Jack 'The Hammer' Finlayson!"

The man looked up at Mark, his eyes warming. "Been a while since anyone called me by that name, kiddo." There was a US accent, but it was blended with English, as if the man had lived on these shores for some time.

"Who?" asked Robert, genuinely confused. In the space of a few moments they'd gone from trying to kill each other to discussing the man's identity.

"What do you mean who? The Jack-Hammer – as in 'he'll hammer all comers into the floor'. Only one of the best wrestlers on the circuit!"

"Wrestler...?" But the more Robert thought about it, the more it made sense. The fighting techniques this Finlayson character had been using were very much in keeping with that particular sport.

"I saw tons of your matches, some on the sports channels, but my Dad used to take me to..." Mark let the sentence fall away, his brow furrowing. It was the first time Robert had heard him mention his parents, let alone his father. For some reason it hurt him just as much as it must have done Mark. The boy caught Robert looking at him and carried on, as if nothing had fazed him. "You should have seen him against Bulldog Bramley at the Sheffield Arena, he tore that guy apart!"

"I always thought that stuff was faked," Robert countered.

The wrestler sneered. "Maybe in some places, but not when I was in the ring. Back then it was about as fake as the little tussle we've just had, fella."

"So you can vouch for him?" Robert asked Mark.

"He signed me an autograph once, on the way back to the dressing rooms. They didn't all do that."

"That doesn't mean a thing these days. Everything's

changed." But Robert could see now there was a kindness to Finlayson's face as he smiled at Mark – even though the guy probably didn't remember giving him that signature. Plus which, Robert was starting to get a feeling about him. It was the sort of judgement call he made all the time back when he was a policeman. The kind of instinct that had told him Granger was okay. Realising this, it made him even angrier to think he'd fought Finlayson. "I could have really hurt you – that was a stupid thing to be doing, walking around in here."

"Hey, you started it," Finlayson pointed out. "You were about to ventilate me, pal. Never heard of asking 'who goes there, friend or foe?'"

Robert had to concede, he'd been ready to shoot the man just because he figured it was De Falaise who'd sent him.

"I'm sorry," said Robert quietly. He stuck out his hand and the big man took it. Robert almost went down again when Finlayson used it to pull himself up.

"Thanks," the large man said, brushing himself down and picking up his baseball cap. "Hey, you know, you would've made a pretty decent go of it on the circuit yourself. I'm a bit out of shape, granted, but no one's given me a run for my money like that in quite a while."

Robert was more than flattered by the comment. "If Mark here says you're all right, that's good enough for me." He caught Mark's chest swelling when he said this. "Let's hear your story, Finlayson."

Finlayson had grown up on the rural outskirts of upstate New York. "It was too quiet there for me, man. And the winters were harsh." He explained that his father would make him chop wood for the fire during those snowbound months, something that gave him a taste for exercise and honing his body. "I began weight training before I hit eleven. Not with real weights, you understand – with anything I could get my hands on: engine parts, rocks, the wood I was choppin'. 'Course, I was also growin' some by then. My old Mom, God rest her soul, used to joke that I'd fallen from a beanstalk when I was a baby and her and Pop had adopted me." It had been his father who'd taught him the basics of wrestling, one of the few pastimes they had out in the sticks. "I remember the first time I beat him as well. The look on his face!" Finlayson laughed.

He'd begun to find rural life too stifling and, when he was old enough, Finlayson went in search of the great American dream. He wanted a taste of the bright city lights, so he got a job in a gym, mopping up at first in exchange for the use of their equipment. "All kinds of people would train in there, footballers, boxers, wrestlers. It was those who interested me. I got talkin' to some of them and they suggested I should try out for some of the local matches, maybe even get a manager. I did all right over there, but I was a small fish in a very big pond."

It was on a visit to the UK one summer as part of a tour that he fell in love with the country. "Must have seen most of what there is to see of Britain, but I always loved this part especially. So, I decided to stay. Oh, they tried to get me to go back to the States, but over here I could actually be someone – perhaps not on the scale of those WWE big shots, but in my own way I'd be recognised." Finlayson smiled again at Mark, who grinned back. "I carried on doing the circuits for several years, places like Lincoln, York, Leeds, Doncaster, Manchester, and closer to home in Nottingham and Sheffield, which is I guess where you caught up with me, huh kiddo?"

Mark nodded.

"Quite a few of those matches were televised, as well. I used to send tapes to my Pop. I think he was proud of what I was doing. Towards the end though I began to think: what am I getting in there, getting myself all banged up for? Counting the bruises at weekends, having to visit the doc more and more often. That's when I began to pull back from it all a bit."

"So what were you doing when the virus hit?" asked Robert.

"Working in a gym again, believe it or not. I was teaching classes at a Health and Fitness Centre this time – qualifications in wrestling, no less."

Finlayson told them what had happened when the virus had hit. It was the same old story. The people either clogging the doctors' surgeries or hospitals, taking to their homes, or dropping in the streets. Robert listened, trying not to let his mind go back to his own experiences, trying not to think of Stevie and Joanne. After The Cull, Finlayson, like so many others, had taken off for a quieter spot. "Guess I finally saw the wisdom of getting away from it all like my folks had done, all those years ago. Things were gettin' too, I don't know, out of control in the towns and cities."

"Didn't you have anyone... anybody that you left behind?" asked Robert, then immediately said: "Wait, don't answer that. It's none of my business."

Finlayson didn't seem to mind. "You mean a gal, a family and such? No woman's ever been able to pin me down, if you'll pardon the expression. As for family, they were all the way over in the US. Like I say, my Mom died before all this, thank the Lord. My Dad... He wouldn't have made it."

"How do you know?"

"Wrong kinda blood."

They sat in silence for a while then, before Finlayson

broke the quiet.

"I sometimes get to thinkin' about what happened over there, what it's like back in the States. You know anything?"

Robert shook his head. "I've been a bit out of touch. You never thought about returning, to see for yourself?"

"It's not my home anymore. This is. Which brings me to why I'm in Sherwood Forest. Word's spreadin' about what's gone on here. Stories about a hooded man helping the communities, about how he took on a bunch of men single-handed at a market and won. About how he gave back food and supplies to those who've been robbed by that son of a bitch holed up at the castle, pardon my p's and q's. I figure that you've got a cause I wouldn't mind fighting for."

Mark must have caught the look of shock on Robert's face, because he added, "You can't be that surprised they've heard of you. There aren't too many people, too many communities left."

"Not only have they heard of you," Finlayson chipped in, "some of 'em want to join you. Not many folk care for a bully. Anyway, I thought to myself, hooded man in Nottingham... in Sherwood... hmm. I'm pretty damned big, maybe I ought to be in the runnin' for one of the starring roles in that flick."

Robert quickly glossed over the obvious reference. "We thought you were one of De Falaise's men. We thought you'd come here to kill me."

"Nope," Finlayson confirmed. "I came to offer my services."

"So why the fight, why creep up on us like this?"

"To show you what I could do. And to see just how good the set up was, if the stories were true about you... Like they say, you never really know a man till you fight him."

"What's that, some kind of mystical thing?"

"Actually, it's from one of them *Matrix* movies," chuckled Finlayson. "Man, I really miss films, don't you?"

Robert found himself laughing, too. It felt weird, alien even. But good. He stepped forward and offered his hand again; this time in friendship. Finlayson shook it immediately.

"I won't let you down."

"I know," came Robert's reply. He looked at the staff he was holding. "I think you might be needing this. It's more you than me, anyway." He handed Jack the weapon and the man smiled. Out of the corner of his eye he could see Mark grinning wildly. "Right, well, I think we ought to introduce you to a few people."

Robert ushered the big man into the forest and then waited for Mark to fall in behind. If Finlayson was right, if there were enough people like him willing to fight, then maybe things could go their way after all.

And if the struggle against De Falaise could be turned around, well, maybe a few other things could be too.

CHAPTER TWELVE

After a while you grew accustomed to the screams.

De Falaise had learnt this fairly early on in his career. He was damned sure Tanek had as well. In fact, the huge slab of a man in front of him had probably been born with the capacity to shut out the cries of pain. Or was it more than that, was it that sometimes you could grow to actually enjoy hearing them, find them just as pleasing as a Beethoven symphony?

When it came right down to it, this represented everything De Falaise was about. The strong having control over the weak. And he had all of his troops' lives in the palms of his hands, could send for any of them at any time and just pop a bullet into their skull as an example. But there was something infinitely more satisfying about doing it this way. It was the difference between a nuclear explosion destroying a city, killing millions, and a laser cutting out a tumour. Meticulous work. De Falaise had observed Tanek's technique on many occasions. He'd seen Tanek extract information from the most reluctant of sources, men De Falaise thought would never crack. In the end they all did, it was just a matter of pushing the right buttons.

Which brought him back to the screams. Down here, away from prying eyes, and illuminated by a jury-rigged lighting system, Tanek laboured at his work. The subjects this time: two men and a woman. All were hanging in chains. None of them knew each other, but they did have one thing in common. They'd all been turned in for speaking about The Hooded Man: at markets, gatherings in villages, on street corners. De Falaise had his spies, so scared to put a foot wrong they'd rather turn in those who had befriended them than risk being brought down to these caves themselves.

The reports that were filtering back were displeasing. Yes, people were frightened of the Frenchman, as well they should be. A legend was forming around De Falaise, of what he did to anyone who opposed him, what he did under the castle with his prisoners. But the stories of initial attacks on villages by his men had only been rife for a short time. Now other tales were being spread.

These new stories revolved around Henrik and the tank, around Javier's incompetence in the forest (for which he'd not only lost his ear, but his freedom down in these dungeons). This last outrage had made De Falaise so angry that in a fit of rage he'd ordered the statue outside the castle to be torn down...

Word had also spread about the soldiers who'd swapped their allegiance. De Falaise had put paid to any such ideas of resistance amongst his own men quickly enough, by stringing the bodies of the soldiers who had returned with Javier up on posts in the courtyard for all to see. He'd even called a gathering to say a few words about their presence. "This is the price of failure," he'd shouted. "Look upon it, and mark that it is not yourself next time!"

But if De Falaise was inspiring dread among not only the populace, but his own army, then this man who was following in the footsteps of an old legend was sending out another message. One of hope, of freedom.

And hardly surprising: in the past weeks since De Falaise had lost Savero – another one of his elite – and the goods he was carrying, there had been more attacks, more losses. It was clear that if something wasn't done soon, the tide could very swiftly turn against him.

"I will not lose everything I've worked so hard for," he'd screamed at Tanek, "not because of some half-breed savage with a knife and a bow and arrow!"

It was clear that this man – whose real name De Falaise did not even know – had learned a lot about him, and his plans. De Falaise intended to redress the balance.

Hence these three prisoners had been cherry picked because they were shooting their mouths off about the hooded man. They'd been bundled into the backs of jeeps under armed guard, brought to the castle, and deposited here in one of the dank chambers De Falaise had requisitioned for his needs. Or more specifically for Tanek's.

The girl he'd taken as his plaything would end up in the dungeons soon, too, De Falaise thought to himself. He was growing tired of her. The limp rag doll impression he'd found such a turn on at first was growing wearisome to say the least. While it was true he preferred no resistance, he was not a huge fan of necrophilia, either.

Another scream brought his attention back to the prisoners. Tanek was applying a hot iron to the oldest of the men, rubbing it up and down his thigh. He'd worked his way up the leg and would soon reach a place that would cause the maximum amount of pain. De Falaise had no sympathy for him. It could all end now if the prisoner would only tell them what he knew of the renegade... the renegades, he should say.

For they now knew that the man in the hood was no longer alone, after Javier had spilled his guts about what had happened in the forest. There were at least two trusted aides it would seem.

"A holy man, you say?" De Falaise had questioned, rubbing his chin.

"The... the one from Hope, my Lord," Javier spluttered, the side of his head a mess of dried blood.

De Falaise struck him. "You no longer have the right to call me that!"

"I'm sorry... I'm so sorry..."

De Falaise had leaned forward. "What was that, I didn't quite catch what you were saying?"

"I said I'm sorry!" Javier hissed, spittle flying from his mouth. "I was scared..."

"More scared of your 'maker' than you are of me?" De Falaise said. "Why?"

Javier couldn't answer, he just stared at De Falaise.

"Do you not understand, is it not apparent to you? Around here I am God! Your allegiance is to me! It is too late anyway for you to make your peace with whichever deity you choose to believe in. You've travelled too far down another path for that. The holy man lied to you if he was offering you salvation, you stupid turd. But I will keep you alive until you have learned your lesson, Javier. Which starts with telling me more about this Hooded Man's gang."

De Falaise had listened as his former major described a man in a checked shirt who carried a shotgun, someone small he hadn't got much of a look at, and now Granger, the halfwit they'd picked up down in London.

"Ah, yes, him," De Falaise had nodded knowingly. "I thought he might be trouble eventually."

Even including the men he'd commandeered from Savero, the man in the hood couldn't have much of an army... Unless more joined him from the villages.

It was nothing compared to De Falaise's militia, but it was still a worry.

Tanek left the man he was burning and turned his attention to the woman. "Please, I've told you everything I know," she said, sniffing back tears. "He lives in the forest somewhere. I haven't even seen him!"

"No need to cry," De Falaise said softly. "No need at all." A sharp nod of the head and Tanek was reaching for his knife – not the one he usually carried, the soldier's knife.

This one was more like a scalpel. He brought the blade up with one hand, cupping the back of the woman's head with the other. His hand was so big it covered almost the whole of her scalp. Then Tanek jammed the blade into her left eye and scooped out the orb. The woman screamed, the cry louder and much more piercing than the man who'd endured the iron.

"You see," commented De Falaise. "No more tears now. Much better."

Tanek flicked the eye from the knife, then made to take out the other one.

"For pity's sake!" shouted the younger man.

"Pity?" asked De Falaise, turning towards him. "Pity? Pity is for the feeble and the foolish. You do not know this, which is why you are the one in the shackles, mon ami."

Tanek finished up with the woman. When he moved to the side De Falaise could see the holes in her face where the eyes had once been. Her scream had turned into a low moan. De Falaise gestured for Tanek to tackle the next subject.

"And it is also why, you see..." the Frenchman continued, stepping aside so that Tanek could get past – his next implement of torture ready, a drill. "...you will be next."

The man began screaming even before Tanek drove the drill bit into his kneecap.

The three prisoners told De Falaise nothing he hadn't already known. The people feared and hated him, they admired and cheered for The Hooded Man.

"Something has to be done about the situation," De Falaise commented when they exited the chamber, leaving the half-dead bodies behind them, "before it gets out of hand."

"What?" Tanek asked, climbing the steps behind De Falaise.

"I have an idea. You see it strikes me that if we cannot take him in his native environment, we must smoke him out somehow, non? And the way to do that is to eat at his conscience. You do know what that is, don't you?" said De Falaise laughing. Tanek didn't even crack a smile. "Yes, that is it. Tanek, if all goes to plan then we will soon bring down this 'hero' and his band. We will rewrite history, and I will have his head before the summer is out!"

CHAPTER THIRTEEN

Today had begun much the same as all the others since the world ended.

Though, to be honest, things hadn't really changed on the farm much anyway; work-wise at any rate. She still got up at sunrise, still fed the pigs and chickens at the same time, tended to the fields, saw to the bees in the back yard. Life was pretty much how it had been for as long as she could remember. Apart from the fact that her brother and father were gone.

Mary Louise Foster looked out over the tracts of land that formed the backdrop of her house. It was an inherited property, which strangely enough she never thought would be hers – and certainly didn't want to come by in the way that she had. Her mother left when Mary was only small, unable to cope with the lot of a farmer's wife, and the two kids that farmer had given her. In many ways Mary resented the fact she'd disappeared like that, leaving her father to cope on his own. In some ways, though, she totally understood. However, it meant that Mary and her sibling, David, had to grow up fast. They'd been set to work on the farm, David taking to it like one of their pigs to muck, while she always felt oddly out of place. And always scrutinised. In their eyes she could never lift as much as David or her father, could never work quite as hard as they did. So the older she became the more she was expected to do what they called the 'woman's work', cleaning the house, making the meals.

Then one day Mary decided enough was enough. She'd told them out and out that they had to do their fair share of work around the home.

"Only if you do your fair share out there, Moo-Moo,"

David had replied, using her nickname, a contraction of Mary-Lou.

"Fair enough, then, Diddy," Mary responded, folding her arms and using the ridiculous childhood name she, in turn, had saddled him with.

So she'd rolled up her sleeves and joined them again out on the farm, resolving to work not just as hard as them this time, but harder. She hadn't given up, not even when her limbs ached and her feet were sore. Mary lugged bales of hay, learnt how to drive the tractor, got stuck in with the pitchfork and, in return, demanded that David and her father get in the kitchen from time to time and learn exactly how a Hoover operated. The older of the two refused, no matter how hard Mary toiled. Bernhard Donald Foster was stuck in the past, and not just because he liked to collect his precious historical memorabilia. No, he came from a different generation, who had buried their heads in the sand when it came to treating women the same as men. He had taken his lead from his own father, and his grandfather before that, who thought their wives were put on this Earth just to serve them. Which was probably why Bernhard had spent so many nights alone in that big double bed. Sometimes she'd hear him tossing and turning in the small hours and her heart would go out to him. Then he'd get up the next morning and ask her what was for breakfast, when he could expect it, and all that sympathy would vanish.

David, on the other hand, had admired his little sister's tenacity: so much so that he began to help out with the cooking, did the dusting on a Saturday and even – shock, horror – gave a hand with the washing-up from time to time. Her father looked on this with great disdain but said nothing.

Before Bernard died of a massive stroke at the age of fifty-five, David and Mary had developed an extremely close bond. David had just turned twenty, so he took on the legal guardianship of Mary. Both agreed they didn't want to look for their estranged mother – who'd already been written out of the will. They'd be okay, here, together. They didn't need anyone else.

Like David before her, Mary attended the local school, only she excelled in the arts. When the time came to choose, though, between moving away to attend college and remaining on the farm, Mary stayed with David. He hadn't pressured her, but she'd felt it was her duty nonetheless. There was a big part of her that really didn't want to leave him, anyway. Every year that went by, however, it grew tougher and tougher for farmers. For them. She continued to draw and often wondered what it would have been like if she'd made it to college. Would she have had a successful career in graphic design, met the man of her dreams that she'd been saving herself for?

But then, looking back, none of that had mattered in the end. Because of The Cull.

The first they'd heard about the virus, living all the way out here, was when David had returned from trying to sell the pigs at auction.

"They're all talking about it. They're saying maybe it's come from the animals. Like Foot and Mouth, only worse, spreading to humans.... People are getting real sick, Moo-Moo."

"There's nothing wrong with our animals!" Mary said defensively.

"I know that! I'm just telling you what they said."

But nobody knew where the virus had come from. The television threw back images of cities in chaos, of throngs of people desperate to get somewhere, but not knowing where. Mary and David locked themselves away from the outside world, pretending it didn't exist.

Then, one morning, David began to cough.

"Look, I'm bleeding, Moo-Moo." She could see that for herself. The blood was all over the towels in the bathroom, all over the floor. Mary had cleaned him up as best she could, helping him back to bed. She had no formal training in nursing, but had done a few courses in first aid and learnt what she could from books. She was also used to looking after two grown men who insisted they were dying every time they came down with something. The only difference this time being David actually was.

They had all kinds of medicines in the house – oh, the Fosters were very self-sufficient – and she tried him on antibiotics, anti-inflammatories, whatever she thought might help. Nothing did the trick.

The phone lines were all busy, the emergency services non-responsive. Mary thought about running David into the nearest town, but by that time he'd deteriorated rapidly. He probably wouldn't have lasted the journey. All she could do was sit with him and hope he made it through the night.

He did, but only just. Delirious, he kept asking for their father in the final moments, wanted to tell him he was sorry for abandoning the farm. "It's down to you now. There's only you left. You have to promise me, Moo-Moo. As long as it's still... still standing."

"I promise, Diddy," Mary had said, tears streaming down her face.

Then she realised he was already gone.

Mary buried David out by one of his favourite trees, where he used to read on summer days when they'd take picnics into the top field.

It still made her sad that she'd never gone off and started a family somewhere, but Mary had made her peace with the life she'd chosen – wouldn't have missed spending those final few years with her brother for anything.

Besides which, in retrospect, what might have happened to that family even if she'd started it? She'd probably have had to say goodbye to a husband she loved, to children. She couldn't even begin to imagine what that must be like; what it could do to you.

Mary never really questioned why she didn't get sick. She just assumed there was something inside her stronger than David. In the end she'd been proved stronger than both him and her father, had been bequeathed the entire farm and its lands.

And today had begun just like any other day: she'd done quite a few of her chores and was now looking forward to a nice bacon sandwich.

No sooner had she put the pan on the range, standing with her long, dark hair tied back in a ponytail, than she heard the sound of approaching engines. Apart from the tractors, which she'd used sparingly since David passed away – conserving the fuel they kept out in the adjourning garage – she hadn't heard a car engine in longer than she could remember. It sounded strange to her; not just the noise, but the connotations of it. That people were, in fact, out there in the world.

That they were heading her way.

Mary rushed to the kitchen window, craning her head to try and see up the dirt track leading to her farm.

They were dots to begin with, no bigger than the bees she tended to outside. But they were growing larger with each metre of road they devoured. Mary hadn't encountered another human being in all this time, and now she was about to meet several, all at once. She counted two jeeps, three or four motorcycles and a truck.

What do I do? she thought to herself, realising her hands were shaking. *Hide? Pretend I'm not here and hope that they'll just go away?* But she'd done enough of that already. It didn't sit right anymore. This was her farm now and she should see what they wanted. After all, they looked sort of official. Perhaps civilisation was piecing itself back together? Perhaps they were here to help?

It wasn't long before the vehicles were in the yard: the chickens in the run protesting, the pigs in the sty oinking for all they were worth. Mary hung back at the window, crouching and peering out through the netting. The men wore uniforms but they weren't like any she'd seen before. They looked as if they'd been standing in an Army & Navy store when a hurricane hit: each soldier sporting items from different branches of the forces. The man stepping down from the driver's side of the truck was wearing a peaked cap – obviously the guy in charge.

He reached into the truck and pulled out a megaphone, as more of the soldiers came to join him. Each one was heavily armed, she noted, holding machine guns close to their chests.

"If there is anyone at home here, please come out with your hands where we can see them," the man shouted. His accent betrayed him; definitely not from England, though Mary couldn't place where it had originated.

They don't sound very friendly, Moo-Moo... came the voice of her brother in her head. It didn't freak her out at all, because she knew – hoped – she wasn't crazy, just imagining what he might say if he were here. *No, I definitely don't like the looks of this.*

Neither did she.

"If you don't come out we will be coming in. We are here under the authority of the new High Sheriff of Nottingham."

The what? said David in her head. *He's got to be kidding, right? Have we just gone through a time warp or something?*

Mary watched as the men spread out, investigating the chicken run, the sty. They reported back to the fellow with the peaked cap. She watched, horrified, as one of the soldiers stepped into the run, grabbing a chicken and snapping its neck. Mary had just about got over that when she heard gunfire coming from the pigsty, a rat-ta-ta-tat noise as someone massacred the helpless creatures. Her hand shot to her mouth.

They're going to do that to me, too, aren't they?

Probably, Moo-Moo. I don't think you should hang around to find out, do you?

Mary came away from the window and noticed the smoke; the bacon had burnt to a crisp. Then the smoke alarm went off, proving that even if everything else in this world had gone to crap then at least one thing could be relied on. The incessant beep-beep-beep gave her away, and she knew she didn't have long before they stormed the house.

Mary ran from the kitchen into the hall, passing the crossed broadswords that hung there, on her way to the combined study & living room . She hurried to the desk at the back, her father's antique desk. On her way something caught her eye through the window – figures rounding the back of the house, ensuring any escape route would be cut off. Mary yanked open the drawer nearest to her. There they were, lying in the bottom, shiny and fully loaded, with packs of bullets next to them. When they'd been little her father had kept them safely locked away, only bringing them out to admire and clean when they were in bed. As they grew, he'd been less bothered about safety, even letting them hold the pistols when they were unloaded. David had always looked at them like he was handling live snakes, but Mary had felt the weight in her hand comforting. Whereas most farmers might have a shotgun to protect their land, Bernhard Foster had two replica Smith & Wesson Peacemakers, and he knew how to use them. Mary had watched him out in the field sometimes, able to knock nine out of ten tin cans from their perch on top of a wooden crate at thirty paces or more.

She'd watched and she'd remembered.

When the handgun ban had come into effect in the UK, David had wanted to take them in. But she argued against it, saying that it was one of the few things they had left of their father, but really just wanting to keep them around the place. She felt safer with them in the drawer. There was a reason she'd looked after them and kept them loaded ever since David had gone. A reason she'd practised with the tins just like her father had when she was young. This was the reason, she understood that now.

Taking them out, her fingers curled around the handles, and it gave her confidence. Mary felt like she could do anything now, anything at—

There was a banging on the front door – which she had a clear view of from her position. Placing one pistol down on the desk momentarily, she emptied out bullets and stuffed them into the pockets of her jeans, as many as she could cram in there. Skirting back around the desk, she used the living room door jamb for cover and risked a glance out. Heavy boots were stamping against the wood of the front door, but it was holding for now. It wouldn't for long.

Just like Custer, eh? Dad would've been proud, said David.

Great, thanks...

The door was splintering at the lock and Mary knew in seconds they'd be through. She slid down the wall, breathing heavily, waiting to act until she heard the door give completely. She heard it smash open, and turned to fire upwards – assessing the situation quickly before pulling the trigger.

The soldiers burst in and she let them have it. Because of the awkward angle she was at, her aim was a little wide, ricocheting off the stone wall above the door. Nevertheless it was enough to force a retreat.

She smiled to herself – that wasn't so hard. But then a hail of bullets filled the hallway; Mary only just managed to roll back into the living room and avoid them.

"Tin cans don't do that," she muttered to herself.

Luckily they were aiming high, the soldiers either not that well trained or hampered by the smoke that was wafting out of the kitchen and filling the hall, masking her from sight.

Mary looked around for an easy exit. The enormous back windows were probably her best option, but even now she saw shadows there as more men ran around the back of the house, trapping her.

She heard the shattering of windows elsewhere too, possibly the dining room that lay on the other side of the hall. The stairs were between there and here, so a dash for the landing or bedrooms was out of the question. Mary shuffled up against the living room wall.

First order of business was to defend the front door – they'd be coming through that again any moment. Mary rose, twisted her head, and peered around the jamb. Sure enough she spotted figures there – responding to orders given by their commanding officer outside – and she fired blindly through the smoke. Mary dived when the muzzles of their machine guns flashed again, rolling as she did so to reach the other side of the jamb.

There was gunfire at the back of the house as well, raking the stone, shattering the glass of the living room window. Mary fired a couple of shots in that direction to try and ward off any soldiers entering that way.

She risked another glance into the hall, and it was at this point she saw something rolling towards her. It was small and black, ball-like but metallic; it rattled along the wooden floor as it went.

Move, Sis! Get out of there, right now!

"Oh shit!" she cried, scrambling to her feet. Mary was about halfway across the room, already diving for the shelter of the desk, when the grenade exploded in the hallway. The force of it flung her the rest of the way, bouncing her off the top of the desk and pitching her against the far wall, as most of the room appeared to follow behind her.

Mary landed on the other side of the desk, protected from the resultant blast but barely conscious.

Moo-Moo... Wake up! You've got to wake up... Those men are in the house and they're going to hurt you! Please Moo-Moo!

So, her mind was still working then, still keeping up the imaginary dialogue with her dead brother? She drifted in and out of wakefulness, desperate to keep her eyes open. Mary could hear sounds, men calling out to each other. A creaking from above, someone walking on the floorboards upstairs. They were searching the house from top to bottom.

"All clear," someone called.

She blacked out for a few moments, then another voice not far away was shouting, "In here... Look."

"Careful, she's still alive."

"Call Colonel Rudakas, quickly."

Mary was aware of hands on her, of being lifted up – but she couldn't do a blessed thing about it. Again, a few more seconds of blackness, then she felt her face being slapped.

"Hey! Wake up!"

Another slap, followed by a shake – rough hands holding her on either side were pushing her forwards, then backwards, in quick succession. Mary screwed her hazel eyes up tight, then opened them. The figure in front of her was blurry, but she could tell by the peaked cap it was the man in charge, this Rudakas guy.

She was shaken again. "I'm awake," Mary burbled. "Stop shaking me."

"Good." He smiled. "This is quite a place you have here..." He waited for her name, but when Mary didn't offer one, he proceeded. "Hidden away, miles from civilisation. We almost missed you on our spree today."

Mary struggled against the men holding her, but they had a firm grip.

"You're headstrong, I'll give you that – but it will fade soon enough. You're also very beautiful." Rudakas looked her up and down. It made Mary feel sick to her stomach. "My Lord De Falaise grows weary of the companion he has at present. He is in need of some fresh company."

"Who... who are you people?"

"Us? Have you not heard? No, I do not imagine you have. We are the new order, we are your new masters."

"You're not my anything." Mary scowled.

Rudakas toured around the room, approaching the desk that had shielded Mary after the grenade went off. When Rudakas turned back to her, he had both the Peacemakers in his hands.

"Collector's items, I believe. Where did you come by such magnificent pistols?"

"They were my father's," Mary told him reluctantly.

"Ah, a family heirloom then... Like all of this, I presume." He gestured at the room, the house. "I must apologise for the untidiness, but you left us little choice. Had you made your presence known, surrendered earlier then... Well, things might have worked out a little differently. I am not an unreasonable man; nor is the Sheriff."

"Sheriff? I don't understand."

"It's quite simple, really. My Lord has taken over these

lands and appointed himself their keeper. Which, put simply, means that everything found on said lands belongs to him. These," he lifted the pistols, "your property, such as it is... Your animals, which we have already begun slaughtering for meat. Your crops and, finally, you, my sweet."

Mary stiffened.

"I take it you do have a name?"

She clamped her mouth shut.

"Tell me, for that too belongs to him."

When Mary defied the man, he stuffed one of the pistols into his belt and then punched her hard in the stomach. The breath exploded from her, but she wasn't allowed the luxury of doubling over – the men holding her on either side saw to that.

"Now, I ask again, what your name might be?"

Tell him, Moo-Moo. Tell him or he might do something worse. "Ma...Ma..." was all she could manage, but it wasn't just the effort of speaking when winded; it was the principle that was sticking in her throat.

The man grabbed her just under the chin. "We have all the time in the world, but it would go easier on you if you just told me right now."

Mary spat in his face.

Rudakas recoiled. "You fucking bitch! I will teach you some manners before dragging you to the castle." He pulled back his fist again, and was about to strike Mary when there came a noise from outside.

It was the sound of gunfire.

"What is that? Are there more of you here?" When he got no answer, he said to the men, "Hold her until I return." Rudakas strode off up the hallway.

Mary's face stung and her stomach was killing her. But she recognised an opportunity when she saw one. Feigning weakness, she lolled forward, forcing the men holding her to yank her back again. As soon as they did, she made her move. Mary stamped on the foot of the soldier to her right. He was wearing boots, but then so was she, and Mary dug the edge of her heel in hard for maximum effect. The man let go and, as soon as he did, she swung her newly-freed arm around and smashed a fist into the face of her other warder, giving a satisfying grunt as his nose shattered.

Without anyone to hold him, the man did double over – so she punched him again, this time at the temple. He toppled over sideways and didn't get up.

Mary suddenly felt arms around her. The first guard, who'd got over her treading on his toes, had wrapped himself around her, clasping his hands together over her chest. Mary dropped, letting go and turning into a dead weight, slipping out from under his grasp. On her back, and on the floor, she brought up her left leg and swung it over her head, kicking the man squarely in the crotch.

He fell backwards with a loud yelp. Mary ran to the smashed window at the back of the living room. More of Rudakas's people were standing guard there but, as she watched, something very strange happened. Out of nowhere came an object, a spinning thing flying through the air. It hit one man at speed, wrapping itself around his neck, the twine whipping round until the stones attached to each end came together. He reached up for this throat, unable to call out, choking as other newcomers approached.

One of them was a huge bear of a man wearing a baseball cap. He came up behind a soldier and swung what appeared to be a staff, knocking him into a beehive.

What's going on, Diddy?

I'm not sure, but I think they're here to help, Moo-Moo.

Then she heard the second explosion of that day, and

the house rocked with its intensity.

Rudakas hated having to leave the girl, especially at such a crucial point.

He knew De Falaise would not want a woman who would spit and fight back – he preferred them to be docile. If he could tame this one, he'd be in his Lord's good books for weeks, or at least until he grew bored of her too. Not that it was always a good thing to be among De Falaise's most favoured, mused Rudakas. Just look at Javier. He'd brought their leader the last girl, and in return had been rewarded with a very 'special task'.

Rudakas wondered absently how well he might have fared in the forest against the Hooded Man. Surely he would have done better? He pushed such thoughts aside, concentrating on the here and now, on the fact that the woman back there was not as alone as she seemed. He looked down at the pistol he held in his hand. "They were my father's," she'd said, and he'd assumed the man was dead, just like most of the population. But what if she'd meant him to think that? What if her father had seen them approach and hid, maybe in one of the barns? Maybe in that rickety old garage joined on to the house? Or perhaps a brother or cousin, if the father was no more? Anything was possible and someone was certainly causing a ruckus outside.

The door had swung to again, so Rudakas pulled on the handle to see what was happening. Once more he heard gunfire. He looked outside and couldn't believe what his eyes were telling him.

His unit was under attack, but not just from one man – or even a couple. Gunfire emanated from the bushes that ringed the fields, from behind the barns, even from behind their own vehicles. They were being hit by an organised and motivated group. One of his own soldiers dropped, falling from a shoulder wound. Another was hit by something much cruder – a stone, flung with force.

"Pick your targets," shouted Rudakas. "Watch for muzzle flashes and–"

Something embedded itself in the wood of the door jamb, inches away from his head. He examined the arrow, obviously handmade, but lovingly fashioned and extremely deadly. Then he traced its trajectory back to the person who'd fired it. He was standing on top of their truck, head down, a hood covering much of his face. The bow he was holding – a strong wooden longbow – was still reverberating from the shot.

Be careful what you wish for. You wanted to know how you'd fare against The Hooded Man – well, now you will find out.

The figure on the truck, set apart from the rest of the battle, and barely seeming to take much notice of the bullets flying back and forth, raised his head. From beneath the cowl Rudakas saw two of the most penetrating eyes he'd ever had the misfortune to gaze into. It was as if the man had fixed on him, and him alone, for his prey.

Rudakas was suddenly conscious that the only guns he had on him were the Peacemakers he'd taken from the woman. With one in his hand already, he snatched the other from his belt and raised them, moving forward at the same time.

The Hooded Man smiled, a grin only just visible beneath his beard. And like a blur, he was reaching for another arrow from his quiver, jumping down onto the hood of the truck, with an aim to hit the ground running.

Like gunfighters from an old western movie – quite appropriate considering the weapons Rudakas held – they faced off against each other. The colonel fired, expertly aiming and yet somehow missing the target every time. The Hooded Man let off a couple more arrows, one of which scraped Rudakas's thigh, the other only just missing his head.

"Fuck!"

Rudakas fired again, The Hooded Man mirroring his actions. This time a bullet nicked the latter's shoulder: a flesh wound, but enough to ensure the man's aim was off.

Rudakas grabbed his chance. Raising both the Peacekeepers he fired directly at his enemy's head. Both pistols clicked empty. He'd become so used to automatic weaponry, easy to reload and discharge, that he'd forgotten he was holding revolvers – and that the woman had already fired off a number of bullets at them as they broke into her home.

The Hooded Man, however, still had one arrow left in his quiver. Rudakas swallowed dryly as he watched the man reach for the projectile. The arrowhead was aimed right between Rudakas's eyes. But he refused to close them; he'd always told himself he would meet death with his eyes wide open and, if need be, his arms too.

The Hooded Man's fingers twitched on the bowstring.

Rudakas waited for the end – and if time had slowed before, then it practically ground to a halt now.

But when it lurched forward again, the colonel was surprised to see The Hooded Man's aim shifting, the bow and arrow pointing several metres to Rudakas's right. He looked over, saw that one of his men had a grenade and was about to toss it into the middle of the fight; not the most sensible thing to do, as that would cause the Colonel just as many problems as the arrow, but in the end it proved a satisfactory diversion.

The arrow caught the soldier just below the collarbone, with such force that it went right through to the other side, pinning him against the wooden doors of the garage. The grenade slipped from his fingers and rolled underneath the gap at the bottom of the garage doors. Both Rudakas and The Hooded Man looked on as the man struggled to free himself, understandably not wanting to be anywhere near the grenade when it went off.

The soldier frantically tugged away at the arrow, an expression of pure horror on his face, then finally he pulled it out of the wood, bringing his shoulder with it. He had little time to celebrate, though, because at that point an inferno was unleashed behind him. The explosion blew the doors off their hinges, lifting the man, and some of the ground, into the sky. He cooked instantly in the blaze.

Rudakas wondered what exactly had been stored in that garage. Explosives? Hardly likely. And it was too strong for just a vehicle's petrol tank. Then what? Reserves of fuel?

There was no more time to think about it, as the wave of heat came their way. The Hooded Man stood planted to the spot, mouth open, as if he'd seen the Devil himself in those flames. Rudakas, saved from certain death by the arrow, wasn't about to waste the gift of life. He dived back into the house, into the hallway, just as the shockwave hit. The house, as he was to discover not long afterwards, wasn't that much safer because it was connected to the garage, but it would provide temporary shelter. While his enemy out there was still gawping at the mini-Armageddon.

Rudakas covered his head and laughed.

Robert couldn't move.

He was back again outside his house so long ago, as the

men in the yellow suits burnt everything he ever cared about. He screwed up his eyes, waiting for the blast to hit him...

NO!

Maybe before, when he was on his own, hiding away from the rest of the human race. Hiding away from his destiny. But not now. There were people relying on him, just as they had when he was in the police. Whereas before he'd hated his survival instincts for keeping him alive when all he wanted to do was curl up and join Joanne and Stevie, now Robert willed them to kick in – to save him from the explosion that was about to tear through him.

He opened his eyes, turning to run at the same time. It was too late. The blast scooped him up, then slammed him down on the hood of the armoured truck. He rolled over onto the ground at the other side, hitting it hard. If the petrol tank hadn't been shielded, that would have gone up as well, but as it was it at least provided some cover from the explosion.

Robert ached everywhere, drifting in and out of consciousness, his mind replaying the events that had led him here...

The noise of gunfire had attracted them initially, forcing them to break off from the delivery of more stolen goods back to the people.

"Sounds like trouble," Jack Finlayson had said.

"And where there's trouble these days, you can probably count on the Frenchman's involvement," Robert had answered.

They'd ditched the truck and spread out, approaching the farmhouse via the fields: Jack taking a few men round the back, Robert leading the rest in an assault on the soldiers scattered about the yard. There was no way they'd even have known the house was here if they hadn't been attracted by the noise. It was completely cut off, a place where he himself would gladly have lived out his remaining years up until recently.

Robert had been proud of the way his men had fought, doing just as he'd taught them in the short time they'd been with him – using their environment to conceal themselves, never showing their hand too quickly. Some he'd even begun to train with the bow and bolas. For his part, he'd picked off choice targets, hoping to draw a more worthy prize out of its own hiding place.

Then he'd seen him: the man wearing the peaked cap emerging from the farmhouse. Robert delighted in letting him know just who was behind it all.

The first arrow was a message, the next few intended only to slow the man down. Though Robert hadn't had time to study them closely, he saw that the man's firearms were quite unusual: old-fashioned, but still in perfect working order. Enough to wing him and throw his aim, anyway.

Then, when his enemy had run out of bullets and Robert had just one arrow left, he knew it was his lucky day. Except for the fact that out of the corner of his eye he saw the soldier with the grenade. It had been pure instinct to fire at him instead, a case of dealing with the most severe crisis first. That was when his luck had run out.

He tried to raise himself, failed, and slumped back down. Robert could see more of the soldiers – he couldn't tell whether they were De Falaise's or his – lying face down not far away from him. With a shaky hand he reached out and grabbed the dirt, attempting to pull himself along and back round the front of the armoured truck.

He made slow progress, desperate to get a better view of the scene – to find out who was still standing, who had fallen. Who had won the battle.

"Going somewhere?" The voice had a nasal quality, instantly dislikeable, and Robert wasn't at all surprised to see De Falaise's minion standing over him. "You do not look like a legend now, my hooded friend. You look like the worm you are," the man continued. He had his hands behind his back and Robert assumed he was holding the pistols, reloaded and ready to fill him full of holes.

However, when the man brought his hands back round, Robert saw he was hiding a broadsword instead. Different era, different weapon, but no less deadly. Where was he getting this stuff from?

"After all I had been told, I was expecting some kind of indestructible super-being. You are nothing of the kind. It will be my pleasure to put you out of your misery. There's a saying in my country, a curse: Let the earth swallow you!"

The man hefted the sword, preparing to bring it down, to embed it in Robert's cranium.

I can't fight it anymore. Finally I'm going to join them.

The man juddered, then stopped, like a robot that had rusted stiff.

Come on, if you're going to do it just get on with it!

Slowly the man looked down at his chest, where a crimson stain was blooming on the material of his uniform. Then the fabric split as something very sharp, and very long, was pushed through his torso.

That sword fell out of his hands and dropped with a clatter to the ground. Robert flinched as it landed just inches away. The impaled Colonel dropped his weapon, managing only a thick wheeze as his eyes rolled back and he collapsed sideways – the foreign object pulled wetly from him as he dropped.

A woman with dark hair, her cheek bruised but with a determined look on her face, stood looking down at the corpse, a dripping sword in her own hand. She looked at Robert and gave him a brief nod as if to say: 'That's another job done.'

"Are... are you all right?" he managed, then groaned loudly.

"I think I should probably be asking you that question. You look terrible."

With shaky fingers, Robert reached for the sword the man had dropped, wrapping his fingers around the handle, struggling to get it beneath him.

"Here," said the woman coming over to him. "Let me help."

She steadied him as he used the sword as a crutch, and he almost fell again. "This...this is your place?" he asked, every word hurting him.

"It is..." She looked back at the remains of the garage, the fire spreading to the farmhouse, spreading through it, smoke billowing out of shattered windows. The alarm had given up the ghost long ago. "It was," she said sadly.

"I'm sorry." His breathing was uneven, his chest hurt when he spoke. "I know what it's like to lose your home."

She looked at him, and gave the faintest of smiles. "I made a promise a long time ago that I'd stay here, alone, run the place while it was still standing. Something tells me it won't be for much longer."

Behind them Robert's men were coming closer, including Jack Finlayson.

"You came here to help me, didn't you?" she asked, looking at the men clearing up.

Robert could barely nod, all his strength leaving him.

"That's what you do, isn't it, help people? Hey, easy, take it easy," said the woman, bearing more of his weight. "So I guess you know all about this Sheriff? And that would make you–"

"It's all pretty much over," Jack interrupted. "De Falaise's remaining men have been rounded up... Robert?"

"Give me a hand, would you."

"Who're you, little lady?" asked Jack.

She nodded towards the dead man. "I'm the 'little lady' who did that. Now stop asking stupid questions and help me – he's been pretty badly injured."

Jack did as he was told, then said, "We'd better get him back to Sherwood."

"Sherwood, right, of course..." She rolled her eyes. "Oh, hold on, could you take him a second?"

"Sure," said Jack, puzzled, watching as she rushed back into the house. She emerged a couple of seconds later, tucking one of the Peacekeeper pistols into her jeans, and holding the other.

"There might still be some wheat and corn left in the barns if you want to tell your men, and we can load up the animals those scumbags slaughtered. No sense in wasting the meat, we might as well salvage what we can."

"Wait a second," said Jack. "You're coming with us?"

"Yeah, well... you have someone who can look after him?"

"Can you?"

"I've done my fair share of tending to the sick," she answered.

As they began to carry Robert away, he turned to the woman and asked weakly, "What's...what's your name?"

The woman gave him a worried smile. "Mary. My name is Mary."

CHAPTER FOURTEEN

Again, the dream...

Robert somehow knew that he was unconscious rather than sleeping, but that didn't appear to matter. It came anyway, different as always.

This time he could see more faces belonging to the people who stood by him at the lake. The large figure of Jack Finlayson with his staff, for example, more defined than he had been before. Now there was Mary, standing holding those Peacekeepers of hers – with Mark hiding behind, peeping out.

He looked down into the surface of the lake – while it still was a lake – and saw his reflection, the Stag-Man from the last dream staring back up at him.

What am I? asked Robert. *Who am I? Why do you keep showing me this?*

The reflection didn't answer, but Robert knew what it would have said. He was tied to this place, connected. Then the reflection vanished, consumed by the fire that accompanied the Frenchman's walk across the lake.

Even before Robert could reach for his bow and arrow, De Falaise was firing into the crowd, randomly hitting Robert's men. There was confusion as his people panicked, each one trying to find cover. He saw them diving to the ground, throwing themselves behind bushes and reeds.

When he looked up again, De Falaise had a hostage.

It was Mark.

The Frenchman laughed as he held the gun to Mark's temple.

No! screamed Robert. He attempted to move forwards, ignoring his fear of the fire, his only concern being to rescue Mark. But Robert found he couldn't shift. Looking down, he saw that he'd caught several bullets when the Sheriff's weapon had discharged. He fell to his knees, tears flooding his eyes. Robert reached out to Mark, his form flitting between Stevie and the boy he now knew.

Robert fell backwards, gazing up at the clear blue sky. He felt pain, but it was an odd sensation: disjointed, like the wounds didn't really belong to him.

A face hovered into view above him, concerned, frightened. It was Mary. She was asking if he was all right, then telling him to keep still, that she was putting pressure on the bullet-holes, stemming the blood flow. Promising him that he'd be okay.

But even as she uttered these words of comfort, her own appearance was changing. Suddenly the words were being spoken by Joanne, the face that of his dead wife. He began to shake, twitching as he lay there bleeding to death on the bank of that flaming lake, the heat reaching for him. Joanne was trying to hold him down, pleading with him to keep still. Her face pulled out of his line of sight for only a second, but it was enough for the features to change again.

This time, when she dipped her head again, it was a skull – not white and bleached like you might see in a science lab, but faded and yellowing, with shreds of skin still hanging from it.

Robert struggled to get up again, but the skeleton – a real, honest to God skeleton now – was holding him down with more strength than he could find in his weakened condition.

The skull drew closer to his face, coming in for a kiss. He brought up his hands and tried to fight it off, but as it filled his field of vision, the blackness of the eyes obliterated everything else.

Until there was nothing left...

Robert's eyes snapped open.

It was dark, very dark. But that was only because his vision was still adjusting to the half-light; torchlight under cover. His head was pounding and his body ached. But it was his arm that throbbed the most. He was suddenly aware that he'd been stripped down to his boxers, his bottom half covered with a blanket. The familiar 'ceiling' of the makeshift tent that served as his home slowly greeted his eyes, and he relaxed slightly. Tentatively reaching across he felt the bandage around his arm, where the bullet had grazed him. Only a flesh wound, but sometimes those can hurt the most.

There was something wrong with his face; it felt strangely naked and exposed. Robert touched his chin, his cheeks. His beard was gone. For some reason this was even worse than being in his underwear. He couldn't believe that had happened while he'd been unconscious, and wondered just who would have had the balls to do it anyway.

He heard a rustle and sat up, seeing the figure at the other end of the tent. He squinted and Mary's face came into focus. She was holding a clipboard and writing on it. Robert pulled up the blanket, trying to hide his semi-nakedness.

"Hello again," said Mary looking up. She gave a little laugh when she saw his actions. "Don't bother on my account. Who do you think it was undressed you? Had to if I was going to wash your clothes. They really stank."

Robert rubbed his chin again, furrowing his brow.

"Oh, yeah, that too. I figured you'd never let me do it while you were conscious. Don't worry, I'm very good at it. Used to have to shave my dad all the time when I was growing up – never used a knife before, though. And that hair could use a bit of a trim at some point as well."

"What... what happened?"

Mary placed the clipboard under her arm and crawled over beside him. He pulled back slightly. She noted his discomfort and increased the distance between them a little. "It's all right, you know. You haven't got anything I haven't seen before... Under that beard, I mean." Mary smiled. "You shouldn't cover it up; your face. You're quite good looking, in a sort of mean and moody way."

"You didn't answer my question," Robert said, feeling the blood rush to his bare cheeks.

"The short answer is, you passed out in the truck. Had a bit of a turn actually – put the wind up that mate of yours, the big guy."

"Jack," clarified Robert.

"Right, Jack. In fact you scared me a bit too. You even stopped breathing at one point."

Robert's frown intensified. "I dreamed I was dying."

"It was no dream. We had to give you the kiss of life."

Robert looked at her.

Mary closed her eyes slowly, then opened them again. "All right, I had to give you the kiss of life. Don't worry, I knew what I was doing. I have some medical knowledge; I looked after my brother when he got sick... And the animals, of course... not that I'm comparing you to... oh, you know what I mean."

He continued to stare, saying nothing.

"You're very welcome, by the way," said Mary, her tone hardening.

"Er, thanks," said Robert.

"That's better. Now, how do you feel?"

"Strange. A bit out of it; sluggish."

"That'll be the sedatives. The injections I've been giving you."

"What?" He clutched his arm.

"There was all kinds of good stuff in the medical packs from the trucks. Helped you sleep, helped with the pain... The priest guy–"

"Tate."

"Yeah, Tate – I'm getting there with the names – he showed me where everything was. To be honest, it's a wonder you didn't fry when my garage blew."

"What was in there anyway?"

"Fuel for the tractors. We always made sure we had a good stock in and I've only been using it when necessary. Fields don't plough themselves, you know."

She leaned over to examine his arm and he shuffled backwards, recalling the skull-thing from his nightmare.

"Hey, what's wrong? I've been looking after you for two days now and–"

"Days?" Robert couldn't believe what he was hearing.

"Your body needed time to heal itself," explained Mary. "You took a bit of a tumble."

"That's one way of putting it."

"Not for the first time, by the looks of it. I always say that there's nothing a good long rest won't cure and this is a perfect example. Don't worry about what's been happening out there, your men seem to have everything under control. They're still delivering stolen stuff back to people it was stolen from..." Mary thought about this for a second. "If you see what I mean."

"You talk a lot," said Robert.

"Not really, that is not usually. Not that there's such a thing as usual in this case. Sorry, I'm rambling again, aren't I? What I mean is, I think I'm making up for not having talked to anyone for so long, not since my brother..." She let her silence say what she couldn't.

"I'm sorry," Robert said.

Mary looked down. "Yeah, well, I'm figuring that it happened to a lot of folk. Especially talking to some of them around the camp."

Robert nodded. "What were you doing when I woke up just then? Looked like you were making notes or something." He gestured to the clipboard under her arm.

"What? Oh, this..." She took it out. "It was the only spare paper I could find; the back of some inventory or other." Mary turned the board around and Robert saw sketches of himself; not lying unconscious as he had been for a couple of days, apparently, but upright head and shoulder views: one of him with the hood, one without. The one without looked just like him... and again the beard was gone. He took it from her and examined it more closely.

"You're very good," he said.

Mary shrugged. "Had to do something to while away the hours." There was a pause before she spoke again, changing the subject. "Tell me something," she began, then shook her head, not wanting to continue.

"What?"

"No, it's really none of my business."

Robert moved forwards, letting the blanket drop a little. "What?" he repeated.

"Who're Joanne and Stevie?"

Robert's lips tightened.

"I only ask because you said both their names when you were out of it. Practically screamed them, in fact. I asked round camp but nobody's called Stevie and there are definitely no Joannes. No one seemed to know who—"

"You did what?" Robert's voice rose and he threw down the clipboard.

Mary recoiled. "I'm... I'm sorry I just—"

"Just what? Thought you'd try and find out about my past? I hardly even know you!" Robert was edging forwards now, his face red with anger. "I want you to leave now."

"No," she snapped back, folding her arms. "No, I won't.

One thing you ought to know about me right off is that I will not be bullied – my father and brother found that out. So did that colonel back there at my farm. Now, I know you came to my 'rescue' and I really do appreciate it, but I saved your life. Twice. You of all people don't get to speak to me like that."

Robert rubbed his forehead with his hand. "Please, I just want to you go." His tone had softened and he was trying hard not to let Mary see him cry.

This change of tack seemed to throw her. "I didn't mean to upset you, honestly. I was just curious, that's all. It's really nothing to do with me."

Robert looked at Mary. He did owe her a lot, but did he owe her an explanation? Could he bring himself to tell anyone about what had happened?

Tate's words rang in his ears, "And those people back there, do you not think they would give everything they have to turn back the clock? Don't you think that they lost people they loved as well?"

Mary had lost her family to the virus, and now her home to fire. What made his suffering any worse than hers?

"I should go, like you said," she said softly. "Leave you in peace."

She made to get up, and he suddenly found himself reaching out a hand and placing it on her arm. Mary turned and looked into his eyes.

"Wait," he said. "I–"

"Robbie! Robbie!" Jack's deep voice interrupted him. It was coming from outside the tent at first, then seconds later it was inside, along with Jack himself. He stuck his head through the gap. "Robbie... Oh, I didn't realise I was interrupting something."

"Mary was just..."

"...checking on the patient," she finished for him. They

shared a look of complicity, with just a dash of guilt thrown in.

"I see." Jack seemed far from convinced. "Like the new look, by the way. Very smooth."

"What exactly do you want?" asked Robert.

The big man faced Mary. "Is he up to coming outside, little lady?"

"I'm up to it," Robert cut in before she could answer.

"Good, because I really think you should see this, buddy."

When Mary left Robert threw on some clothes, which he noted had been washed, wincing as his body protested. He probably shouldn't be going anywhere, still needed to rest, but Jack's tone told him that he was needed urgently.

In the middle of the camp a few of the men had gathered around. Slowly, Robert made his way towards them, waving down both Jack and Mary's offers of assistance. Inside the circle was a man, probably only in his thirties, but he looked much older: he was losing his hair rapidly, there were heavy bags under his eyes, and he had a ripe, purple bruise on his forehead. His hands were shaking as he sat on a log, a blanket covering his shoulders. Tate was filling a bowl full of stew from the campfire to feed the man. When he took it, and the spoon, he nodded a thank you to the Reverend. Robert noticed that his hands were still shaking as he took the food and began to eat.

"What's going on here, who is this man?" Robert asked.

"Robert, you're up." Tate turned towards him, concern etched in his face. The rest of the men there did the same, their fascination shifting from this poor wretch to their resurrected leader. It made him uncomfortable, the way they were staring at him: some of them no doubt saying to themselves, So, he can be hurt after all – he isn't invulnerable. Others were probably thinking exactly the opposite, that he'd been caught in the explosion and lived to tell the tale.

"Yes and I asked a question," he replied, trying to deflect the attention away from himself.

"His name's Mills, comes from a community just outside Ravenshead," said Bill, who'd been leaning on a tree at the back. "We just delivered there week before last; De Falaise had left 'em starving."

"He says he's got some very important information," Jack added.

"Okay," said Robert, "I'm listening."

"Allow the man to eat." Tate let his stick take his weight. "He's about ready to pass out."

Mills held up a hand. "It's all right... really... I need to tell you all this..." He looked around at the faces present, then settled on Robert's. "It happened late last night. They... they came without any kind of warning... started... started..."

Robert came closer. "Who came? What did they do?"

"For Heaven's sake, Robert, can't you see the man's distressed!" Tate snapped.

"Yes, I can. And I want to know why."

Mills was choking back a sob. "They took my Elaine. Came into the village and just took her... right out of our house. I'd only just found someone who..." He sniffed back another tear, then said with hatred in his voice: "It was the Sheriff's men."

It still amazed Robert how easily that name had come back into usage, and how rather than some comic strip villain it now stood for everything that was wrong in this world – striking dread into the survivors of the virus. "They've taken people before," Robert commented, not wishing to sound cold but regretting the words as soon as he'd said them.

"Not on this scale." Mills sighed heavily. "They took at least seven people, maybe ten, and they told those who were left behind that they were going to grab more from different villages. Places loyal to you." It might have been Robert's imagination but had there been a veiled accusation in that sentence? All he'd been trying to do was help them, protect them from this monster that had taken up residence in the castle.

"What do they want them for?" asked Tate, his voice gentle but firm. "Slave labour?"

"They... They said they were going to kill them... unless..."

"Yes?" coaxed the holy man.

"Unless The Hooded Man surrenders himself to the Sheriff."

Robert had been expecting this. De Falaise was a chess player and this move was intended to draw his enemy right into the middle of the board.

"They have only till the weekend to live, then the Sheriff will begin executing them," Mills blurted out, "publicly, by hanging them in the grounds of the castle. Beginning at daybreak on Saturday."

Jack whistled, and immediately apologised for his tactlessness.

"He can't do that," Mary said, then turning to Robert, "Tell me he can't do that."

"Oh, he can," Robert assured her, "and he will. Unless I give myself up to him."

"Now hold on there just a goddamn minute," Jack said, "if you do that, who'll be left to stand up for these people? The Frenchman will just walk all over them again."

"Jack's right." This from Bill. "The whole thing'll start over again. Everything we fought for will have bin for nothin'."

"And," chipped in Granger, who had been standing

silently in the crowd till then, "the Frenchman is just going to kill the villagers anyway. The guy's a psycho."

Robert stepped even closer. "You say that they're doing this all over the region?"

Mills nodded.

"How many people do we have out there at the moment, delivering to villages?"

"Not that many, why?" Jack said.

"Why? Because they're in danger. More than they ever were before. The chances of our men and the Sheriff's men running into each other are much higher."

"Oh no," said Bill, standing upright.

Robert hobbled over. "What is it?"

Bill gazed at him, wide-eyed. "We have a team out deliverin' not far from Newstead today. They set off early this mornin'. Tony Saddler's leading it, you know, the ex TA bloke we recruited from Kersall."

"Newstead? That's only a stone's throw from Ravenshead," Robert said to himself. "We have to radio and warn them."

"That's not all."

"Go on." said Robert.

"Mark's wi' that team."

Robert's mouth fell open. Mark. Snatches of the nightmare came back to him, glimpses of De Falaise clutching the boy, holding the gun to his head. "How could you have let him go off like that?"

"How was I supposed to stop him? Lad's got a mind of his own. 'E wanted to help, an' I figured he'd be safe enough in Saddler's group."

Robert said nothing, just stared at Bill in disbelief.

"Mark's bin lookin' after himsen for years. I thought it'd be all right. I didn't bloody well know about all this lot, did I?"

Robert turned to Jack. "Get on the radio, find out

their location. Warn them they might run into some company."

"I didn't know..." Bill called out after him.

But Robert wasn't taking any notice, he was too busy following Jack as the big man took off his cap, placed a set of earphones on his head, and worked the radio he'd cannibalised from one of the stolen vehicles (as a kid shortwave had been one of his hobbies, and a way of keeping in touch with the world outside upstate New York). "Come in Green Five, are you reading me? Over." Jack listened intently, one hand on the left earphone. He repeated the message.

"Anything?" Robert asked after a few moments.

"Not yet. I'm having trouble raising them. It's just static on their wavelength. Could be that they're just in a black spot."

"Or something else. Keep trying."

"Hey, sure. I like the little squirt. He's my biggest fan." Robert patted him on the shoulder and staggered back to the tent. Mary chased after him.

"I hope you're not thinking of doing what I think you're thinking of doing."

Robert stopped, turned, was about to say something, then didn't bother. He reached inside, bringing out his bow and quiver.

"You're crazy," she told him. "Look at you. You can barely stand."

"I can manage," he assured her.

"Like hell!"

He began to walk away from her, but she raced around the front and stood in his way. "Mary, please. I have to go. I have to try and warn them."

Robert saw her checking his eyes for any sign of relenting. When she found none, she said, "Right, well, you're going to need a driver then."

"I said I can manage," he told her, then missed a step and almost keeled over. He recovered before Mary could grab him.

"Either you let me drive or I'm going to fetch that sword. Right now. I mean it."

Robert sighed again, then nodded. She fell in alongside him as they made their way out of the forest towards the confiscated jeeps.

Mary wasn't the only one who'd insisted on tagging along. Bill, who didn't come right out and say it, but was obviously feeling guilty about Mark, caught up with them as they were climbing into the vehicle. Robert didn't say anything. He just gestured for Mary to start the engine. She was well used to driving Land Rovers and the like, she told them, so this was no problem for her. In fact, Robert had to admit he was impressed with the way she guided the jeep over fields while he consulted the map – steering clear of the roads as much as possible in case they were seen.

They covered the distance cross-country quite quickly, keeping in touch with Jack to see if he'd been able to contact Green Five. Robert had personally okay'd their leader after witnessing how he handled himself when defending his own community against the Sheriff's men. Robert and his group had come in on the tail end of the fight, but when it was over and the invaders had decided to take flight, Robert asked Tony Saddler if he would consider joining them. "We can always use someone with your expertise," he'd told him. The chestnut-haired man had needed little persuasion to put his training to good use. He was an experienced soldier, who'd been serving in the Territorial Army when the virus hit. Mark should be in safe hands with Tony.

So why did Robert have such a nagging feeling that something had already gone disastrously wrong? Was it just the dream, or something else? The radio silence? Could be just out of range as Jack said, or even that the equipment at their end was broken. But Robert doubted it.

When they reached Green Five's last known location, Robert's worst fears were confirmed. As they made their way down one last dirt track, they saw the smoke rising above the trees, into the early evening sky. The village Saddler and his team had been delivering to was pretty much like any other in the region, and had no doubt once been beautiful in its heyday. Quaint cottages lined the roads even before they got to the main street, but now they were either in ruins or the walls were dotted with bullet holes.

It was even worse in the centre of the village. A truck had jackknifed, blocking off the road, though Robert couldn't tell if it was one of theirs or De Falaise's – seeing as they'd originally stolen their vehicles from him. Here and there were upturned motorbikes. And bodies, plenty of bodies.

"Judas Priest!" said Bill as they edged closer.

"Bring us in slowly, Mary – and keep your eyes peeled." Robert glanced over and saw her take one hand off the steering wheel to pick up a Peacekeeper. He gripped his bow tightly, though there wasn't enough room to prime it. Mary braked gently when they arrived at the truck, bringing the jeep to a stop but not putting on the handbrake in case they needed to beat a hasty retreat.

"Wait here," Robert said to Mary, "Keep the engine running." He opened the door and hopped down, still wobbly but feeling better for the fact that he could now use his bow. Bill joined him, shotgun at the ready. They advanced together.

It was no longer a peaceful British village in the countryside; now it resembled the streets of some foreign war-torn land.

Some of the bodies Robert recognised, though they were in terrible condition. These were his men, all right: what was left of Green Five. *My God! Mark...* he thought, scanning the ground to see if he could spot him, but hoping against hope he wouldn't.

What he did see was Saddler. The man had made it several metres from the truck, crawling, leaving a streak of blood behind him. He had given up when he came to a grass verge and simply collapsed onto it.

Bill covered him as Robert crouched down to feel Saddler's neck. There was nothing. He shook his head and caught the look in Bill's eye.

They noticed movement across the street and both Robert and Bill swung their weapons in its direction.

The figure coming towards them had its hands in the air and was shouting: "Don't shoot, please don't shoot."

Robert could see now that it was a young girl of about fifteen. Where her face wasn't covered in freckles it was dirty, the pale yellow dress that she was wearing was ripped in places.

"Who are you?" shouted Bill.

"My name's Sophie," she told him. "I live..." She looked around at the devastation. "I live here. He's... he's The Hooded Man, isn't he? Like in the stories..."

There were more people emerging from the damaged houses. They ranged in ages from the elderly to some as young as Sophie.

"What happened here?" asked Robert. "What happened to my men?"

"The Sheriff," she said.

"Your people were in the middle of giving us food and

blankets," a man with a shock of white hair told them, "when the attack came. They didn't stand a chance."

"How long ago?" Bill asked him.

"Not long. Two, three hours. They took quite a few of our people with them. Kidnapped them, bundled them into the backs of their trucks. They said that unless you surrender yourself to—"

"Yes," Robert broke in. "Yes, I know what they want. What happened to the boy?"

The old man looked confused.

"About this high. Mop of dirty blond hair, wearing a tracksuit. Always carries a backpack."

"Mark!" said Sophie. "You're talking about Mark."

"That's right. You know him?"

"Only a little," Sophie said. "The men were going to take me away, but he gave himself up instead, told them to take him. He protected me, even when they tried to..." Sophie swallowed hard. "We were in the house back there when they came, you see. I was fixing him a glass of fresh apple juice – they grow not far away in the orchard..."

"Hold on, so the Sheriff's blokes didn't know the lad was one of us then?" said Bill.

"I... I don't think so," Sophie replied. "I didn't tell them, anyway."

Bill turned to Robert. "That's summat at least. If he's just another villager to them, it might keep 'im alive."

"For now," Robert reminded him.

Mary joined them. She went over to check if anybody had wounds, if they needed help. Robert watched her for a moment or two, then limped across to sit on a wooden bench.

Moments later, Sophie followed. She stood in front of him. "I've heard about the things you can do. You're going to save him, now, aren't you? You're going to bring everyone back? Rescue them?"

Mary came up behind and put her hands on Sophie's shoulders. "Come on, let's get you cleaned up," she told the girl, ushering her away before Robert could answer.

Sophie looked back over her shoulder as if still waiting for him to shout his reply. Robert let his head drop, the words still echoing in his ears, tinged with the naivety of youth.

You're going to save him, aren't you?

Aren't you?

CHAPTER FIFTEEN

They'd been waiting in the truck now for about twenty minutes.

Mark especially. Waiting, tensed, picking at the material of his empty backpack.

He looked round at the faces in here, each one the same tangle of anguish. Every prisoner asking the same thing. Were they going to get out of this alive? All of them had been bound at the wrists with plastic ties, so tight they cut into the skin. The people who'd been collected in this particular truck had been bundled in any which way, face down, sitting, on their knees: manhandled by the Sheriff's men on their rounds amassing hostages.

That's why they were standing now, engine idling, as the men with machine guns ravaged yet another village known to have been accepting help from The Hooded Man. Mark shut his eyes, but then the memories of the attack rushed back. He'd been helping unload goods and distribute them. Jacob, one of the guys who'd been shanghaied into the Sheriff's army, and was now glad to be out of it, had nudged Mark and pointed across at a local girl staring at them. She was wearing a yellow dress and had freckles on her cheeks.

"Think she likes you. She's been gaping over all the time we've been here." Jacob grinned.

"Get out of it," Mark had replied.

Jacob had made a kissing gesture then and Mark hit him on the arm. "Hey, I was only playing with you – should count yourself lucky if she does. Pretty girl, that."

She was. Though he still considered himself too young for all that kind of nonsense, Mark had done quite a bit of growing up in the last couple of years. Had been forced to. So while he was still a kid in many respects, he was more mature than many thirteen year olds. And he had begun, finally, to notice the opposite sex. Maybe Jacob had a point in his own clumsy way, and you could never have too many friends. So, he'd nervously met her eye a few times as Tony Saddler continued organising the drop. Mark had been sad when he looked up at the end and found the girl gone.

"Good work, guys," Tony told them, "take a breather."

Mark looked around for the girl again, but it had been her who found him, tapping him on the shoulder and saying hello. She introduced herself as Sophie and asked if he wanted a drink after all that hard work.

Mark nodded shyly, then followed her into the house where he assumed she lived. "It's not mine, of course, but I chose it when I came here." He remembered thinking that maybe he wasn't the only one who'd had to mature quickly; at just fourteen Sophie was running her own little household by the looks of things. She'd originally come from West Bridgford, she told him, just the other side of Nottingham: a small place that had been taken over by gangs and thugs believing they owned the joint. They had driven her out, and she'd begun the journey further north, hoping to find somewhere quieter; somewhere safer. On the road she'd hooked up with a group of men and women doing the same, and fell in with them. Then they'd settled here.

"It was peaceful for a while," she told Mark as she fixed him his drink. "We got on with our lives, made plans, began to imagine the future might be different. But then the Sheriff's men came."

"Sounds familiar," he told her.

She shrugged. "We got off lightly compared to some I've heard about. They just took things, not people. So," Sophie had said as she offered him a seat, "what's he like?"

"Who?"

She laughed. "The Hooded Man, silly."

"Oh," said Mark, deflating somewhat. "He's... well, he's pretty cool, really."

"Is it true he once took on fifty of the Sheriff's men single handed?"

Mark stared hard at her. "Erm..."

"That he's seven foot tall with a square chin and broad shoulders?"

Mark squirmed in the chair; he hadn't been expecting to be fielding questions about her crush on Robert. "He's quite old," Mark informed her. "Old enough to be my... well, your dad too, really."

She seemed a little disappointed by that. "Really? I heard he was about nineteen, twenty."

Mark shook his head. "But you do know I'm like his second in command, don't you?"

Sophie seemed to perk up at that. "Really?"

Mark nodded. "He runs everything by me. I'm his official advisor as well, his PR man, the works."

She pulled up a stool and brought it round the side of the table to sit near Mark. Sophie was only a few inches away and, without realising it, he found himself breathing in and out a little too quickly. "Tell me more," she said, bubbling with excitement. "Have you been in many battles with him?"

"Oh yeah, course. Loads."

Sophie practically jumped up and down with delight. "So, go on, I want to hear about the best one."

Mark thought for a moment. "Well, there was this one time at market when—"

He hadn't got any further before he heard the gunfire. Both he and Sophie rushed to the window and looked out, in time to see Tony Saddler and the other men dropping to defensive positions as bullets whistled around them. They were being picked off one by one, sitting targets in the middle of the road. Someone started up the armoured truck, but before they could pull away, an explosion flipped it onto its side. Mark pulled Sophie from the window just as a hail of gunfire shattered the glass, spraying them with fragments.

"Get back," Mark shouted to her, and she nodded, terrified. What had been just stories before, entertainment and excitement, was suddenly real and happening right now. More bullets ricocheted off the door of the house – and then suddenly there were soldiers, forcing their way inside.

"Get behind me!" Mark shouted to Sophie, his voice cracking, adrenalin pumping through him.

"Hey, what do we have here?" The lead soldier, a youth with a scar running across his jawline, sneered at them both. "Two little muppets playing happy families."

"I dunno, Jace," said the man behind him, "the girl's fit enough."

Jace tramped towards them, grabbing Mark and swinging him out of the way. Mark hit the wall, bouncing off it and into a chair. "Yeah, you're right there, Oaksey. I definitely vote she comes with us." Jace laughed raucously.

He reached out for Sophie and took hold of the top of her dress. He pulled and the fabric tore easily. They appeared to have forgotten about Mark.

He got up, running at the thugs, grabbing the lead one by the waist and sending all three of them sideways – while Sophie fell back onto the floor. "Fuck me!" Jace called out as he toppled over. Mark had seen Jack use that wrestling move more times than he could remember, but never thought he'd have to put it into practice.

Other soldiers came in, and pulled Mark off – though

not before he got a few good kicks in.

"Quit goofing around," one of the newcomers told Jace and his mate as they scrabbled back to their feet. "Let's get these two into the truck."

"Just one from this house, remember?" said another soldier.

"Right." Jace turned the rifle on Mark. "Bye-bye, muppet."

"Wait," Mark said, waving his hands. "Listen to me, The Hooded Man you're looking for. I've seen him."

"Here?" asked Jace's friend.

"He was here, yeah. Just before you came."

"Bullshit." Jace jammed his gun in Mark's face.

"Wait, we'll take him anyway. He might come in useful, plus kids make good prisoners."

"But what about her?" Jace whined, thumbing back towards Sophie.

"Leave her. There'll be more skirt, and closer to your age."

Jace considered this. "I guess you're right." He grabbed Mark roughly by the collar. "Come on, you little prick."

Mark just had time to look back at Sophie, who mouthed a silent thank you. Then he was being shoved outside, where the fight was all but over. Those men remaining from his group were either dead or badly wounded. Mark saw Jacob lying on the concrete, covered in blood. He just about had enough strength to look up at Mark, a pitiful expression on his face, then one of the Sheriff's men came up behind him and emptied a full magazine into the youth.

Mark bit his lip, unable to let himself cry, unable to even show that he'd known the dead man, let alone that they'd been kidding around together not long ago.

"Move it!" Jace pushed Mark hard, almost sending him over. If he was honest, Mark was glad to get away from the scene, because the more he saw of it, the more he knew it would stay with him for ever.

When they got to the prisoner truck, out by the road, Jace pulled the bag from Mark's back and began rooting around inside it. "Got anything valuable in here, shithead? Any weapons maybe? Bet you'd just love to stick me with something, wouldn't ya?"

Mark's eyes narrowed. You'll get yours one day, Jace. Don't worry about that.

Jace emptied out the backpack, tossing it into the rear of the truck. He ate the chocolate bars and cast aside any items he deemed to be rubbish. "Ah, what's this?" he said finally, pulling out a small photo album. He opened it up, flipping through the pages. They showed pictures of Mark when he was younger, during happier times: birthdays, holidays, bonfire nights, Christmas.

"Leave that alone," spat Mark.

"I'll do whatever the fuck I want," Jace snarled back, tearing the clear plastic of one page like he'd pawed at Sophie's dress. He took out a photo, dropping the rest of the album on the ground. Jace spun it around, showing Mark the picture of himself with a man and woman in their late thirties, standing with their hands on his shoulders. They were all dressed in walking gear, wearing backpacks and woolly hats. There were fields behind them, and a couple of mountains. "Who're these boring twats?" Mark wasn't about to give him the satisfaction of saying, but Jace guessed correctly. "Your folks, right? S'pose they bought it when the virus came, huh? Personally I was glad to see the back of mine, the interfering... Do yourself a favour, muppet. Let it go. They're fucking dust." He began to tear the photo in half and Mark snatched at it. Jace smacked him to the floor, then he threw the photograph over his shoulder before binding Mark with the plastic ties.

As he was thrown into the back of the truck, after

his backpack, the vehicle was already filling up with other captives. Mark stared down at the ground, at his belongings there – gathered over the course of his time on the streets – and the photo album being trampled on, kicked around: the picture in two halves ground into the concrete by heavy boots. He fought back the tears. It was like having his childhood taken away from him a second time.

But there was nothing he could do, as the doors of the truck were closed and they trundled away.

Those same doors opened again now, as the waiting was over, and the soldiers directed more people to climb inside. Mark sprang for the exit, attempting to squeeze through and run away. He knew he only had a slim chance, but how many times had he escaped the crazies in the cities, in the towns, on his quest to pick up items for the market, in his quest to stay alive?

He could do it, just this one last time – escape and find Robert, bring him back here so that he could free these people. He only made it as far as the door when the barrel of a rifle appeared.

"Ah-ah-ah," said the soldier – not Jace, but they were all beginning to look the same to Mark. He knew there were good amongst the bad, those who Robert had brought over to his side were testament to that. But there was precious little evidence here today, just men who followed the orders of De Falaise blindly, and to the letter. "Get your scrawny little arse back inside the truck, or I'll fill you so full of metal you'll need a can opener to take a dump."

He pushed Mark backwards, where he landed on someone's legs.

Once the last prisoner was on board, the doors were shut again. The truck's engine revved, getting ready to set off again. There couldn't be many more stops on the journey to the castle, Mark realised that. No more chances, if he was being realistic.

Mark wondered what was happening back at the camp, whether they were aware of the massacre yet? Did Robert know – and what would he do when he found out? Contrary to what Sophie, and many others, believed, he wasn't some kind of superman. The state he'd been in the last time Mark had seen him proved that.

But, nevertheless, Mark had faith. He'd seen Robert do amazing things since he'd met him.

The Hooded Man, as he'd come to be known, was really and truly their only hope.

And Mark wouldn't – couldn't – give up on that hope.

CHAPTER SIXTEEN

By the time they got back from the village, the rest of Robert's men already knew what had happened. A sombre Bill had radioed and told Jack he could stop trying to raise Green Five. On the return drive, the atmosphere was tense. Bill and Robert only had one brief conversation, which turned into an argument.

"You should never have let Mark go with them," Robert said again.

"I've known the lad longer than you have," Bill had retorted, "and when Mark sets his mind on somethin'... Anyway, ye can talk – never really wanted him around in the first place. Didn't want any of us, if the truth be told."

"Shut your mouth."

"It's true – look at ye, playin' the hero. Didn't want to get involved, though. Not really. Wanted to hide and hope everything would go away."

"I said, shut your mouth or God help me I–"

"Boys, boys," broke in Mary, who was trying to concentrate on the dirt track ahead of her. "We're all on the same side, right? I know you're both worried sick about Mark, but how is fighting among yourselves going to help?"

Robert and Bill settled back into their respective seats, sulking.

"We need to keep a level head," advised Mary, not even sure if they were listening to her, "figure out what to do next."

"Didn't hardly know the lad," Bill took great pleasure in pointing out.

"Maybe not, but I've seen the way things work in that

forest; you're a team, and if one of you is in trouble, the rest rally round."

"Reckon you're part a the team, now, eh? Only bin 'ere five minutes, lookin' after lover boy there."

It was Mary's turn to answer him back. "Look, I didn't ask to be dragged into this. But the Sheriff's men destroyed my home, I very nearly ended up like Mark – I think that entitles me to be a member of your exclusive little club, don't you?"

Bill said nothing.

Silence reigned then, but what Bill had said played on Mary's mind. What right did she have to interfere? Yes, she'd saved Robert's life – but he'd saved hers as well, just by showing up. And sure, she'd gone with them to look after their leader, but wasn't there a huge part of her that tagged along because she wanted to fit in somewhere again. Because she was tired of being alone, tired of talking to an imaginary dead brother in her head?

Hey, I object to the word imaginary. I'm as real as you are, Moo-Moo.

Mary ignored the voice, focussing on her driving and getting them all back to the camp before a scrap broke out.

When they returned, Tate was to the first to greet them. "So?"

Robert waited for the rest of the question.

"Are we finally going to do something about this Sheriff, once and for all? Are we finally going to go in there and get those people out?"

"Like your Gwen, you mean?"

"Who's Gwen?" Mary wanted to know.

"Someone I failed," explained Tate. "Someone else the Frenchman took, like Mark – except she's been there so much longer. They took her to be with him." His face fell at the thought. Mary's hand went to her mouth and he saw it. "What, child?"

"It's just... just something that Colonel said, the one who came to my home with his soldiers."

Robert and Tate frowned.

"What did he say to you?" Robert asked.

"I was to be her replacement, I think."

"What?" Tate moved forwards.

"He told me that the Sheriff, De Falaise, was growing bored of the woman he has... He called her a 'companion'."

"I think we all know what's meant by that," said Bill, not helping matters.

"What exactly did he say, Mary?" Robert coaxed. "It might be important."

"Something along the lines of De Falaise needing fresh female company, and he thought he'd found it. I was a little too 'headstrong' though, apparently – maybe he can't handle strong women?"

"This is gettin' us nowhere," Bill moaned, "what're we goin' to do about Mark?"

Robert rubbed his neck. "I need time to think."

As he walked off, pulling the hood over his head, Bill called out after him, "Time's summat we don't have. You heard what that there Mills said: the weekend. We need a plan, bloody quick."

But Robert was already disappearing into the foliage. Bill looked like he was going to go after him, but Jack stopped him. "Ease up on him, eh, fella? Let the guy do his thinking." Bill didn't argue, just gave him a stern look and tramped off.

Mary watched Robert go. She'd heard Jack's words, too, but something was nagging at her to follow. As the rest of the group went back to the fire, in preparation for the night ahead of them, they left her gazing out into the forest.

Then, once she was alone, she disappeared into it herself.

Mary soon regretted her decision. The further inside the forest she went, and the darker it became, the more her imagination began to play tricks.

There was no sign of Robert. He was like a spirit who'd suddenly decided to leave this plane of existence. Mary blundered onwards, pushing back leaves and banging into tree trunks. Though she'd spent much of her life outdoors, these surroundings were alien to her – nothing like the open fields she was used to.

There was a strange noise off to her left. She looked down and found that she'd instinctively drawn her Peacekeeper.

Another sound, and Mary turned again – her gun hand shaking. She had absolutely no idea where the camp was now, and couldn't find it again even if she tried. Light was waning and the shadows the trees cast in the moonlight made her shiver.

Crack! – off to her right, this time. She cocked the pistol, but stopped herself from firing. What if it was someone from the camp, someone who'd had the same idea? It might even be Robert for all she knew.

Or someone else, Moo-Moo. Could be one of De Falaise's men.

They wouldn't be that stupid, she told him. Mary had been told about the times they'd been totally humiliated by Robert. Now that he had more men on his side – some of them the very soldiers that were sent in to catch him – they wouldn't dare enter. Especially at night.

But are you sure? Better be sure, Sis.

Mary headed in the direction of the noise. David was

right. What if it was one of their enemies creeping through the forest, on a mission to kill them all? She couldn't just let them get on with it.

"Reckon you're part a the team, now, eh? Only bin 'ere five minutes..." Bill's offhand comment came back to her, reminding her that she barely knew these madmen living out in the back of beyond. Yet she'd felt a kinship with them from very early on; even Bill. They were banding together to fight a common foe, one that she'd had a run-in with herself. She felt a loyalty to them, even if this place was yet to feel like any sort of home.

Mary tried to be as quiet as she could, heading in the direction of a clearing. The trees were parting, offering her a view of something ahead: the thing that had been making all the noise. It looked like something out of a horror movie, dark horns, a snout: demon-like in its appearance.

She let out a gasp, startled by the shape no more than a few metres away. Her gun hand was shaking as she brought it up to aim.

There was someone beside her, at her ear – someone she hadn't heard approaching. Someone raising her gun arm into the air and snatching the Peacekeeper from her in one quick movement. Mary looked sideways, terrified, seeing only another dark shape there.

"Ssshhh. Watch."

The same hand that had taken the pistol from her pointed towards the clearing, at the creature now illuminated by the moonlight. It bathed the animal in its rays, uncovering it as it did so. Another gasp issued from her as she saw the stag in all its wonderful glory.

It looked towards her, fixing Mary with its ebony eyes. Then, as suddenly as it had appeared, it was gone. Still shaken, she looked again at the shadowy figure beside her. A hooded man.

"Robert?" she whispered.

"Yes." He raised the hood and his features caught the moonlight too.

"Why did you follow me, Mary?"

She shook her head, at a loss to explain it to herself let alone him. In the end she decided to just change the subject. "What... what just happened here?"

"Couldn't you feel it?" Robert replied.

She had felt something; the seconds slowing down to match her heartbeat, the fear of the beast and a stranger beside her, giving way to a sense of supreme tranquillity. "It was the most beautiful thing I've ever seen."

"You almost killed it."

"I'm sorry."

"Don't be. I almost killed it myself, once." Robert handed her back the pistol. Then he left her side and walked into the clearing.

She watched him standing there, as he looked up at the moon. Unlike her, he was totally at home here. This was where he drew his energy from, where he felt at peace. She understood now why he'd come so deep into the forest to think.

"Who are you, Robert?" she said.

"I've asked myself that question a lot recently. I used to know, implicitly, who and what I was. Now..." Mary walked over. "Sometimes I..."

"Go on," she encouraged.

Robert let his head fall, shaking it. "It sounds ridiculous when I say it out loud."

"Tell me."

"Sometimes I feel as if the forest is speaking to me. Like just now, and in my dreams." He let out a weary laugh. "Does that make me a lunatic? Lord knows I've been through enough to send me crazy."

Mary laughed herself. "I'm afraid I can't really judge. I

hear the voice of my dead brother in times of stress. Now you think I'm crazy."

Robert turned. She could feel his gaze on her and looked away, though only for a moment.

"I guess Tate is right when he says we've all been through our own personal tragedies."

"And what did you go through, Robert? What made you run away?" Mary stepped closer to him. "Joanne and Stevie, right?"

Like the stag, she was expecting him to bolt. She felt him tense, but he didn't move. Finally, he spoke. Opened up to her, told her all about what had happened: having to watch his wife and child die, powerless to help them. Waiting to die alongside them, but being denied even that. Then he told her about the men in yellow suits, what they'd done to the house, to Max. How it had driven him almost over the edge, driven him into the heart of this place so he could wait out his life alone and be with them again. It hadn't quite worked out that way.

Tears tracked down her face as Mary listened to Robert's story – a tale he'd kept from the closest of his men, but which he was now revealing to her.

When he was done, she put an arm around his shoulder, pulled his head down and held him to her. He didn't resist, but she felt him shaking as the tears came.

"It's okay... It's okay," she repeated over and over, realising that the words sounded so hollow. It wasn't okay, nothing about what Robert had been through was. But destiny, or whatever you wanted to call it, had given him a new identity, a new purpose. Where he hadn't been able to protect his family, he could still protect the people of this region from De Falaise. It was what he'd been doing these past few months, and it was what he had to do now as they faced their toughest challenge.

Slowly, Mary eased him back when she felt the sobbing

subside. "You didn't come out here to think at all, did you?"

"What do you mean?"

"You know exactly what to do – and your men know it too. We just have to figure out a way of doing it that'll work."

"Mary," he said, wiping his cheeks, "if I didn't think you were crazy before – I do now."

"Then we make a good team, don't we?" she said, quickly adding, "we all make a good team. In fact, no, we're not a team at all..."

"No?" said Robert.

Mary shook her head. "Uh-uh. We're a family. All right, maybe we're a little heavy on the testosterone." She laughed. "But still a family. And a member of that family is missing."

"Then there's only one thing to do," said Robert, pursing his lips, "isn't there?"

She nodded.

"Yes, Mark is..." Robert paused, as if he'd just thought of something. Then, suddenly, he was taking her by the hand. "Come on, let's get back to the camp. I have to talk to the rest of my... family."

Mary grinned. "Lead the way, then, seeing as I wouldn't be able to find it even if I fell over it."

He began to march off back into the forest, pulling her with him. She thought then how much stronger he looked than earlier on that day. Invigorated was the word she was looking for.

"Oh, and Mary," he said, glancing back. "Don't tell any of the men you saw me crying, okay?"

She laughed again, and this time Robert laughed with her.

"Funny kind a thinkin', that," Bill said to no one in particular as Mary and Robert arrived back at the camp together. Robert looked down, realised he still had hold of Mary's hand, and released it.

"What did I say about ridin' Robbie," Jack warned Bill, stomping up alongside him.

"I'm not the dirty bugger doing the ridin'," he replied.

Mary ignored the comments as Robert called for his men to gather around. "I've reached a decision regarding what to do about the villagers and, of course, Mark."

All the men leaned forward so they could hear, with Mills on the front row.

"As you pointed out yourselves, it would be foolish to give in to the Sheriff when all he would do is carry on as he has been doing, taking what he wants from the people, ruling through fear, spreading like a disease through..." Robert stopped when the significance of what he was saying struck him. Mary placed a hand on his back to steady him and he turned to look at her. She stepped back again when she felt he was okay to speak. "The point is," Robert went on, his voice gaining strength again, "he must be stopped. And stopped for good."

"What are you suggesting?" asked one of the group at the back.

"He's talking about a full-frontal assault," Jack answered before waiting to hear what Robert had to say, "aren't you?"

"Not exactly. Attacking the castle head on would be suicide." There were definite mumbles of agreement from the camp. "It's been attempted in the past and a lot of people have died in the process. That's why De Falaise chose the place, because it can be defended so easily."

"Anyone entering the city would be spotted right away by lookouts," Granger chirped up. "Then there's that sniper on the rooftop."

"Yes," said Robert, "I know. That's why I'm going to give them the one thing they want. Me." He went on to outline his plan, then added at the end. "Now, you all have your reasons for wanting De Falaise brought down. But this isn't going to be easy, and it's going to be extremely dangerous. So I wouldn't force anyone to join me. That's not my way, it's the Sheriff's way. But I am going in there to put a stop to this, once and for all, so any help would definitely be appreciated." Robert looked around at his men, the people Mary had called family. He waited for someone, anyone, to say something.

"That's probably one of the craziest, most cockamamie notions I've ever heard in my life." This was Jack, who pushed the cap back on his head as he spoke. "But you can count me in, Robbie. I wouldn't miss it for the world."

"You know my feelings on the matter," Tate then said. "I will be by your side, Robert. And I feel sure God will, too, if that means anything to you."

Bill raised his hand. "I've come this far," he said. "An' there's Mark to think about."

"I'm not mad about the first bit," Mary told him honestly, and in fact she hated it with a passion. Robert was just going to hand himself over to them, with no guarantees of his survival. When she could see he was waiting for her to say something else, she tacked on: "But you know I'll stand by you."

He nodded, satisfied. "Granger, how about you?"

The young man looked unsure at first. "If you'd asked me that question not long ago, I'd have said no. But being here, being a part of this... It has to be a yes, don't it? Besides, I have a score to settle with the Frenchman."

A show of hands was called for, and though some of the men were reluctant at first, all of them supported Robert and his idea. Mary could see the pride in him, the fact that he'd inspired them, brought them together. He'd set an example, as every good leader should, whether he realised it or not.

"Thank you," he said to them. "Thank you all."

"Mills," asked Jack of their guest, "do you think there might be support in the villages for this?"

"I'm sure there would be. We all want the people we care about back."

It brought it home again to Mary when he said those words that while she'd been hiding herself away from everything in the farmhouse, the world had carried on turning, people had found each other, cultivated new relationships, tried to rebuild what they'd lost – for good or for bad. It was what had happened in the forest thanks to Robert: a small, but determined band who would not bow to dictatorship.

"Then it's settled," Tate said, "we have until the weekend, everyone."

A few days. Not long to properly plan what Robert had in mind.

Are you sure about this, Moo-Moo? Are you sure about him?

Mary couldn't answer, because she didn't know.

But something had brought her here. One thing Mary was certain of was that she still had a part to play in this story.

A very important part.

CHAPTER SEVENTEEN

The dreamscape, the arena – and a challenge now accepted.

Here, Robert and De Falaise faced off against each other. No preamble this time. No symbolic nonsense or veiled meanings, just raw hatred and a sense that this was all building to a climactic head.

Though they had never met in the flesh, they felt like they knew each other inside out. Villain and hero, though each would disagree with those descriptions, they circled each other. Stripped of weapons, they had only their hands to attack with... which they did, De Falaise coming in fast and low, Robert blocking his punches.

They fought, growing closer and closer, arms and hands a tangle, until they were at each other's throats. Each looked into the other's eyes, recognising the fury there, reflected back. Could one exist without the other?

De Falaise tightened his grip on The Hooded Man's throat, and Robert did the same. They were choking the life out of each other at the same time, with the same force. At this rate they would cancel each other out.

Still they continued, both hoping that their opponent would show a chink in their armour, offer up a hint of weakness.

Who would win? Who would lose?

It was a question that would soon be answered...

She could tell by his breathing that he was asleep. In the darkness of the small hours she listened to the sound, guttural at times as he began to snore. The very noise caused her stomach to do somersaults. She felt like she was going to be sick, in fact. And not for the first time since she arrived here.

Like all those other times, however, Gwen had fought the sensation. Fought all sensation, all feeling, all awareness. She'd made the decision very early on that if she allowed herself to be conscious of what was happening to her, she might just go stark, staring mad. Like if she thought about what had happened to Clive back in Hope, when that murderer Javier had put a bullet in his head. Gwen felt the nausea rising again, and swallowed to try and halt its progress. It was little comfort to her that the man was now being held down in the caves after failing De Falaise; as far as she was concerned, if he'd been stripped of his skin and then made to roll around in vinegar it wouldn't begin to make up for what he had done.

Javier had handed her over to the disgusting man with yellow teeth lying by her side.

"You had better not try anything like you did with me back there. He likes his women to be seen and not heard. Compliant, if you know what I mean, Señora," Javier had explained on the drive back to the castle.

Oh, she'd complied all right. Not because she feared what might happen to her if she didn't – though the thought of being handed over to that animal they called Tanek far from appealed to her – but because she was biding her time until she could have her revenge.

That time had almost come, necessitated by the fact that De Falaise was becoming bored with his possession.

"She is beautiful, that is not in question – it is why I have kept her around for so long, non? But it is as though she is not really here at all," she'd heard him tell Tanek one time. "She is somewhere else entirely."

That was true. Gwen had shut herself off, retreating to the darkest corners of her mind when the Frenchman wanted his 'fun'. Switching off as he dressed her up in those ridiculous costumes, while he pretended to be some kind of time traveller, an historical conqueror who'd taken over this land and its women. She'd had to pretend herself while he did this; pretend she was some place safe – with Clive.

"I'll avenge your death," she'd tell him. "I promise."

"I know you will, sweetheart, I know."

Javier would get his in time, but she was closer to the man who'd given the orders right now, the man who'd orchestrated this whole affair. She'd begin at the top and work her way down. To that end she'd waited, patiently and silently – so silent he believed that her spirit was crushed. Little realising that she was lulling him into a false sense of security.

It happened bit by bit, leaving her alone in the room for ten minutes to begin with (possibly testing her at first to see what she would do), with no guard inside or even on the door. She'd done nothing, sometimes not even moved between the time he left and the time he got back. He'd begun to spend the night with her after doing what he needed to, the exhaustion of his efforts causing him to fall asleep. Again, at first he would doze very lightly, then when nothing untoward happened he'd eventually relaxed more fully.

In addition, Gwen had kept her eyes and ears open on her tours round the castle. De Falaise no longer kept her under lock and key, knowing that the place was so well guarded she could never possibly escape. And no one really noticed her anyway as she drifted through rooms, along corridors; all they saw was De Falaise's broken play thing. No threat to anyone. As long as she was back in the room when De Falaise was in the mood, there wasn't a problem – and she knew his routines well enough by now.

The soldiers who brought her food barely acknowledged her. They just left the plate, picked it up again half an hour later; unless, of course, De Falaise wanted to dine with her – which again involved a change of outfits and a small banquet on a wooden table. Many of the men didn't even want to be here – she'd got that from listening as well – let alone scrutinised what she was doing with her meals.

So, yesterday, she'd decided to take a gamble. Gwen had hidden her knife, hoping against hope that the soldier wouldn't take a blind bit of notice when he came to retrieve her tray.

She held her breath as he picked it up. Gwen tried to act casually as he bent and grabbed it, but she overdid it, and he caught her looking at him as he turned around.

"What?" he asked. "What's wrong with you?"

Gwen didn't reply, hadn't spoken for so long, in fact, she was frightened her vocal chords might have seized up.

"I asked you a question." The soldier didn't look much more than about eighteen, she surmised. Had probably never had a woman, either in the pre-virus world or in this one. Thinking fast, she got up and went over to him, letting the loose robe she was wearing open just a fraction too much. His eyes flicked down to the curve of her breasts, then back up again. Smiling, she'd reached out a hand, brushing his arm with her fingertips. He looked down again, right down inside her robe. Then her hand had reached lower, brushing against his stomach. Before it could move further down, the soldier stepped back. "I... er... that's enough. You go and sit back down again and... er..." His face was crimson, his gait half slouching. "Sit back down or I'll have to report this... I..." He backed up against the door, reaching for the handle and pulling it open, desperate to get out of there. The soldier said nothing more, he just left in a hurry, probably not quite sure what had happened.

But he wouldn't report it. Gwen had bet her life on that. For a start, who would believe him? *The zombie woman came on to you? Piss off!* Even if they did, he wouldn't want it getting back to De Falaise or he might find himself down in those caves.

Flustered, he would return the tray to the kitchens and with a bit of luck the missing knife would go unnoticed. Gwen waited most of the afternoon for someone to come back and accuse her of hiding it, but they didn't. She then began sharpening the implement, using a rock she'd picked up on one of her 'outings'. By the time she was done, the labours focussing her attention in a way nothing had since she'd been dragged here, the blade was rough but sharp.

She'd had to hide it quickly when De Falaise returned, inside a cushion belonging to the couch she was sitting on. Her 'master' had been dressed in the garb of a general or admiral (she wasn't very good with ranks), medals splashed across his chest. It looked like a hybrid of styles, which had become the trademark of De Falaise's army, but was in keeping with his abnormal personality.

He'd looked at her strangely from the doorway, as if trying to read her mind. Then he smirked and threw a dress at her: blue silk. "Put it on. We are going for a little stroll."

At this point any normal man might have turned his back, or exited the room, but De Falaise wasn't an ordinary man. He liked to watch his plaything disrobe and put on new outfits. This was all part of the game.

His eyes traced every contour of her as she climbed into the dress, which should really have been worn with a corset beneath, though that didn't appear to bother De Falaise. "Hurry," he snarled when she was taking too long and she did as she was told. Then she joined him at the doorway, walking that zombie walk she'd perfected. Taking the part of his pet.

Putting on his sunglasses, he led her outside and along the East Terrace. "Did I ever tell you the story about King John and what he did along here?" She didn't say a word. "Non? Well, John was the brother of Richard the Lionheart, as you may know. When Richard went away to fight in the crusades, John tried to take over the country, using this as his base. He'd always had a soft spot for this castle, you understand, in fact his father had bequeathed it to him before his death. Needless to say, when Richard found out he was, how you put it, more than a little pissed off with his sibling. Having only reached Italy, he returned to see to his brother himself. That happened here in 1194. Richard got into the Outer Bailey and rounded up all the people he could find – not just soldiers, but families of the garrison, tenant farmers – and he hung them, just strung them up. John's men didn't surrender at this point, not until the archbishop threatened them with excommunication. They then abandoned John and he was put into exile. However..." De Falaise held up a finger at this point in the lecture, halting their walk, "when Richard died John returned and used the castle as his permanent residence, the only king to do so. Which brings me to the story I originally wished to relate. It was here that John hung twenty-eight Welsh boys over the side of the rocks after inviting them along for dinner. They were the sons of Welsh barons and John did it because of a disagreement with their fathers over the Magna Carta. Ah, those were the days, non? If someone disagreed with you, you hung them. If there were traitors in your midst, you simply disposed of them."

Gwen was almost certain that he had found out about the stolen knife, why else would he be giving her a speech about traitors? Was she to suffer the same fate as those poor people at Richard and John's hands? She considered running, but knew she wouldn't get twelve paces without being gunned down by one of his men. There were a good dozen in sight along this section of the castle alone.

De Falaise held out his hand for them to begin walking again down the East Terrace, towards the steps guarded by twin lions. As she reached the top she realised her mistake. The recently mowed field below had been practically cleared of vehicles and was now was filled with people, all bound, all standing with heads bowed.

"Behold, the traitors of our time," announced De Falaise. "Those who have accepted aid from our friend, The Hooded Man. Those who have shielded him from me, who conspire against my new regime."

He's insane, thought Gwen, as if only just realising it for the first time. *He's completely lost his mind*. Of course she'd heard about the Hooded Man, the one who had stood up to De Falaise and was rallying support to his cause – in fact she'd mentally punched the air a few times when she'd heard of his victories over the man standing next to her. But she had no idea the stakes had been raised so high. There were children down there, children just like Luke and Sally who she missed so much. Gwen's eyes settled on a boy near the front. His dirty blond hair was ruffled, the tracksuit he wore tatty and torn, and he was clutching an empty backpack like a security blanket.

Looking at the people before her she understood that De Falaise was going to kill them all. And he'd think nothing of it. In a way they were just as much his toys as she was, as they all were.

It was then she knew she had to strike that night. This monster had to be stopped.

So, once he'd had his way with her again, the thrill of the imminent executions obviously arousing him – and she'd blotted it out the same as always, retreating to that place in her head where Clive waited – Gwen lay awake and waited for him to drop off. Then she'd waited some more until he'd drifted further into sleep.

Experimentally, she eased her shoulder away from his. Gently... Gently... she told herself, struggling to keep her own breathing even. Now she moved her left foot, the one furthest away from him. If she could only slide it down and feel the floor, she could manoeuvre the rest of herself out of the bed more easily. Her heel reached the end of the mattress and she allowed it to drop slowly, anchoring herself, pulling herself, straining with her calf muscle.

Almost there... almost–

De Falaise rolled over with a snore, arm flailing out and landing on her. It felt like a bolt sliding across a cell door. Gwen lay stock-still. De Falaise murmured something and his right foot kicked out, twitching in his sleep.

Gwen bit her lip hard. How the hell was she going to get off the bed without waking him? And even if she did get the knife and use it, how was she going to get out of the castle, past the guards? And how would she find this hooded man?

De Falaise muttered something and rolled onto his back, withdrawing his arm. Gwen let out a long, deep breath. Then she looked across at him. His head was cocked back, neck exposed. A thought suddenly occurred to her...

Why do you even need the knife at all? You could do what you should have done a long, long time ago. You could wrap your hands around that neck and just squeeze.

There'd be less chance of him waking up before she could do the deed. All she had to do was roll over and grab him. But was she strong enough? Could she kill him before he came to his senses and fought back? It was risky to say the least.

Risky, but oh, so tempting.

Yes, I'm going to do it, she told herself, even as she was turning over, hands reaching out, ready to encircle his neck, thumbs itching to press down on his windpipe with all her might.

He felt the hands around his neck and immediately snapped awake.

In the darkness a figure was on his chest, looking like some kind of ghastly apparition. But the pressure around his throat was real enough. He felt the hands gripping tight, and shock more than anything prevented him from fighting back.

You're going to die. If you don't do something right now, then you're going to be throttled to death!

The figure above was replaced with patches of deeper darkness that began to cloud his vision as his brain was starved of oxygen.

Do something...

He clamped his hands around his attacker's wrists and tried to pry the grip free. But he couldn't budge them.

"I'm sorry," he heard. "I have to do this."

He brought up his knee, hard. There was a grunt, but the assailant didn't shift. He did it again. This time it worked and his twisted the figure onto its side. He shook his head, clearing his vision. Bringing a knee round, he shoved it into his attacker's side, winding them. They grappled with each other for a moment, both on their sides now. Then suddenly the roles were reversed and the victim was on top. He struck out with a punch that caught his attacker across the jaw, enough to stop their struggling.

The voice came again. "I'm... I'm sorry." A whimper this time. "My Elaine... I... I had to do something."

Robert kept the man's hands pinned down as he heard voices outside the tent. Light filled the space, torches shone in. "What's going on?" asked Jack. Robert turned, though it hurt his neck to do so, and saw Tate there too – plus a couple of his other men – alerted by the sounds of the struggle. He opened his mouth to speak but found it hard to get the words out. Luckily, the man he was holding down answered their questions quickly enough.

"Dead or alive... that's what they said. The Sheriff doesn't care which," gibbered Mills, the man who'd come into the camp and told them about the raids. Only he'd withheld that one crucial piece of information.

"Jesus," Jack whispered. "You traitorous–"

"I did it for my Elaine," protested Mills. "They're going to kill her. And... and your plan, it's never going to work in a million years."

Jack huffed. "You think so?"

"I know so. They'll be expecting something... De Falaise will murder the hostages."

"Weren't..." croaked Robert, then coughed. He turned to the man again. "Weren't you listening earlier? He'll murder them anyway."

Mills shook his head, not willing to accept the truth. The next stage was lashing out again. "It's your fault they took her in the first place! All this is your fault. It's you he wants! If only you'd left them well enough alone to do what they wanted."

"You'd have been even further up shit creek, pal," argued Jack, then looked over at Tate. "Sorry, Rev."

The holy man wasn't really listening, he was too fixated on the scene before him.

Robert rolled off Mills, and rubbed his windpipe. The man didn't try to get up, didn't even try to escape. Jack and the others came and grabbed hold of him, dragging him away from Robert. "Don't hurt him," their leader managed.

"Hurt him? I know what I'd do, given half a chance," Jack told Robert.

"He was just scared for the person he loved."

Another snort. Then Jack told them to take Mills away and put a guard on him. He knew too much about what they were planning for them to just let him go.

Tate came fully inside, leaning heavily on his stick, and waited for Robert to look up. "If..." Robert coughed. "If that's an... an example of support in the villages, we don't stand a chance."

"You don't believe what he said, do you?"

"Trying to assuage your guilt, Reverend?" Robert said in broken words, massaging his throat.

"Guilt?"

"About persuading me to do this – setting all this in motion." Robert coughed again.

"It wasn't me who persuaded you, Robert."

He fixed Tate with a stare. "People are probably going to die because of me. You do know that, don't you? Maybe even Mark."

"And how many live today because of you, answer me that? How many of the men out there have a purpose now?"

"I'll probably get them killed as well."

"It's their choice to follow you. Their decision. In a broken world like this, you should feel proud of that."

There was someone else at the flap of the tent, a female face, and Robert looked past Tate, locking eyes with Mary. "I just saw that man Mills being taken away and..." She rushed over and knelt down beside Robert. "You're hurt."

He waved a hand to let her know he was okay, aware

of the half-smile on Tate's face. "Remember what I said, Robert," said the Reverend, then left.

Mary watched him go. "What's he talking about? What went on here?"

But Robert didn't answer her, because he didn't quite understand it himself.

It was somehow connected to a dream he'd been having before he felt Mills' hands at his throat, that much he did know.

Though whether good or evil had won this particular battle, he couldn't really say.

The knock roused him from his slumber.

He saw a shape almost on top of him – looming over. Hands were reaching down. It brought back flashes of the dream he'd been having. A struggle of some kind, a fight with The Hooded Man. They'd had each other by the neck, each fighting to squeeze the life out of the other.

But this was no man – it was the woman from Hope. His doll. And she wasn't trying to strangle him, he saw that now. No, she was shaking him, rousing him even further from his sleep. Pointing to the door.

Or was that just a cover for what she'd really been about? It was unlike her to be so animated, certainly in the bedroom.

De Falaise looked at her suspiciously. Then he rose, pushing her to one side.

"Oui, oui... I am coming," he shouted, pulling on his gown as he marched over to the door. "This really had better be good."

Tanek was standing there. "It is."

For the briefest of seconds De Falaise noted the bigger man's interest in what was beyond him: the body of the naked woman on the bed. That made him feel good, the fact that even his right hand wanted what he owned. Perhaps he would hold onto her just that little bit longer – especially if she was becoming more... responsive.

"So?"

"A boy," Tanek said simply.

"What?" De Falaise rubbed his tired eyes. "What are you talking about?"

"Javier recognised him when we brought the new prisoners through."

De Falaise frowned. "As who?"

"One of Hood's gang."

The Frenchman beamed from ear to ear. "Really? You are sure? Give me a few minutes to get dressed and I will be with you."

De Falaise closed the door and clapped his hands. "Did you hear that, mon cherie? It would appear that we have an added bargaining chip." He began to put on his clothes, looking up only once or twice at the woman. She was leaning against the headrest, knees pulled up close. She regarded him with an odd expression, somewhere between defeated and catatonic.

"I will return," he promised her. Then he exited the room and closed the door behind him.

Gwen clutched her knees, pulling them even tighter to her body.

She'd been so near to grabbing him, a fiery strength rising in her. She could have done it, and done it easily – but the knock at the door had thrown her into panic.

In an instant she had altered her stance, from attacker to concerned 'companion', rousing him. Had he bought it? There was no way of telling, but the news about the boy had probably chased any immediate thoughts about her from his mind. The very idea that they'd stumbled upon one of The Hooded Man's gang, and completely by accident, was nearly enough to make the Frenchman dance a jig on the spot.

Gwen knew which boy Tanek had been talking about, as well. It had to be the young kid with the tousled blond hair. Good God, what on Earth would that maniac do to try and get information out of him? Let Tanek loose? Would he do that?

Of course he would – the man had no scruples.

It was at that point, as she imagined Luke or Sally in his place, Gwen began to cry. She'd never cried for herself in all the time she'd been at the castle, but she did then.

Because she knew in her heart that she had failed.

CHAPTER EIGHTEEN

The weekend, they'd said.

A couple of days now to turn the men into the finest troops Sherwood had ever seen – able to face a superior enemy, with superior firepower. Could it be done? Possibly, but only if they returned once more to the basics of fighting.

Robert had already been giving some of his men lessons in the use of bow and arrows, even how to make their own. Granger had proved the most proficient, and volunteered to oversee the development of those particular skills. Obviously it would be madness to send the men into battle against machine guns without them being similarly armed... But Robert's own preferred weapon had the added advantage of being quiet and the ability to take out a target from a surprisingly long distance. He'd proved this again and again on strikes against De Falaise's troops.

For his part, Tate was teaching the men hand-to-hand combat. They'd had virtually no training in this while in De Falaise's army, the Sheriff preferring instead to rely solely on firepower. That was all well and good when your enemy was far enough away, but what about when they were on top of you? Robert couldn't help grinning when he watched a pair of younger men try to take Tate down.

"Come at me, then, let's see what you're made of," the Reverend had said. They were on the floor in seconds, with the minimum of effort, the holy man hardly having to move. "I see... It appears we have quite a lot of work ahead of us, then."

On that first day after the plan had been outlined – and

after the attempt on Robert's life – two people came to him for a talk. The first was Bill.

He began in his usual gruff way. "Judas Priest. Sure ye know what you're doin'?"

Robert shook his head and regretted it immediately. He coughed loudly.

"Aye, I heard about the Mills thing. Shoulda been more grateful for what we were tryin' to do. For what you've done for all of 'em... All of us." He looked at Robert then, seeing whether his roundabout way of apologising had worked. Robert nodded to tell him it had, and that he was grateful. Men like Bill very rarely said they were sorry, if ever. This was the closest he was ever going to get.

"He thinks the world of ye," added the farmer, "Mark."

Robert closed his eyes, picturing the boy's face – trying not to imagine what he must be going through at the castle. Hoping he could hold on until they mounted their rescue attempt.

"We're goin' to bring him back," continued Bill as if reading his thoughts. "Bring 'em all back."

"I hope you're right," said Robert.

"Aye. Listen, I've bin thinkin' – you'll need a way of knockin' out that pillock on the castle roof an' his pop-gun." Robert would hardly have described the high-powered sniper rifle De Falaise's man had as a 'pop-gun', but then compared to that cannon Bill carried around with him...

"Have any ideas?"

Bill smiled. "As a matter o' fact, I do. Care to go for a little drive?"

Robert was reluctant to leave the forest at such a crucial point, but Bill promised him it would be worthwhile. So they'd taken one of the jeeps out, travelling east. Bill had refused to tell him where they were going, leaving it as a complete mystery. "Just hope no one's got to 'em first or wrecked the place," was all he would say.

"Look, are you going to tell me where we're heading?"

"Towards Newark – that give ye any clues?"

Robert didn't need any, especially when they turned off, following the brown and white signs which eventually led them to a large car park and concrete runways. He stuck his head out to get a better glimpse of the corrugated metal hangars, camouflaged grey and khaki aircraft left abandoned outside to rust. The air museum, once a thriving tourist attraction built on a former World War Two airfield, was now empty and neglected. It was somewhere Robert had always intended to take Stevie but just never got around to it, never found the time. How he would have marvelled at the planes. Robert felt a twinge of guilt as they drove in, because it was way too late and the only reason he was coming here now was because he needed to save another boy.

Bill parked the jeep in the virtually empty car park. Anyone with any sense working here would have returned home to be with loved ones when the plague hit, the owners of the few cars that remained probably left it too late. Whether they'd see any bodies here today depended on if the clean up crews had bothered with this place. Robert just hoped it hadn't appeared on De Falaise's radar.

Thinking along the same lines, Bill took out his shotgun as he climbed from the jeep. "Can never be too careful," he said, as if Robert needed telling. He already had his bow raised.

As they walked over towards one of the hangars, Bill pointed to various aircraft.

"See that, it's a BAC Canberra bomber. In service up until the '70s. There you have a BA Sea Harrier. A Vertical Take Off and Landing aircraft, it was still in service with the UK and US Marines up until... well, y'know. Best all round fighter-bomber in the world. Oh, that there's an Avro Vulcan bomber. Superb British heavy bomber in service until the 1980s, last used against Argentineans in the Falklands Campaign, the nuclear bomber of the UK. An' over there's an Avro Shackleton. Old turbo-prop bomber..."

Robert gaped at him, astonished.

"What?"

"Aeroplanes? I just never..."

"Wouldn't have pegged me as an enthusiast?" Bill tutted. "Have to say, I'm not really. Me uncle was ex-RAF, nuts about these things. Taught me all I'll ever need to know, even took me up on a few flights in his civilian life. This place was like a second home to him, God rest his soul."

"And you know how to fly these things?"

"Aye." He closed his eyes, imagining the cockpit. "Airspeed indicator, heading, altimeter, fuel gauge, landing gear, throttle." With his finger he traced the position of each instrument. He finished with a tap in the air in front of him. "Yoke. Simple."

"So, your plan is to take one of them up and what? Strafe the castle? Use a few of those relics of missiles they have here?"

"Naw," Bill replied, as if he'd even considered it as a serious suggestion. "This is a museum, lad, not a military installation – leastways it hasn't bin for a good many years."

"Then what? He'd see us coming a mile away in one of those things!"

"Who said I was thinkin' about a plane?" Bill winked.

He directed Robert across to one of the hangers and smashed open the locks. They stepped inside – the light from windows above illuminating the scene. Robert saw more aircraft: one grey, one red and blue, another silver and yellow, all remarkably untouched. He guessed the survivors of the virus had other things on their minds than visiting air museums.

"I did think about an early Gazelle. The Sud Aviation SA 341 Gazelle prototype they have here, but this is more manoeuvrable." He strode over to a helicopter, which had a huge see-through bubble on the front. It was a bit like those Robert had seen in old reruns of *M*A*S*H*. "Westland Sioux Scout/Trainer. Very quick, very small. Somethin' to draw his fire, but hopefully avoid it."

The doors opened wide and Bill undid one, swinging it outwards. He climbed inside it and stuck a thumb up to Robert, who followed him.

"She's not fuelled," Bill called to him, "but I daresay I can scrounge up some aviation fuel from around here somewhere. They used to have demonstrations all the time."

"And how do you intend on getting it out of here?" said Robert, asking the obvious.

"Same way they got her in." Bill pointed down. "She's on wheels, look. Once we clear some space, we can tow her through the hangar doors. Bit of an effort, which is probably why no bugger else's bothered, but it can be done."

"This is insane," said Robert.

"More insane than what you're plannin'?" Bill asked, not expecting a reply. "Look, we've got the element of surprise – that bloody Frenchman 'asn't got anything that flies."

"As far as we know," Robert pointed out. "That doesn't matter – the sniper will shoot you out of the sky before you can get close."

"I may look as rough as a badger's arse, but I'm pretty nifty once I get up there. Besides, while the bastard's shootin' at me, he's not shootin' at anyone else."

Robert had to concede that. At the same time he also had to wonder just why Bill was so eager to launch himself – literally – into this suicide mission... not that he could talk. Was it because he felt bad about what had happened to Mark? Or did he really think he could pull it off? Robert didn't question him, just helped Bill to get the chopper out into the open, using the jeep to tow it from the hangar. The side caught on the nose of a plane that was a little too close for comfort, but in the end they managed it.

"We should have brought more men," Robert complained to Bill.

"An' take 'em away from their trainin'? They need all the help they can get. Anyway, it's like I said: a surprise."

After that Bill filled the chopper with fuel they managed to scavenge: enough to get the thing home – and both of them – plus stocks of it for the Nottingham run. Robert stared at the flying machine in front of him. He'd never flown before, apart from three or four holidays abroad with the family. He definitely hadn't been suspended above the ground in a bubble and didn't relish the prospect now.

"It'll be fine," Bill assured him. "A doddle. Tell ye what, I'll show ye."

And he did, beginning with the main differences between how a plane and helicopter fly: one creating lift by angling the wings, the other by manipulating the rotor blades to change the angle at which they meet the air. He took Robert through the pre-flight checks, explaining briefly what the main controls did – from the collective control stick through to the cyclic control joystick and, finally, the tail rotor pedals on the floor. "So, no accelerator?" enquired Robert, only to get a groan from Bill.

Next he walked Robert through the instruments,

stopping when he noted the man stifling a yawn. It was as if Bill needed an outlet for all this information, like he'd been bottling it up inside for years and it was all coming out now he had a captive audience. "Anyway, ye get the general idea. Time to go."

He made Robert strap himself him in, warning him that it had been a while since he'd done this.

"How much of a while?"

Bill didn't answer, instead he put on the earphones and instructed Robert to do the same. With nothing else to occupy him, and more to take his mind off what was about to happen than anything, Robert watched Bill as he started up the chopper. Bill patted the instrument panel that lay between them. "At-a-girl." When he noticed Robert looking at him, he explained: "They can be very sensitive, needs a light touch. The biggest mistake new pilots make is to 'over control'."

Robert had to admit, the take-off was incredibly smooth. Even so, he gripped the end of his bow, squeezing tightly until they were up in the air.

It was an odd sensation and Robert wasn't sure whether he loved or hated it. He thought that it would be interesting to fly the length of this land, see what had become of it. See who had survived where – and what had been destroyed.

It was a land worth fighting for, Robert finally realised as he saw it stretching out in front of him in all its beautiful patchwork glory. It was a land worth keeping free. If ever the human race was to get back on it shaky legs again then men like De Falaise had to be defeated.

"All right?" asked Bill beside him.

"Just drifting."

"Aye," said the ruddy-cheeked man, coaxing more speed from the chopper as they headed back to familiar forest terrain.

Once they'd landed on the outskirts, Robert and Bill made their way back to the camp to find new faces waiting for them. Strangers in their den. Robert's first instinct was to bring up his bow, but Jack raised a hand, jogging over to explain.

The men and women were from communities the Sheriff had terrorised, communities Robert had been trying to help. Though these were new, and small, they represented the first seeds of rebuilding this part of England. The people that made up their number had found each other, in spite of all the odds, and built new friendships, relationships and homes. Now those they cared about were in danger and they wanted to do something about it.

"We found them gathering at the forest's edge," Jack explained. "They're volunteering, Robbie."

"For what? To kill me in my sleep?" Robert said, slowly lowering his bow.

"Mills were just one man," Bill threw in. "Look at 'em, they've had enough of bein' scared. They want to fight."

Jack nodded. "They want to help."

Perhaps they do at that, thought Robert. "Okay then, start training them up. But first, see if any of them have combat experience. You never know, we might drop lucky again and find another member of the TA or something. Or, who knows, maybe even a Kung Fu clergyman or ex-professional wrestler?"

Jack laughed, clapping Robert on the shoulder. "We might at that." He began to walk back to the crowd, then remembered something. "Oh, I think Mary's been waiting for you to get back. She wants a word."

"What about?"

Jack shrugged. "None of my beeswax, Robbie. None of my beeswax."

"Best not keep the lady waitin', then," Bill told him.

Robert didn't have to look far to find Mary – she was just outside of camp, practising with her own bow and arrow, aiming for a target notched on a tree trunk. She was holding the weapon awkwardly, her aim off. Robert came up behind her quietly, so quietly that she started when he reached around and took hold of her arms.

"Robert!" she cried, turning round. "I wish you'd stop doing that, you nearly gave me a heart attack."

He could feel Mary shaking and regretted not announcing himself. He still wasn't quite used to how stealthy he'd become. "Sorry, but the way you're holding the bow... May I?" He could feel her arms relax slightly, the muscles still bunched but more flexible, allowing him to guide her aim. "Don't think about the shot too much, just let yourself feel it. Feel the arrow against your fingers, that's how you're going to guide it to the target." Robert brought up her bow arm a touch, bending down to look along her line of sight, squeezing one eye shut to get a better view. "Nice... Nice..." he murmured. "All right, now just pull the string back, feel the tension building. Can you feel it?"

"Y-Yes."

"Now just let go." She did. The arrow didn't hit the carved circle dead on, but it was pretty close. "There, you did it."

"Yay me."

Robert let out a small laugh. "Yay you." He realised that even though the arrow was embedded in the tree, he was still holding Mary's arms, his chest pressed up against her back. He moved to step away, but she moved with him. She was quivering again, but this time it wasn't because of the fright.

Robert was trembling too.

"You took off before I could talk to you this morning. About Mills, about what happened," she said. "Tate told me about it."

"What's to talk about? People try to kill me all the time these days. Since I decided to become a recluse, I've never been so popular."

Mary turned. "Don't joke about it, Robert. You could have died last night and I might never have..."

"Might never have what?"

Mary looked right at him. "Had a chance to tell you how I feel."

"Mary, listen. I think you–"

She dropped the bow and put a finger to his lips to stop the flow of words.

"You can feel the tension too, can't you?" She placed her hand on his arm. "Now just let go..." Mary kissed him then. Gently and briefly "There. We did it. Yay us."

Robert shook his head. "I... I can't. You know why."

"I do." Mary's eyes were glistening. "At least I know what my head is telling me... But this..." She placed her hand on her chest. "Well, that's telling me something entirely different. I'm sorry." Mary let her head drop, though Robert wasn't sure if it was because she didn't want him to see her cry, or she was embarrassed.

Robert lifted her chin. "Hey, you have absolutely nothing to be sorry about, Mary. You're wonderful. I've never met another woman like–" He stopped himself short. "In another time, another place, and if things weren't so screwed up..."

"Yeah," she said, sniffing, then pulled back from him.

"Don't be like this. We're friends, Mary. At least I

thought we were."

Robert made to move towards her, but she halted him with a: "No, please."

"Mary–"

She rounded on him, eyes red. "Oh, what does it matter anyway? What you're planning on doing... You're going to get yourself killed, you know that, don't you?"

"Thanks for the vote of confidence."

"You're walking into the lion's den, Robert. What do you expect me to say: Good luck and goodbye?"

"It's something I've got to do, don't you see? For Mark, for all the people mixed up in this."

She didn't have an answer to that, probably because she knew he was right. But after a pause Mary came back with: "It's what you've wanted all along, isn't it? To be with them."

"What?"

"You want to die, don't you? You have done all along."

Now Robert kept quiet. He was frightened that anything he might say would give away the truth. That there was a part of him that still desperately wanted to be with his family again. But there was also a part that recognised he had a new family, that people were relying on him. That he had to focus on those who were still alive.

"Well, you're about to get your wish I think," said Mary, the tears coming more freely. "I hope it makes you happy." She picked up her bow and ran. Robert started after her, then decided to let her go. There was nothing he could say that would make things better. He couldn't tell Mary what she wanted to hear, couldn't back out of what he was going to do. He could only watch her disappear into the forest – his forest – and hope that someday she might find it in her heart to forgive him.

CHAPTER NINETEEN

"So, how does it feel to be in favour again?"

He'd first been asked that question in the small hours of the morning, by the guard who'd come to collect him. Javier, his wrists still bound, had instinctively touched his wounded ear, remembering what it was like to be 'out of favour'. He had to admit, it felt good. And all because of his saviour: the boy.

Javier hadn't recognised him to begin with; hardly surprising seeing as he'd only gained a glimpse of him once. It didn't help that the kid had been thrown into the dim caves along with the rest of the villagers De Falaise's men had captured. The place was packed with them in fact, hardly any room to move even an elbow or a leg. It reminded Javier of the illustrations he'd seen as a child from Dante's Divine Comedy by Gustave Doré. One of the levels of Hell with naked bodies piled on top of each other, the masses suffering for their sins. The only difference was in Dante's Inferno they didn't have men with automatic weapons guarding the exits, ready to shoot you if you made a wrong move – there were no exits.

It was a stark contrast to the early days after the virus. Back then you'd be lucky if you saw one person a week, let alone dozens all crammed into one tight spot. Javier had been dumped here after De Falaise and Tanek had had their fun with him, most of which he'd tried to blot out, and every day that passed he'd been fully expecting them to return to finish off the job. Nothing they'd done had resulted in any permanent damage, just some flesh gouging, a few broken ribs, plenty of burns, and a scar in a particularly delicate place that he doubted would ever fade. The ear he had lost before he'd been dragged back up to the castle. How could he have feared the wrath of God over that? What possible pain could any deity inflict that would match Tanek's skills? Yet he'd felt he had no option but to talk back there in the forest. Not only had there been the constant bombardment of scripture – the threat of The Almighty's wrath taking him right back to his formative years when his grandmother would quote from the 'Good Book' – but he'd also felt the weight of the place pressing down on him. It seemed ludicrous now, but it had almost been like the trees themselves were watching him, pressuring him to comply.

But what had made him think De Falaise would be lenient? In his mind's eye, had he pictured a scene where the Frenchman would simply rap him on the knuckles for what he had done and then let him get on with his job – or let him go, free to wander wherever he wished so long as it was out of the Sheriff's sight? The truth was he hadn't really been given a choice. Those fuckers back in the forest had more or less forced him to return with his tail between his legs, an action which was rewarded by seeing his men shot dead in front of his eyes and his ear ruined.

Of all the things he had endured since his fall from grace, though, the waiting had to be the worst. Not knowing when his former leader would return and what things his right hand man would have in store this time. Agonising weeks, with only the scraps of food the guards tossed to him and whatever bugs he could find crawling around on the cave floors to sustain him. Javier's belly had never been so flat as it was right now, not even when he was a youth in the military.

How proud his family had been of him then, as he worked his way up the ranks, before he'd been arrested on suspicion of dealing in black market goods and drummed out. The only reason he hadn't been tossed in jail as well was that his superiors hadn't had any hard evidence. Left with his career in tatters, he'd pursued the only option available to him, becoming a gun for hire. Those had been dangerous times, but Javier fought dirty and always got the job done. The rewards had been great, allowing him a luxurious lifestyle and all the women he could ever desire. Yet something was missing. No matter how much he pretended to be the big shot – growing bigger every day, literally – it was all an illusion. He'd never make Major in any army, because they simply wouldn't have him. And though he'd led men into 'battle', most notably those skirmishes in South America, they'd showed him no respect. It wasn't an official army, just a bunch of mercenaries doing what they were being paid to do.

With De Falaise it was different. Javier was feared by the men they'd commandeered, that they'd enlisted to their 'cause'. He'd agreed to follow the Frenchman because there was something about the way he talked, just as persuasive as the Reverend. He had a vision, and he wanted Javier to become a part of that. They would have power, wealth, sex, whatever they wanted. There was just one downfall. If you let him down, there were no second chances. Usually.

Javier had failed him so spectacularly that he didn't think this would ever be a possibility. That is, not until the Mexican had spotted the boy, his eyes now accustomed to the gloom. The tiny figure had been swimming in a sea of people, struggling not to drown. Javier might not even have noticed him if it hadn't been for that backpack he was clutching in his hands: a makeshift float to stop himself going under.

I see you, little man, he thought to himself, smiling at how appropriate that phrase was this time. *I know who you are.* He remembered the battle, the fighters involved.

One of them had been smaller than the rest. The more he thought about it, the more he remembered seeing...

A backpack, Javier had spotted a backpack.

Sure, there must have been thousands that looked like the one the kid was gripping. But somehow Javier was sure it was him. There was only one way to prove it, however.

Though he was weak from lack of proper food, Javier had pushed himself forwards, propelling himself through the arms and legs of the prisoners. Some complained, but not for long – he headbutted one and poked another in the eye. Javier had to get over to where the kid was, see his reaction when he caught his gaze. Only then would he be a hundred per cent convinced. Determination drove him onwards.

Sure enough, the boy looked across in his direction. Nothing unusual in that, Javier was causing quite a fuss. But when he stared right at him, Javier saw the fear in his eyes. The boy knew him all right. Even in this half-light, the look of recognition was unmistakable.

"I see you, little man," he said out loud. The kid with the backpack attempted to scramble away. "Hey, you, come back here. You're my ticket out!" There were more shouts of alarm and protest, the other prisoners unable to fathom exactly what was going on.

Finally, Javier came within snatching distance. He reached out with his bound hands and his fingers snagged the strap of the boy's backpack. Summoning all the strength he had left, Javier tugged the boy towards him.

"No!" he shouted, but it was too late. The kid had no footing to lose and so fell easily into the Mexican's clutches.

"I have you now, don't I?" Javier whispered in his ear. "Your friends have caused me much pain."

"I... I don't know what you're talking about."

"I think you do. They don't know who you are, do they? De Falaise? Tanek? Otherwise you wouldn't have been dumped in here with the rest of the dregs." This gained him one or two severe looks from the prisoners, but they did nothing to antagonise him.

"I still don't know–"

"Quiet! We will soon see what you know. Guard! Guard!" Javier began shouting, his voice echoing through the caves. It was crazy to think that his whole survival depended on one of the runts he'd once commanded, one of the men they'd picked up on their rampage through Britain. Javier just hoped that the fuckwit had enough sense to listen to what he had to say. "Guard!"

He saw one of De Falaise's men appear at the entranceway. He flashed a torch into the caves. "What's all this shouting about?"

"It is I, Javier."

"Who?"

"I used to be a Major in your army." *I used to command respect, and fear, and wish to again – so listen to me, hear my words...* "I need you to fetch De F... the Sheriff. Fetch him quickly."

"Are you off your fucking head? Do you know what time it is? He'll have my balls for breakfast."

"He will have them anyway if you don't give him my message. I have identified one of Hood's men." The guard passed his torch over the boy Javier was holding and cocked his head. The Mexican rephrased what he'd just said. "One of his gang."

"Fuck off. Him?"

"He was with them when they attacked us. I saw him," Javier explained. "Now go and fetch De Falaise."

The guard looked again at Javier's captive, then seemed to think about the consequences if he was wrong. "I'll...

I'll fetch Tanek," he told Javier.

So he did. Javier didn't know what he'd said to the big man – and wouldn't like to have been the one to rouse the brute – but within ten minutes the swarthy giant was down in the caves with them.

"It's true, I tell you," Javier promised. "Why would I lie?"

"To get out," Tanek stated without missing a beat.

"Tell him." Javier shook the boy. "Tell him who you are."

The kid remained silent.

"I recognised him. Please, you have to believe me. What harm would it do to make sure?"

Tanek nodded. "Pass him over."

Javier began to ease the boy across, but he struggled. Not only that, some of the people in the cave were aiding him, getting in both Javier and Tanek's way.

They're helping him because he's with The Hooded Man, realised Javier. *My God, are they that stupid to risk their lives for him?*

Apparently so, because Tanek took out a pistol and began to shoot those closest to him. He put bullets into two people before the crowd began to relent. "Better," said the big man.

He reached over and grabbed the boy by the collar of his tracksuit top, holding him off the ground. Then he put him down and pushed him towards the stairs.

"No... No, wait!" shouted Javier after them. "Where are you going? Tanek... Tanek don't leave me down here with these people!"

But Tanek was gone.

The prisoners mourned for their dead. Then they looked to Javier for revenge. He lashed out at them, warding them off. But the sheer force of the throng was too much. They pulled him down into their sea, hand upon hand, bodies climbing on top of him until he could barely breathe.

Then, just as he thought it was all over, there came a voice: "Let him go. De Falaise has ordered it." It was the young guard again, Javier saw through a crack in the bodies. He was pointing his rifle at the prisoners and they understood what would happen next if they didn't comply.

Javier was spat out of the mass, thrown onto the cold floor in front of the guard. As he was helped to his feet, Javier spat into the crowd, who bayed for his blood.

The guard led Javier up through a corridor in the cave system. It was then that the question was asked of him a first time: how did it feel to be in favour again?

Javier had answered honestly, after touching his wounded ear. "It is better than being dead."

The guard led Javier up and out, through into another part of the caves. It was a place all too familiar. Tanek's torture chamber.

He saw the boy first. Too small to hang in the chains they'd fixed up, the ones Javier knew intimately, they'd tied him to a wooden chair instead, hands strapped to the arms. He looked up as Javier and the guard entered, eyes already wide with panic.

Then Javier saw the duo of De Falaise and Tanek. Like Victor Frankenstein and his hideous monster, they loitered in their underground lair. The difference was that where the famous doctor sought to bring about life, albeit misguidedly, these two brought only suffering and death.

"Major Javier," De Falaise said in greeting. "How nice to see you again." He gave a chilling smile, lips pulling back over those yellow teeth, black eyes twinkling. "Now, is it me or have you lost weight?"

Javier bit his tongue. This kind of goading was De

Falaise's speciality. To put a foot wrong now would see him back in the caves with those bloodthirsty villagers.

"Well, do not simply stand there – come inside and make yourself at home. Ah, I forgot, you are already familiar with the surroundings, are you not?"

Javier held his silence.

"What's that?" De Falaise cupped a hand to his ear. "Would you like me to speak louder? Is that it?"

Javier shook his head. "I hear you just fine."

"I am sorry. I do not think I caught that properly." He turned to Tanek. "Did you catch that?"

Tanek admitted that he hadn't.

"I hear you," Javier repeated, but now added, "Sir."

"Sir will suffice, I suppose. But also acceptable would have been 'My Lord', or even 'My Lord High Sheriff.'"

Javier grimaced, remembering it was he who'd told De Falaise about that name on his return from Hope. Absently, he wondered what had happened to the woman he'd brought back from there, and whether the Frenchman had dispatched her yet after having his pleasure.

"And how is your relationship with your God, these days? Do you still fear his retribution more than mine?" De Falaise laughed. "Look at you, mon ami. How you have changed. But then, you know what they say: easy come, easy go." De Falaise approached Javier. "I do have one thing to thank you for, however, and that is giving me this important bargaining chip. If it does turn out that the boy belongs to 'Hood', then you will have done well."

"N-No..." stuttered the blond-haired lad.

De Falaise spun around. "So, it speaks, oui? Are you begging for your life already? Come now, the night... or rather the day is young."

The boy was shaking but he got the words out. "No... Nobody belongs to him. P-People aren't property."

That's exactly what the woman's boyfriend had said back in Hope, thought Javier, and look what happened to him.

"Quite right," snapped De Falaise. "They are pawns. Pawns in my game!" His eyes narrowed. "But the way you jump to Hood's defence like that, it makes me think Javier was not just trying to save his own skin after all. That you may well be in collaboration with my enemy."

"It is as I told you," Javier insisted.

"You are not vindicated yet, Major." De Falaise strolled over to the prisoner. "He still has to admit that he is one of Hood's gang, that he has been plaguing my efforts over these past months. Are you ready to do that yet, boy?"

"Mark... my name is Mark."

De Falaise nodded. "I see. But don't think that a name makes you any more of a person to us. You are a handy tool. You serve a purpose. Right now that purpose is information."

"I don't know anything. I was taken from my village by your men..."

"And is it not correct that you told them that you'd seen The Hooded Man?" De Falaise turned to Tanek. "A fact that has only just come to light, although the soldiers in question have been reprimanded for their forgetfulness."

"He was with the troops bringing us food and supplies."

"So what happened to him when my men got there? He wasn't killed with the rest of the scum, that much I am certain of. My soldiers would not forget to tell me that or they'd swing with the rest of your kind at the weekend."

Mark gulped. "He took off."

De Falaise grabbed the boy by his collar and pressed his face up close. "Liar! If there's one thing I do know about my nemesis, it's that he wouldn't abandon his people to their fate. It is something I am very much counting on at the moment. Unlike myself, he has principles. But then you'd know that, being so close to him."

"I-I've never met him..."

That was enough to set De Falaise off. He back-handed Mark across the face, his rings opening up cuts on the boy's cheek. As Mark began to cry, the Sheriff said: "This will not go well for you if you insist on withholding the truth."

De Falaise threw a look back over at Javier who was standing uneasily, watching.

"What is the matter, mon ami? You gave us this child, did you not, to do with as we will? Or is that another sin in the eyes of your God?"

Javier didn't know what else to do but shrug. Inside, though, he was beginning to doubt himself again.

"If so, then what we are about to do to the boy will really piss Him off." De Falaise called for Tanek to approach. "I suggest you answer my question truthfully this time," the Sheriff told Mark, "or I will instruct Tanek to do something thoroughly unpleasant."

Mark looked from Tanek to De Falaise, then finally across at Javier. His eyes were wet, pleading for help, but Javier kept his mouth shut.

As did Mark – an act for which he paid dearly. Tanek got down on his knees in front of him and held up his leg. Removing the boy's shoes and socks, he placed the heel in one hand and then took out a small needle, barely big enough to sew a button back onto a shirt. Without further ado, he shoved this into a chosen spot on Mark's sole. The boy let out a scream.

Javier cringed.

"You see, Tanek has been trained in both reflexology and acupuncture. Techniques which, in the right hands, can heal or harm. He knows just where to inflict the maximum of pain with the minimum of effort," De Falaise explained to Mark. "All the other nonsense with chains and knives and red hot pokers... well, he mainly does that just for kicks." The Sheriff glanced down at Tanek holding Mark's quivering leg. "If you'll pardon the pun. So, I ask again – are you a member of Hood's gang?"

Gritting his teeth, Mark shook his head violently. De Falaise nodded at Tanek, who repeated his procedure. Another yelp came, less piercing than the last, but no less disturbing.

It took several jabs with the needle, on both feet, before Mark would admit to De Falaise's accusation, and then all the Frenchman got was a slight tip of the head that could just have been the exhausted boy drifting into unconsciousness. Not that De Falaise would allow that, of course. He was there, all the time, slapping Mark on the cheek to wake him – just in time for another fresh bout of agony.

They continued like this for a good few hours, De Falaise asking questions, Mark refusing to answer at first, then finally giving in when he couldn't hold out any longer. Tanek appeared to be able to reach every single part of Mark's body from that one spot, as Javier noticed arms, shoulders, torso and neck all spasming in turn. Mark eventually told the Sheriff how many men Hood had, what their capabilities were, and about the main members of his team – complete with descriptions of Bill, Tate and newcomer Jack. When it came to the exact location of the camp, however, Mark kept shaking his head.

In the end they called a break. "My, is it afternoon already?" De Falaise exclaimed, looking at his watch. "Time flies when you are having such fun, does it not?" He directed this at Javier. "Are you pleased with our progress, Major?"

Javier, who had witnessed so many shocking things in his time, but nothing quite like the last half a day – a torture that left no physical scars, but had obviously taken its toll on the boy – responded with a weak: "Y-Yes."

"Good."

Food was brought down and they ate in front of a starving Mark, De Falaise biting into chicken legs, wiping the grease from his chin. Tanek tucked into a practically raw steak, dribbling blood as he shoved each forkful into his mouth. A plate of eggs and bacon was placed in front of Javier and though his bonds were cut, for the first time since he'd come back to the castle – for the first time in his entire life – he found his appetite gone. He should have been wolfing down the meal, but every time he looked at it, then at Mark, he felt his stomach give a lurch. *It's just because you haven't eaten in so long*, Javier told himself. But was it? He thought back to the way Tate had gotten information out of him, a hardened soldier. The holy man had needed no needles, no pain – just the right combination of words, the right things to play on the guilt Javier had buried. Though the Reverend had wanted to do more – and who could blame him? – he hadn't. He'd shown the kind of compassion that was lacking here today. The torture of a boy... a fucking boy!

What had you expected them to do with him? Give him an ice cream? It was that same stupidity which had hoped De Falaise would forgive him for failing to kill The Hooded Man. For singing like a bird about their operations. He'd seen an opportunity for getting back in their goods books and selfishly taken it, relished a bit of revenge on one of the people who'd put him here in the first place.

But Mark wasn't much older than his little brother had been when Javier left for the army. A little brother who was now dead and gone. No matter how tough he acted,

Mark was scared and vulnerable.

The image from Dante's Inferno flashed through Javier's mind once more, bodies writhing. He imagined what it would be like to experience what those prisoners were going through for all eternity.

"You want some, eh?" De Falaise called across to Mark. The boy regarded him with disdain.

The Sheriff tossed across the bone from the leg, which hit the boy in the chest and dropped into his lap. Even if he hadn't been bound, there was no meat left on the thing. De Falaise had picked the drumstick clean. "He'll come for me, you know," Mark promised them. "Then you'll be sorry."

"You don't seem to understand, I want him to come," chuckled De Falaise. "But he will be the sorry one." He turned to Javier. "What is the matter? Eat, Major. We have a long session ahead of us and must keep our strength up."

A long session? Only because his 'leader' was watching, he forked some of the egg into his mouth. It tasted like ashes.

De Falaise left them alone for a while – Javier suspected he needed to work off other appetites, though he had no way of proving this and wasn't about to ask – but when he came back, the questioning began again.

"Where is Hood's camp located in Sherwood? Is it central, on the outskirts, where?"

Javier knew the information would do them no good anyway, because even if they were to send a whole battalion in there, the men would come back defeated. It was his turf, and his alone. There were traps, lookouts, probably guards. He was as safe there as De Falaise was in his castle.

Mark held out for a long time and, by the end of it all, he could do nothing but mumble. "We will get no more from him," said Tanek. Javier wasn't sure whether the man meant today or ever.

"That is a pity. But we have one last thing we must attend to. I wish to send The Hooded Man a gift, a souvenir if you will. Something belonging to the boy that he may remember him by." De Falaise went over to where Tanek kept his instruments of torture. He picked up a set of bolt cutters. "Major, would you care to do the honours?"

Javier touched his chest. "Me?"

De Falaise nodded forcefully, as if he wouldn't take no for an answer. Javier walked across to him, his movements slow. In the end, De Falaise grew impatient and covered the rest of the distance between them, slapping the cutters into his hand. "There. Now, which do you think? Finger or toe?"

Javier's mouth dropped open. He could not be serious, surely?

He was. "I think a finger. We have done enough with his feet already, non?" De Falaise chortled. "So, which one? Little finger, index, or how about a thumb?"

Javier was rooted to the spot.

"No suggestions? Then I will decide for you. Hmmm... little finger it is, I think." He took Javier by the wrist and curled his fingers around the handles of the cutters. Then he got hold of Mark's little finger and placed that between the blades. The boy woke up then, realising what was about to happen. He shook his head, mumbling something that sounded like: "Please."

"I know how weak you must be, but it will take only the slightest of pressure – the mechanism is spring-loaded. Do it, Javier," ordered De Falaise. "Do it and prove that you are one of us again."

Javier saw the bodies in his mind's eye, saw flames this time accompanying them. Saw Tate, heard his words about damnation. "God will punish you for all you have done wrong. Repent, repent!" He felt the throbbing in his ruined ear.

His hands shook, causing the blades to scrape against the sides of Mark's finger.

"Do it!" De Falaise screamed. "Do it or I will blow your brains out all over the wall." The Sheriff had snatched Tanek's pistol and was aiming at Javier. This was no bluff. He would shoot if Javier defied him.

Clenching his teeth, Javier snapped the blades together. The little finger fell to the ground. If Mark had howled before, then that had been nothing compared to what he did now. Bucking in the chair, his head rocked backwards, the intense pain causing him finally to black out.

Javier dropped the cutters. He took a step back.

De Falaise clapped, then began to laugh. Tanek came over and stemmed the bleeding. They didn't want Mark to die quite yet.

"Good work, my dear Javier. You overcame your fears. He was only a boy when all was said and done."

No, not just a boy – a man today ("Your friends have caused me much pain, little man."). *More man than you'll ever be... My...My God, what have we... what have I done?*

It was then that he was asked the question again, now by De Falaise. "So, how does it feel to be back in favour once more, Major?"

Javier stared at De Falaise. If he was honest, he felt damned. More damned than he ever had before.

"He'll come for me," Mark had said. "And then you'll be sorry..."

Right now Javier didn't fear De Falaise with all his men and firepower, didn't fear God with all of His angels and the ability to cast Javier down into the pits of Hell.

He feared The Hooded Man.

And what would happen when he finally did reach the castle...

CHAPTER TWENTY

The training continued on into the next day, though by noon Robert and his men had things on their mind other than the battle to come.

One of the lookouts reported that a uniformed man on a motorbike had skimmed the border of the forest at about 11.30, acting strangely. The rider kept making passes at the perimeter but never actually came in. He then took his rifle and fired into the air. The lookout almost fired back, but then saw him sling off a backpack and toss it into the forest, riding in the other direction as fast as he could. The lookout assumed it must be explosives of some kind and raised the alarm.

Robert was called and, along with Jack, came to investigate. They got close, but not close enough to get caught in a blast if there was one. Both men recognised the backpack, and knew who it belonged to.

"Doesn't mean it isn't going to blow," Jack reminded him. "Haven't you ever seen those spy films with the briefcases?"

Robert gave a shake of the head. "It's not a bomb." He began walking towards it.

"For Pete's sake be careful," Jack called after him.

He watched as Robert paused by the backpack, then as he toed it with his foot. "There's something inside," Robert reported back. "Square but remarkably light. Doesn't feel heavy enough to be an explosive device."

Robert opened up the bag, taking out the cardboard box inside.

"Don't you go opening it, now, Robbie," warned the big man. "I don't want to be scraping you off the trees."

Robert ignored him, pulling open the lid. He gazed at

the object inside, then blinked once, twice, as if making sure what he was seeing was correct.

"What is it?" Jack shouted, curiosity now getting the better of him. When Robert didn't reply, he came over – but soon wished that he hadn't. Inside the box was a severed finger packed in cotton wool. The stump end was caked in dried blood, and the whole thing had a rubbery quality to it, like one of those joke fingers people once bought to scare their friends. But this was real; it smelt bad, like it had been detached for a while. Jack honestly thought he was going to throw up. *It's Se7en all over again*, his mind kept saying, but he shouted it down – this was no time for stupid movie references.

There was a note next to the finger. It read: *See you soon. D.F.*

"The sick... You don't think that's really–"

"It's his," Robert stated.

"So they know about Mark. That poor kid. Holy shit, Robbie! How do we fight people like that?"

Robert rubbed his forehead, and for a moment Jack thought he was going to run off and punch a tree, or do something to vent the feelings that were building up inside him. Instead, he put the lid back on the box, replaced it inside the pack, and began to walk off into the forest. Jack didn't question this, didn't ask if he was okay – Hell, he wasn't okay and he hadn't known the kid half as long as Robert.

Your biggest fan, eh, Hammer? Went to your matches... Now he's at the castle and they're cutting bits off him. Jack shook his head as he followed Robert. He just couldn't believe anyone could do that to a child, just to send a message.

Not a message: A warning.

It was designed to put Robert and his men on the back foot, to make them think twice about trying anything stupid. Now the more Jack considered the plan, the more unwise it seemed. He had come up against some vicious opponents in the ring, some of them bigger and stronger than him – hard as that was to imagine – but even the mightiest crumbled if they showed even a hint of self-doubt. If, psychologically, you could trick them into thinking you were playing for keeps, they'd slip up somewhere down the line. That's what De Falaise was hoping with Robert, that he'd think twice. That he'd realise the Frenchman was playing for keeps.

When they arrived back at the camp, Robert wouldn't – couldn't – answer any of their questions. He left Jack to handle all that and retreated into his tent. Jack thought it best to just let people see for themselves.

Tate crossed himself and Bill swore. If De Falaise had been around right then, Jack knew Bill would have blown his head clean off with that shotgun he carried around. Granger wasn't surprised at all by the sight.

"He's even more twisted now than when I was at the castle," was his reply. "We should think about moving the camp – the kid may have told the Frenchman where to find us."

"No," Jack said with confidence. "He wouldn't have done that, no matter what. Besides, they'd be mad to come in here and risk being picked off. Not when they're banking on Robbie coming directly to them."

"Should someone go and see how Robert is?" Tate asked.

"Best to just let him gather his thoughts, I reckon," Jack told him. "Unless... has anyone seen Mary around today?" She'd be the only one who might be able to comfort him right now. Jack had noticed the way they'd been together lately, the body language. They seemed closer to each other than anyone else in camp, that was for sure.

"She was training with a bow and arrow last time I

saw her," offered Granger. "But that was last night sometime."

"Fair enough," said Jack.

"I still can't get over that poor mite back at the castle," lamented Tate, who'd been left holding Mark's bag.

"The best thing you can do is pray for him, just like you've been doing for that gal the Sheriff took." Jack straightened his cap. "And the best thing we can do is prepare for what's to come. You all know what you have to do."

They did, and they got on with it – more so now because of what they'd seen, throwing themselves into training to take their mind off it. Jack got on with the task of teaching some of the men wrestling moves.

But all the time his mind kept flashing back to that box, to the finger – and he couldn't help wondering how Robert was.

And how it would affect them all come the morning.

By evening Jack wasn't the only one worried.

At various moments other members of his gang had gone to the tent and asked Robert if he would like something to eat, if he wanted to see how the training was going. They'd received no response. Finally, Bill had said: "To buggery with this…" and gone inside. He emerged a minute or so later with a confused expression on his face.

"What is it?" Tate asked, limping over.

"The man's gone."

"What?" Jack came to join them now. "How can he be gone? We all saw him go in there."

More of the group stopped what they were doing and came over, desperate to find out what had happened to

Robert.

"Disappeared," reiterated Bill. "Bloody well vanished."

Tate looked for himself, not doubting Bill but needing to see it with his own eyes. "He's right," said the Reverend when he came out again.

"But... but where?" Jack said.

"'How the hell should I know?" said Bill. "Judas Priest! That's just effing great, that is. Eve of the big day and he's gone walkabout."

"He wouldn't do that," argued Jack.

"Wouldn't he? Perhaps what happened to Mark affected him even more than we realised..." Tate clicked his fingers. "Or he's gone off to try and rescue him alone. I do know he was having misgivings about dragging the rest of you into this."

"Is he off his head?" Granger said.

"It's been said before..." came a voice from somewhere. It was difficult to pinpoint, seeming to originate first from the left, then the right. "And to be honest, right now I'm not even sure myself."

Jack gave a grin. "Robbie."

"Where are you?" Tate shouted.

"I'm over here..." That definitely came from behind them. "Or am I here?" That was in front. The men looked first one way, then another.

When they turned back to the middle of the camp, though, there was Robert –leaning on his bow. They gazed at him, then at each other, unsure how to respond. Should they clap, as they would after a magician's trick? In the end Robert spoke up and saved them the trouble of deciding.

"Misdirection. It's the one thing we have on our side, the one thing that might help us to pull this off. While you were all busy training, not one of you noticed me slipping out, did you?"

There were mumblings, shakes of the head.

"When people are busy, they take their eye off the ball. I'm banking on that tomorrow. But I'm giving you one last chance to back out. I have to do this now, especially after..." He couldn't finish. Under his hood, they all knew the sadness that must be reflected on his face. Robert kept his 'mask' in place while he talked. "If anyone has cold feet, I wouldn't blame them."

No one said a thing, there weren't even any murmurs from the crowd.

"You're good men. You've restored my faith in human nature, something I never thought would happen. You give me a sense of hope, and I thank you for that."

Just then there was movement at the rear of the crowd. Everyone turned to see Mary standing there.

After a beat, Robert continued. "You all know the plan. You all know your roles. I know you won't let me down. If I should fall, you have to get the villagers... get Mark out. That is imperative above all else. I may not see you again, but you'll all remember what we did here in our time together, what we are about to do. And know that you have right on your side. Good hunting."

They did clap and cheer then – none of them caring whether the noise could be heard from outside the camp, possibly even outside the forest. It reminded Jack of soldiers from olden times before heading off to fight. We're about to do our Lord of the Rings thing, he thought.

Eventually the crowd broke up. The Hooded Man cast just one look back as he returned to his tent, over at Mary who was still watching him.

Then he disappeared inside.

He waited for some time, almost gave up on her – but in the end she came, as he knew she would.

Robert was sitting cross-legged on the floor, head down, hood covering his features. When Mary entered he didn't even look up, just said: "You came back, then?"

"Yes. I promised I would stand by you – that I would help in whatever way I could. I don't break my promises." There was a steely quality to her voice tonight that hadn't been there when they'd spoken yesterday. He recognised it, because he'd used it himself before.

"Actually, I'm not so sure you should have."

"You know, for a hero you really can be a wanker sometimes," she snapped.

Robert raised his head at that. "Is that what you came to tell me?"

"No." Mary dawdled at the entrance, not wanting to come too far in, but not wanting to be outside either. "I came back to wish you luck."

"Thanks..." He looked up at her properly now. "Mary, listen, when I said I'm not sure you should have come back I meant... I know you can take care of yourself and everything, I just wouldn't like to see something... I wouldn't want anything to happen to you."

"Like it has with Mark, you mean?"

He didn't answer.

"That's sweet, but I make my own decisions in life. You're about to go and get yourself captured or killed. Why shouldn't the rest of us? Why shouldn't I? Give me a reason, Robert."

"Because–" He said it a bit too forcefully, too hastily, then took an age to finish the sentence. "Because... I care about you."

"Yes. I know. We're friends, right?" Mary sighed. "That was quite some speech you gave out there, you know? You certainly have a way of rallying the troops."

"I just wanted them to know how... how much I've come to think of them."

"As for that little trick with the voice throwing; pretty nifty. Then appearing in the middle of them–"

"You were watching?"

"A-huh," she admitted. "I've been watching all day, saw you set the rope up – just like you've been teaching them. When you asked if anyone had seen you leave the tent; I did. I saw you Robert. I wasn't preoccupied."

Robert got to his feet.

"One day you'll be a legend, Robert Stokes. One day stories will be written about you, just like they wrote about him."

"Him?"

"You know who I mean. Your... predecessor."

"Oh."

Read to me Dad... Read some more...

Mary came a little more into the tent, hands behind her back. "I didn't just come here to wish you luck," she admitted at last.

"No?" He got up and moved forwards.

"No. I came to give you this..." She brought her hands out where he could see them, and she was holding one of the broadswords from her home. "You may as well look the part."

"I... I can't take that," said Robert.

"Yes you can. They might not let you keep it, but you never know. They might not even see it as a threat."

"One hell of a hunting knife, though," Robert said, with a lightness of tone that had been absent during the rest of the conversation. "Thank you."

"No need. Just take that stupid hood off and let me see you."

Robert pulled it back. "I meant what I said, you know. About another time and place..."

"I know." Mary smiled weakly. "But this is the only one we have."

He opened his arms and she walked into them. They held each other and both knew that this might be the last time they saw one another alive. Mary kissed him on the cheek. It felt like the end of everything, and in a very real sense it was. By that time tomorrow everything would have changed.

"I'm sorry," he whispered.

Mary whispered it back.

CHAPTER TWENTY-ONE

The two men remained like that for some time...

Hands at each other's throats, neither one willing to give ground. This was the final fight, their only 'real' fight in fact, and both men were desperate to win. The Hooded Man because he saw it as his mission to rid the world of this new infection; the Frenchman because he needed to pluck this thorn from his side before he could rule completely.

Tighter and tighter they grasped each other, spinning in the dreamscape – the fire on the water raging higher all around them.

Then one of them removed a hand. It was the Frenchman, reaching down, grabbing a hidden knife and bringing it up. It was too quick for The Hooded Man to block and he looked down, eyes wide, as the blade slid into him. It pierced his stomach, slipping through flesh and into him almost up to the hilt. He gave a cry and coughed up blood, his grip on his opponent's throat weakening.

Neither of them said a word; they didn't have to. It was obvious what had happened. The darkness had triumphed, winning out overall.

The time of the hero had almost passed.

And The Hooded Man would pass just as quickly into the arms of death.

De Falaise had woken with a smile on his face.

He couldn't remember all of the dream but he recalled the ending, recalled sliding the knife into Hood's gut and killing him.

Au revoir, he said to himself, *you've proved a worthy adversary, but it is time for this whole affair to draw to a close.*

The Frenchman looked over and saw the woman from Hope lying there, asleep. He contemplated waking her so that he could begin the morning by celebrating, but he had so much – too much to do. There would be time later, when he'd dealt with his enemy. All the time in the world, in fact; perhaps even time for a change. When she'd been getting dressed the last time he'd noticed his plaything was putting on a little bit of weight. He was obviously feeding her too well.

He'd got to bed late last night, after overseeing the last few hours of construction himself: the culmination of two days' labour. The men had worked hard, but then so they should have. They were doing it for their Sheriff. The platform and gallows were crude but sturdy. A series of six in a row so they could get through the executions as fast as possible, regardless of whether Hood showed up – though De Falaise was positive he would come. The platform, located out on the grass where Middle Bailey had once been, was high enough to accommodate the trap doors. These could be released by a single lever. That idea had been his and he'd explained in great detail how it could be achieved, muttering afterwards about the shortcomings of the British school system when it came to carpentry and woodwork.

What a sight it all was when it was finished, much better than simply hanging bodies over the sides of the rocks. This had style, flair – panache, as his people would say. It would be a spectacle; just one of the things that he would be remembered for. De Falaise had even appointed an official photographer, a soldier named Jennings who had an interest in such things and could develop film as well as take the actual photographs.

His inspiration had been the photos down in the basement of the castle, depicting all those different eras. One day, he realised, people would look back and remember what he had done here and applaud him for having the vision and bravery to pull it off. They would cheer his achievements, bringing Britain together again – perhaps even under a different name? Yes, something more fitting like... like Falaisia. That had a certain ring to it.

But he was taking small steps: towards a much larger goal. The only thing standing in his way was Hood and his malcontents. Once they were out of the way he could rule this region however he wanted. Build his army up even more, spread out and conquer from this one, fortified base.

It was his right, and his destiny.

One day those who came after him would look to his lead in governing their own lands. Just as he'd drawn from the past to establish his empire.

He'd left the woman and gotten into the outfit he'd handpicked for the day's proceedings – the red dress uniform adorned with medals and topped off with a ceremonial sword. Practically ignoring the new guard on duty outside his room De Falaise made his way down into the basement one last time. He had examined the history of this castle and its surrounding areas frequently, but only today did he feel like he was making a contribution to the museum. He would have his men erect some kind of memorial to his achievements before too long, continuing on the story of Nottingham and its castle.

De Falaise paused to examine the model of the place he now called home. Bending, he placed both hands on the glass cabinet.

"You are not just living history, De Falaise, you are

making it," he said to himself.

Next he made his way upwards through the castle and onto the roof, putting on his sunglasses as he went. He walked across to where Reinhart was camped out. He'd been up there for two days straight, watching the city – if not with his sniper's scope, then with the binoculars De Falaise had left him. The Dutchman was like a machine, never complaining, never faltering. Just watching, ever vigilant.

"Anything to report?" De Falaise asked.

Reinhart shook his head. "No unusual activity at all."

"And our scouts in the city?"

"Checking in as usual – once every half-hour."

"Good, good. We will begin the executions within the hour. If you see any sign of The Hooded Man..."

"I will let you know, my Lord," Reinhart promised, holding up his walkie-talkie.

So that was that. It only remained for them to ready the prisoners, roust them and get the first batch onto the platform. De Falaise would allow most of his men to watch, those who were not busy patrolling the walls, that was. It would serve as both example and, he hoped, entertainment. There was so little on TV these days.

As for The Hooded Man...

De Falaise would await his presence with eager anticipation.

Gwen felt De Falaise shift about in bed first thing, then heard him laughing as he woke. His dreams had obviously amused him. He'd been restless prior to that, though, just like he had been the night she missed her opportunity to kill him. She hadn't been able to find the right moment since.

She'd feigned sleep in the hopes that he would leave her alone, knowing that nine times out of ten he'd do whatever he damned well pleased, not giving a toss whether Gwen was awake or not. This was the tenth time, obviously, because he got up and got dressed, barely making a sound. If he had tried something then she might well have reached for the knife now under her pillow, ramming it into his throat as he groped her. He was clearly waiting until after the day's events for that particular 'delight'.

Not that she had any intentions of still being here then.

Not that she had any intentions of still being alive. Her plan was simple. Free the prisoners, kill De Falaise. Yes, she was aware she was just one woman. Yes, the odds were impossibly against her, but still she had to try.

She couldn't leave that young boy to his fate. Hopefully, he could lead them all back to his hideout where they'd be safe (*if you can get them past that nutjob on the roof with the sniper's rifle – don't forget about him, Gwen.*)

They had to make a run for it, at least. They'd be dead anyway if they stayed here.

She was surprised, given his heritage, De Falaise hadn't insisted on a guillotine. But then, they'd executed the nobility that way, hadn't they – and that's what De Falaise aspired to be. Hanging was for peasants and criminals, historically speaking. Today, it would be used to put an end to the lives of people like she'd known in Hope, who just wanted to get on with their existence from day to day; just wanted to forget about the horrors that had befallen them during The Cull.

You're thinking too far ahead, Gwen, she told herself. *First things first... The guard.*

She got up off the bed, grabbing her robe. She didn't have too long before she'd be expected to join De Falaise at the ceremony, wearing yet another ornate dress he'd picked out. Gwen had other ideas. She slipped on the silk, hastily fastening the dressing gown with the belt around the middle, and made her way to the door. Controlling her breathing again, she took hold of the handle and turned it, opening the door a crack.

There was the guard, sitting opposite and to the right: a yobbish-looking youth today with a scar across his jawline. He didn't appear to notice the door opening – obviously the perfect choice for a guard – so she had to cough to get his attention. Now he looked up, then stood, raising his rifle as he did so.

"E-Excuse me..." she said in a low voice.

"What are you doing out? It's not time for you to come out yet. The boss will go spare."

"I-I don't want to come out. I want you to come in." Gwen let the door open a bit further, hoping she'd read this one as well as the shy boy. The thug in front of her was a different kettle of fish – no virgin, and probably cut from the same cloth as De Falaise.

Well then, let's give him what he wants, shall we?

"You what?"

She crooked her finger. "I said I want you to come in, pass the time a little."

He licked his lips. "I-I can't. The boss would kill me. He was bad enough when I forgot to tell him about..." The soldier realised he'd said too much and shut up.

"About?"

"Doesn't matter."

"Is that why you pulled guard duty?" A blink of the eyes told her it was. "Can't be much fun, playing nursemaid."

"Isn't."

"Bet you'd rather be out there getting ready for the executions."

He nodded, grinning.

Oh, you're a piece of work. I might enjoy this after all.

"De Falaise has left me all alone, he's too distracted with the preparations. Didn't even have time to see to my needs. A woman has needs, you know." As before, she let her gown fall open a little way and she saw his eyes flash downwards. Unlike the other guard, though, they stayed there. It made her feel sick, but she knew it was just a means to an end. "What's your name?"

"Jace," he told her, eyes still cast downwards.

"That's a nice name, I like it. Why don't you come inside for a minute or two, so we can talk properly. Doesn't have to be long. No one will know. You can keep an eye on me much better from in here."

Jace looked left and right. "All right," he finally said.

She allowed him in and his eyes lit up when he saw the unmade bed. "I've heard what they say about you," he told her.

Gwen smiled, getting more and more into the part with each passing second. "And what do they say?"

"That you let him do things. All kinds of things to you."

She closed her eyes slowly and opened them again. "What would you like to do to me, Jace?"

His cheeks were glowing bright red, but there was none of the hesitation of the other soldier. Jace planted a kiss on her; rough, without any feeling. Gwen tolerated it, putting her arms around him, more in an effort to lead him to the bed than anything else. They inched their way across with her guiding him, until the backs of his legs hit the mattress. Gwen pushed him onto it, climbing on top.

Jace lay back, rifle still in his grip, so she bent down to kiss him again. Her robe fell open even more and his eyes were glued to her breasts. "That's right," she said seductively. "You get a good look..." Gwen bent further down, and while he was distracted she snaked her hand under the pillow and brought out the knife. She held it against his neck and, for a second or two, he didn't even realise what was going on. "Move and I'll slit your throat. I mean it!"

With her other hand she reached down and relieved him of the rifle.

She rose from the bed, putting the knife in her pocket and training the weapon on Jace. "Now, stand up and get undressed."

Jace still seemed bewildered, as if he couldn't quite understand how the situation had gone from one thing to the other.

"Fucking well get undressed!" she hissed, jabbing the barrel of the rifle in his direction. "Lose the sidearm first." Jace scrambled to his feet. With fumbling hands he undid the belt of his holster. "Slowly," Gwen warned him. He dropped it to the floor with a clunk, then began to take off his clothes. "All of them..." Gwen ordered, then laughed as he took off his boxers. "I don't know how you were expecting to do anything with that maggot."

"You fucking bitch!"

Gwen hefted the rifle and hit Jace squarely in the face with its butt, and with enough force to knock the beret from his head. He collapsed onto the bed, unconscious.

Quickly, Gwen took off her robe and began to get dressed in the uniform. It was loose in places, but would disguise her well enough to get to the caves. She tucked her auburn hair up into the beret, strapped on the holster – hiding the sharpened knife away in a front pocket of the combat trousers. Then she left Jace behind, opened the door a crack again to check that nobody was around, and slipped out.

Gwen was already on the ground level, so only had

to make a bolt for the exit to get outside. Rifle over her shoulder, she skirted the building, keeping her head down and praying that nobody would notice her. Thankfully everyone was busy today, men dashing to and fro, and hardly anyone gave her a second glance. Once she was on the other side of the castle, she saw she was too late.

The prisoners were already being led out from the caves under heavy guard – up the steps and into the light, hands shackled in front of them, shielding their eyes from the brightness. Gwen scanned the line as the soldiers forced them up at gunpoint, but she saw no sign of the boy.

Dammit, I waited too long...

What she did see, however, at the end of the line, was Javier. A thinner, more defeated-looking version of the Mexican, with a large plaster over one ear. But it was him. She'd never forget that face. What was he doing out of his makeshift cell? He was in uniform, too, but didn't look to be giving orders. If anything, he was just milling around observing what was going on. He didn't even appear to be armed.

Gwen ground her teeth. There was no way she could take on all the guards and free the prisoners, much to her regret – it would just get them killed all the quicker – but the temptation of taking some kind of revenge on Javier was simply too much to resist. Head down again, she made her way across to the far end of the line, striding confidently as if she belonged there.

Coming up behind Javier, she took the pistol out of its holster.

"Hello Major," she whispered, jamming her weapon into his ribs.

"Who–"

"Quiet..." she growled. "Let the soldiers go on ahead,

you're coming with me. We have unfinished business."

As the string of people and soldiers headed off in front, she steered Javier to the side and then marched him back down into the caves.

"And how is our prize this morning?"

Mark grimaced at the man who'd entered the upstairs room, the Sheriff as he called himself. He'd ordered Mark to be kept inside the castle for the last day or so, too valuable to be lumped in with the rest of the bunch. Tanek had kept a watchful eye on the pale boy, now strapped to another chair, to keep him from falling into unconsciousness, perhaps even dying. De Falaise couldn't have that... Not before his time, at any rate.

"Are you ready to be our star attraction?"

"G... Get stuffed," Mark managed, croaking out the words.

Tanek pulled his head back by the hair. "Show some respect."

De Falaise waved his hand. "It is all right, I understand totally. The boy is upset. But do not worry, you will soon see your beloved Hood again. If he doesn't just leave you here to hang."

Mark scowled.

"Bring him," De Falaise said to Tanek. "It will soon be time."

Tanek undid the bonds tying Mark to the chair and the prisoner almost collapsed. Picking up his crossbow, the big man dragged Mark to his feet and half carried him out of the room by the scruff of his neck, following the Sheriff to the landing. They made their way down the stairs, and out onto the eastern side of the castle. De Falaise led them towards the stone steps, overlooking where Mark and the other prisoners had been examined when they first arrived.

Now that area was looking very different. The platform for the gallows took up much of the space, with men still making final adjustments to the structure.

"What do you think? I may even leave it there for future occasions." De Falaise mused out loud.

Mark was quiet.

"I think our star attraction is lost for words, Tanek."

The big man nodded.

"In awe, I'd say," De Falaise went on. He bent, smiling. "How would you like to be the first to try it?" The man talked as if he'd just unveiled a new theme park ride.

Mark attempted to break free of Tanek's grasp but even with all his strength present he wouldn't have stood a chance.

"Better hope The Hooded Man comes for you, then," said De Falaise, chuckling, "but I'll let you into a little secret, shall I? It doesn't matter anyway. You are still going to die. You all will. Now come along, do not dawdle. We both have a date with the inevitable."

Gwen forced Javier back down the steps and into the now abandoned cave system. There were no soldiers or guards down here, as there were no prisoners left. It was just the two of them.

"Am I at least allowed to see who my executioner is?" he asked as Gwen ushered him onwards.

She stepped down and spun him around. "There – remember me now?"

He screwed up his eyes in the half-light. "Yes, I remember you."

"Then you remember what you did, to Clive... to me,

back in Hope."

Javier's eyes brushed the floor.

"He... He was the one good thing that's ever happened in my life," Gwen said, raw emotion in her voice. "He never mistreated me, never used me. He just wanted to give me the life I'd always dreamed about. But then you came along, you and the Sheriff."

"The 'Sheriff' is totally insane," Javier replied. "I once believed in him, but I was wrong. I was frightened."

"So you did it to save your own skin, is that it?" Gwen raised the gun higher, hand trembling. "Just like you turned the boy over to him."

Javier appeared shocked she knew about that, but he nodded a third time. "What can I say? I am a weak man. A selfish man."

"You enjoyed the power, though, anyone could see that. And you enjoyed killing Clive."

"No. That was an accident. If the holy man hadn't–"

"He was trying to stop you."

Javier shook his head. "If your friend hadn't argued in the first place..."

"He was protecting me, you idiot! He was killed because he was protecting the woman he loved, the place he loved. And now..." Her hand grew steadier, her aim true as she pointed the gun at his head. "Now you're going to feel what it's like to have your own brains blown out, Major."

Javier winced. "That is the second time I've heard such words in as many days, Señora."

"And what, you're scared? Good!"

He shook his head once more. "I am not scared of you. But I am scared of what waits for me when I die."

"Judged by a higher power, is that it?"

"Yes. That is why I say to you, put down the weapon. If you kill me like this you will be damned just as surely as

I am." He held out his hand for the weapon.

Gwen's laugh was harsh. "You've got to be kidding me!"

"No. I wish to save you this."

Her gun arm began shaking again, and it lowered a fraction. Only a fraction. Maybe he's right; are you really a killer? she asked herself. Won't that make you just as bad as him, as De Falaise? Isn't that why after all this time you still couldn't murder the Frenchman? Couldn't stick the knife in him and twist it? Not even to rid the world of his sickness?

Gwen shook her head. No, she had to do this. Do it to avenge Clive, for her own satisfaction – even if the man in front of her in no way resembled the bloated slug who'd driven into Hope. First Javier, then De Falaise.

She made her mind up.

Closing one eye, Gwen took aim.

The people from the villages were being herded onto the field by De Falaise's men.

One man looked over at the gallows and made a run for it. He didn't make it as far as the pathway before being gunned down. De Falaise clapped at the action, nodding curtly to the men who'd opened fire. Then he motioned for Tanek to bring Mark up to the platform.

Jennings, who had been taking shots of the crowd and capturing a general sense of the occasion, began to snap De Falaise.

"Where is that woman?" De Falaise said under his breath, hardly breaking his camera smile. "I told her to be here for the pictures."

"Shall I send someone for her?" asked Jennings before Tanek got a chance. This earned him a hateful look from the Frenchman's second.

"No, no, no. It is high time we started. It is her own fault if she misses it. I will think of a suitable punishment later." De Falaise called for five 'volunteers' from the crowd. The soldiers pushed forward the handful of people, at gunpoint. They were forced to climb the steps to the raised area, where a couple more soldiers placed their heads in the nooses. Tanek brought down the rope so that he could shove Mark's head into the gap.

The first six were ready.

"This is an historic occasion," De Falaise said, walking along in front of them, looking down at the faces of those who would be next and the soldiers he had allowed to watch. He resembled a game show host in front of an audience. "The first hangings in your country for over forty years. And not a moment too soon, I say. Stop jostling down there! If you are well behaved I might still let some of you live to tell of what transpired here today." De Falaise turned to the poor unfortunates about to be executed. "If any of you have anything to declare, it is too late now anyway." He tittered to himself. "I suppose I am not alone in my disappointment that the man you put so much stock in has not even bothered to show up. At least it tells you all that your faith was misguided. He is both a coward and a murderer, responsible for all your deaths."

De Falaise looked across at the soldier holding the lever. He held his hand up, ready to give the signal.

When his radio crackled into life.

"My Lord..." came a voice over the airwaves. De Falaise raised an eyebrow, looking down at the walkie-talkie hanging from his belt. "My Lord, The Hooded Man is here. Repeat: The Hooded Man is here!"

CHAPTER TWENTY-TWO

Reinhart couldn't figure it out.

He'd had his scope trained on the city below, moving left and right, taking in as far as a mile ahead of him. None of the teams had reported anything suspicious, all checking in on their half-hourly rota as per normal. Then, suddenly, there he was. The Hooded Man. As large as life, walking up Friar Lane towards the main entrance to the castle. Reinhart blinked several times. He couldn't believe what his eyes were telling him. It was as if the man had just appeared out of nowhere.

In reality, he knew Hood must have come out of one of the buildings nearby when he wasn't looking. But how had he come this far into the city without any of them knowing?

Reinhart watched as the man proceeded slowly up the road, bow and arrows on his back, that trademark hood of his pulled down over his face. There was something dangling at his hip as well, which glinted in the morning sunlight. It was a sword. So this was the person who had caused them so much trouble? Hardly looked like a threat at all. Why, with one bullet Reinhart could just end his life right there and then. No more problems. De Falaise would probably thank him for it.

Or would he?

The Dutchman knew his superior wanted to do that job personally. Had arranged all this just for that purpose, in fact. Quickly, he snatched up the radio and called it in.

Within seconds De Falaise had answered him back. "You are quite sure?"

"I am," confirmed Reinhart.

"Very well. Keep your eye out for anything else

suspicious." Reinhart heard De Falaise switch to the other channel, ordering his men at the gates not to open fire on pain of death. He was glad now he hadn't acted so rashly.

By this time Hood had reached the entranceway, passing beneath a tree briefly, then vanishing out of Reinhart's sight at the gatehouse.

But he heard the knock as The Hooded Man demanded entrance.

De Falaise gazed down the incline, towards the gatehouse.

They all heard the banging on the old doors, a fist smacking the wood.

He was aware that his free arm was still in the air, frozen at the moment of ending the six prisoners' lives. Slowly, he withdrew that arm – staying the execution for now. He had other – more pressing – things to deal with first.

Even if he hadn't just aborted the hangings, De Falaise doubted whether the order would have been obeyed. The soldier at the lever was staring down at the gate as well, along with the assembled crowd.

The banging came again.

"Sir..." A crackle over the radio reminded him he still had it in his grasp. "Sir, should we let him in?" This was a soldier at the gate.

The Sheriff brought the radio to his lips. "Yes, of course, you imbecile. Open the gate. This is what I have been waiting for. He is just one man, alone. He is not to be interfered with."

De Falaise walked to the very edge of the platform, Tanek joining him.

Several men ran out of the buildings at the gatehouse,

clambering to undo the huge doors.

"Come on, come on!" De Falaise said under his breath.

The doors opened wide and The Hooded Man stood there, a dark figure in the shadows. He took a step forward, then another. The men at the gate watched him pass.

In spite of the fact The Hooded Man had his bow slung over his back and a sword at his hip, the men there did nothing to take them. They'd been told not to interfere with the visitor, so they didn't. It wasn't as if the man could do anything with such antiquated weapons anyway, not before being gunned down.

The Hooded Man strode up the pathway, his gait confident, his head bowed so that they still couldn't make out much of his features.

He began up the incline, and as he did so De Falaise's men at the rear of the crowd ran to the edge and trained their guns on him. The Hooded Man gave the war memorial on his right a glance, then continued up the snaking path, until finally he reached the summit – steps that led up to the East Terrace on his left, the crowd and the platform on his right.

"So," shouted De Falaise, holstering his radio, "you finally came."

The Hooded Man moved forwards, still with dozens of guns trained on him. One false move and he'd be torn to pieces, with no forest to cover him or swallow him up this time. Now he was on De Falaise's home turf.

A strange thing happened as he walked towards the crowd. To begin with, the nearest few people moved aside – they didn't really have much of a choice, as the man was coming no matter what. It caused a ripple effect, and soon another path had been created for him up towards the platform. Like a human version of the Red Sea, the people – soldiers and prisoners alike – parted almost as one, creating a safe passageway for him.

The Hooded Man walked through them, looking neither left nor right. But the people stared. If there was to be anything worthy of record today, then it was this – something Jennings also recognised as he snapped off several pictures of the event. De Falaise glared across at him and he lowered the camera slowly.

"Sorry."

"Take as many as you like when I kill him," said the Sheriff.

The Hooded Man was almost at the steps to the platform. He paused there, looking up slightly at the wooden construction. At Mark, slumping in his noose; it was the only thing keeping the boy on his feet.

"Do you like my new little toy?" De Falaise asked.

In a low voice, The Hooded Man replied: "Every pantomime villain needs a stage."

De Falaise pouted. "Why do you not come up onto my stage, then, and participate in the production."

The Hooded Man accepted this invitation, but drew out the act, taking one step at a time. For De Falaise, the wait was agonising, and he nearly ordered Tanek to put a bolt through the man's head immediately. But he wasn't quite finished with Hood yet – not after everything he'd put him through. For one thing he needed to see his face; needed to look into his eyes. If he was to let some of these peasants go today to tell the tale, he wanted them to spread the word about the death of Hood. How the Sheriff of Nottingham – *by Christ, of Britain!* – humiliated him first, then shot him... no, wait, slit his throat... no, perhaps strangle him? De Falaise realised he'd given absolutely no thought whatsoever as to how he would actually finish this. How he would see an end to The Hooded Man, who was still wearing that damned piece of clothing even now: his trademark, his mask. Then he remembered the sabre hanging from his hip. It mirrored Hood's own sword, one which he would never get to use. That was a good way – with Jennings documenting proceedings for posterity.

De Falaise realised that up until now The Hooded Man had stolen most of his thunder. Walking through the streets of Nottingham, only letting himself be seen when he wanted to, that business at the gates, even the crack about pantomime villains. But he would have the last laugh. He would win, just like he always won.

"Good. And now, I think it is time," De Falaise began, "time that we all saw what The Hooded Man looked like. Time to see that he is not a legend at all, far from it. He is just a man. Just a man."

The two faced each other on the platform, just metres apart. De Falaise stepped forwards, hands raised. His enemy was being covered, not only by the men near the platform, but also Tanek with his crossbow and Reinhart above since Hood had come into the grounds. He felt safe enough approaching his enemy. But before De Falaise could get close enough to do the deed himself, his rival reached up and grasped the sides of the hood.

It fell back, revealing more delicate features than De Falaise had been expecting. Much more delicate – beautiful, in fact. Full lips, chiselled cheekbones, and the deepest hazel eyes he'd ever seen. As the hood dropped a length of long, dark hair fell with it, trailing down the back.

De Falaise removed his sunglasses slowly and dropped them on the platform.

The girl stared at him and said: "I hear you have a problem with strong women?"

The Sheriff looked at Tanek, as if expecting answers from him. "What is this?"

But before anyone could reply, and just as he was turning back to face the woman who had pretended to be

Hood – who surely couldn't be Hood? – the first gunshots were already being fired.

It had been their signal to move.

Seeing Robert through the binoculars, approaching the gates, knocking on them – knowing most of the eyes at the castle would be on The Hooded Man at the other end of the wall, it was their opportunity to make a break for it. Though Granger had serious doubts about whether Tate would be able to make the short sprint across the street to the Trip to Jerusalem pub; then, skirting the sides of the buildings through the Brewhouse Yard, before breaking cover so that they could gain entrance at the barred door of the caves. It was fortified now, Granger knew that, men posted on guard round the clock. But they had the element of surprise on their side.

That had been part of the plan Robert outlined, inspired by Mark's hidden incursions into the towns and cities. To use the buildings of Nottingham to hide their own journey – going through them rather than around them. "The quickest way between two points has always been a straight line," Robert had told them. "Like an arrowhead passing through a target."

The teams had entered during the night, silently picking off or capturing the lookouts placed around the city and leaving some of their men behind to answer the radio check-ins. They'd reported no activity, every half-hour, while the rest of them had made their way through the buildings that hid them. It was just like being back in the forest, except it was concrete and stone now masking their presence rather than wood and foliage. The same principles applied, though. And that psychotic on the roof of the castle, who would definitely be on the case today, wouldn't even see them coming – hopefully – until it was too late.

For his part, Robert had entered the city alone. He would wait until it was time and then make his appearance, at which point they would make their move.

It was risky, crossing the street and heading towards Brewhouse Yard, but worth it if they could get into the castle that way.

Tate had surprised them all, moving pretty sprightly for a man with a stick. Now that would be used as a weapon, the only weapon he would carry in fact. It was his choice.

Granger wondered if he would have felt better using a rifle at this stage of the operation, but understood the reasons why Robert suggested bows and arrows – so as not to tip off the rest of the soldiers inside the castle too early.

The barred door usually had about three guards on it, but when the group of eight men reached the edge of the rock and Granger grabbed a quick look around the corner, he saw that number had tripled today. De Falaise was obviously taking no chances with security – and who could blame him? Granger held up fingers to show how many guards there were.

The only thing they had in their favour was that to all intents and purposes, none of Robert's men had joined him on his lonely walk up to the castle. As far as anyone knew, he was all alone.

"When we do this," Granger whispered, "we have to do it quickly. We can't afford to have any gunfire alerting the rest of them."

The men nodded. He felt like he was finally in charge again, at least of his squadron. It was payback time for Ennis and the other Jackals. "Ready?"

More nods.

"Wait a moment," Tate said, gripping his arm. Granger thought there was something wrong, or someone had seen them, but then the Reverend closed his eyes and said a prayer. He finished it by crossing himself.

"Nice to know we have the big guns on our side," said Granger, smiling.

"Always, my son," Tate told him. "Always."

Granger slipped an arrow into his bow. "Right, let's do it." He came out from hiding, loosing the arrow as he ran. It hit the first of the guards, a man he actually recognised now the closer he came as Oaksey – a nasty piece of work. It caught him in the shoulder, though Granger had been aiming lower, and he went spinning back into another guard. Meanwhile, the men behind Granger were all letting off their arrows as well, with varying degrees of success. Some found their homes in legs or sides, others in upper arms. Only one guard fell right away, when an arrow shot straight into his throat.

None of them had a chance to fire back. They didn't even have the opportunity to raise their rifles before the hail of projectiles thumped into them. Now those who were wounded were too preoccupied to think about their guns, crying out in pain at the wounds the arrows had inflicted.

Well, that was a piece of cake, thought Granger, then saw that the extra guards outside weren't the only security measure De Falaise had added. There was a flash of a muzzle from inside the barred door. The bullets howled past Granger, taking down a man to his right, killing him outright.

"Get down!" Granger called back, but knew they were sitting ducks out in the open. Lying down, they couldn't fire back with their bows and arrows. Not that they had to anymore. Shots had been fired, the cat was out of the bag, and his men drew their pistols, primed their own rifles – firing back at the door in the cave. Their own bullets sparked off the rocks which protected the men inside, none of them hitting their targets.

Shit! Granger tried to wriggle backwards, but enemy fire chipped away at the floor around him. We're going to die out here.

So much for having the Big Guy on their side. Just like before, there was nobody who would help Granger except himself.

Even here at the end, when he was a part of this, whatever it was, miles away from his 'home', he was going to die alone.

Jack peered out of the window.

He'd been looking out long before Robbie broke cover, mainly because there was nothing else to do while he was stuck here. They'd entered the building from the rear, knowing it was directly opposite the metal gates at the side of the castle, and afforded a view of what was happening in the grounds too. Jack had seen the preparations for the hangings, seen the prisoners being led out on the grass, followed by De Falaise and the man he knew as Tanek, dragging Mark up onto the platform. The kid looked as white as milk, hardly surprising after what he'd been through. But, as if that wasn't enough, they were now fixing to put his neck in a noose.

Jack had almost charged out there with his team right then. Even if he hadn't had the handful of fighters with him, he probably would have done it anyway. He felt like he could just rip down those metal side gates and take on the whole of De Falaise's army single-handed at that moment.

But he had to wait for Robbie, had to do this the way

they'd discussed. The kid meant more to him than any of them – and vice versa Jack suspected. He had to give Robbie the chance to act. So what was keeping him?

Finally, just as the six people – including Mark – were about to be executed, Robert appeared. Hood drawn as usual, he'd made his way coolly to the main castle gates. Jack had watched, anxiously, as De Falaise countered the order to hang them, and he breathed a deep sigh of relief.

"Here's where all the fun begins, guys," Jack said over his shoulder to his team. But as he kept watching, waiting for his cue, he could tell something wasn't quite right. It was to do with Robbie's walk, his height. In fact, the more closely Jack looked, the more convinced he became that it wasn't his leader down there after all, but an impostor.

The question was: *Who?*

That particular mystery was cleared up when the person in the hood stepped up onto the platform and revealed their face.

Jack let out a sharp breath. "Mary? What the blazes is she doing in there?" As far as he knew she was with one of the other strike teams about to hit the front wall of the castle, or at least that had been the strategy. When had that changed, and how come Robbie hadn't informed the rest of them?

Where the devil was he, anyway?

The sound of gunfire broke into his thoughts. Mary or Robbie, it made little difference to the plan – it was still a distraction. What could mess it up completely would be if their men were already being shot at, as appeared to be happening somewhere.

"Time to kick the bad guys' butts," he shouted and opened the door. The men behind Jack covered him with a hail of bullets and arrows, as he ran and tossed two grenades at the barricade. The explosion blew the metal inwards, buckling it and causing the side gates to swing back on their hinges. Jack ran towards them, staff in hand. Two soldiers with rifles were firing at him through the smoke, but he dropped to the ground, rolled, and came up sharply – jabbing with his staff to catch one in the face, then swinging it around and knocking the legs out from under the other.

"You've just been Jack-Hammered!" he said to the felled soldiers. Then he rose and led his team into the grounds of the castle.

At the same time all this was going on, three more teams were making their assault on the castle from the front, springing from buildings that ran adjacent to the wall.

Reinhart could see them, but couldn't take them all out at once – especially when he had his rifle trained on the site of the old Middle Bailey. He was only one man. Then there was the explosion, and more of The Hooded Man's – woman's? – men were pouring in from the side entrance. It was impossible to keep up with what was happening in several different locations at once.

You should not be here – any of you! Reinhart shouted inside his own head. He was used to one, two, maybe even three or four targets at once, not multiples from many different angles. Luckily there were men on the walls that were shooting at the other assault teams; they could hold them off for a little while. That's what this castle was good at, defending against invaders.

Just then he heard something – a faint sound in the distance. He turned to see the dot on the horizon... which was reducing the distance between them fast.

And there was the distinctive sound of helicopter blades cutting through the air. *They must have been keeping low, out of his range, waiting, hiding, before rising up to let themselves be seen, Reinhart thought to himself. Clever. Very clever.*

But it did mean that his targeting options were now more simple. He had to focus on the helicopter, which was obviously designed to give support to the men on the ground. They didn't have anything they could put in the air to meet it and no one else was ready to fire on it. He couldn't take the chance that it wasn't armed, either.

The choice had been made for him.

Reinhart swung his rifle around. He looked through the scope to see a man in a checked shirt, with a tatty tank top pulled over it, piloting the chopper. The scope was so good that he could even see the man's ruddy features, an indication that he'd spent a lot of time outdoors – a lot of time at Sherwood. But he wasn't alone. In the passenger seat was another man, younger, wearing the cobbled-together uniform of De Falaise's men, albeit slightly bloodstained. Another traitor to the cause? Something told him different. It wasn't just the fact he had a bow and arrow with him, because many of Hood's men were carrying those ridiculous weapons: it was something about the way he held it, something about the steely look of determination in his eyes.

This was Hood, the real one. Reinhart had never been so sure of anything in his life. He aimed at the man, then remembered De Falaise's orders about wanting to take out his enemy himself. Were they still relevant now that chaos reigned down there?

And what about afterwards, when they're all dead and you have to explain to De Falaise how you killed his prize? What will he do to you then? Reinhart thought. *Take down the chopper, but don't kill them. Cause them* to make an emergency landing and then radio De Falaise to let him know.

It was a plan indeed. After all, what harm could they do from this distance? Put an arrow in him? Hardly.

Reinhart smiled and closed one eye, aiming for the side of the helicopter. "Time to bring you down to earth now, birdy."

He squeezed the trigger.

A couple more shots rang out in the cave entrance. Granger saw the muzzle flash and ducked, but nothing flew past him. Raising his head slightly, he heard more bangs – saw the cave light up – and it was then that he realised the shots were on the inside.

Then there was silence.

Nothing moved in the cave entrance, no rifles poked out and took pot shots at the men spreadeagled on the ground.

"What's happening?" shouted one of the men behind him.

"Not sure," Granger called back. "Stay down." He got up, keeping his bow raised in case a sudden volley was let loose – and wondering what good it would do him anyway. Then a figure appeared at the gate, a woman with auburn hair that he recognised.

"Hold your fire," he called out.

"Gwen!" This was Tate, who was already getting up, albeit with a little difficulty, using his stick for support.

"Reverend?" came the reply.

Granger watched as the woman who had been De Falaise's love slave worked to open the door with keys she'd taken from the felled soldiers. He motioned his men to move forwards, but still keep low.

When Tate reached the gate, Gwen had it open already and she fell into the holy man's arms.

"My God, I can hardly believe it. Are you all right?" he asked her when they separated, but she didn't answer. Instead she shouldered the still smoking rifle she'd used to dispatch the men laying on the floor, and pointed up the sandstone steps.

"You can get into the grounds this way – it's pretty clear. I got rid of any soldiers you might run into between here and there, but can't say there won't be more once you leave the caves. They're bound to have heard the shooting." When Granger and the other men looked at her blankly, she said. "Look, follow me. But promise me one thing when we get there."

"What's that?" asked Granger before Tate could.

She looked at him. "I know you, don't I?"

"I used to be here at the castle before–"

"Yes, I thought so." Gwen unslung her rifle, as if to shoot him.

"Wait, wait..." Tate put himself between them. "Things have changed since Granger was in the Frenchman's army. Unlike the Sheriff, Robert – the person you know as The Hooded Man – gave him a choice. A real choice," Tate explained to her. "Granger's here of his own free will. He's here to fight De Falaise. So are all these men who once served him."

"He killed the best friend I ever had," Granger told her. "I'm sorry I couldn't do anything to help you when you were here, but I'd have been killed on the spot. You know yourself that he never needs much of an excuse. But..." He shrugged. "Well, I'm here now."

"I could have... should have been dead by now," she said, but Granger saw her eyes soften, and the rifle lowered. "We'll discuss this later. We're wasting time." Gwen turned to lead them up the steps.

"Hold on," said Tate. "You didn't finish what you were saying, Gwen. What did you want us to promise?"

The auburn-haired woman cast a glance over her shoulder. "To leave the Sheriff alive," she said in a serious tone. "At least until I get to him. He's mine!"

De Falaise had flinched when he heard the first round of gunshots. But that was nothing compared to the explosions down below at the castle's side gates.

The woman in front of him had used the distraction to knock an arrow and aim her bow – shooting at the soldiers closest before they could do a thing. He thought he heard her say something that sounded very much like, "Yay me." Though some went wide, as if she hadn't quite got the hang of it yet, most of the arrows found their mark, diminishing the numbers around the platform.

A much smaller arrow whistled past her, and when De Falaise looked he saw that Tanek had taken the shot with his crossbow. But what should have gone into her cranium missed because of the boy. Perhaps spurred on by what was happening, Mark had somehow found the strength to raise his hands, lift his head out of the noose, and then swing over to where Tanek was standing, letting go when he reached the right spot.

The lad flopped onto the larger man rather than landing gracefully, and although he spoilt Tanek's aim, couldn't hang on to him. Mark slid down the length of his body – helped by a shrug from the giant himself.

Just as Tanek was about to stamp on the boy, a second man – who matched Tanek in height – leapt up onto the platform. He was carrying what appeared to be a staff in one hand.

"I'd advise against that, buddy," said the guy in an American accent. Then he smacked Tanek across the face with a balled fist. Tanek took the blow, his face shunted to the side, though not by much. Then he hit the man wearing the cap, squarely in the chest – and he went back by a couple of steps. It was like watching a colossal clash of the titans.

Tanek raised his crossbow to take a shot at the other giant, but before he could fire another bolt the man lashed out with his staff, knocking the weapon to the floor. Tanek ran at him, nimble for a man of his size, and swatted the staff aside. Both fell backwards heavily onto the already creaking platform.

The other villagers waiting to be hung, seeing now that there was a chance of escape, as well as a possibility that the soldier with the lever might accidentally get knocked and pull it anyway, followed Mark's lead. Unhooking themselves with their bound hands, they leapt from their places, fleeing the scene as quickly as they could. The soldier in charge of the lever – seeing no further use for his services – hopped off the back of the platform, swiftly followed by Jennings and his camera.

Which left De Falaise facing the woman, the impostor who had started all this. In the absence of Hood, he decided to take it out on her. Afraid of strong women, indeed, she had simply thrown him momentarily...

He drew his sabre and slashed it through the air, catching her bow and sending it flying out into the panicked crowd. It was difficult to see now who was guard and who was prisoner, mixed up as they were, but every now and again there was a hint of uniform, a rifle barrel to show allegiance.

The woman, unperturbed by losing one weapon, drew her broadsword. She met De Falaise's strike with not inconsiderable strength. The two of them came together, hilts of their respective blades sliding upwards, and he only just managed to back away before she kicked out – hoping to catch him between the legs.

De Falaise's face soured.

"Not used to fighting a woman, are you?" she goaded him. "Used to them playing nicely, eh?"

He came at her again, the sabre swishing as it narrowly missed her. She leaned first one way, then another, countering his next swing with one of her own, before hefting the sword and almost opening up his belly.

There was a sound from above, heard even over the rage of gunfire. The thrump-thrump-thrump of a helicopter. It had been so long since De Falaise had heard the noise of rotor blades that he stopped what he was doing and looked. Shots rang out from the rooftop of the castle, hitting the side of the machine, but as De Falaise kept his eyes trained on the scene, someone leaned out of the side of the chopper and attempted to fire a bow and arrow.

When he looked down again, he saw that the woman was also gazing upwards – mouth wide in surprise. He took his opportunity, to make her as 'compliant' as the others females he had known, to knock the fight out of her as someone should have done long ago. De Falaise gripped the handle of the sabre and punched her with the hilt, splitting her lip open with the guard of the blade.

Her cry was music to his ears. She toppled backwards, losing her grasp on her sword. De Falaise grinned wildly. Whatever else was happening around them, he was winning his particular fight...

"How's the head?" Bill asked as they'd manoeuvred in and out of buildings, keeping low to avoid detection.

Robert let out a soft moan by way of a reply. Whatever

Mary had stuck him with had left one stinker of a headache behind. The last thing he'd remembered was them hugging goodbye, then something in his shoulder – the prick of a needle.

"I'm sorry," she'd said, as he slumped forward into her arms. But all he could think was: *why are you doing this? Had she been a spy of De Falaise's all along? Impossible. The Sheriff's men had been attacking her when they arrived at the farmhouse.*

Then there were no more thoughts, just dreams. The same one he'd had many times before, where he'd faced De Falaise. This time the balance was shifting, the darkness was winning.

He'd come to at some point in the early hours of that morning. Sitting up in the tent, he felt his head spin and nausea rise. What had she injected him with, that same stuff from when he'd been shot? Or something else, something stronger she'd found in the supplies?

"There was all kinds of stuff in the medical packs..."

Whatever it was it packed more of a punch than any fist.

Robert looked down and realised that his clothes were gone again, stolen. He glanced to his right and saw the clipboard with the sketch on Mary had drawn. Him with and without his hood. It was then that he'd had the first inklings of what she was intending to do. "No... Mary, what were you thinking?"

Snatching up his bow and arrows, and the sword she'd given him, he'd staggered from the tent wearing virtually nothing. It didn't matter, because there was nobody in the camp apart from a sleeping Mills, tied to a tree. All Robert's men had left to put the plan – his plan – in motion. The only problem was they'd left without him!

He looked up at the sky and saw the first hints of light there. Whatever Mary had used had put him out for most of the night. But there was still a slim chance. Robert raced round, grabbing clothing where he could find it – spare bits of uniforms mainly. Then, though his head was pounding fit to burst, he ran through the forest he knew so well, taking a short cut to try and reach Bill. With a bit of luck he wouldn't have set off yet.

Robert just about made it, propelling himself from the trees just as Bill was preparing to take off. He'd waved his hands to attract the man's attention, but when that hadn't worked, Robert had fired an arrow across the front of the helicopter's nose bubble. Bill had looked over, mouthing the words 'Judas Priest!' when he saw Robert.

"Yer supposed to be in the city," he said as Robert climbed inside and put on the headset. "Left ages ago."

"That was Mary," explained Robert. "I'll tell you about it when we get in the air." And he had, waiting until they were well on their way before offering his hypothesis.

Bill tutted. "What's she playin' at? Lass'll get herself killed."

Robert knew exactly what she was doing, and why, but he didn't say anything. He just instructed Bill to follow the plan as if nothing had happened. They'd assess the situation when they reached Nottingham.

They came in low over the city. If all had gone well then De Falaise's spotters on the ground had now been replaced by theirs, but they couldn't risk using the radios to check in case frequencies were being monitored.

"We 'aven't been shot down yet. That's a good sign," Bill commented. He kept low until dawn had broken completely, then he lifted the helicopter up above the rooftops and began their run.

By the time they reached the castle, everything was kicking off. "Looks like the party's already started." Bill pushed the chopper forward, dipping the nose to gain more speed.

Robert had his face pressed against the glass, looking down at his men attacking on several fronts – Jack from the north; Granger and Tate from the south; the rest from the east. It was the latter who were encountering the most resistance from the soldiers on the walls firing at them. Robert also saw the crowd and the gallows, making out the figures of De Falaise, a huge man who had to be Tanek, a smaller figure who was undoubtedly Mark – and a person dressed in his clothes. "Mary," he said.

Even as he watched, he saw Jack tackle Tanek – quite possibly the only man who could stand a chance against him at close range – then De Falaise and Mary's duel begin.

There was a heavy ping as a bullet ricocheted off the side of the Sioux. "That were too close for comfort!" Bill exclaimed. "Looks like we got our man there's attention."

Robert took his eyes off the scene below and refocused on the castle rooftop. There was the sniper Granger and the others had told him about, and he had his weapon trained on them.

"Think you can keep us alive long enough for me to take him out?" Robert asked Bill.

"Aye."

Bill zigzagged the chopper and Robert saw now what the man meant about manoeuvrability. If they'd attempted this in any one of the planes from the museum they'd have crash-landed.

Robert opened the door of the helicopter, wrapping one thigh around the safety belt and using it to hold him while he leaned out. He didn't dare look down, and kept his mind totally on the job at hand. This was a tricky shot, especially while the chopper was moving, and with the sniper still firing at them, but Robert shut everything else out apart from the gunman and the threat he posed.

Time slowed down; he was back in the woods, in the forest, hunter versus prey. Robert slipped an arrow into his bow, drawing it back as far as he could.

Bill helped him by bringing the chopper sideways on, though he couldn't hold the position for long. It would be a case of who fired first, and who was the most accurate shot.

"Now! Y'have to take it now!" Bill shouted.

Robert let out the breath he'd been holding, then let go of the arrow. At the same time the sniper fired off another shot.

The sniper's round grazed the back end of the Sioux, but it was Robert's arrow that had the most impact. It rocketed through the sniper's scope and straight into his eye. The man let out a howl that could be heard above everything else. Flailing around, his hip caught the edge of the roof's wall and he went over.

"Shot!" Bill clapped Robert on the shoulder as he eased himself back inside.

The helicopter made a strange noise that sounded like a cough. That cough turned into a splutter and Bill wrestled with the controls.

"What's happening?"

"Must've nicked somethin'," Bill told him, stating the obvious.

"Can you get us in lower, I need to help Mary and put those soldiers on the wall out of commission."

"We'll be goin' in lower, all right," said Bill as the chopper took a turn downwards.

It was the speed they were coming in at that Robert didn't care for. He glanced at Bill, who threw a look back, and they both focussed their attention on the ground that was coming towards them fast.

They saw no more soldiers on their way up through the caves. Only when they reached the exit did some of De Falaise's men begin shooting.

Granger and his group returned fire, picking them off with bullets and arrows alike. It was Tate who pointed out that the men on the walls needed to be incapacitated first. "Try just to wound or injure if you can. The fewer deaths the better," advised the Reverend.

"Tell that to them," replied Granger, nodding at the soldiers with machine guns. "They're not holding back on our men outside." But they took it on board and, where possible, fired to debilitate rather than kill.

Gwen ran off ahead on her own, desperate to reach the Middle Bailey and find De Falaise. Tate limped after her, knocking one soldier out with his stick and taking another one down with a series of simple judo moves.

"Gwen, wait! God will provide his own revenge," promised the Reverend. But just then he got caught in a crossfire of bullets and was hit in the shoulder. Gwen turned and doubled back to check on him. She pressed his own hand against the shoulder and told him to keep pressure on it.

"I have to go," she told him firmly.

"Gwen..." mumbled Tate, but she was already on her way to stop De Falaise.

CHAPTER TWENTY-THREE

Gwen strode through the grounds of the castle, spraying bullets from her rifle as if she was dealing with a bug infestation.

She was out of ammo by the time she reached the Middle Bailey where the bulk of the action was taking place. So she cast the rifle aside and took out her pistol – the one she'd used to murder Javier.

No, she hadn't simply killed him outright in the end, had she? Appropriately, it had been more by accident than intent. Just as she'd been wrestling with what to do, gunfire had echoed through the caves: Granger and Tate attacking the south side entrance. It had proved enough of an interruption for Javier to make a play for the gun, spluttering that he mustn't die, couldn't risk what would happen to him if he did.

Javier had grabbed the weapon and they'd wrestled with it. He'd almost turned it around on her when she summoned strength from somewhere, jostling him back against the wall. His hands had closed around the pistol, forcing her finger on the trigger and the sudden bang had made them both jump. Her because of the noise. Javier because the bullet had entered his chest.

She backed away from him as he clutched at the wound – tried to stem the blood pouring from it – then he reached out with one of his shaky hands. "You... You must forgive me, señora... please... before it's too late."

Gwen shook her head firmly. "Damn you."

He smiled, though it was more of a grimace. "I... I am already damned..." The light went out in his eyes, and he slumped to the floor.

Gwen stepped over the body. "For you, Clive," she whispered. Then the sound of gunfire came again, snapping her out of her daze. The castle was under attack. It had to be Hood's men, an attempt to stop the executions. She had to go and help.

Holstering the pistol, she'd unslung her rifle and followed the sound to the fight. Before long Gwen came upon the soldiers defending the lower cave entrance. They'd turned in her direction, but before they could fire she'd pulled the trigger of her own rifle, filling the cave with light and sound.

It had paved the way for Granger and his men to enter, for them to begin taking down De Falaise's regime. Whether or not Granger could be trusted still remained to be seen – he hadn't lifted a finger to help her when she was being held captive – but she'd deal with that later. Right now, she had a mission... a promise to keep.

And absolutely nothing was going to stand in her way.

Jack wrestled with Tanek on the platform. He tried using some of his moves on him, but the olive-skinned man had a few of his own.

A swift elbow in Jack's stomach saw him releasing his grip. In seconds, Tanek was up and had a dagger drawn. He was just about to plunge it into Jack when he paused, his eyebrows twitching. Then he looked down.

Jack's eyes followed and discovered what had made him hesitate. There was a bolt from a crossbow sticking out of his calf. Tanek scowled, but before he could do anything, another bolt hit him – this one in the side. Jack traced its trajectory to Mark lying on the floor. Resting on his stomach, the boy had the crossbow propped up and was shooting at Tanek.

Jack took the opportunity to rise and land an uppercut

– not a legal move in wrestling, but something that came in handy when the referee wasn't looking. Tanek reeled backwards, but didn't fall. Instead, he cleared his head, then threw the dagger in Mark's direction. It missed the boy by inches as he rolled over, letting go of the crossbow in the process. Jack came at Tanek again, but this time the giant sidestepped him, bringing down his own fist on the base of Jack's neck – sending him crashing into one of the wooden gallows.

Tanek stalked over towards Mark, snatching up the crossbow where it had fallen. Jack attempted to get up, but failed. All he could do was watch as Tanek picked out the bolts like splinters, still not making a sound even though he must have been in agony.

Tanek looked down at Mark and pulled a strange face – halfway between a smirk and a scowl – then he turned the crossbow on the boy who'd caused him so much trouble.

Now that the gunmen on the walls were falling, Granger saw that their own men had begun climbing up the other side using grappling hooks and ropes. They were swinging over the tops and taking out more of the guards.

In the grounds, confusion reigned supreme. Gunshots were ringing out and nobody really knew who was firing at who. De Falaise's army was bigger, but they were panicking.

Granger spotted Tate as he was making his way towards the Middle Bailey. The Reverend assured Granger he was okay, and begged him to go after Gwen, so he left one of his squad to look after him.

She didn't take much finding. The auburn-haired woman was striding through the mayhem, shooting at anything that moved until her rifle was spent. Granger ran off after her just as she was pulling out her pistol.

But there was a soldier behind her, off to her right, aiming his gun at her head. Quickly, Granger loaded an arrow and pulled back the twine. He let the projectile go and it embedded itself in the soldier's side, causing him to fire up into the air. Gwen heard the noise and turned, saw the arrow and mouthed a thanks to him.

Then she turned back to get on with her task.

Granger began after her again, but before he'd got three steps an arc of bullets patterned the sky above him – then lower, hitting him in several places all at once. He seemed to go down in slow motion, holding the bow close, feeling the red-hot blood leaking out of him.

He toppled to the floor, vision blurring.

Granger could just see the figure of the woman heading off towards the platform, off to do what he'd been trying to stop her from doing – though would have done himself given half a chance.

"Go... go on girl... do it for E-Ennis..." he managed. "Do... it for m–"

Granger closed his eyes and lay still, while all around him the battle raged on.

She saw him – there he was.

The man who'd left her in bed that morning, the man who'd done all those things to her. The man who'd given the orders for Javier to follow. Gwen approached the platform. A soldier came up on her right and she shot him in the leg without even blinking.

"I've heard what they say about you... That you let him... do things. All kinds of things to you."

Not anymore. Now it was payback time.

De Falaise was terrorising some other woman now, she saw. A dark haired girl dressed in green and khaki. They were looking up at something, and though Gwen registered the sound of the helicopter she didn't take any notice. Then the Sheriff punched the woman in the face with the hilt of his sabre.

That did it.

Gwen rushed up towards the platform, pistol drawn. *"FRENCHMAN!"* she screamed, mounting the steps.

De Falaise looked over and puckered his brow. Perhaps he didn't quite realise what was happening, how she could be here in uniform, brandishing a gun – instead of in a nice dress by his side. "My dear..." he began.

"Don't!" she warned him. "I'm going to kill you now, just like I killed Javier." Gwen pointed the gun at his head.

"Then by all means get on with it," he said snidely.

Gwen's hand shook. She remembered what Javier had said about sparing her from what he was to go through, about saving her soul.

"You cannot do it, can you?" De Falaise grinned that smug grin of his. "You cannot just kill me like this, defenceless."

Gwen pulled the trigger.

The gun clicked empty.

De Falaise's eyes widened, then he began to laugh.

Gwen saw red. She threw the useless pistol at him and took out the knife from her pocket, the one she'd originally intended on using.

"I am afraid that mine is much bigger than yours." He held up the sabre to illustrate.

Gwen didn't care. She ran at him anyway, shouting at the top of her voice.

She was stopped in mid-lunge by something hard plunging into her shoulder, sending her spinning. It was De Falaise's second in command, firing one of his crossbow bolts at her – the only thing causing him to miss, a young boy hanging on to his leg.

Gwen toppled sideways, falling away from the laughing Sheriff. He was slipping out of her reach. But before she fell off the side of the platform completely, she threw the knife with her one good arm.

It landed in De Falaise's thigh.

As she dropped, uncertain of where she would land, she at least had the satisfaction of hearing the Frenchman let out a shrill yelp.

Then she was tumbling away, falling and hitting her head. Before she lost her grip on consciousness, she looked up, and it was then that she saw the helicopter flying overhead, much closer than it should be to the ground.

The Sioux came in to land with a bump, not far from the war memorial.

Robert and Bill jolted forwards, but both chopper doors were wide open within seconds, while the blades were still turning. Bill took up his shotgun, Robert had bow and arrow ready again.

On their sprint up the incline, Robert bagged a couple of soldiers and Bill opened fire over the heads of two more, causing them to drop their rifles and run off in alarm.

They ran up the path – back up towards the platform and the scene they'd just passed over. "I'll take the left, you take the right," Robert told him.

On the right, there was Tanek, reaching down to grab Mark again – to shoot him finally with a bolt to the head. On the left were De Falaise and Mary.

Bill aimed his shotgun at the bigger man and ordered him to let Mark go. The olive-skinned giant looked at him like he was speaking gibberish. Then he pointed the crossbow in Bill's direction. He fired, but at the same time Mark produced Tanek's own discarded dagger and rammed it with all the strength he had left, through the man's foot.

Tanek did make a noise this time, but it was more a growl than a scream.

The bolt hadn't flown straight, though it had found Bill – lodging itself into his pelvis. As he dropped, though, the farmer squeezed his own trigger. The blast hit Tanek in the middle of his chest, sending him reeling backwards with a grunt. The whole platform shook when he fell, but he didn't get up again.

Robert, meanwhile, had an arrow trained on De Falaise's head. But the Frenchman already had a dazed Mary pulled close to him, and he took this opportunity to bring the sabre up to her throat.

"The real Hooded Man, I presume." said the Sheriff.

Robert's eyes narrowed. "You know who I am. And I know you."

"Indeed." De Falaise kept Mary between him and the line of arrow fire. "You care for this woman, I can see that. I can use that." He looked all around him at the devastation, looked back over his shoulder to see Tanek lying on the deck, then he added: "And much as it pains me to leave before we have had a chance to get properly acquainted, there is a saying that seems appropriate: Prudence est mère de sûreté; Discretion is the better part of valour. And so I will live to fight another day, non?" He began to drag Mary backwards with him, limping – a knife still in his leg. Robert kept his arrow on him the whole time, but couldn't risk a shot.

He dragged Mary down the rear set of steps, disappearing

from sight. Robert skirted around the side of the platform, missing only a few moments. But by the time he rounded it, De Falaise and Mary were almost at the farthest end of the lawn; almost at a truck parked there.

"You've got to let her go to climb inside, you bastard," said Robert under his breath.

But De Falaise managed to keep Mary in front of him as he got into the cab of the truck, sitting her on his knee. The engine started up, the vehicle shuddering.

"Damn it! Jack... Jack, get Mark off the platform – right now!" Robert kept a bead on the vehicle as it powered towards them, but also kept an eye on what was happening on the gallows. Jack had managed to drag Mark to the edge and then over it, both of them tumbling off the right hand side of the platform. The truck clipped the left hand side, ramming through it, just missing Bill and a prone auburn-haired woman. Robert barely had time to dive out of the way, rolling as the truck tipped over the incline and drove down past the helicopter, scattering people as it went.

Robert raised his head in time to see the truck power through the devastated side gate and out onto the street.

His eyes flicked back to the helicopter, its rotor still turning. "Bill..." he called out on his way over to the man. "Are you in a fit state to fly?"

"Does it bloody well look like it?" Bill replied, nursing his wound. "Judas fucking Priest, I can't even get up!" He thumbed back towards the helicopter. "And I doubt if she will, neither."

Robert ground his teeth. The truck could be heading in any direction, even if he could get to a jeep or truck in time to follow. The helicopter was the only option if he was to find De Falaise and stop him.

Bow in hand, he began down the path, ignoring the calls from Bill and Jack.

What are you doing? What exactly are you doing, Robert? he asked himself. He couldn't fly, not even with a chopper that was in any fit state to get off the ground. Robert knew all this and still he had to try.

It was Mary's only hope. God alone knew what would happen to her once she no longer served her purpose as a hostage. That lunatic De Falaise...

He tried not to think about it as he threw the bow into the cockpit, then climbed in himself. Closing his eyes he visualised what Bill had done before take off, remembered what he'd said about lightness of touch.

With one hand on the collective and one hand on the cyclic, he attempted his first ever take off.

For long moments nothing happened, and Robert wondered if this was because of the state of the battered machine. But then, all of a sudden, and with a lot of mental encouragement from its pilot, the Sioux lifted a few feet off the ground.

"At-a-girl," said Robert, coaxing more height from her. Once he was high enough to make it over the castle entrance, he pushed the chopper forward, practically kangarooing it, bouncing onto the other side. It would never get up to the height it had before, but Robert was hoping he could get at least high enough to see where the truck was going.

As he lifted away, he saw the devastation of the battle he was leaving behind. His men were pretty much mopping up, and those soldiers who were left were surrendering in droves since De Falaise had cut and run. There would be time for sorting all that out later – time to find out how Mark was later. Right now, all he could think about was getting Mary safely back.

CHAPTER TWENTY-FOUR

Wake up Moo-Moo – you're in serious trouble. Even worse than the last time.

She heard David's voice rousing her, but it seemed so far away.

Moo-Moo, please wake up. The Sheriff has you as a hostage. You're driving through the streets of Nottingham in an army truck and when you get far enough away he's just going to kill you and dump you. Moo-Moo, are you listening to me! Mary! MARY!

That did it. David very rarely called her by her proper name, only when he was angry with her about something. Right now, that would appear to be because she was going to die. Mary opened her eyes a fraction, looking to the side. She saw De Falaise in his dress uniform, hunched over the wheel of the truck. A knife was buried in his leg, but he didn't seem in any rush to take it out. Beyond him she saw buildings going by. He took a right at speed, almost causing the truck to tip over. It was all Mary could do to keep quiet.

Good, said David. *He still thinks you're out of it, so there's no reason for him to question otherwise, is there? He also thinks you're unarmed. Oh God, Moo-Moo, however did you get yourself into this mess? Because you thought you felt something for someone you hardly even know? Because you always said to yourself even though you were hiding away that one day the perfect man would come along and you'd know it instantly?*

Mentally, she told him to shut up. Mary needed to concentrate, which wasn't easy when you were pretty sure your nose was broken and your head was splitting. She waited, watching De Falaise through the slits of her barely open eyes. Waited for him to turn the wheel again, so that she could use it as a cover to flop a hand below the seat. Then, with his attention still on the road, she reached that hand up behind her, reaching under the bottom of Robert's hooded top, reaching for the Peacemaker she had tucked away there, hidden in the folds.

She wasn't expecting to still have the gun by this late stage in the game – just how stupid were the soldiers under the Frenchman's command? – but then she wasn't expecting to fight De Falaise, get knocked senseless, and get dragged along for the ride in his mad dash for freedom.

And he was mad, no mistake about that. As Mary and the others had suspected all along, this guy was a total loon, playing out his fantasies of being a dictator in a world where he thought nobody could stop him.

He was wrong.

Mary had her fingers curled around the handle of the gun, her thumb ready to cock it. She wasn't thinking about what would happen once she'd shot him, whether he'd crash the truck and kill them both, she just wanted to end this right here and right now.

"Merde!" She flinched at De Falaise's raised voice, thinking that he must have noticed what she was up to. But he had caught sight of something out of the corner of his eye in the wing mirror. Something following them. Mary could just about make out the shape of the vehicle from her angle – but it didn't look like any car or jeep or truck she'd ever come across. "The cretin does not know when to give in. But I will show him."

"Robert," she whispered, too quietly to be heard.

Yes, said David. *He's come for you, Moo-Moo. He's come for you. Perhaps you were right after all.*

De Falaise stamped on the brakes, sending her back

into her seat as the low-flying helicopter crashed into their rear.

Robert grappled with the controls. It was taking all his effort and concentration just to keep the Sioux several metres off the ground, but it had done its job – got him high enough to pinpoint where De Falaise was going, heading blindly towards the market square. Then, having little choice in the matter, he brought the damaged chopper back down to hover as near to the ground as he could. The landing gear scraped the road, causing sparks.

Knowing De Falaise's direction helped Robert to take a short cut, emerging from one street just in time to see the truck go by. He was then in full pursuit.

Robert kept just a little way back, trying to hide behind the vehicle and hoping that the Sheriff wouldn't see him. But it had to happen eventually, and so Robert found himself having to pull on the collective control quickly, as the truck braked, slamming into the front of the helicopter. Then it rose, groaning in protest, but just about made it above the height of the truck, settling down on top of it as it accelerated again.

The truck wove this way and that, trying to shake the chopper. Robert fought to keep her level with the vehicle below him. They were driving down a road heading along the tram tracks when De Falaise pulled his braking stunt again.

This time, the helicopter shot forward and over the front of the truck, and suddenly both vehicles clipped the side of a building. They crashed through overgrown foliage onto what had once been the fountain of the square. Robert attempted to disentangle the chopper, but that only made matters worse, and soon they were heading towards the Council building.

Grabbing his bow, Robert opened the door of the chopper. He was just about to jump clear when he remembered something else he'd brought with him, and leaned across quickly to retrieve it. He dove out just as the truck rammed into one of the once majestic stone lions, a match for those back at the castle. Whether De Falaise had been deliberately trying to crush the chopper was unclear, but Robert hit the concrete and rolled, feeling something pop in his shoulder as he did so.

From his position on the floor, Robert raised his head and looked up at the mess of twisted metal. The truck and the helicopter were fused together like a piece of modern art. A river of diesel ran all the way across the market square like a slug's slime trail. And it was spreading into a lake...

"Mary..." groaned Robert. He had to get her out of the truck.

Hauling himself to his feet, he slipped the broadsword he'd grabbed into his belt, and staggered across to the wreck. He'd only got a few feet when two figures came into view around the side. It was the Sheriff and Mary, the former holding his sabre to her throat again, the latter still out of it.

Robert slotted an arrow into his bow and raised it, wincing at the pain from his shoulder. The pair moved sideways like a crab, De Falaise dragging Mary away from the truck as if he still thought escape was an option. Robert moved with them, keeping his arrow on the pair, but not being given the opportunity to take a shot.

"Let her go!" ordered Robert as they hobbled away, though his voice lacked any kind of authority.

"I think not," replied De Falaise.

"Look around you, it's over. You're done."

"Non. It is only just beginning, mon ami. We are–" De Falaise's face crinkled up, then he let out a piercing cry.

Robert glanced down and saw Mary's hand, twisting the knife still embedded in the Frenchman's leg. She'd only been pretending to be unconscious, and was now fully awake, intent on causing De Falaise the maximum amount of torment.

He threw her roughly to the side and she hit the ground, rolling over twice. It was as she came to a stop that Robert saw what she had in her hand. Her Peacekeeper, trained on the Sheriff.

"Mary, no...!" But she didn't hear him in time. Mary fired at the Frenchman, missing him, but hitting the truck some way behind them, igniting the leaking fuel tank.

De Falaise looked behind him, looked down at the trail of diesel, and began to limp quickly away. Robert ran for Mary, but the resultant blast as the truck and helicopter exploded knocked him off his feet – pitching him backwards into the middle of the square. A streak of heat whooshed between the two enemies as the diesel caught fire, then fanned outwards.

Robert slipped in and out of consciousness. He was back in the dreamworld suddenly, back at the lake of fire – then he was here, at the market square. There seemed little difference. The Sheriff came at him, but he couldn't tell whether it was real or an illusion. The man appeared out of the flames, burnt, his clothes smouldering, but he wasn't stopping.

It was only when his sabre descended that Robert realised this was no dream. He rolled over and the blade connected with the concrete, clinking loudly. Robert struggled with his own sword, but couldn't disentangle it from his belt at this angle.

De Falaise struck again. "I will kill you," he said, his face wild.

Robert kicked out, knocking his attacker backwards and reversing the descent of the sabre. While De Falaise wobbled back, Robert clambered to his feet, and finally pulled the broadsword from his belt. When the Sheriff attacked this time, metal clashed against metal. The strokes were clumsy – only to be expected from such inexperienced swordsmen – but any one could have ended the fight, skewering through flesh.

Neither man had the strength to really fight anymore, so in that respect they were evenly matched. After several slashes at each other with the swords, they grabbed one another's wrists at the same time. Robert squeezed as hard as he could, forcing De Falaise to let go of his sabre, while his opposite number followed suit, wrenching Robert's arm forward and aggravating his shoulder. Robert let go of the broadsword and it landed with a clatter.

They locked eyes, set against a backdrop of flames. It was clear that they recognised this scene, and knew what came next. Letting go of wrists, they went for each other's throats. Both men found reserves of energy, just enough to try and choke the life out of each other. Robert had a slight edge, and could feel De Falaise's grip on him weakening.

Too late, he remembered the dream – and what the Frenchman had done in it. Robert let go of De Falaise's throat, just in time to move back and see the knife as it was shoved into him. The crazed Sheriff had torn the weapon – a sharpened table knife – from his own leg and had been aiming for Robert's gut. It embedded itself in his side instead, but was no less painful.

Their faces centimetres apart, the Sheriff snarled. "And so it ends, English."

"Everything ends eventually." Robert headbutted De Falaise, causing him to let go of the knife and stagger backwards.

At the same time, Robert reached into his quiver, taking out an arrow. He held it as he would have done a dagger, then shoved it into De Falaise's open mouth, ramming it home.

The Sheriff's eyes widened and he clawed at his throat, choking as he might have done on a fishbone.

"That was for Mark. This is for Gwen and Mary."

Robert took out another couple of arrows, and this time shoved them into those eye sockets, snapping off the ends as he did so.

De Falaise couldn't scream, so he just gargled in agony, toppling to the floor, where he writhed about.

Robert stood above him, holding his side. "And this," he said, pulling out a final arrow. "This is for the rest of us."

De Falaise held up a quivering hand, but Robert ignored it, bent down, and plunged the arrowhead into the man's heart, hard and deep. The Sheriff twitched for a few more moments, then lay still.

Breathing heavily, Robert rolled off the corpse, still holding his side. He lay beside the Frenchman, not able to move any more – and to the casual observer there might have seemed hardly anything to choose between them. Two dead men, covered in blood.

But one was alive. Even after everything he'd been through – even after willing it to happen – Robert was still alive. The difference was, today he was glad of the fact.

He felt something, someone at the side of him. If he'd had the energy he would have brought up the knife still in his side, defended himself in case it was another attacker. But he didn't. So he was glad when the face that appeared above him was a familiar, friendly one.

"Yay you..." said Mary half croaking out the words. She wasn't in a much better state, her face all banged up, dried blood at her nostrils – yet it was still beautiful in spite of all that.

Robert laughed at her words, coughing, and when he did his shoulder and side felt like they were on fire, while the actual fire on the square was seemingly burning itself out. "Yay... Yay us," he managed.

Mary smiled and kissed his forehead, her hand reaching down and helping to stem the blood flow at his side.

"You... you finished with my clothes now?" he asked her.

"Why, you going to need this old Hood again, Robin?" she asked him.

He smiled weakly, the sound of vehicles in the distance reaching his ears. Maybe it was De Falaise's men fleeing? he thought. But when he saw Mary waving he knew it had to be his own men, drawn to the place by the smoke from the crashed vehicles.

It could mean only one thing. The battle for the castle, for Nottingham and the region, was finally over. Certainly the villain of the tale was dead...

But what of the war?

What of the future?

Those were questions for another time, another day, he told himself as he closed his eyes.

Yes, those were questions for another day entirely...

CHAPTER TWENTY-FIVE

If he hadn't wanted to be found, he wouldn't have let her.

But Robert was getting better at allowing Mary to track him down these days – getting better at letting her in. It would still take time, and she knew that. This wasn't some magical fairy story, and he couldn't simply erase the past. She wouldn't expect him to. Though yesterday seemed increasingly distant the more time that passed and the more time he spent with her.

"They said you'd come to the forest." Mary joined him in the clearing. It was the same one she'd followed him to that night, when they'd both seen the stag – except now the leaves were turning autumn gold. He knew that once she would have said it all looked the same, but now she actually recognised the place... he could tell from her expression.

"They were right," he said.

"You're waiting for it to come back again, aren't you?"

Robert sighed. "It won't, I know that."

Mary closed the gap between them. "You miss this place..."

He nodded. It had been two months since they'd taken over the castle, but he'd come back here often. He just couldn't settle. Bill, Jack, Tate, they had things running pretty smoothly now they were all fully recovered – thanks in no small part to Mary's attentions and a few other medical people who'd stepped forward. The soldiers who hadn't fled had been either placed under arrest until they worked out what to do with them, or offered a minor post in their ranks... under supervision, of course.

The dead, like Granger, had been buried – not cremated, Robert hadn't allowed that – and words had been said by their graves in the grounds, near to the war memorial. They'd done this for their men and for those who'd sided with De Falaise. After all, many of them hadn't had a choice. Some had, of course – some wanted the power that came with serving their demented master. Men like Tanek, whose body could not be found anywhere after the battle ("There's no way he was getting up after what I did t'him," Bill said, but still there was no sign of the man...). At any rate, word had gone out to the villages, and through the markets, that there was a new force in Nottingham, a force that wouldn't tolerate violence or stealing or attacks on the communities it sheltered. If the region was to stand again on its own two feet, it would need policing; it would need defending. And they were the ones to do it.

Still he'd been thinking about coming back, even though he hadn't said anything aloud. But every time he stepped foot inside the forest, he felt it. Something was missing; something had changed.

"You don't belong here anymore, you know," Mary said, her little finger brushing his. "What you came here to run away from..."

"Mary, don't," he said, but she pressed on anyway.

"What you wound up doing here... It's over. You have a different life now, a chance at a new beginning."

(Robert had a sudden flash of De Falaise in his head then, heard what he'd said during their last fight. "It is only just beginning, mon ami...")

"There's no need to run anymore. And they need you back there," Mary went on. "Mark needs you." Now Robert saw a picture of the boy... the man who'd had to grow up so fast. He remembered the first time he got a chance to speak to him after the battle, once they'd both rested up and gained their strength back. Mark's hand was bandaged, so was Robert's side. A right pair they'd made. Robert told him how very proud he was of him, how brave he'd been holding out under torture. Mark looked at him, fighting back the tears, then he'd hugged Robert – so hard he had to suck in a breath from the pain, but he'd endured it gladly. For a little while the child in Mark had returned; it was nice to see.

"They all need you. And... and I do too."

Robert nodded slowly. "How's Gwen?" he asked, changing the subject.

"The Reverend's looking after her. She's really starting to show now; late bloomer I guess. She's still convinced it's Clive's, though. A legacy of their love."

"Better for her if she carries on thinking that." Gwen's would be the first baby born in the castle, but the more time his men spent out there in the villages, the more relationships were blossoming. It wouldn't be long before other children came along. Each one would give them all new hope.

"And how's your side today?" she asked him.

"Better. Still twinges, especially now it's turning cold, but it's okay." Mary had seen to that too. A proper little medico she'd become, whether she intended to or not.

"You'll live, eh?" She smiled. "That's my Robert... So, are we going back to the castle or do I have to stick a needle in you again?"

"I still haven't forgiven you for the last time." He laughed softly and took hold of her hand.

Mary looked down and squeezed it. "Come on, there's still lots to do – and it looks like it might rain anytime. Let's go home." Now she tugged on the hand, and for a moment or two he held fast. Then he relented, turning, walking with her out of the clearing, back towards their jeeps on the outskirts of Sherwood.

There was a noise behind them, something in the undergrowth. Robert looked over his shoulder quickly and caught a glimpse – or was it his imagination? A flash of antlers against the green. Then it was gone.

"What is it?" Mary said craning her neck to see.

"Nothing," he told her. "Nothing at all."

As they walked, Mary chatted, but he wasn't really listening to her. He was taking in the trees, remembering the first time he came here. The reason why he'd hidden away...

Suddenly he recalled what Stevie had said the first time he'd finished reading him his favourite storybook.

"Is that it? Is that the end of the adventure, Dad? What happens to them all afterwards?"

Robert couldn't answer him, nor the many times after that he'd asked, because he didn't know. Robert still didn't know. What did come after the end? Peace? Love? Or would they find themselves having to deal with another threat one day? What came afterwards?

What came next?

With his free hand, Robert reached up and pulled his hood over his head.

Then, falling in step with Mary, he walked to the edge of the forest without looking back.

Knowing that there was one – and only one – sure way to find out...

THE END

PAUL KANE has been writing professionally for twelve years. His genre journalism has appeared in such magazines as *The Dark Side, Death Ray, Fangoria, SFX, Dreamwatch* and *Rue Morgue*, and his first non-fiction book was the critically acclaimed *The Hellraiser Films and Their Legacy*, introduced by Doug 'Pinhead' Bradley. His short stories have appeared in many magazines and anthologies on both sides of the Atlantic, in all kinds of formats (as well as being broadcast on BBC Radio 2), and have been collected in *Alone (In the Dark), Touching the Flame* and *FunnyBones*. His novella *Signs of Life* reached the shortlist of the British Fantasy Awards 2006 and *The Lazarus Condition* was introduced by Mick Garris, creator of Masters of Horror. In his capacity as Special Publications Editor of the British Fantasy Society he worked with authors like Brian Aldiss, Ramsey Campbell, Muriel Gray, Graham Masterton, Robert Silverberg and many more. In 2008 his zombie story 'Dead Time' was turned into an episode of the Lionsgate/NBC TV series *Fear Itself*, adapted by Steve Niles (*30 Days of Night*) and directed by Darren Lynn Bousman (*SAW II-IV*). Paul's website, which has featured guest writers such as Stephen King, James Herbert, Neil Gaiman and Clive Barker, can be found at www.shadow-writer.co.uk He currently lives in Derbyshire, UK, with his wife – the author Marie O'Regan – his family, and a black cat called Mina.

ACKNOWLEDGEMENTS

A big thank you to Trevor Preston for all the sound military and weapons help, and for answering all my niggling little questions; you're a complete star. Thanks to the staff at Nottingham Castle for the tour around the caves and especially to Pete Barnsdale who took us round the castle early in the morning before the crowds arrived. Ditto to the people at Sherwood Forest Visitors Centre and Rufford Abbey Country Park, plus thanks to Nottingham County Council for the use of the quote at the beginning of this book. Thank you to David Bamford for the help with checking historical details. Thanks to my friends and family for all their support not just while writing this, but during the last twelve years as I've been making my way in the writing biz. A special thanks to John B. Ford who gave me that all important first break and has been encouraging me ever since. A huge thank you to Jonathan Oliver who saw the potential of the idea, and Mark Harrison for bringing my protagonist to life. Thanks to Simon Spurrier for letting me play in his sandpit, and to Scott Andrews and Jaspre Bark for the opportunity of being part of something bigger than the whole. Thanks to Richard Carpenter for creating what will always be, for me, the definitive Hood in the 80s; without him my version would not exist. And lastly a 'words are not enough' thank you, as always, to my wife Marie. The first person to read this and offer such excellent advice. Love ya, sweetheart.

Now read the first chapter in the next exciting novel
in *The Afterblight Chronicles* series...

THE AFTERBLIGHT CHRONICLES

OPERATION MOTHERLAND

Scott Andrews

COMING MARCH 2009
US RELEASE DATE TO BE CONFIRMED

ISBN: 978-1-905437-90-0

£6.99 (UK)/ $7.99 (US)

WWW.ABADDONBOOKS.COM

CHAPTER ONE

Lee

I celebrated my sixteenth birthday by crashing a plane, fighting for my life, and facing execution. Again.

I'd rather have just blown out some candles and got pissed.

"Hello? Is anybody there? Hello?"

"Lee? Oh thank God."

"Dad? Dad is that you? I can hardly hear you. Where are you?"

"Still in Basra, but we're shipping out soon. Listen, I don't know how much time I have. Is your mother there?"

"Er, yeah."

"Put her on, son."

I'd been scanning the terrain for about ten minutes, looking for a decent place to land, when small arms fire raked the fuselage.

Stupid, careless idiot; I'd been flying in circles, just asking to be shot at.

I'd managed to fly thousands of miles, refuel twice without incident - if you didn't count that psycho in Cyprus, but he wasn't that much trouble - and make it to my destination unscathed. Then, on arrival, I descend to within shooting distance and wave my wings at anyone who fancies a potshot.

I bloody deserved to be shot down.

I pulled hard on the control column, trying to raise the plane's nose and climb out of range, but it didn't respond.

"Oh shit," I said.

I was at 500 feet and descending, nose first, towards a suburban street littered with abandoned cars and a single burned out tank. I tried to shimmy the plane left or right, pumped the pedals, heaved and wrenched the control column, anything to get some fraction of control. Nothing.

Too low to bail out, nothing to do but ride the plane into the ground and hope I was able to walk away.

My arrival in Iraq was going to be bumpy.

"Jesus Dad, what did you say to her? Dad, you still there?"

"Yeah, just... I, um... listen, Lee, there's something I have to tell you."

"Ok."

"The plague, from what we've been hearing here it's sort of specific."

"Eh?"

"You only get it if you've got a particular blood type. No, that's not right. You don't get it if you've got a particular blood type. Everyone who's got blood type O Negative is immune, that's what the doc here told us."

"And everyone else..."

"Is going to die."

I was coming in clean towards the road, lined up, by pure chance. If the road had been clear, and if I could've got the nose up, I'd maybe have had a chance. But I was heading straight for the fucking tank, and no matter what I did the plane was just a hunk of unresponsive metal.

There was another burst of gunfire, and this time I could see the muzzle flash of the machine gun on a rooftop to my left. His aim was true and the plane shuddered as the bullets hit the tail, sending fragments of ailerons flying into the tailwind. I yelled something obscene, furious, defiant, and pulled the control column again, more in frustration than hope.

And, hallelujah, it responded. That second burst of fire must have knocked something loose. I never thought I'd be grateful that someone was shooting at me.

Of course, at twenty feet and however many knots, there wasn't that much I could actually do.

The nose came up a fraction, but that was enough to change the angle of descent from suicidal to survivable. Not enough to actually stop my descent, though.

I'm pretty sure I was yelling when the tail of the plane slammed into the turret of the tank, snapped off, and pitched the aircraft nose first into the hard packed earth.

The world spun and tumbled as I screamed in tune with the crash and wrench of twisting metal. The plane somersaulted, over and over, down the road, bouncing off cars and buildings, losing its wings, being eroded with every revolution, until it seemed there was just a ball of warped metal and shattered plastic enclosing me like a cocoon as it gouged the ground, ricocheting like some kind of fucked up pinball.

Eventually, just as the darkness crept into my vision and I felt myself starting to black out, the world stopped spinning.

My head was swimming, there was blood in my mouth, I was upside down, the straps of my harness digging into my knotted shoulders, but I was alive.

One more life used up, Nine Lives, whispered a familiar, sarcastic voice in my head. I told it to piss off.

Then I realised that I was wet. I reached up and wiped the slick liquid from my face. When my eyes could focus and my dizzy brain began to accept input, I realised that I was soaked from head to toe in fuel.

I heard gunfire in the distance, as someone started taking shots at what was left of my plane.

And I couldn't move.

"All of them?"

"All. Lee, you're O Neg. So am I."

"And Mum? Dad, you there? I said what about Mum?"

"No."

"Oh. Right."

"Now listen, she might be safe if you can just quarantine yourselves. Don't leave the house, at all. For any reason."

"But what about food? The water's been switched off, we've got no power, there's these gangs going around attacking houses, Dad, they've got guns and knives and..."

"Lee calm down. Calm down. You mustn't panic, son. Breathe... You okay now?"

"Not really."

"I know. But you've got to be strong, Lee. For your mum."

"She's going to die isn't she... Dad?"

"Yes. Yes, she probably is."

"But there's no doctors, you know that right? The hospital's been closed for a week. They put these signs up saying to wait for the army to set up field hospitals, but they haven't shown up. They're not going to, are they?"

"No, I don't think so, not now. I know it's hard, but it's all up to you, son. You're going to have to nurse her. Until I can get there. I'm coming home, Lee. As fast as I can. You've got to hang on, understand?"

"But what if you're not fast enough? What if something goes wrong? What if I'm left here, alone, with... with... Oh god. She's really going to die, isn't she?"

I reached across and unclasped my harness. It snapped free and I slumped, shoulder first, into a mess of tangled metal. I screamed as my left shoulder ground into a sharp metal edge. Something felt wrong about the way it was lying. I tried to move my left arm but all I felt was an awful grinding of flesh and bone.

It was dislocated.

Add that to the disorientation, which would probably give way to concussion, and the numerous possible wounds that I'd yet to discover, not to mention the chunk of my lower lip that I'd bitten out with what remained of my teeth...

Actually, I thought, I'd got off pretty lightly all things considered. Now if I could just avoid getting burned to death this might even qualify as a good day. I squirmed in the tight embrace of the cockpit's carcass, trying to find a gap through which I could wriggle, some way to gain purchase, something I could use to lever myself free. It was agony; every move ground my shoulder joint against the slack, useless muscles, causing shooting pains so intense that they made my vision blur.

I could hear cries from nearby streets, and more gunfire, as men closed in on my position. I really needed to move.

Finding nothing that offered any chance of escape, I braced myself as best I could and pushed hard, using my full body strength to try and force my way out, like a wounded bird kicking its way out of a metal egg. My spine cracked like a rifle, and my legs burned with effort. My shoulder joint minced the flesh that surrounded it, and I screamed in impotent fury until, finally, I felt something near my feet give ever so slightly. I redoubled my efforts, taking every ounce of strength I had in my small, wiry frame, and mentally concentrating it in my feet. Oh so slowly I forced a metal strut backwards as it groaned in protest.

Eventually it bent far enough to let in a small circle of sunlight. I squirmed again, rotating inside my shell, until my head and shoulder were positioned beneath the opening.

I gritted my teeth. This was really going to hurt. I closed my eyes, and pushed myself upwards, squeezing my agonised shoulder through the tiny gap. I felt something rip inside my arm and I screamed again. Once my shoulders were clear I was able to pull my right arm through and use it to push myself free.

Just as my feet emerged, the mass of wreckage beneath me shifted under my redistributed weight, pitching me forward. I lost my balance and tumbled to the ground.

I lay there on the dusty earth and I smiled though the pain.

This dirt was Basra.

I'd made it.

"Lee, focus, you've got things to do."

"Right. Yes. Okay."

"Now we're shipping out of here before the week's out."

"Back to England."

"Yeah."

"So, what, I should see you in ten days or so?"

"I'm afraid it's not quite that simple. They're not just letting us go home. I'm still a soldier and I still have to take orders. If I try to just come home I'll be shot as a deserter. They executed one of my mates yesterday. He wanted to stay here, got a local girlfriend, kid on the way. Tried to slip away, got caught. They shot him at dawn."

"Bloody hell."

"Apparently there's some big thing planned for when we all get home, but nobody's telling us anything."

Before I could gather my wits and rise to my feet, someone started kicking the crap out of me.

I tried to roll away from the kicks, raise my good arm to protect my head, find some space in between the blows to reach down and grab my Browning, which was tucked into my waistband. But with one arm useless, and my head woozy with shock and pain, I ended up just curling into a ball and letting the blows come. My attacker was shouting and firing his gun in the air, laughing as he kicked me to death. Luckily he was wearing converse sneakers, not hobnail boots. So it was going to take him a while.

Then, what was left of the plane exploded. The shockwave actually rolled me along the ground a bit, like a balled up hedgehog. The kicking stopped. I cautiously removed my arm and saw my assailant sprawled on the floor beside me. There was a short metal stanchion protruding from his forehead. I uncurled myself, lurched upright, reached down and gingerly took the AK-47 from his still twitching hands.

He looked younger than me. Bum fluff moustache, dark skin, khaki pants, plain white t-shirt, head swathed in cloth. He lay there on the sandy ground, staring sightlessly into the sky. My first victim of the day. I hoped he would be the last, but I didn't think it likely.

A rattle of gunfire from the far end of the street reminded me that he had friends. I had to move. I staggered as fast as I could in the opposite direction to the gunfire. I had no idea of the layout of this town; they no doubt knew it like the backs of their hands. I was one wounded boy with a useless arm, a half empty machine gun and pistol with a couple of clips; there were bloody loads of them, and they were armed to the teeth. I had salvaged no water from the crash, the midday sun was beating down on me, I was losing blood, sweating as I ran, and had no idea how to come by safe drinking water.

I was so fucked.

I wished I had some of Matron's homebrew drugs on me. In the heat of the battle for St Mark's a shot of that had kept me fighting despite shattered teeth, a broken arm and more blows to the head than I could count. But I'd left without really saying goodbye. I regretted that now; I'd almost certainly never see her again. Still, it seemed like the right thing to do at the time. After all I'd probably have ended up blubbing or, worse, trying to snog her, and that would have been excruciating.

A bullet pinged off a brittle brick wall next to my head as I dodged down an alleyway, weaving in between burned out cars and abandoned barricades. This was pointless. If I could get far enough ahead of them I had a chance, but I just wasn't capable of any kind of speed. I'd never outrun them.

I had to go to ground.

"So what do I do?"

"You go back to school."

"What?!"

"Listen, some of the teachers stayed behind didn't they? And some of the boys?"

"Yeah, but..."

"No buts. It's the only safe place I can think of. They've got weapons there, in that bloody CCF armory, haven't they?"

"Uh huh."

"Then get back there, join up with anyone who's left, arm yourselves, and wait for me."

"You promise you'll come?"

"No matter what happens, Lee, I'll be there. It may take a while, that's all. If you're at St Mark's you'll be as safe as houses and I'll know where to find you. Promise me."

"I promise, dad."

I emerged from the alleyway into a housing estate. Residential tower blocks rose up in front of me, some burnt out, some with great gaping holes punched in them by depleted uranium shells, one even reduced to a pile of rubble. Their balconies were festooned with clothes, bedding and the occasional skeleton. This desolate, abandoned maze of passages, flats and stairwells was my best chance of eluding my pursuers.

I stumbled across the churned up paving stones, heading for the doorway of the block that seemed the most intact. The sound of gunfire and pursuit echoed eerily around the long deserted concrete wind trap estate, making it impossible for me to know how many there were, or where.

The blue metal door to the block lay half open. I shoved it, using my good shoulder, but something inside was blocking my way, so I had to shimmy through the narrow gap into the musty, fetid darkness of the stairwell. My foot sank into something soft and yielding. I felt something pop beneath my boot, and a pocket of evil smelling gas was released that made me gag and choke. I tried to free my foot, but it was caught on something hard. I looked down to find that I was ankle deep in a bloated corpse, my lace end snagged on a protruding edge of fractured ribcage.

After I'd dry heaved for a minute or two I slung the machine gun over my shoulder, reached down and gingerly unsnagged the lace, smearing my fingers in vile black ichor as I did so. I limped away from the unfortunate wretch, wiping my fingers on the wall as I went.

That man - had it been a man? I couldn't be sure - had been dead for some time, but he'd outlived the plague. He still had a gun in his hand, so I assumed he'd died fighting. On the evidence so far, it looked like Basra was still as violent and deadly a place as it had been before The Cull.

And I'd come here by choice. Bloody moron, Keegan.

The stairs were littered with junk. Toys, prams, CDs, DVDs, clothes, a bike, some chairs, computers, TV sets; this place had been comprehensively looted, but it seemed like most of the stuff had just been thrown around for a laugh rather than salvaged and squirreled away.

I negotiated the wreckage and made it to the third floor without stumbling across any other recent casualties. I risked a glance through a shattered windowpane, and could see a group of three young men, machine guns at the ready, cautiously quartering the courtyard below. It wouldn't take much for them to realise I'd come into this block; one whiff of the doorway should do it.

I needed a hiding place, fast. I ran down the corridor, trying to decide which flat to hide in. Some still had their armour plated doors firmly locked shut from the inside, entombing anyone who'd sheltered within.

One door was decorated with a collection of human skulls, hanging from hooks in the shape of a love heart. I gave that one a miss. Eventually I just ducked inside a random door, and pushed it closed behind me. I was about to slide the large metal bolts home when I realised that the bolt housings had been ripped from the wall when someone had kicked their way inside.

I turned to explore the flat, and found two long-dead bodies lying sprawled on the sofa. The one in the dress, with the long red hair, had a bullet hole in the middle of its skull. The other, presumably her boyfriend or husband, still held a pistol in its boney fingers, the muzzle clasped between yellow teeth. The flesh was long gone, all that remained were tattered clothes and bones picked clean by rats that had long since moved elsewhere in search of food. I imagined that most of the locked doors in this block, and all the others, contained similar tableaux.

The world hadn't ended with a bang; it had bled out in an orgy of mercy killings and suicide pacts.

"And Lee, listen, your mother..."

"Yes?"

"I've seen what this disease does. And I want..."

"No."

"Lee, I wouldn't ask..."

"Dad, no. Please. Don't ask me to do that."

"But..."

"No. I'm not like you dad. I couldn't do something like that. I just couldn't. I won't give up hope."

Right. First things first. Before they found me I needed to sort out my shoulder. I did a quick walk through of the flat but found nothing surprising, just the abandoned fragments of other people's lives. I looked out the bedroom window, and found myself staring down at a sandy expanse of scrubland. It took me a minute to realise what I was looking at, but when I did it was all I could do to stop myself throwing up.

Lined up on the ground were row upon row of impaled corpses. Maybe thirty or more people, all with their hands tied behind their backs, lying with their faces skywards, sharpened wooden stakes protruding from their shattered ribcages. The stakes had been dug into the ground and then the victims must have been flung onto them. And pushed down. Recently, too; the flies were still buzzing, hungrily.

I'd seen some pretty horrible deaths in recent months. I'd been responsible for a few of them. But this was far and away the most awful thing I'd seen.

I stood at the window for a minute or two, transfixed. I could feel the first stirrings of panic.

After all that had happened to me in the last hour,

it took a field of impaled sacrifices to make me start panicking. That's a good indication of how fucked in the head I was at this point. Running, hiding, fighting for my life, killing people who were trying to kill me - all this had become part of an ordinary day. A year ago I'd have been a shuddering, stammering wreck. But now none of that stuff even touched the sides. I just got on with it.

A few weeks previously I'd stopped looking at myself in mirrors, started actively avoiding my own reflection, scared of what I'd see. I just kept telling myself to get on with it, things to do. I'd sort it all out later. I think I imagined some sort of quiet solitude, a retreat or something, where I'd go and try to get my head straight once I'd got everything done, ticked the final item on my list of jobs (take out milk bottles, finish geography homework, defeat army of cannibals, iron shirts, fly to war zone and rescue dad from enemy combatants who like impaling people).

I suspected that if I allowed myself too many moments of introspection I'd go mad.

I shook my head, impatient with myself.

Stop being maudlin.

Things to do.

Fix my shoulder. I was pretty sure it was only dislocated, not broken, and I knew how to sort that. You just grit your teeth and shove your shoulder really, really hard against a wall or something and, voila, it just snaps back in. Simple. I'd seen Jack Bauer do it on 24.

It'd most likely hurt a lot, so I picked up a piece of wood from the floor, part of a smashed doorframe, and shoved it into my mouth. I didn't want any screams bringing my pursuers right to me. Then I stood before the bathroom wall and calmed my breathing, focused, and slammed my dislocated shoulder into the wall as hard as I possibly could.

The pain blinded me and I was unconscious before I hit the floor.

"All right, Lee. Look, I gotta go. Look after your mother. I love you."

"I love you to, dad. And make sure you come find me, 'cause if you're not back in a year I'm going to come find you!"

"Don't joke. If I'm not back in a year, I'm"

Click.

"Dad? Dad, you there? Dad?"

When you've been knocked unconscious as many times as I have you learn a few tricks. The most important is not to open your eyes until you're fully awake and have learned all you can about where you are and who's there with you.

I was bleeding, hungry and thirsty, and I ached all over from the crash and the kicking, but I was still alive.

The most obvious thing was that I wasn't lying on a tiled bathroom floor. I was sitting up, with cold metal cuffs binding my hands to the chair back. Someone had found me, then. I probably screamed as I passed out and they found me where I dropped.

The second thing was that my shoulder hurt like hell and I still couldn't move my arm, so I hadn't managed to relocate it. Thank you, Jack Bauer. Thanks a fucking bunch.

Note to self: really must stop thinking that life is

anything like telly.

The air was still and dry and there was no wind, so I was indoors. I listened carefully, but I couldn't hear anybody talking or breathing. I risked opening my eyes and found myself staring down the lens of a handy cam.

It took a minute for me to realise the implications. I craned around to look behind me, and saw that I was sitting in front of a blue sheet backdrop with Arabic script on it. That's when I really started to panic. Could I really have flown halfway round the world just to end up in a snuff video?

It took a lot of effort to regain my composure, but eventually I calmed myself down, got my breathing under control, forced down the panic and concentrated on the details of the room. Dun, mud brick walls, sand floor. Single window, shuttered. Old, tatty blue sofa to my left, sideboard to my right. Lying on the sideboard was a big hunting knife, its razor edge glinting at me like a promise. The handy cam was a Sony. Behind it there was a metal frame chair with canvas seat and back, the same as the one I now occupied. Next to that was an old coffee table on which were piled digi-beta tapes. The last thing I noticed, which made the panic rise again, was the dark red stain on the floor, which formed a semi circle around my feet. There was a splash of the same stain across the floor in a straight line and onto the wall beside the sofa. That would be the first gush of arterial blood from the last poor bastard who'd sat in this chair.

I remembered the siege of St Marks, two months earlier, walking into the Blood Hunters' camp, all cocky bravado, baiting the madman in his lair. I remembered the plan going horribly wrong, and the moment when they forced me to kill one of my own men. I remembered holding the knife as I slit Heathcote's throat, and felt the blood bubble and gush over my hands as I whispered pleas for forgiveness into the ear of my dying friend. I remembered the hollow ache that had sat in my stomach as I'd done that awful thing, the ache that had never left me, which still jolted me awake in the middle of most nights, sweating and crying, reliving his murder over and over. He had not died easily or well. When the siege was over, and the school was a smoking ruin, I had found Heathcote's body, in amongst the mass of slaughtered, and dug his grave myself. I had a broken arm so it took me two days, but I wouldn't let anyone else lift a shovel.

It was as I placed the plain white cross on his grave that I realised I could not stay. All my decisions, all my plots and schemes and plans had just brought the school to ruin. It would be better for everyone if I left Matron in charge and gave the school a clean start in a new home. I was cursed. I stayed long enough to heal the arm, and then I just walked away.

Dad hadn't shown up, and it had been nearly a year. Time for me to come good on my promise. Time to fly to Iraq and find out what had become of him. I had little expectation that he was still alive, but I had to try. So I found myself a little Grob Tutor plane, the one I'd been taught to fly by the RAF contingent of the school's County Cadet Force, plotted a route via various RAF bases where I thought I'd be able to find fuel, and set off.

All that distance from Heathcote's grave, all that effort just to put myself in a place where I could suffer exactly the same fate. It seemed only fair. Inevitable, even.

Poetic justice, Nine Lives, said the voice in my head. I couldn't really argue with that.

I heard footsteps approaching and low, murmuring voices. The door opened and two men stepped inside. They wore khaki jackets and trousers with tatty, worn out trainers. Both had their faces swathed in cloth, with only their dark eyes visible. They stopped talking and stood in the doorway for a moment, just staring at me. Not long ago I'd have wracked my brain for a quip or putdown, but there'd come a point some months back where I'd heard myself saying something flippant to a psychopath and I'd realised that it didn't make me cool; it just made me sound like an immature dick who'd seen too many bad action movies and was trying way too hard. So I just told the truth.

"I have no idea who you think I am," I said, trying to keep my voice even and level. "But I'm not your enemy."

They ignored me. The taller one moved to the handy cam and hunched over it, preparing to record. I wondered how he'd charged the battery. The shorter one checked the sheet behind me before picking up the knife and taking his place at my side, still and silent like a sentry.

"I'm just a boy from England looking for my dad," I went on hopelessly. "Just let me find him and I'll fuck off out of it, back home. I promise."

No response, just a red light on the handy cam, and the whirr of tiny motors as it opened to receive the tape.

Of course, it could be that they didn't even speak English.

"Look, there's no media any more anyway. There's no Internet or telly. So what's the point of cutting my head off on video? Who's going to see it?" I thought this was a pretty good point, but they didn't seem to care.

The cameraman slid the tape into place and snapped the handy cam closed. A moment's pause, then he nodded to his companion.

I tried to calm my nerves, tell myself that I'd been in situations like this before, that there was still a way out. But no one knew I was here. There were no friends looking for me, no Matron to come riding to my rescue. I was thousands of miles from home, in a country where I couldn't make myself understood, and I was about to be executed as part of a war that was long since over.

I supposed it made as much sense as any other violent death.

I felt a tear trickle down my cheek, but I refused to give them the satisfaction of sobbing. The weird thing is, I wasn't sad for myself. I'd faced death many times, and I'd got to know this feeling pretty well. I was ready for it. I just felt guilty about my dad. He'd never know what had happened to me, and I'd never be able to tell him about what had happened to me after that phone call. I'd been looking forward to that conversation. I missed him.

The man standing beside me began to talk to the camera in Arabic. I made out occasional words - Yankee, martyr - but that was all. At one point I gabbled an explanation to the camera, drowning out his monologue. At least that way anyone watching it would know who I was. I had no idea where this video would end up, so it was worth a shot, I supposed. Nothing else I could do.

"My name is Lee Keegan," I shouted. "It's my sixteenth birthday today, and I'm English. I flew here to find my dad, a Sergeant in the British Army, but my plane crashed and these guys found me. If anyone sees this please let Jane Crowther know what happened to me. You can find her at Groombridge Place, in Kent, southern England. It's a school now. Tell her I'm sorry."

The guy with the knife punched me hard in the side of the head to shut me up. He finished his little speech and then there was silence, except for the soft whirr of tiny motors.

I stared straight into the camera lens, tears streaming down my face. I clenched my jaw, tried to look defiant. I probably looked like what I was - a weeping, terrified child.

I felt cold, sharp metal at my throat.

Then the guy behind the camera stood up straight, unwrapped his face and took off his jacket, revealing a t-shirt that read: Code Monkey like you!

"Hang on," he said. "Did you say your name was Keegan?"

And that's how I met Tariq.

For more information on this
and other titles visit...

THE AFTERBLIGHT CHRONICLES

The CULLED

Simon Spurrier

Price: £6.99 ★ ISBN: 978-1-905437-01-6

Price: $7.99 ★ ISBN: 978-1-905437-01-6

Also Available

THE AFTERBLIGHT CHRONICLES

KILL
OR
CURE

Rebecca Levene

Price: £6.99 ★ ISBN: 978-1-905437-32-0

Price: $7.99 ★ ISBN: 978-1-905437-32-0

THE AFTERBLIGHT CHRONICLES

SCHOOL'S OUT

Scott Andrews

Price: £6.99 ★ ISBN: 978-1-905437-40-5

Price: $7.99 ★ ISBN: 978-1-905437-40-5

THE AFTERBLIGHT CHRONICLES

DAWN OVER
DOOMSDAY

JASPRE BARK

Price: £6.99 ★ ISBN: 978-1-905437-62-7

Price: $7.99 ★ ISBN: 978-1-905437-62-7

TWILIGHT of KERBEROS

SHADOW MAGE

MATTHEW SPRANGE

Price: £6.99 ★ ISBN: 978-1-905437-54-2

Price: $7.99 ★ ISBN: 978-1-905437-54-2

TWILIGHT of KERBEROS

THE CLOCKWORK KING OF ORL

MIKE WILD

Price: £6.99 ★ ISBN: 978-1-905437-75-7

Price: $7.99 ★ ISBN: 978-1-905437-75-7